Above Ground

Above Ground

Jack Ludwig

Introduction by Margaret Laurence
General Editor: Malcolm Ross

New Canadian Library No. 100

McClelland and Stewart Limited

The Canadian Publishers
McClelland and Stewart Limited
25 Hollinger Road, Toronto

Printed and bound in Canada

IN MEMORY OF

Misha Ludwig
Fannie Ludwig
Joannie Ludwig

For Bobby

who mourning could not mourn

In a time of famine the only crop which men could harvest and eat drove them instantly mad. So they ate, but they were commanded to record and remember they were mad.

Introduction

Joshua, the protaganist of *Above Ground*, learns very young and very thoroughly a basic fact of life – all living creatures are mortal. Death, not as something which happens only to the very old, but as something which can happen anytime to anyone, enters his consciousness truly and permanently when, at the age of five, he has his tonsils out and begins hemorrhaging. Joshua's grandmother died when the boy was three, but death for him did not yet have a name, and possibly in his first hospital experience at five, it still does not have a name, but it is there and is felt, the darkness which he senses when he knows he is bleeding uncontrollably. Jack Ludwig does not dwell on the (literally) gory details of this first scene. He does not have to. Our first glimpse of Josh is of a child in hospital, more frightened than he even realizes himself at the time.

Some years later, the boy fractures his hip. Treatment is bungled by the first doctor and the bone does not mend. Then begin the long sessions in the enclosed world of the hospital, "a city within a city." Here, Josh experiences great physical pain and the fear of death or mutilation (at one point, being taken into the operating theatre, he is convinced that they are about to amputate his leg; no one has thought to tell him that they are going to put it in a cast). He also experiences others' pain, and witnesses the death of Mac, one of the nearby patients, after an operation. The saving elements in the situation are the kindness and even affection of nurses, all of whom Josh falls in love with, and the visits of his family, especially his Uncle Bim, with his enormous gusto and appetite for life. Uncle Bim has "two categories, *live* and *dying*," and to his nephew he imparts some of his stubborn will to survive, to live joyously, to rise, to fly.

It is typical of the older Joshua, the narrator of this novel, that he recounts the grim hospital scenes with an incisive and ironic humour – not the saccharine humour of sentimentality, not in any sense a down-playing of the realities of pain and death, but the humour of survival. In fact, this survival humour is one of the marks of Jack Ludwig's writing, not only one of his greatest technical strengths but also an unstated theme in itself. Man, it is said, is the only creature who knows he must die. Man is also the only creature (or at least as far as we know) who laughs. For Ludwig, the two facts are not unrelated. It may be as well to point out here that Ludwig's humour is not "sick humour" in the contemporary meaning of those words. It is not cruel or malicious humour. It does not seek to destroy – my sense of it is that it seeks to build, to mend, even to heal.

The type of Ludwig's humour in *Above Ground* meshes perfectly with the general theme of the novel – a person who lives with the knowledge of the reality of death is a person who may be capable of living most fully. Josh's hip never does heal properly. For him, life is a gift. He takes nothing for granted. Uncle Bim sums up this double consciousness when he proposes a toast at Josh and Maggie's engagement party, a toast to all, and "to the angel of death," who "looks just like the angels of life."

Josh's awareness of the fact that he is, fairly miraculously, alive and on his feet, makes him constantly aware of the life around him, both its ugliness and its splendour, and here Ludwig communicates, through Josh, a keen and detailed sense of place and time. Whether in descriptions of North Winnipeg streets in the Thirties Depression years, or the Second World War years, or the good sand beaches and repulsively artificial apartments of California, or the concrete deserts and few human oases of New York, Ludwig can paint the picture of a specific place in incredibly few words, so that the reader can see and feel and hear the scene.

Josh does not have an answer to death – who could? But he does have a cry of defiance, and even, in one sense, a kind of magic charm against it. The ancient charm. For Josh, as for every human since our legendary father Adam and mother Eve, probably, the act of love is a defiance of death. It is a talisman, a rune, an act not only of the flesh but an act of faith as well. Josh differs from most humans only in the way that he knows and verbalizes this aspect of our lives, our deaths. Josh falls in love frequently, but he is no cynical collector of the sexual equivalent of scalps. Which brings us to an interesting aspect of this novel. I would guess that I am fairly alert to most kinds of putdowns of women, in fiction as in life, and in *Above Ground* I get no sense of women being regarded as objects. On the contrary, each of the women with whom Josh makes love has a totally recognizable individuality; one doesn't get them confused; they speak in their own voices, and what is more, they speak intelligently. When Josh says he loves them, he means it. He does love them, and keeps on loving them even when the affair is over, and with one exception, Mavra, they do not rely on him to make or save their lives. Zora, the flamboyant girl in Winnipeg, with whom Josh makes love on the evening of his engagement to Maggie, and who, many years later, he meets again and is saddened by the inevitable fact that she has grown older; Maggie, the constant in his life, whom he marries and who has a daughter with him; Alvira, who loses vast amounts of weight in order that she may experience sex, even if not love, and with whom Josh makes love at least partly out of pity, although he denies this is so; Nina, the Russian woman whom he meets in California, and who remains to him some kind of ideal, a dream-person whose tough-minded reality he sees but does not want to recognize; Gyla, who as a Jewish child in Europe during the war was left with nuns and told by her mother to kiss the cross, for survival; and finally, the incredible Mavra, disturbed to a degree, Mavra of many roles and faces—I find all these women understandable and believable.

Perhaps one of the most interesting women in the novel is Maggie, Josh's wife, about whom less is said than about most of the others. Maggie is aware of each of Josh's affairs, and is angry, but never so angry that she considers leaving him, partly because she cares about him but also partly because she is shrewd and intelligent, and she knows a lot of things about Josh. At one point, during his affair with Mavra, Maggie says "You still believe a great love could heal a hip." We are shown the transformation of Mavra from the rather kooky but pathetic young babysitter who latches onto Josh and Maggie and their infant daughter, Bailla, into the desperate and compulsively promiscuous woman who begs Josh to save her, and who is so far gone in being spiritually maimed that she cannot for one instant see outside herself, not even to recognize Josh's pain when his father dies. But long before Josh finally comes to see that Mavra's spiritual disease is one which can infect and destroy others, Maggie has seen it. Maggie is, as far as the portrayal of her goes, totally believable, and yet I feel somehow that there are whole areas of Maggie's responses to life which aren't dealt with. I have the sense that Josh, as narrator, is both protecting her and shying away, for his own protection, from some of the aspects of Maggie which might be too upsetting for him to face. Wasn't she ever interested in another man? I can't believe it. Ludwig tries occasionally to get inside the consciousness of Maggie (as he does, once, with Mavra, in the bar scene) but I don't think these attempts are entirely successful, partly because they aren't probed far enough and partly because in a first-person novel this method of taking on another person seems, at least momentarily, to threaten both the narrative flow and the authenticity of the single voice. With this reservation, however, about the character of Maggie not being looked at deeply enough, I still have to say that the women in this novel are never stereotypes and never caricatures. Josh values these women both as sexual partners and as people. I really like the sex in this novel—there is always a warmth and tenderness about it. Ludwig's portrayal of women is as far from the Bunnygirls of *Playboy* as a field of wheat is from a plastic daffodil.

But if love is Josh's talisman against death, Death is still a constant presence. Life, for Josh, does not mean merely drawing breath. There are two people who live on but do not survive, Evvie and Tamara, both of whom become insane and live out their lives in institutions, the one terrorized by sinister voices despite a lobotomy, the other an inert vegetable. A great many of the characters in *Above Ground* are touched by the angel of death, either death-in-life or actual death. These portraits are done with such a sense of caring, such ironic humour, and in such brief and telling brushstrokes, that it becomes plain that this kind of character portrayal is Ludwig's finest talent. Wilkoh Joe, who hangs himself because he cannot understand English and imagines the doctor is telling him he has TB; Bibul the fruit peddler, with his old horse and wagon; the Chemistry professor, Grover, in the horrific hypnotism scene, who "woke us all" but not quite in the way Grover imagines himself to have done; Uncle Baer and Aunt Teena in California, who in their hatred of one another must carry on the pretense of a perfect marriage, except when the masks slip; Hettie Karousel, who "bought apartment blocks the way some bought coins," and who is run over accidentally by Levitt, her abject husband; Fran, damaged irreparably by her puritanical family; Carson, who can't accept that he's survived the war and who only gains peace when he becomes crippled with polio; and perhaps more than anyone, Mavra, whose urge to destroy spiritually both herself and others is so strong that nothing can abate it. All these people suffer, are maimed, and yet the general feeling of the novel is not despair. Once, making love with Nina in the sea, Josh cries "What a way to go it would be." Nina says, "In the midst of this much life, why death?" Josh can only reply, "A passing thought." For him, the thought passes across his consciousness often, maybe always. And because it does, life is not diminished – in fact, the exact reverse.

The final portion of the novel, which includes the death of Josh's father and subsequently the death of his mother, counterpointed with letters from Mavra which are idiotic and repellent and yet somehow touching because of their very vulgarity and tactlessness – this constitutes the most moving part of the novel, and one which draws all the threads together. Josh's father dies, quite unexpectedly, of a heart attack, when it is Josh's mother who has had a stroke and is in hospital. The human condition is borne in upon Josh all over again at that moment.

> "Irreversible death. Knowledge that flays. I could not to be to my father as if he were Lazarus."

No one can save anyone else. We can only try to make them aware of our caring. And yet, when Josh's mother dies, Josh is not there. He has gone back to New York to see Mavra, and doesn't return to his childhood home in time. Josh's aunt Beatty tells him that his mother has said, "Tell him how hard I waited." Beatty says that "She had a crazy thought in her head – she believed you could keep her alive." Josh says, "Beatty, I couldn't."

Not will, nor love, nor faith, nor any mortal thing can stop Time. Death will not fail to happen. This may seem obvious, but it is not. Some people never know it until death surprises them. Maybe they are the lucky ones, and maybe not. But for Josh, the goal is to stay above ground for as long as possible, hopefully with whatever love it may be his to give and to receive. On the night of his mother's death, Josh thinks of his Uncle Bim, who died some years before " . . . old eaglefaced man, waving his arms to discount the finite." With the constant knowledge of death, perhaps the only way to live is as though we were going to live forever.

Something about legends interests me in *Above Ground*. Ludwig, from time to time, brings in references to classical myths – Orpheus, Aeneas and Queen Dido, Theseus and Ariadne. I have the feeling that these references may be somewhat extraneous. The true ancestral references are made in this novel, it seems to me, without any comment and without naming sources, and these work very well – these ancestral references, of course, are Old Testament ones, and this is not only because Ludwig is writing out of a Jewish background, but also because for most of us in Canada, I suspect, the Old Testament legends have more relevance than the classical ones. At one point, Josh says "Miracles I carry in my bones. Not when voice spoke out of whirlwind; or seas parted; or man was swallowed then spewed by whale." But the voice that spoke to Job out of the whirlwind, saying *Where wast thou when I laid the foundations of the earth?* is a voice that one feels this contemporary Joshua would recognize, if not in a purely religious sense, then at least in his realization of the fleeting quality of human life. When the Red Sea parted, and Moses led his people into the wilderness, on the way to the promised land – Josh, like nearly everyone in our land, would recognize that parable, ironic though some of its aspects are. As for Jonah, who was swallowed by the whale – Josh, to use the words of Carl Sandburg, " . . . was swallowed one time deep in the dark / And came out alive after all." Josh, when explaining to Mavra why he has not kept in daily touch with her whilst in the prairie city at the time of his father's death, says "There was a time to think about you and a time that swept you and everything else out of my mind." The echo there is from Ecclesiastes, *To everything there is a season, and a time to every purpose under the heaven; A time to be born, and a time to die* . . . Josh's words catch that echo and use it like his natural inherited speech. The Biblical Joshua, remember, was he who crossed Jordan and entered the new and ancient land. Josh, in *Above Ground*, speaks in his own idiom, for his own time, and miracles he does carry, literally, in his bones. But he also speaks out of his ancestry, and that ancestry is the Old Testament.

Ludwig is doing something else with legends. Some of the characters he portrays – Josh's mother and father, Uncle Bim, Dobrushyn, Uncle Baer, Joseph Czernowski, and many others – these people are a part of our own legends, our history, our ancestors, and Ludwig, like a number of Canadian writers at this point, is giving to them a form and a voice.

The main theme of *Above Ground*, however, remains that of how to live in the face of an everpresent awareness of death. It might have been an exceedingly sombre novel, but sombre it most certainly is not, and the reason that it is not is only partly due to the swiftness of the currents of humour within it. The other aspect is summed up in the novel's last line – " . . . I fly eastward, where sun rises tomorrow, as I hope to see."

Margaret Laurence
Peterborough

. . . so all women are one woman . . .

T. S. Eliot

NORTH

memos of a messenger

I WAS born in a cold city to a beautiful warm mother and a handsome father whose life began again every time he met a beautiful woman. His seemed the right way to me. I learned to talk only to say what was on my heart to beautiful women. I spoke to them exclusively. Not till I was five did I speak to a man other than my father.

The first strange man in my life was a doctor. He came to ask me what hurt. I said my throat.

"Tonsils," he said. "Away with them."

I went to a hospital of beautiful nurses. One sat by my bed for hours. I fell in love. She came to truss me up for surgery and I smiled calfishly; I mooned my way onto the operating table and swooned out, only partially influenced by ether.

I woke up bleeding.

I bled and bled and bled.

The doctor must have been in love with my nurse and in need of vengeance.

My nurse sweetly packed choking sour cottonballs down my throat to stanch the blood. Her I would have let do anything.

My father came in.

I was bleeding.

He fainted.

My mother and my aunt detached themselves from duty and packed my father off home in a taxi. My nurse left. The bleeding stopped. I was alone in darkness.

Out on a porch, in gray light cut by one yellow beam let in by an open door, close to nurses slamming charts together, metal on metal, I heard a scratching.

Under the bed. Again. Soft, silly, irregular. I inverted my head over the side of the bed, carefully.

A tiny mouse hung in the light's yellow path, paws under its chin in fright. An alive mouse. He was no toy. A tiny speck of spider web was caught on his nose, like spectacles. I smiled at the mouse, braced myself on my outspread hands, arms stiff to brake my sliding.

I couldn't think what one says to a mouse: "Psst"? "Chkchk-chk"?

Hanging over the bedside my head felt odd; I grew dizzy; my face throbbed.

"Hey, mousie," I tried to say softly.

I couldn't.

Something was happening.

Between my hands on the gray stone floor a bright red raindrop splattered. A second.

Four drops, five. My hands were red with blood. The mouse cowered in the yellow light, examining me through his spectacles.

A nurse rushed into the room.

My mouse fled.

"Doctor, doctor," I heard her shout, "our boy is hemorrhaging!"

It was not a pretty word. I don't like it any better now. And it drove my mouse away.

I cried all night for my mouse. Cried while wheeled down a corridor, cried on the white hard table. Unseen nurses soothed my wet forehead but could not soften my sorrow.

I remembered my mouse forever; trying to run up a flat wall.

He was a messenger to me, gray and tiny-tailed. Gray and red. I love the colors together. In the combination, gray more than red.

On the seventh day I rose from bed whitefaced, and cried no

more. I was out of tears. Beautiful nurses comforted me and cradled me. But I wanted the world outside the hospital windows. I said reluctant farewell to my nurses and fell in love with my kindergarten teacher.

Miss Landy was her name. She seemed tall. She smiled all the time, warmly, inclining her head. Her voice was low and shivery. I dreamt of her the way she was in life. We went on walks together. When it rained I sat beside her and listened to that thrilling whisper in her voice. In my dreams she sang to me and told unbelievably beautiful stories about kissing and hearts and arms around.

I was faithful to Miss Landy. She married, though, and left the school.

I met her many years later.

Older.

My mother and father were European. They loved each other. They kissed. They played instruments. They sang.

I grew up singing.

What I loved I sang to, and what I sang to I loved. I mean whom. I mean beautiful women. My sorrow over Miss Landy's fickle heart lasted a short time. I fell in love with a girl my own age, with long golden hair. Whenever I saw her watching me I did something daring. I dived into water over my head. I shied a rock over the sun. I did flips and handstands. I leaped over any available obstacle. No fence seemed too high.

Yet one was.

I tripped, fell, and fractured my hip. For love it was necessary. I have no regrets. I concluded something I hold up as a possibility: ALL FOR LOVE, or, A BROKEN HIP.

A broken hip combined with blood from the throat suggested I was short on luck. Not to my mother's Uncle Bim. He sat at the head of my bed, his profile humped and heaped on my covers as I hung in traction. A bald eagle. He looked mournful. He stooped. He was long. I thought of him moving with a flap of his Russian cloak.

"My hip is not good, Uncle."

"You will glow, like sun in rubies."

"I don't like hurting."

"Days will pass. You will sparkle, shining, like blood."

Uncle Bim was a misunderstood man. His children thought him vulgar. He did not bathe much, 'twas whispered; sometimes he forgot to wash before eating. He had a terrible way of clearing his throat. His children said he humiliated them when they were in need.

Probably his children were right.

But when Uncle Bim stretched his long arms the way ancient birds beat their wings to soar their tired heavy bodies high over intervening mountains, he made you want to devour life.

Bite chunks of blue out of the sky, I mean; flare up on fire to where the sun sits spinning. He made you want to wrap your arms around spring greenness, imprison in your ear the cry of waking birds, love and be loved by a loving lovely girl.

Uncle Bim was a presence.

This *imitatio* I live is a shifting fickle thing; but when I turned messenger I leaped to stride in Uncle Bim's footsteps.

He was fantastically gaunt, my Uncle Bim, with huge hands and feet, a careless aristocratic bearing. He wore a stained gray fedora low over his glinting gray eyes day and night, summer and winter, eating, napping. It shadowed a sharply cut face, thin skin, a map of veins I read as rivers and streams. His chin was short but deeply cleft, his full moustache straggly as Einstein's.

He flourished in icy winter. Out of the snow, a huge dark shadow in long black greatcoat and gray karakul collar, his Russian galoshes buckled high up the calf, crusted with gray snow cracked and cratered. His entrance was a stomp of overshoes, a beating together of fur mitts, a white blast of fogging breath.

He ate rye bread of a dark and snapping-crisp crust; grated black radish and Bermuda onions covered with oil and coarse salt; his taste in salami was hot, hard, dry, garlic-loaded; he prepared pickles in dill-and-red chili pepper; laid his own wine, red sweet and powerful.

His beaked eagle's nose demanded a third dimension of the world; his singing voice mocked silence; his shining gray eyes and red-veined cheeks forced color into day. I loved his walk — stiff-legged, hurrying, a dark pursued ostrich. I loved his gestures, his windups, his hands shooting up to express surprise, hugging himself to express horror.

He demanded nothing, expected nothing. His arrival caused as much excitement as a prince's. Kettles banged against taps, cube-sugar rattled in china bowls; silverware anchored freshly sailed-out tablecloths.

He smoked the strongest Turkish tobaccos, handmade cigarettes held between his teeth from lightup to snuffout. His vest was a dark burial ground for scattered ash memorializing countless cigarettes long ago cremated.

He was ruthlessly partisan toward his children, his grandchildren, other people's children. Those who were beautiful, gifted, he saw; others he did not. He hated safety, anonymity, measure, good sense. He had two categories, "live," and "dying." His choosing was Paris's apple.

Beside my bed he sprang at me the bait of life. When I closed my eyes I soared on his voice over deserts and mountains; he spoke with a rush of whirlwinds and a touch of deliverer zephyrs.

But he could not mend my broken hip.

Nor could my love for that girl with long gold hair.

I lay in traction a winter's length and tried to find patterns in new flyspecks on my room's small windows. Any voice was a line in a part-song I sang with through the long night. My fingers played soccer, hockey, football, true to the seasons. Everything lived in my imagination, except my nurses.

Month after month they came and went, dayshift nurses, eveningshift, nightshift. I was always in love with at least three. Hospital procedures interfered with my heart's choosing. My nursing loves were routinely transferred to obstetrics. But no eight-hour shift found me without a nurse I loved. If they were beautiful my open eyes stared gratitude; if they were less than beautiful, half-closed eyes and an open imagination brought love up to a snapping level. I inhaled their womanly warmth under masking greensoap. I soared out the narrow windows on a multicolored Persian carpet, my only passenger a dark-haired nurse. We rode together to Paris and Rome, climbed to the top of the Eiffel Tower, threw mad kisses at St. Peter's from St. Paul's.

Love was not the business of that hospital world. Life was there, on the wind and on the wane. When harsh bells ended visiting hours, or hard light the fantasy of a chrysalis, I knew I was only in bed, much strung up on bare wood two-by-fours and pulleys. Puppeted, from waist to toe.

White walls did not a prison make, but did set terrible limits to the universe. Seven men were in the room with me. I had to make a world with them. One was a penitentiary guard who wept for his wife at night. Once a week she came to visit.

"I'm dyin' for it."

"No worse than me, Bill."

"Find a way, love."

"Where can we go?"

"Nowhere."

There was a rummy among us, "Three Star" Hennessy, who faked collapse outside the hospital gates each November, and spent winter in the "Florida" of our warm flat. Spring, like an open window to a carrier pigeon, called Three Star back to the world. He began to eat, recover, and prepare for a summer of panhandle and drink.

A nurse brought him his torn mackinaw, baggy trousers, worn lifeless tweed cap, stiff Relief workboots laced with dirty knotted string. He sat in the center of the room, rotating on his bottom, like clockhands.

"Cheaters overrun the world, lad. Rob an ailin' man of his new clothes. Look at these rags, will ye? For a man collapsed in the lungs! My kids will think the old man pawned his Burberry for vintage wine. If it teaches *you* to be wary, lad, my sorrow ain't wasted."

One old man cared for nothing in this life but ripe cherries. His wife selected them by hand, each of a size, dark black-red. She sat with a stiff cream damask napkin and polished his cherries. One by one. Never eating herself. Popping them carefully into his mouth. He chewed silently, slowly, thoroughly. The pits he squirted back into her hand were buffgray, quite dry. He had a magnificent sense of timing, my cherryman. No matter how many she brought him, no matter how long she stayed, the last pit dropped from his tongue and lips at the visitors-out bell.

The retired railroad construction foreman had a daughter who visited weekly, but never came in from the hall. She was blonde, with hair long and sundrenched. I fell in love with the foreman's daughter. Her eyes were a light blue, and always teared-over. She wanted her father to invite her in. He never did.

He was a big Belgian, with huge moustaches, and a brooding anger in his ducked-down head. Hatred lived in the stoop of his shoulders, violence in the flick of his fork.

He came home unexpectedly one night and found his daughter on a man's lap, her large breasts quite bare. His fists battered the man severely. He insisted the man should marry his daughter. The man considered the request premature; he had barely begun his passionate address when the old man intervened.

The girl was left alone.

With her father, I mean. He didn't talk to her again, ever.

If I had been the man with that girl on his lap I think I would have listened to her father.

She was beautiful.

One man played the zither. Much of the day. Western tunes.

I was there. I'll tell you how I know.

A passing doctor, with eager medical students and internes in his progress, stopped in the doorway, stared at me, pointed. His devotees ranged themselves along his finger, as if they were sighting with a rifle.

"That boy is septic," he said.

His voice was resonant. Bass.

"No, sir, he is not," said my resident.

"Are you sure?"

"I'll check it again, sir."

"I'd be willing to bet."

He turned away. His flock followed. In the marble corridor their feet sounded marchtime, but his shoes, which I heard clearly every morning after, had small metal taps on the heels, and cut through the anonymity of the marchers, rolling over the stone floor, echoing in the halls hollowly, taking a long time to recede.

One man frightened me, because his eyes were yellow. In evening light they glowed that color dandylions reflect on children's chins in the game, "Butter, butter, do you like butter?"

His name was Mac, Macdonald, and he lived on a big wide farm. This was his first time in any city. He had no visitors ever. His wife knew Mac's yellow-eyed sickness was serious, but she had chores to do, he said, and his kids needed schooling.

Mac's friend was the Frenchman. Together they sat at the scaffolding over my bed. Mac had a son my age, the Frenchman a daughter.

We lived together in a city within a city within a city. The real sun through glass was smoky bronze, and unreal. The real buildings outside the windows were unfamiliar, pasteboard, mean. The hospital's labyrinthine corridors might never lead back to an open door.

In our lonely world Mac had the dignity of the helpless. His bony face and long scrawny neck sunbeaten, wrapped in a foxed hospital robe, bluegray, with faded Indian designs. His hands were tanned yellow red, thicknailed, veins raised, gray at the fingertips.

He always cleared his throat before speaking.

"It's only that they never really talk to a feller. Questions about liver ain't talk. I mean sky and snow and people — doctors get outside. They know about things."

The Frenchman bounced his crutch in agreement.

"You right. God you right. I tell you about that one, eh? Who say 'Cut,' after I freeze the toe. 'Cut, what the hell cut? *Me* cut?' He say, 'It have to be, Frenchie. You got the gangrene. You dumb to pedal the bike in thirty below.'"

Mac stretched his fingers over his head. His bathrobe sleeves fell away. His skinny arms crisscrossed in silhouette against our windows.

"You can't rightly *ask* them, you know. I worked out hired hand one Christmas and the boss's kids laid a present for me under the family tree. It would have to come like that."

"Next time they gonna cut the everything. I show lady doctor where. She turn her back, by God."

"Come fall, they need help on my farm."

They came for me on a morning and loosed me from the puppetstrings. They dressed me in a starched gown that gaped open at the back, wheeled me into a large room crowded with students.

Lights came on. The tape on my legs glared blue-white. Boys in dark suits, and stethescopes crowded him who had framed himself in the doorway, whose bass voice boomed arrogance and taught pride.

He picked my leg up absently.

"What was that guess, sir?" he said with a shake of his head. "T.B. *after* a fracture? What if T.B. were there *before*, undetected, causing bone degeneration?"

"What is the classic treatment, sir?"

"Bed rest. Six months to two years in the San."

Students crowded in, poking. Words showered over me, "the San," "T.B. T.B." "the San." The sanitarium, doorless, high on a hill, to which fathers couldn't come, and mothers couldn't come, nor Uncle Bim, where nurses were nuns in steelrim glasses and didn't sit on beds and hug and kiss, and I wanted back to my own barewood rack, with my mother there and my father there and Uncle Bim.

"T.B. can be masked in a thousand confusing ways."

"Doctor."

"What is it, son?"

"Please, you're hurting my leg."

"Couldn't possibly be."

He let my leg drop without warning.

His feet were too long for the stretcher.

He wanted to be wheeled out sitting up. A whitehatted nurse touched his shoulder. She had a gauze mask under her chin.

"Lie down, Mister Macdonald."

She smiled. Mac waved as he lay back, and disappeared through the door.

A bald orderly shuffled in with a white metal rack chipped black, rusting; he yawned, rocked the stand till it steadied, came in again with a thick brown stand for the other side of Mac's bed. He caught my eye as he shuffled out, and shook his head.

My dayshift love swept into the room. She was my darlingest. I deeded her to Mac for the day.

She hooked a plasma bottle to the top of the white rack, something colorless to the top of the brown. The door bumped open. A larger stretcher on heavy rubber wheels came like a ship into the room. Mac was asleep, his head flat. Three doctors, heads bound, and masked, raised him gently into his bed. One pressed a needle into Mac's left arm, another into his right. They slipped out of the room noiselessly.

My nurse sat, head to one side, fingers on his pulse, her lips moving in count.

"Mister Macdonald, wouldn't you like to wake up now?"

She sang.

"Mister Macdonald, rooster crowed hours ago. Come, now, wake up."

She sat back, folded her arms again.

"How did the operation turn out?" I whispered after long silence.

"Grand."

"Please wake him."

"I will."

"He'll love seeing you. You're more beautiful than flowers."

"I'll kiss you for that, dear boy."

She stood up.

"Mister Macdonald, Mac, slugabed, sleep away the sun? I'm a farmgirl, you can't fool with me."

She took his pulse again.

"Mac," she said, "I need you up. Come now — one two three."

Her hand shook his shoulder.

"Mac, I'll be late for *my* chores. You wouldn't want that?"

She slapped him on the cheek, playfully, then urgently, hard.

"Mac," I blurted, "how are you, Mac? You're back with us."

"Mister Macdonald, someone is asking how you are."

Mac's feet stirred. His voice came from somewhere.

It frightened me more than his sleeping.

"Not bad for a feller, you know. Not too bad at all."

"Rest easy, Mister Macdonald. I'll be back in a second."

She looked at me.

"I haven't forgotten that kiss."

I leaned up on one elbow. Mac was still.

He turned suddenly. The bottles clanged on metal.

The Frenchman looked black with sorrow.

"How are you, Mac?" I whispered.

"Not too bad, nossir. Not too bad."

"Need anything?"

"A feller could do with a drink."

I pressed my buzzer. A strange nurse hurried in. She stopped halfway to his bed, tiptoed one step forward, one step back. My nurse came running. Nobody offered Mac water.

The surgeon stole in, booted like a deepseadiver. The sheets he pulled back were dark with stain.

"How's a feller doing, doctor?"

"Fairly well, Mister Macdonald."

My nurse flapped a change of sheets.

My throat was tense with unyawned yawns. One by one the red and colorless bottles were hung. The surgeon came back, looked, took the needles out of Mac's arms. Nobody read. Nobody spoke. The Belgian man smoked with his head down. The man with the zither silently tightened strings.

I aimed my love at Mac. Borrowed back my love for my mother and my father and Uncle Bim, took back my love from all my nurses. Threw love Mac's way with two hands, as if I were bailing water from a terribly leaking boat.

He sat up suddenly, his eyes on the ceiling.

"Mac," I said, "keep your head down."

"That's proper, I guess."

"How are you feeling, Mac?"

"Pretty good, pretty good."

"Shall I ring for the nurse?"

"Can't rightly think of a thing I need, sonny."

He fell back.

The yawns in my throat pulled tight.

Mac's head turned toward the window. A church slate roof, silver in dusklight, the sun blocked out by its belltower. Weak, sinking sunlight struggled free of brick, reached for the window, came into the room on motes of red dust.

Mac rose suddenly, a poor skinny man on his knees to touch the sun. His body bent forward. The Frenchman hollered, the prison guard swore. Mac lunged for the sunspot near the window, missed, hit his washstand. His alarm clock skid crashing to the floor.

"Mac," I shouted.

He hung down the side of the bed like a warrior thrown dead over his horse.

A squarewheeled stretcher they must have used, clattering, banging doors, beds, clanking against stands of metal. I hid my head under the covers and imagined whiterobed aviators, goggled menacingly, with great white packs on their backs, white boots laced to their thighs.

"When I got the call to bring the covered wagon I had a feeling this was the guy. What a noise we kick up."

"The customers never complain."

"He's long."

"Pack him neat."

"Look at the gore. Somebody pulled the plug, I betcha."

"How do we dump the mattress?"

"Pitch it over the covered wagon. He won't mind."
"I'll run ahead and close doors. Scares everybody to see one."

That alarm clock ticked all night under the stripped bed.

My nurse had fine taste. She never offered me that promised kiss.

I had a feeling about the resident. He spoke to Mac in a loud toneless voice. He had sandy hair and a drunk's cheeks. His face looked swollen, his eyes a fighter's, beat-up. I had a feeling about him, but no power.

He came to do a job, with written orders. I should have been happy. The adhesive bandages that held the strings that supported the weights, he would cut them off.

He held shears. He didn't look at me.

"The ether?" I reminded him.

"To put you to sleep?" He laughed.

"To unstick the adhesive."

"More trouble than it's worth."

"I don't mind the trouble."

"Ether is messy."

"I've got hairy legs. Every other time the interne used loads of ether."

"I'm a resident, not an interne."

My alarms rang. He blew on a nurse's flatnosed scissors, slipped them quickly between the adhesive and my skin. He worked slowly, expertly, snipping in a jagged line, down one side on one leg, down the other on the other. He put the scissors down.

"How will you take the stickiness away?" I cried.

"Like this!"

My skin tore like canvas. I screamed. That rasping sound set my legs on fire. Lengths of adhesive curled with hair, trailing skin.

"Please, not the other leg!"

He grabbed a loose end of adhesive. The fire jumped from one leg to the other.

"Stop that screaming. If something bad happened you'd be bleeding. Here, this will help."

"I am bleeding!"

He sprinkled a powder over the fire. An irritant! I felt the pain catch at me like an open flame, a knife under a fingernail, a bone shattering.

"Shut up, you baby! You just want to make trouble!"

"Stop the burning. Please stop the burning."

I bear his scars.

The chief orthopedic surgeon came in, sorrowing.

"De Sade," he said, "only de Sade knows about this. Get him out. Get them all out. Sonny, in a month it will be all healed over. Just the marks will stay. We all must have marks."

Soon it was spring. Free of bandages, strings, weights, pulleys. My scars were healing. A spring of nurses came to the ward. The man with the zither played recognizable Neapolitan tunes. The railroad foreman's daughter ran off with a jockey. The prison guard kissed his wife for one whole visiting hour.

I loved a nurse whose hair smelled of the sea.

I loved another whose eyes were miniature mosaics, finely cracked greengoldhazel glass.

I loved my nightnurse, who glided in like a phantom, and didn't rustle the starch of her aprons. I hugged her in the darkness.

She didn't believe Mac was better off dead.

I was in a lover's paradise.

And my hip didn't heal.

One long foolish April I luxuriated, but X-rays found me out.

I was no better. The old orthopedic surgeon came and looked. I begged him not to string me up again.

They came on a night, the same orderly with the same equipment they used on Mac his night before. Next morning I got no breakfast. A strange nurse was in the room.

"What's the doctor planning, Nurse?"

"You'll find out."

"Do my parents know?"

"I suppose."

"They didn't say anything."

"It's a secret, between them and doctor."

"Please let me call them."

"This early? You'll scare them half to death."

"Am I going to be cut?"

"Silly boy — so much talk — now stop it."

"O.R. on your cap. Operating Room. That means cutting."

"Doctor knows what's best."

"Were you in there when they cut Mac?"

"Who?"

"Mister Macdonald."

"We see dozens every day, sonny."

I wanted to shout to the prison guard I was being kidnapped. Someone should phone my parents.

Politeness hid my terror. I tried to smile the abstracted nurse over to my side.

I thought of my mouse, and the blood. I had played Isaac to one surgeon, and his knife slipped.

"Miss, there's a phone across the way. Can you lend me a nickel?"

I was wheeled past the phone booth swiftly, down a stone corridor, into a phoneless elevator.

"Nurse," I shouted as we moved through opaque glass doors, "I have to go to the bathroom — badly!"

The glass doors closed behind her. I was over the line.

Basins, instruments, cabineted walls full of silvery devices. Sinks with footpedals. Voices. Water rushing. An opaque door with moving shadows. I pushed my head back, up against the nurse's soft belly. She pulled away.

The door swung open. Two hairy arms took hold of my stretcher. Wide awake I lived out the strangling nightmare of trying to shout for help.

Nothing familiar. Masks. No shape, no face. Not a sound.

On a white tablet stiff and solid as stone they placed me, a thousand lights over my head, mocking mirrors telling my littleness.

Whitegowned man, whitegowned woman, plead for me when he comes, the masked man whose knife slipped at my throat. Find a ram's horn. Make a sign in the thicket.

Lights turned on, I stepped into the blinding sun.

The mask would be next. My nose would be covered, my lungs sealed.

My gown was yanked free. A sheet flew over me. I smelled something weird — neither ether nor chloroform. I was jacked up, wrapped in roughness. My legs. My belly. My chest. I opened one screwed-shut eye. I was encased in gray felt. A huge man with a mask on his chest held two pieces of black iron riveted into a cross. He pressed the cold metal into my hipbones. He measured. One leg. The other.

Amputation. They were measuring. Catch the falling blood.

I had nobody to shriek my fears to.

Three black iron rods swung across the table. Another large man pressed them against my sides, from armpit to ankle, from groin to heel. Feet shuffled. That strange smell grew stronger.

"Quick, wrap it fast before it sets."

Something wet and clammy touched my instep. I opened my eyes.

I was spun in wet plaster, wound white like a silkworm spinning a long sleeve. Behind the two huge men was the old orthopedic surgeon, his glasses reflecting me and the thousand lights. I was built into a white iron lung. Stiffening. Stiff. Hard as the iron rods. A paralyzing cocoon but for one leg left free.

"My bad leg's the one you covered," it sounded as if my voice said.

"Sonny?"

"The bad leg. You covered it."

"We'll make it as good as new."

"You're not going to cut the other?"

"Cut? What gave you that idea?"

The cast was heavy. It ran from my armpits to my hips and continued down one leg. I could not turn without help. To write or draw I had to be lifted, set against a backrest propped with cushions. Often I fell over on my back, stuck.

I was committed to that fake healer, Time, and sent home.

One window at my head, opening onto a verandah I cased quickly — two chairs, a puffy green couch. Once I had seen them it seemed silly to twist my head to look behind.

When I was carried to the verandah windows I rediscovered the framed world. Milkmen, breadmen, phonemen, deliverymen, neighbors.

I could almost see blades of grass lengthen. I knew every spill of tar on the road, the stain of dripping oil. I knew who had thrown what cigarette cardboard where, and what car ran over it when. I lived the routines of sparrows and robins, believed in their choices. I read wind in the motion of trees, rain in the darkening of clouds. A candy wrapper blown on stage was the gallop-past of a horse and strange rider.

Later in life I could afford to differentiate. Then, it was Either/

Or. Light or no light, sound or no sound, a human being or none at all. One window. No more. That much space. Nothing wider.

I couldn't rouse Mac or the Frenchman, talk to the prison guard, read my cherryman or the old Belgian. I was grateful for the rattle of a manhole cover two blocks away, and prayed the passing car might turn down my block. Any stir started my heart pounding — slamming car doors, banging screens, the clop-clop of old horses pulling the few ragwagons left on streets.

Two houses to the west lived Mrs. Stevens, very large, very fat, who wore white bowling shoes winter and summer, and wept because her only son was "nervous."

There was Mrs. Moroz with her raspy voice, a condemner, complainer, and great wisher-of-harm. I loved Mrs. Moroz, and her miserable ways. She broke the blankness of my wall, the dead silence. I grew tired of painting worlds for myself. I wanted color and action in my room. Mrs. Moroz was my great Queen Bess arrested on a progress. I encouraged her worst side, because it kept her going longer. I smiled when she blistered her boarders, clucked sympathetically for the roomatiz killing her shoulder.

Her face was Indian, coarse black hair in a heavy bun wisped silver, small inky eyes squinchy with complaint, squinty from the sun. Her skin was grained and dark. Her crooked teeth had great gaps her tongue played like a cricket chorus, cheery chirps which punctuated her lamentations as irreverently as a birdsong cutting Hamlet's soliloquies.

When she talked she pulled her dress closed at the throat, left deep fingermarks. She was in terror of "consumption," which she thought a spitting boarder had sprayed through her house.

She told great stories.

"My brother's wife's uncle got a fly in his eye —"

"Which?"

"Left, I think. Fly got in this eye and go to his brain. Poof! He finished. Well, I go now, sonny."

"Poof? From a fly in the eye!"

"A tiny one so big like this piece fingernail. I have time I tell you more."

"People get flies in the nose?"

"Every day ten, at least. You heard from bean in ear?"

"Somebody died from a bean in the ear?"

"You don't believe?"

"You tell me, I believe, Mrs. Moroz."

"Over on Magnus a Ukrainian lady get one small breadcrumb under her nail. It get in a vein and run up her arm to the —"

"The brain?"

"Never! Breadcrumb gots to her heart."

"She died?"

"You betcha," Mrs. Moroz said with that chirping flourish.

Next door lived Mr. Boyczuk who in my cold city grew fruit trees, fed them pig's blood he dug into the rich black loam with his fingers; when snow bent boughs low Mr. Boyczuk wired them and crutched them. He was bald and didn't like to wear his false teeth; we were allies, he and I, his grimaces through my pane of glass said so — a man with lumbago understood a broken hip.

His trees bore fruit in summer.

Uncle Bim kept the unsimple world near.

There was a side to him flared with hatred. Dobrushyn. As a small child I read the signals — the brim of Uncle Bim's fedora rising in agitated rhythm, his arms apart, pumping, his fingers stretched.

"Twenty people Dobrushyn wrote one letter: 'Don't send me money for steamship tickets and I drown myself. I stand at the sea till I hear from you. Me and eight potential orphans.'"

Uncle Bim's wife and Dobrushyn's wife were first cousins. The feud their husbands carried on was shame to them, and a big bore.

The feud claimed precedence, nurtured like love, satisfied like success, was self-engrossing as sleep. Together on hatred Uncle Bim and Dobrushyn soared high above land, family, children. The true cause of the feud — something about those steamship tickets — was forgotten. Like courtiers, Uncle Bim and Dobrushyn could hate on a straw, war over an eggshell.

Dobrushyn was as short as Uncle Bim was long. He drank tea not from a saucer, Uncle Bim's way, but out of English bone china cups, his free hand waving a long elegant amber cigarette holder. Smoking he leaned back, the holder between his small even teeth. His cigarettes were initialed, made by his wife each morning and packed into his initialed gold case. His shirts were monogramed. His maroon custom Chrysler had a huge Old English "D" on its front doors. His hair was cropped short, military, his Oriental golden skin creased in mocking and ironic expressions. He often closed his slanty eyes and seemed asleep, to open them suddenly, a startling blue.

His vests hung heavy goldlink watchchains, matching his heavy gold cufflinks. His shoes gleaming patent, his shirt collars starched stiff, his trousers sharply creased. Silk handkerchiefs flowed from his breast pocket.

He, like Uncle Bim, never learned to drive a car. Uncle Bim rode in the front seat of his touring Studebaker, its celluloid sidewindows yellowed, the leather top torn and worn. Dobrushyn settled back in the raised custom cushions of his Chrysler and directed his chauffeur sons.

He considered his genetic message garbled. Any question about his children Dobrushyn met with a grimace, and closed eyes. Only Leeba, his one daughter and eldest child, found favor.

"She's a crook. I have her manage my books. She steals, and she knows I know — that's the beauty. Those idiot boys steal with tails between their legs. Leeba has a power."

"General" Dobrushyn's bad eyes and weird gargly strained voice passed to his children. His wit, his charm, his vitality, his wise worldly ways, not. Leeba was supposed to make up for all that: Leeba married a truckdriver type called Ziff.

"I told her," I once heard Dobrushyn say, "you want a ruffian in your bed, I'll fix you a place to knock stuffing out of mattresses. Marriage is something else. A doctor or university genius we need. I'll set a brain up like a prince. Even if it doesn't stand by him."

Ziff was chosen, most of the time, to be chauffeur. With his sons Dobrushyn backseat drove, tonguelashing them from stopsign to stopsign. Ziff the old man lacerated.

Summer cooled the feud. Dobrushyn offered Uncle Bim's relatives rides to the beach.

He kissed on the cheeks. Wet, gluey, lasting. It wasn't polite to rub off after Dobrushyn kissed. One wore his lipmarks like an ignored housefly.

My brother and I, before my fall, huddled on the Chrysler's jump seats to stay out of range. Peppered with instructions, Ziff drove over country roads. Dobrushyn bounced off the back cushions, hanging onto a plush handstrap like a subwayrider. This one morning he was in a great mood, telling of his triumphs and wicked trades.

One tale was never finished. The Chrysler jumped, veered, skidded, almost ran off the road; Ziff, like a champion racer, wrestled the wheel. The car stopped inches short of a deep ditch. We wanted to cheer.

Dobrushyn's face was sickeningly yellow.

"Roughneck, what did you hit?"

"Nuddin'."

"Nuddin'? Ape, does a car get thrown around by nuddin'?"

"We got a blowout. Is it my fault?"

"Did you check the tires before we left? Your life is worth nothing. You should respect the rest of us."

Like abused Caliban Ziff growled his way onto the road.

Dobrushyn stepped out, set his shoes down so no dust obscured their gleam.

"Open the trunk, pull out the jack, get the pump, the patching kit — it's your donkey, Leeba. Talk to him donkey language."

Ziff kicked furiously at the flat tire.

"Everybody out," he shouted.

"Don't move, nobody."

Dobrushyn held his hand up with finality.

"You don't understand mechanical advantage? What the hell difference will a few people make to the jack?"

Ziff stomped in the dirt, swore, yanked the trunk open, threw tools into the road. Dobrushyn fitted a cigarette into the holder, deliberately struck a match on the jackhandle.

I felt terrible for Ziff.

Dobrushyn made everybody an accomplice. Even Leeba, who must have dipped into the cash heavily that week.

Ziff jacked the car up high. Every touch of the wheel set the car rocking. He tested the pump with a dustraising blast General Dobrushyn cleverly anticipated, and avoided.

"Here," Ziff shouted, "see, it's done!"

"With a brain you could have done it in a tenth the time."

Ziff knelt at the rear bumper, struggling to free the stuck jack.

"The handle," Ziff said. "The goddam handle."

He poked his head under the car, twisted upward to see what was wrong.

"Idiot!"

Dobrushyn kicked at the jack viciously. The car lurched downward.

"You coulda killed me!" Ziff screamed, and stretched full length in the dirt.

"Clean yourself off good," Dobrushyn said, and climbed back into the car. "You just got taught how to break down a jack."

This Dobrushyn was also pixie.

He played the flute beautifully, and danced a dashing Russian waltz. He loved to give presents, flowers, chocolates, perfumes. He couldn't keep his hands off beautiful women.

The price of the feud was the unavailability of Uncle Bim's four redcheeked, highbreasted, beautiful daughters Dobrushyn in peacetime danced with, pinched and kissed. Each girl took a turn accompanying him on the piano. He played swaying, on tiptoe, his reddish hair fiery in lamplight, his slanty eyes closed. He sang a thousand dirty Russian songs in that wet reedy voice.

Death, marriage, birth ended the feud temporarily. Anything at all set it going again.

Who first said the earth was round compelled the feud to start up over whether it was flat.

Their hatred exploded out of pins, eyelashes, dirtspecks.

Uncle Bim beside my bed would tell me to beware of Dobrushyn. And he, Dobrushyn, on the rare occasions he came, was charming, gracious, lovable, unidentifiable as the tyrant who lamented the joke in his genes.

I put the two of them on stage at night, when everyone slept, and no nurse came, Dobrushyn on a white steed and Uncle Bim, my Don Quixote, sitting Sancho's donkey. They tilted from the front and the back of windmills, never meeting, never hurting.

Mr. Boyczuk had a daughter Katsha I loved as if she were a nurse. Our love was powerful as marriage. Katsha had an uncle, a "wilkoh," Wilkoh Joe, which meant he was, in our way, my uncle too.

Wilkoh's face was burned red from the sun, his forehead a harvester's flour white. He had red flappy ears, a great red nose, grinspread cheeks. He rode a racing bike, wore a broad flat cap with inflated crown, and, on his ankles, bicycle clips. He rose out of the west, his bike's front wheel wiggle-waggling, his hands waving. In front of the Boyczuk gate he vaulted high out of the saddle, hung in mid-air a second, ran the rolling bike up to my window.

My nose pressed against the glass.

"Hallo sohnny, howzda sohnny?"

"Terrific. Howzda Wilkoh?"

"Nor bad, nor bad."

"Hot, you hot, Wilkoh?"

"Terrible hot. I sweat."

Then he came out of the Boyczuk house, pretending not to see me, stop, clap at his head with both hands, push the bike through the gate, jog the front wheel over the curb, rise gently in the air, bang down on the seat, turn to my window, wave, ring flat farewell out of his rusted bicycle bell. Pumping, harder, smaller and smaller, like that tramp in the movies.

Wilkoh Joe and Uncle Bim, I rode off into sleep thinking of them, Uncle Joe, Wilkoh Bim, on a tandem bike, capable as Russian gymnasts, circling the moon.

Wilkoh met a girl.

She had gapteeth, sparkling black eyes, black hair down her back in a braid.

They turned up together first on a Sunday, the bike between them, Wilkoh with his collar buttoned, his Sunday pants free of bicycle clips.

He grinned up at me.

"Howzda sohnny?"

"Great. Howzda Wilkoh?"

The girl stood to one side, grinning.

"Sohnny, meet da Weeky."

"Hello Vicky."

"Hello sohnny. You get bedder right away, hokay?"

"Hokay."

"Sure," Wilkoh said, "sohnny gonna walk goot, like dis."

He aimed a kick at the sky, his head back, the bike swung free of the ground.

Wilkoh married Vicky in the fall. She gave birth late the next spring.

I was in plaster at my window.

Vicky sat on the Boyczuk front steps, the baby in her arms, and grinned up at me. When the baby cried Vicky pulled out her large fair breast, pressed it on the baby between two widespread fingers.

Wilkoh stood proudly patting the baby's head, Vicky's breast, pointing.

I could tell you of those plasterbound days, twenty-four hours by twenty-four hours. It's better to let such time blur.

It turned out, later, that the cast was a big mistake. The man who goofed wanted another chance. Surgery. It was very risky, but important to him. A doctor who has goofed should have a chance to atone.

I did not want to be cut.

Saturday night Uncle Bim came.

"Nobody cuts him," he said.

"The doctor decided we must," my mother said from behind her apron.

"We get another doctor."

My mother called the Chief of Orthopedics at his house. She told him Uncle Bim's son, a medical student, suggested his name.

He bawled her out for calling him at home on a Saturday.

He came, a man with a huge head, moustaches bigger than Uncle Bim's, and a heavy German accent.

"Get out of bed."

"I can't."

I smiled at my mother and father for confirmation.

"I said get out of bed."

I swung my feet over the side of the bed, tried to stand. I crashed to the floor. My mother screamed.

"You two get out of here. This is a professional examination. Or say nothing."

I lay on the floor, stunned.

"Why did you people call me?"

"You're a professor," my mother said.

"I thought this boy was dying."

"They want to operate on Monday."

"Get up."

He yanked me to my feet, steadied me, looked at me fiercely.

"Be in the hospital tomorrow morning."

"To be operated . . . ?"

"Not their hospital. Ours."

I was strung up again. I've told you enough about that.

When I was good and stretched, I stood before a full-length mirror and walked toward myself.

That doctor taught me how.

In gratitude I fell in love with two of his daughters. One was a movie star I never did meet face to face. The other turned up years later, a classmate of mine at the University. I told her I loved her late father, who had raised me from the bed.

She said she heard he helped people sometimes.

I fell in love with her anyway.

The superstitious pinned my misfortune on my brother. Someone had to be blamed. For some reason it couldn't be me. God's harsh judgment was hung on my brother Gad.

He wanted a Roman holiday, a week, maybe a month of unlimited larks. He loved girls. He wanted to take them out in style. He had no money.

The Catholic Hockey League needed players, my brother needed kicks. He adopted the name of a boyhood hero, Scarface Al Capone, made it more Catholic, Scarlatti. Lord of the ice rinks, he took bruising communion Sunday afternoons, Ruby Scarlatti, prince among papists,

I fell in love with every girl he brought home. He majored in college girls, tall and very dark and quite skinny but with huge breasts he swooned over.

All week he suffered the gloom of me in my bed, and the Depression. Sunday he swooped over glittering ice, Ruby Scarlatti, putting on the style. He bragged about his home, and his wild parties.

The older boys trapped him into an invitation.

Ruby Scarlatti who skimmed the cold hazy rink ice had to deliver.

"Tell ma and pa you feel terrific."
"O.K."
"Stop them from going out Saturday night and I'll maulerize you."
"O.K."
"Don't go queer my act like a bloody baby."
"Who's a baby, jerk?"
"Did you call me a jerk?"
"I don't chew my cabbage twice."
"Take it back."
"For you?"
"You nipple — Nip the Crip, that's you, laying there like, I don't know what like."
"Why don't you get me up, Jesus?"
"Did you call me Jesus?"

He thought I was ratting on his Catholic games.

"Jerky Jesus."

He dived at me. I tried to hold him off, but he climbed on the chest of my cast. His knees pinned my upper arms, his hands slapped at my cheeks, left, right, left, stinging, ringing, open-handed, loud, cursing me, his eyes wet, red — I had forced him to fall on somebody helpless, somebody down.

We had no language for other messages. It had to be this, swinging and slapping, writhing, twisting. I knew shame and fatigue would ultimately make him stop.

"Go to hell, you little nipple, go on, cry, you sniveling bastard." I cried.

That beating was so unnecessary. I was dying for a girl party in our still house.

Late Saturday afternoon Ruby Scarlatti took stewardship of the manor. I was in league with him. We were stuck with his bragging.

He who knew nothing about kitchens fixed gooey sandwich spreads. Music called for three of his pals in various beginner stages. Joe played trumpet well enough to vamp for stomping Ukrainian weddings; Ladjoo had two coupons to go in a comic-strip accordion course; David was the fiddler, with soulful Hungarian eyes and a dreamy way of tucking the fiddle under his chin. He was learning what to do after that.

Scarlatti instructed his court musicians. "We play only swing. Polkas are for immigrants, Ladj, you understand?"

Ladjoo was sitting with his feet crossed over, the accordion on his stomach. I lay on the porch behind furniture Ruby and his pals moved out to make a dance floor; I could see Ladjoo chewing gum in his nauseating openmouthed way.

"Ladj," Ruby said, "I would bring this subject up before, but isn't your old man a little bit of a bootlegger?"

Ladjoo tried to throw the accordion at him.

"Calm down — I don't mean he sells to rummies. After hours, classy."

"My old man sells canned heat to people with the arthuritis."

"Could you steal us a couple bottles of whatever smells nicest?"

"What's in it for me?"

"Classy broads. I got one picked out. Blondie with a pair of tits you can tee up your head on. You too, Dave, and Joe. Three extra broads for the musicians."

"How we gonna use 'em if we're playin' music?" Joe asked.

"We'll have plenty of intermissions. O.K.? Ladj, go pinch us three bottles."

Ruby Scarlatti decorated the house with torn sodality bazaar lanterns Joe borrowed from the basement of his church, and flame light bulbs for our empty wall brackets. Thirty cents bought end-of-the-week blocks of half-melted ice, wilted vegetables, turning meat, hardening loaves of bread.

Stewards at the Jockey Club, they covered wide platters of finger sandwiches with damp white cloths, and awaited the arrival of the seignory.

Late evening, when the sun was long gone from Peanut Park, the taxis came.

Darkness helped.

"A whole street of gatehouses," I heard the first girl guest say, "they're divine."

Skirts rustled. Tall bareheaded boys in tuxes. Girls with sparkly combs in their hair.

Somebody came up the dark verandah steps. I ducked down behind an armchair.

"Junk furniture. We have the wrong address."

"I hear a band tuning."

The band was playing.

"Perhaps the main house is behind this one?"

Ruby came running out the back door.

"Hughie," I heard him lie breathlessly, "some dumb guys delivered a carload of old furniture here by mistake."

Joe played "Sugar Blues" on his mute, his third-best number after "The Wedding March" and the Ukrainian national anthem. Ladjoo was vamping off-beat. David's violin scraped Hungarian harmonies waltztime.

"There's the eats," I heard Ruby say in a phony cultivated voice, "I'm tending bar. Go 'head, dance."

"Hughie said something about champagne."

"Go on, dance, it's coming up."

"Gunnie's great at popping corks."

"We keep our stuff on ice in the wine cellar. It would dust up your tux, Gunnie."

"I love exploring wine cellars," the girl said.

"Ours," said Ruby, "ain't much."

The cars kept rolling.

Ruby lost his nerve. He wouldn't let Joe off "Sugar Blues" to try his next best solo.

I didn't hear any feet move.

Hughie called Ruby out to the edge of the verandah.

"Didn't you say bedrooms?"

"Plenty."

"Well?"

"You mean while you're waiting for champagne?"

"Right."

Ruby led two couples into the peach bedroom on the other side of the verandah window. It had no blind. My three-quarter size bed was grabbed by Hughie and his girl; Gunnie and his lady were left with a cot. Hughie's girl was blonde and slim and lovely in a wine velvet dress. The other girl had dark hair and a black velvet gown.

I saw them only a second. The moment Ruby turned, they put out the lights.

At midnight Ladjoo rebelled.

"Nobody's dancing," I heard him whisper.

"Shut up and play," Ruby said, and swung into his vocal.

> *Sugar blues, su-su-su-su-su-sugar blahues,*
> *I left my sugar with those su-su-sugar blahues.*

Couples filed in and out.

Somebody switched on a light and both the wine velvet and black velvet girls were all white.

"Goddam it, Rube, where's my blonde with the big tits?

I need some su-su-su-su-su-shooooooooooooooooogar
Some shooooooooooogar to cure my blahues.

"They're stinkin' drunk on my old man's booze. Look how they don't wait for seltzer."

"People come to a party to do what they want."

"You're running a whorehouse, sucker. Where's our payoff?"

Dave lay down his bow.

"I'm out of resin. My fiddle's squeaking."

"When did you notice?"

Joe slammed his trumpet against his music stand.

"Get them the hell out of here," he said loudly.

"Our guests?"

"They're filthy spoiled kids using this house like a flop."

Joe was a semi-pro; Ruby honored his standards.

"How do I do it?"

"Wake your kid brother and get him to start crying."

"Nah. Crying wouldn't budge them now."

"Let's start a little fire," suggested Ladjoo, born a criminal.

"My brother could burn."

"Don't fool around," Joe said angrily, "turn on the lights, tell them it's finished. I'll do it if you can't."

Ruby Scarlatti, man of honor, did his own dirty work.

An hour later the bedrooms were empty.

David snapped his violin case shut. Joe shook spit out of his trumpet.

Ruby began dragging furniture back. Joe, disapproving, helped carry the larger pieces.

Ladjoo was moving from bedroom to bedroom.

"Ruby," he cried out, "come see. One guy got himself a cherry."

My brother and Joe continued to shuffle with furniture.

"How you gonna explain blood on the bedclothes?" David asked.

"That's my business."

"Change it with the kid's sheets. Say he was picking his nose and bloodies it."

"Thanks, guys," Ruby said graciously, "you played real nice."

Ladjoo paused on the verandah steps.

"Rube, lemme hand you one advice. Next time you give a party, invite yourself too."

I remember that girl in the wine velvet dress.

Toward the end of my final hang in traction Miss MacLendon came on nights. A graduate, with black hair wound on her brow like a tragic actress. Her nose was delicately curved, but turned up. Hers was a night voice, shivery as Miss Landy's. She murmured when she rubbed my back with alcohol, and took a soothing long time drying me off with talc. She stole away the wrinkled oilskin sheet. Once, when I begged, she broke my orthopedic Professor's rule, piled on a chair the heavy weights that pulled on my bad leg.

She forgot to replace them before my doctor made his rounds.

He was angrier than the day he made me crash to the floor.

"Is there someone so ignorant to think this does you service? Give me her name."

I knew nothing.

That night she came and kissed me conspiratorially.

We were allies.

She did for me what Mac wanted his doctor to do. She told me of weather, sports, traffic, people in shops, children in the park, rain, shedding trees on the other side of the hospital, birds in the

City Hall fountain. I held her hand while she sang the outside day,
and oh, loved her. Not as I loved all the others, with a sliding flip-
flop in my throat. Wilder. Needles and pins, crazy rushings to my
throat. I drank her in.

Once I kissed her lips, parted just ever so slightly, and warmly
wet. I thought of those lips all morning and all afternoon and died
for them all night. Her day off was agony. She came back, always,
noiseless as a phantom. I held her lips longer and longer, pressing
slightly, opening them wider.

Her uniform was high-necked, stiffly starched. During one lovely
long kiss I slipped a lone finger into an opening between buttons. I
found the lace edge of a slip, the firmer binding of her bra, her
breast then, soft, small, warm and cool, smooth, her nipple tiny,
firm.

I talked to her about rain in parks. She stretched out till she and
my sheets and strings and I were touching. I slid my hand under
the starch of her skirts, found her thighs, soft and warm and cool
as her breasts; mindlessly, I released her garter.

It snapped loudly.

The man in the bed beside me stirred. Like a cavalier I gallantly
did that garter up. I did not reach for her bare thighs again; it
would have been, I felt then, like singing your love the same sonnet
twice.

She took to kissing with open mouth. Other nurses I kissed too,
but never with passion that made equals.

Miss MacLendon inspired, as the Professor of Orthopedics ordered, my recovery. I thought of sinking down on soft grass and
kissing her bare breasts with my open mouth. When she lay beside
me and helped me undo a button, we were in a park together forever.

The Professor himself took the adhesive wrappings off, brusquely,
with a drench of ether and a swift peel of tape. The mirror he

placed in the room was my guide and challenge. I found my feet. I found my legs. I sat, I stooped.

Unattainable miracles. Climbing a step, going after a rolling ball, visiting a man in another room for a game of checkers.

The Professor brought around the doctor who had put me in the cast. He hid me in a stone corridor, he said as a surprise.

"You remember the boy?" I heard him say.

"Of course. European stock. Afraid of surgery. Just didn't turn up."

I broke from cover. Barefoot I ran like the world's last Olympian carrying a sputtering torch. Ran with a gallop to hide what the cast years did.

Too bad my Professor had to throw me in his colleague's face.

The victory for me was Pyrrhic. I still carried the old orthopod's goof.

Wilkoh danced, threw his cap in the air, hugged me in a wild spinaround, kicked his feet high above his head.

"Footsball, sohnny! You gonna. You gonna also be champeen runner. How much you bet?"

He pressed his huge worn hands over my cheeks, kissed my head like a pecking bird. He shouted, street crier to all the neighbors.

"Look, meesus, come look for yourownsel' sohnny walk."

He made me perform, holding on to fences and him, walking first on one side of the street and then the other. He made me grasp the handlebars of his bike.

"I teach, hah, sohnny? You wanna be teach ride na bike? I teach. You gonna go na Belgium and be champeen."

In the midst of the walking joy lived Miss MacLendon. The night I left the hospital we made plans to meet. Every night at home I thought of her open-mouth kisses and the feel of her breasts.

I wore navy trousers and a matching beret, a white shirt open sportily at the collar, a snappy argyle sweater. It was my first bus trip. My first swing through the city without a hospital or doctor's office as destination.

The sun was blazing. I thought with difficulty of Miss Mac-Lendon in darkness.

Tall and white in shadows, stealing into my room, shutting the door, feeling her way to my bed, stretched out beside me.

By her bus stop I was wild. I all but ran to her apartment. I rang the bell. The door opened. On a tall woman in a dark walking suit, walking shoes with scalloped flaps.

Miss MacLendon.

She was a grown lady.

I must tell you what I wish did not happen. Wilkoh Joe, who after I left my window, still roused me with that rusted bike bell. Through all seasons I ran outside to see his face red against snow or the flowering plum trees.

"Hallo, sohnny, howzda sohnny?"

"Terrific, Wilkoh. And howzda Wilkoh?"

He slapped his hands together, threw back his head, laughing wildly.

"You walk bedder an' bedder, sohnny. I watch. You do goot."

"When you going to teach me to ride that bike of yours?"

"Say na tomorrow, goot?"

"Good."

He began to spit blood.

He tried to hide it. Averted his face when he spoke. Wouldn't take his little girl places. Stopped sleeping in the same bed with Vicky. He forgot, sometimes, to ring that bell; I saw him steal past Elsie's, hesitate, speed by.

My clown with cap like a beefeater's hat, his trousers like bagged-out pantaloons, shrank darkly into himself.

Wilkoh slouched over the handlebars, pedaling hard.

Domyanski, who harvests, has a doctor son, Johann. It will be O.K. Wilkoh speeds up. The bleeding will stop. Wilkoh will dance Vicky and the baby around the room.

He cannot vault up out of the seat. Feet dragging. Barely his leg over the crossbar.

That building. Nice.

No Domyanski. Old man Domyanski said, "Dover. Dr. John Dover."

Wilkoh looks up from his magazine. Nice. Fresh flowers. Big lamp. Pictures.

Nice girl in white. Wilkoh tries to smile. Undress. Girl gone. Gown. Chest against cold black iron. A bell. Hold breath again.

Where to spit?

Wilkoh, in gown, waiting, his head in his hands. Busy doctor good sign.

A door opens. Girl nodding.

Wilkoh holds out hand. Unsmiling. Older than Domyanski's son should be. Wilkoh gives big hello from father. Password. No smile. English questions. Ukrainian, Wilkoh wants. English, wants Dr. John Dover.

Black celluloid picture the girl took. Doctor points. Saying in English. Wilkoh headshake, hunched shoulders, palms out. Not English. Dr. Dover tells in English. Not know. Not know. Please.

Only English.

"Laymen think blood always means T.B. It's an indication, often, but not just T.B. — a hundred other things perfectly harmless. Look at the picture. Why should a cough always mean T.B.? A simple cold, here, see, on my throat, in the picture, this part, the trachea, upper trachea. That's where the blood's coming from. In T.B. blood doesn't come just from here."

Hand on throat, pinching. No smile. Sore?

"Go to the T.B. Clinic. The blood will clear up in a week or so. You've been worried about T.B., you've irritated your throat. Here, take this card, free X-Ray at the T.B. Clinic. No T.B., I assure you. If it makes you feel better, have another picture."

Wilkoh shakes his head. The card to Sanitarium. Doctor smokes pipe, funny sucking sound, hard to hear even English.

Wilkoh over the handlebars, not looking, head barely raised.

That baby?

His neighbors, like his brother-in-law Boyczuk, rush the spring. Already digging. Stormwindows off.

Wilkoh glides by.

His neighbors straighten up, shade their eyes from the sun, listen for that rusty bell.

Wilkoh jumps clear of his moving bike, gracefully sweeps the black clips off his ankles.

"Hey, sport," a man yells, "you stuck-up or something?"

"Joe, you got a big cramp in your gut?"

Wilkoh runs on stiff legs, a speeding crane.

"Vicky ain't home, harvester. Come plant more flowers for me."

Past the front door, and the side, Wilkoh moves, his cheeks bright red. The sun catches his dark back, his head, smoked gold.

"What's with that harvester he don't give me his big hello?"

He hung himself, Wilkoh Joe, stood on his bicycle seat, and let it roll.

When Doctor John Dover was told, he pointed out that the man obviously hadn't understood one word he said.

I was ignorant of the world.

While I was out of the world I did not know I was ignorant of the world. But when I rose, and went out, I met my ignorance face to face.

For four years I saw no river.

Not till I saw the river did I know what it was like to see no river. It shimmered. Striated in evening light like plastic sheets held up to the sun. The river floated bugs and logs and brown-rotted timbers that rocked in a boat wash. The waters smelled of the coolness which overcomes hot August. A finger trailing out of a canoe played tinkly shivering music.

Whatever was where I could not see it or hear it or touch it or smell it, then, when I was set in plaster, was a miracle. A tree I craned my neck to see, or a hydrant, or a fire-alarm box, or smoke from a hidden chimney.

And is still.

I came to a park on the edge of my river, part of a gang, seven in all, and cried taunt at the maids and schoolgirls wandering the lovepaths in two's and three's. The gang giggled and snickered, and I, ignorant, couldn't tell if what we did had style. It seemed babyish. But I had nothing to go on.

I was a stranger in a country rich with customs.

Mikey slid under park benches rocking with lovers and laughed high and hysterical to flush out the semi-clothed.

Johnny threw balled-up newspapers into bush-openings, his target anything white, and moving.

Ladjoo the accordionist, with six others behind him, took the direct approach to a couple:

"Give here that girl."

Three shiners were laid eye-by-eye before he varied the ploy.

My ignorance, I decided, was too vast to be overcome by so excellent a band of tutors.

On a Sunday in dark evening I came back to the park.

I had never been there before, alone.

I had never spoken to a strange woman who wasn't a nurse.

I stood on a grassy hill and looked all around me. I remembered a girl my brother brought home, demure and genteel, who, when my parents were gone, fell on him before he fell on her, straining her skirt and baring her thighs. I wished myself as well.

"The Grasshopper," the park policeman, played his light in the bushes and chained the gates. He had a powerful kick, and moved on seven-league boots. I ducked behind a tree and waited for him to go.

Whistling he wheeled his bike wobbly, its seat jacked to the highest notch. The powerful bike-light searched the dark grass, the darker bushes.

Whirring night insects twisted in smoky spirals. I was frozen in sweat. Chain links ran loudly over gate posts, bump, drrrrrrrr, a loud click, the lock.

The Grasshopper mounted his bike in a scrunch of loose gravel, his wobbly bike-lamp waving farewell.

The news was out.

Silence became whisper. Silhouettes flickered against the river light, twined wraiths separated.

The lawnbowling green was deserted. Moonlight fuzzed the whitewash of its baselines. I imagined large Mrs. Stevens in grunty follow-through, her red face pointing her bowl on its soundless way.

Beyond the low rail fence a man was on the grass, and a moonlit woman.

The children's wading pool, drained, damp, shiny, eerie, sang with crickets. Girls swung easily on baby swings, indistinct in darkness. Bare legs hung moonbathed from the top of the children's slides. Against the darkening sky park bench laths were musical staves with outline devices extravagantly contorted.

I poured perspiration.

"What ya lookin' at, buddy?" said a rise of darkish ground, quite animate.

Two girls walked arm in arm my way. They sat on an empty bench. Sweating vilely, I joined them. One giggled. I moved, to sit near the other.

"Pretty warm night, isn't it?"

Giggles giggled. My lady said nothing.

"Chicago this time of year is worse, you know."

I tried to see my girl in the darkness. Blonde, smiling, hands small, plump little wrists. No stockings.

"Chicago is maybe the hottest place in the world summers."

A man was passing.

"You say Chicago, boy. I like Chicago."

He reached down, separated the two girls, took Giggles by the hand, walked off with her, still silent.

I moved closer to my lady.

"I only like people who resemble movie stars," she said as my hand circled her back.

"That's a good way."

"I look like Sonja Henie. My nose is nicer. Feel it."

Three minutes ago, strangers. Now my hand was under her blouse, feeling a strange woman's body, her warmth.

"Who do you look like?"

"My father mostly."

"I mean movie stars. If you don't resemble a movie star I can't like you."

"William Powell, I look like him."

Her hand investigated my unshaven lip.

"You don't have a moustache."

"I mean before he grew a moustache."

"William Powell always had a moustache."

"At my age?"

As soon as the words were out I realized my mistake. She tried to push my face toward the light. I ducked deeper into the shadow of trees.

"What's your name?"

"Byron."

"That's a fine movie star name, like Tyrone in a way."

"That's who I look like mostly, Tyrone Powers."

"Power."

"What's your name?"

"Steffie. But everybody calls me LaVerne."

"LaVerne. You're prettier than Sonja Henie by ten miles. Let's walk."

I raised her by an elbow in imitation of the man who took away Giggles. My working hand was having trouble with her brassiere catch. LaVerne said little.

On the sloped banks moonlit couples kissed and heaved and rolled together.

"Where's a good place," I whispered.

"For what?" she said too loudly.

A fine screen of bush and tree was a lovers' bed for Giggles and her silent workmanlike friend.

"There, LaVerne."

"Taken."

"How about near the slide?"

"Too open."

Giggles we heard snicker, sniffle, cry. Master-lover was on his feet, and going. We did not stop to comfort Giggles. As soon as she arranged herself and walked crying toward the gate, LaVerne and I slid quickly onto still-warm grass.

I raised her blouse, put two hands to the job of undoing her bra. It didn't budge. LaVerne lay, breathing evenly. Had I been able to free her breasts from thrall-elastic I might have done little else but stroke her softness and kiss her warmth till night passed. Unbudging hooks and elastic forced more. For honor's sake, I switched to her thighs.

"Aren't you going to kiss me?"

It seemed a forward thing for a girl to say to someone she barely knew.

"On the lips."

I raised her up and pulled silk from beneath her.

"If you're gonna do that you have to kiss harder."

"Great."

"Get it right — there — what you got on — O.K. — Byron — hold it — how old are you?"

"Old enough."

"You sound — your voice — it's not settled —"

"Summer cold — open a bit . . ."

She was hot, then moist, after my tongue, and I after her, dizzied, dazzled, the grass prickly on my knees, sharp on my elbows, and I thought of Sonja Henie doing a backward figure-eight, and falling.

Instant Dos Passos-and-Farrell character my lady of the grasses made of me. I came down with crabs.

She and I shared this, as another secret. I would never be disloyal to her, though I really didn't love her half so much as nurses I had seen flash by my door, once only.

When I walked her to the trolley stop and we passed under a street lamp she knew the truth in an instant. But said nothing. It was rather irrelevant by then, anyway. As for me I know I would have taken the subject of my age, at that particular moment, personally.

My father.

He wore the Depression like a cast.

I know about will and way. In plaster, choice led to no good end. The bad times made will and dream equally pointless to my father. He turned salesman, walking the streets of the city, coming to factories and plants to sell shirts and ties out of a satchel. Too much depended on a day's sale. He could not will even that much, a certain number of ties and shirts sold to add up to a day of pay.

He broke down.

Broke down and wept on the bed I had laid in. He cried with his large hands over his sensitive face. His strength ran out in his tears.

I asked him to come to the window and watch me run. His eyes were tightly shut, his lashes gathered in dark wet points.

I couldn't make him rise.

He died in three long stages.

I was the first. I am not crying *mea culpa*. I tell you what I saw, the sag of a gay man. I didn't rise soon enough to make my father believe in risings.

I watched his light go out. Almost every day he wept.

He wept for illness. For lost years. For me down, and for me walking. Weeping webbed his face in shadow.

"Pa," I said, "why are you crying?"

"Everything went on too long."

"I'll make up for it, Pa. I'll fly for you."

"When you leave."

"Pa, I'll never leave."

I leap over the heads of years. I left. He wept. But I left.

This square my hands frame for your eyes is a rear-view mirror. It shows him as I drove away, much later, with a wife and a baby. My father beside a burnt-out patch of brown grass, imprinting my mind and my imagination, his tanned hand waving, his tanned face under white hair, all of him bent, straightening up then, more and more land and less and less him in this rear-view mirror, till his image blurred away in a shimmer of heat.

When I came back to school I became a mark for bullies. I had no school past. I dropped into a room after four years on the moon. My reality had to be tested. The Bully was prober.

He had buck teeth, wore no hat in the coldest days of the long winter, and no coat. A heavy turtleneck maroon ski sweater, leatherpatched breeks, jackboots stiff and ironheeled, laced tight to the calf.

Recess was his game of chess, and all the children pawns. He slid over icy cinders to slam feet together and cause a bloody spill. To avoid him incurred displeasure. Wise kids timed their fall.

My Professor of Orthopedics warned of slips and dangers. I could have claimed exemption from the icy playground. But my strangeness could not afford underlining. I knew what recess might bring. Not I nor any other kid in the room would be a poor-sport pawn, resign from the chessboard as soon as the Bully's game began.

Virtuoso Bully. He once inserted a razor blade in a staircase handrail, disinterestedly. He was no droll sadist; he didn't even hang around to watch. Three children were slashed before the thin silver edge could be picked out of wood and darkness. Blood covered the railing, stained the stone staircase, feathered the cement floor like a rabbit's print. Everyone knew who did it. The Bully bragged of it aloud. But nobody peached.

And the snows came.

The first stormy day, the sun flaked over, on ground grated with heelmarks sharp as cement castings the Bully began his unhurried slide. Those whose backs were turned went down hardest. Those who faced him, and tried to fend him off, were punched and wrestled to the ground.

The Bully's very best move was a sideway sidle, one foot held out like a Russian dancer.

In his community it was best to be maimed and upended quickly. Only, the Bully had a dreadful memory, and often initiated twice. Slings and bandages, certain proofs, granted no exemption. Even being a girl was no way out.

We had malingerers.

But every day somebody had to go out, and get it, boring assault and boring battery. The Bully was too successful to experiment with new techniques.

On a cold day, I gathered my fear around me, and walked out on the frozen playground. The Bully was in a bad mood. He had kicked a girl after she was down.

Up to the moment I saw his lumberjack boots coming toward my uncertain feet I did not know what I would do. I watched him near, his buck teeth biting down on his lower lip. I did what four years in traction and cast ordered — swung my fist at his face with all my strength, timed the blow to meet his powerful skid, my weight against his cheek, his feet still sliding. He went down, and I on him.

It was all luck.

The Bully began to cry. Stretched out full length on the icy ground he held his hurt face between mittened hands.

"Uncle!" he cried.

I did not know the game. It was another void I suddenly stared at.

"Uncle!"

I caught on then.

"Goddam it, say *uncle*."

"I said it twice."

"Say it again!"

"Uncle!"

"I catch you bullying anyone — do you hear, you bucktoothed freak?"

"I hear."

"I'll knock your goddam teeth down your goddam throat."

"I promise."

I rose, hero by accident, but hero nevertheless. I gave the Bully my knightly hand and pulled him to his feet. He was still crying.

I turned my back, walked off with exaggerated limp. I wanted him to think the magic property was in that mysterious leg.

He started a rumor my bad leg was wooden.

I came out one day and discovered a world. The city square. Politics shrilled there; the Salvation Army, pawnshops, beerjoints, a bank, a fourth-run moviehouse, a commercial hotel, three fleabag flops, the town's toughest newsie, his three vanquished rivals, a band of beggars, rummies, whores, pimps, chippies, gigolos, Seventh Day Adventists, Jehovah's Witnesses, pushers of *Pravda, Der Sturmer*, dope, nuns who were mendicants, riot-helmeted policemen, Chinese cooks, Negro barbecuers, Italian barbers, Jewish secondhandclothiers, toughs, hoods, torpedos, rollersofdrunks, bookies, runners, marks, retired railroaders, tourists, schoolkids, sometimes the Mayor, his council, taxcollectors, landassessors, strikebreakers, lumberjacks, social workers, nymphs, dietfaddists, psychologists, insurancemen, morticians, Don Giovannis, Faustuses, Medeas, Cyranos, Tartuffes, Clytemnestras, punks, dolls, queans.

There I saw a husband swear at his wife.

There I saw a Communist blame the Depression on the bosses.

There I saw a young girl zip her dress half-down for one ready-made cigarette. The second took her three-quarters down.

There I saw a drunk try to stop an oncoming police van with an arc of urine. A policeman swung his nightstick.

There, on May Day, I saw ideology fleshed. Whiteshirted Communists marching four abreast on the cartracks, men and women, heads thrown back, singing, and, on the square, truncheoned Nazis in brownshirts and shiny leather roared "Horst Wessel" into the "Internationale." Whitemarching ranks scattered, slats torn from citysquare fences, bricks clawed up from the ornamental garden, policemen riding in, sticks out and swinging.

There I saw a beautiful Russian girl with flowing black hair squat on a Nazi chest; her thighs were bare, his eye skirt-high. Ideology swept aside bourgeois considerations: she clobbered the blonde head immodestly on round cobbles.

There I saw the Salvation Army dodge in and out of the riot with heldout tambourine.

There I saw a blind man step over brownshirt and whiteshirt, his footfall sure and even.

There I found a newspaper and an editor's wise word: he was opposed to dictatorships of both the left and the right.

Through all my discoveries I did not leave love. I gave my heart freely.

I fell in love with a girl who had wild black hair and dark shiny eyes. A girl who had high cheekbones, her hair in a casual pigtail, her arms loaded with books and scribblers. She walked alone, though she was beautiful. She returned my smile graciously, and never patronized my lowerschool status.

I fell in love with a plain girl who always said "Good morning": a tall girl whose father was an alderman. And thirty or forty others.

One there was for whom I felt pity, and rejected kinship.

She was spastic, her legs were in braces. She walked like a scarecrow, legs stiff, arms floppy, her head rolling. Her hair was cropped by a barber who didn't love her. Grayblonde shingles like the tattered edges of a thrown-aside cloche. Her glasses were wire-rim, light-reflecting. Her teeth seemed too large for her mouth, too big a barrier for her tongue. Her voice was edged with hysteria, like a recording, as if she were just learning to produce sounds. I passed her house on the way to the library. She stood at the gate for hours, greeting schoolchildren. Some nodded. A few said "Hello." Most passed by.

She found out my name.

"Good morning," she said.

It came out like this.

"Goo' 'oh'ih."

When nobody was around I waved my hand in greeting.

I'd study in the library two, three hours, return the same way. She was there, leaning over a scrolled wrought-iron gate. Her boy shoes looked too big, her chrome braces massive on her beige cotton stockings. Her doll's head flopped like a Raggedy Ann's.

I found her pathetic, but ominous. That uncontrolled grin, those gleaming teeth, the glinting glasses turned my way. Spy for the league of the maimed and the halt, telling me I must not be apostate. Her doorway led to the underground crippled, sad sentry, with eye like a password, mocking those who were not, yet pretended to be, whole.

I hated her for mouthing my name. I saw her scarily, as horror films transform funhouse dummies, rocking horses, harmless dolls. Sinister Ariadne pretending the labyrinth is a trap and she my guide out when the thread that led from me to her was a chain to drag me out of life.

No one was privy to my fear and loathing.

She needed me, as a bridge into the world. I refused. And wished her away, with finality.

In fall rain one evening I passed her house. Absent in bad weather. And in the library, lost in books, I forgot her. Hurried home over damp leafpapered streets later, when the rain had stopped and air was warm. Red car lights winked off and on in standing pools glazing the streets. Tiny dark raindrops caught the light on leaves. Bark looked shiny, beautiful, fit to eat.

A block away I heard a whimper riding in and out of the sticky sound of tires on wet pavement.

She was stuck.

Her hair was wet, her arms stiff. Jackknifed on the lowest step, her feet sliding on the wet slippery leaves. Caught. On all fours. Crying to the door she could not reach or the someone she knew was passing.

"Help, mister."

I walked on my heels to make no sound.

"I'm stuck. Slipping. Mister, please."

Her crying changed tone. Someone who knows rescue is at hand, hysterical with relief. For one second I hung before her gate. Then bolted.

Refused.

I sped over the dangerously slippery leaves, her cry growing louder behind me. Oh, how I ran, my two feet striking the wet pavement with two unequal sounds.

My life changed when I decided to run.

In the hospital, years earlier, Peter, eleven, or twelve, not yet able to talk, the hospital crowded, Peter an overflow from emergency, who grinned all the time, laughed, or, gasping, jerked his head as if a mosquito stung him.

Three or four of us played at catch, hospital style, throw, miss, and the kids not confined to bed scramble out, barefoot, barebottomed, snatch the ball up, wing it round the room again. That ball came Peter's way. His hands crisscrossed trying hopelessly for a catch. Bouncing up and down in his bed, laughing. Faster the ball whizzed round, richocheting, clangorous on wash basin and metal stand, bouncing off walls, faster, harder.

I catch it. I throw. With all my strength I throw. My white-gownsleeve flaps, my fingers let go. Too late I scream:

"Peter, duck!"

He laughs, bounces, a splat — sickening — his face spurts blood. One hand touches his nose, Peter looks, shows us the red, proud.

That morning the nurse taught him to wash himself. He began slowly, rubbing blood over his face, then quickly, his wrists, his upper arms.

I saw what I wanted to believe I could not cause. We begged and hollered and cried at him to stop, but Peter washed himself thoroughly, in blood.

We pressed our buzzers with one hand. Shrieking nurses swarmed the room.

"Look what Peter did to himself," I think I said, or did I?

I once watched a girl train for the Olympic swim team. She buckled a belt around her waist and attached it by two thick rubber straps to a heavy metal post set in cement at the corner of the pool. While her arms churned the water in simulation of a race the rubber stretched taut. She made no attempt to get out of the training harness till she was exhausted. That took some time.

My mother was tiny. In a photograph album she's seventeen, a wonderful-looking young girl on white skates, a formal skating suit — anklelength skirt, fashionably highbuttoned jacket. Beside it a picture taken the same day; close-up, a girl with a sensitive face, hair curled around in a corkscrew. The man who took the picture thought she was great. Handtinted her eyes, and got their color just right, tawny hazel.

She sang, my mother, in a tiny sopranino voice of perfect pitch — Russian love songs, waltzes, Strauss, Lehár, joined by my father's tremulous baritone. They sang best at night, on the grass in parks, joined by kids and aunts and uncles.

When I was three, and she in her twenties, her mother died. And quickly, her father.

She cut her hair.

When I was in that cast she kept me alive, and wanting life. She and my father and Uncle Bim and Wilkoh Joe. She kept my father alive. He broke. I told you that, but I didn't tell you how. I could begin "Once upon a time," and it would not be wrong. Time is in it.

8:00 A.M. My father ate his usual hearty breakfast of cantaloupe, Scottish oats with heavy cream, whole wheat toast thickly buttered and covered with Dundee marmalade, two cups of coffee, each with two lumps of sugar and a dash of heavy cream.

We play a fast game of tic-tac-toe on the chest of my cast. The cat wins.

8:45 A.M. My father opened the store he manages.

9:00 A.M. His five clerks arrived. Once there were eleven. The boss doesn't come to the store much. He weeps when he reads the news on the register.

12 noon. My father waited for the boss to relieve him so he can go to lunch. The usual parade of unemployed men in overalls and worn Relief boots outside the store. They look in on their way to the soup kitchen.

1:00 P.M. My father phoned his boss to see why he hadn't come in. The phone has been taken off the hook.

1:07 P.M. Shouting in the streets. My father rushed outside. People are running on the sidewalks, on the streets, in front of honking cars and clanking trolleys, people halfdressed, men with tears streaming down their faces.

War, my father thinks.

1:09 P.M. My father stopped a man swinging through the air on crutches. The man cursed at him.

"Now you've made me miss it!"

"What?"

"I wanted to get there before the doors closed."

"Where?"

"Money," yells a riot-helmeted policeman.

"Money?"

"They've closed the banks!"

1:16 P.M. My father stood with a mob trying to pull a guard away from the locked bank door.

1:26 P.M. My father staggered past the city square. A Scottish Communist is shouting at a crowd:

"Wha' d'ye expaict from the C'pitalists?"

1:35 P.M. My father, starving from no lunch, saw a crowd gathered in front of his store. *"Fire?"*

1:38 P.M. The door was padlocked. The five clerks looked up in disbelief. A sign, red on white, scrawled:

BANKRUPT

His raincoat is locked inside, his galoshes, his winter coat, his umbrella, his rubbers, his shaving kit, his tape measures, five clean shirts, his suitcoat. He stood outside in his shirtsleeves.

2:02 P.M. My father came home through the back door. I was propped where he had left me after the game of tic-tac-toe. I was excited to hear him so early. I heard the back door slam shut. From far, or as if I dreamed it, I heard it all.

"Did you take a day off?"

"We're finished."

"What happened, darling, tell me?"

"What's my alarm clock doing in the laundry room?"

"You know I use it to time the washer."

"You don't have other clocks you could use?"

"Sweetheart, what's the matter?"

"Give me that clock!"

"Don't yank it away — here, dear."

"To hell with this clock!"

2:06 P.M. That old-fashioned alarm clock with bells like mouse-ears struck the cement floor. Metal, glass, springs, bells, a clattering disintegration. Two cries.

"I should smash you like that!"

I think I hear a loud ticking.

"Darling, what is it?"

A loud ringing slap.

"Why are you hitting me?"

"For no reason, you hear me — for no reason!"

2:08 P.M. I threw myself over the side of the bed, the weight of the cast unbearable on my spreadout hands and stiff arms. I screamed for them to stop. Blood rushed to my head. I shot over the side and crashed to the floor.

2:10 P.M. My father rushed into the bedroom, strained to raise me up in his arms. His face was a tanned mask of anguish. My mother had her hand on his wet cheek.

"The bank," he mumbled, "the firm, him."

My mother put my father in a bed opposite mine. He slept four days. I couldn't think what to say when he stopped sleeping. On the fifth day he tried to get out of bed, but cried instead. He ate little, cried and slept a lot. Days went by like that. Weeks.

We had nothing to offer each other then. I wanted the world badly. My father wanted it not at all.

Living out the twenty-four-hour day was the task of Sisyphus; sun shining on the huge stone at the bottom of the hill did nothing to make the agony easier.

So he wept, and slept.

I said when she was in her twenties, and I three, it happened, death.

In a day of great crying in a large house with a dark allaround screened porch, my mother and three of her sisters cried on the grass in loveliest sunlight.

Two strange men brought a bed on small silver wheels, the blanket red as a mounty's jacket, striped black and fuzzy. It was empty when they came in, going out they carried grandfather, whose eyes were turquoise, whose face was an owl's. His hair and his beard were dark and wet.

My mother and her sisters followed the two white men down the sidewalk. I had to stay inside.

I stood tiptoe at the front door with my left eye to the keyhole. Air rushing in stung my eyeball. But I saw it. A long white car with a big red mark on the side, and open at the back, like the baker's. Grandfather disappeared in that back.

Grandmother was in that other upstairs room. Her door was locked. I wasn't supposed to go in ever. My mother went in and her brothers and sisters went in but nobody kissed grandmother who coughed. She *used to* kiss all the time and hug, with those earrings tiny, the color of grandfather's eyes.

I heard her cough in the night.

Lillian cried and Gad and Beatty; my mother's crying made her eyes red and her nose red. They stood on the sidewalk waving after the white car with the red mark. They came toward my keyhole, all of them crying.

"Ma, where's grandfather?"

"They took him to the hospital."

"I would like him back."

"They have to operate."

"What's that?"

"Cut something bad out."

"With a knife?"

"He'll be asleep. He won't hurt."

"A knife right into him? Cutting?"

"Maybe he won't be cut."

"Cutting makes you blood."

"Bleed."

"Cutting makes you bleed."

"Sh-sh-sh — you'll make the girls cry."

Nobody told me.

They changed to black.

In that big house with the dark sad screens allaround tears ran.

Tears on Aunty Lillian's ears. Black stains on her black dress, like something spilled from dinner.

They sat on stools. In socks and stockings. Stools left no lap for me. Most of the time they coaxed and I wouldn't sing: if they would stop crying I would sing now.

Big people crying.

My father.

I took his hand with the ring.

"I don't like you to cry. It makes me cry inside."

He couldn't hear. There was too much tears and crying.

I wandered the house. Grandmother coughed. Something was on the floor in the big room, by the big windows.

Crying got louder. My father picked Aunty Beatty up and kissed her. She's eleven. My brother's eight and he's crying.

"Why are you and the big people crying?"

"Grandfather."

"He's in a white car with a red mark on one side."

He ran away from me, Gad my brother.

Big people faces were screwed up tight, like against the sun. A lady was calling Grandfather. I heard her pounding the something that stood on the floor.

"Tell Avrom we miss him," I think she said.

Two men pulled her off the thing on the floor. She was limp, and sleepy from crying.

They went outside. Even my brother.

I stood tiptoe at the front door. Wind blew in thin, like when you cool hot mashed potatoes. My eyeball felt chilled and blinky. A long black car. Windows on the sides. Posts twisted like the legs of the dining-room table. Gold things, candleholders, painted on the side.

I was glad it wasn't that white car.

Something black stood outside my keyhole. It was nice not having the cold wind on my eyeball. I heard Grandmother coughing upstairs. But outside was singing.

A song sadder than crying.

Sob sounds, like an old bird fighting to get higher and higher, wings bent and broke, failing, coming down a shower of black.

The dark outside my keyhole disappeared.

The long black car was moving. Uncle Joe walked behind it, and Uncle Dave, and Uncle Israel, with their hands on their faces, and my mother was with Dave and my father with Joe and my brother and Beatty and the rest of my aunts walking after the long black car, in the middle of the road, right on the streetcar tracks.

You're not supposed to walk on the street.

It came again.

My mother and father carried me out on the verandah, and propped me with pillows.

"Mr. Boyczuk wants you to see it."

A priest in a high hat and a long purple dress, a big silver cross swinging under his long beard. He had a staff in his hands. His voice was terribly deep, as if he sang in a cathedral.

"Gospetepoomela gospetepoomela gospetepoomela."

Wilkoh Joe was crying, his flat cap in his hands, his wet hair parted correctly. He didn't look up at my window. Mr. Boyczuk's daughter Katsha was screaming for her mother. My mother had her arm around Katsha.

A coffin. Six men carrying it. Mr. Boyczuk pointed at me. The men lifted the top. Someone who looked like a tinted picture of Mrs. Boyczuk was inside. A bride kind of dress. Hands crossed with flowers and a white cross.

Mrs. Boyczuk never wore rouge.

I lay in a cold sweat the night Mrs. Boyczuk was buried. Death seeped into my parents' generation.

I prayed all night in my plaster cocoon I would die before them.

I didn't tell my mother or my father what kept me awake that long dark night. I ignored the move to give tic-tac-toe to the cat.

I cried a lot that day, they thought for Mrs. Boyczuk.

The high school.
It had a tower.
I could see it from our kitchen window, on a castle I thought I'd never reach. Chalky red tower, turreted, floated to my bed on cheers and shouts.
I didn't believe I would get there. But the Professor of Orthopedics took that matter in hand.
I entered the high school, on the day we entered the war.

War struck my house.
Long before I was born, on a ship ready for the ocean, Mottyeh, the oldest of my mother's four brothers, watched the gangway being pulled up. Soldiers stopped everything. And took Mottyeh. From his mother and his father and his sisters and brothers. Two days later, weeping on the ocean, they knew of that war.
Nobody saw or heard from Mottyeh again.
The day war came again my mother wept for Mottyeh.
The day war came Ruby Scarlatti was military age.

I kept waiting for the world to change.
We had no air raids. No artillery trained on us. We dimmed our street lights at night. It was all a game.
I studied the sky. Its color should have deepened. The world should have wrapped itself in mourning.
We went to school daily and saw the older boys clean out their desks. We had a brandnew flag on the stage of the auditorium. The principal, a great man, made speeches to us weekly. He got our sharpest attention.
We couldn't believe, from where we were, the war.

Gersh lived in an apartment block. He loved to play tennis,

which his mother considered a bourgeois game. Gersh argued for tennis as a bodybuilder, on the right side of the class struggle. Gersh also said tennis would build up my bad leg and make me eligible for military service.

On the sidewalk in front of his apartment block, Gersh showed me how Tilden served and Budge served and Jack Kramer. His racquet whizzed in simulated overhead smash. He wore a Russian gymnast's khaki shorts, his blond hair long and matted. Thick glasses made him look too scholarly.

A window opened over our heads. A girl with reddish hair smiled down.

"Hi Gersh."

"Hi Maggie."

Gersh stepped deftly to his left, swished his racquet low and stylish, a perfect backhand.

"You should try it that way with a ball sometime," Maggie said.

We all laughed.

"Come out, Mag, and we'll have a fast set."

"What about your friend?"

Gersh looked at my feet.

"He has no racquet."

"He can borrow mine."

She wore a short school tunic, navy blue, with the school crest on it, brown and gold.

Our style with high school girls was to kibitz. Maggie was our age but had a direct manner.

"How's the boy friend?" Gersh said.

I didn't like Maggie to have a boy friend.

"Still in basic training."

"He gonna be a pilot?"

"Or a navigator."

"What would you like to be?" Gersh asked me.

"The guy who runs the airforce. Ping off all the krauts and get back to the serious work of the Depression."

Gersh thought I was talking class struggle.

We drove over to the courts on bikes, I with Maggie's brother's, and her racquet. She stood up to pump, lazily and gracefully, full of a slow vigor. That style of hers was in everything.

"You two play, I'll watch. My wrist is a little sprained."

She sat high on the Umpire's chair, feet together, chin in her hands. Gersh was rich with instruction.

"Keep your wrist lower."

"O.K."

"Hold your racquet down at the end."

"O.K."

"Maggie, get down and show him."

He served the ball with an exaggerated girlish pat. Maggie and I twisted up trying to return it.

"Get serious," Gersh scolded.

"Stop acting like a red rabbi," Maggie said.

We batted the ball back and forth.

"Come back to my place," Maggie said, "I make the greatest hot chocolate."

"Gersh, is hot chocolate consistent with the war effort?"

Gersh saluted.

Maggie's mother opened the door. She held her mouth pursed. She sat in the living room with the *Saturday Evening Post*, her legs thrown over the arms of a blue brocade chair, the ash on her cigarette long.

"Tilden could have beaten 'em all. He didn't have a single weakness," Gersh said.

"Boys," said Maggie.

I fell out of love with the passing girls.

A Greek with many dark daughters had a small wagon on our wide avenue. They sold fried potatoes in long very crisp slices, finely salted in grease-stained bags. They grilled hotdogs till skins curled and broke open and edges smoked with char. The Greek wore a black slouch hat over one eye, and a black satin vest. His daughters were gorgeous. Girls with smile cheeks, warm dark eyes, long hair loose down their backs. Most beautiful among them was Evelyn, who, like the river, I did not know without knowing I did not know.

All walks in the city led to Evelyn. She read everything, the intellectual's dreamgirl. Evelyn knew everybody in the high school, but not me. She wondered if I were a visitor to the city, a cousin of Gersh's or Maggie's.

Evelyn was a dark sunlit girl.

I could not but fall in love with her.

She was older than the rest of us, and important.

One night, after a long walk that ended at Evelyn's open window, where steam rose from boiling oil and Evelyn's creamy skin gleamed in the passing carlights, Evelyn and Maggie and I talked hushedly about Tom Tolliver, and Eustacia Vye. Then we left Evelyn, glowing and shiny.

We wound our way back the long way, on paths that led down to the river, and, outside the park, we watched The Grasshopper rise up on his high seat and go. It was softest summer, and winged insects made soft whisperings around pendant streetlamps. Nightlaughter hushed soft and intimate on the other side of the chain and its lock.

I kissed Maggie as we faced the river.

Her lips seemed tiny, her mouth lovely and warm.

I kissed her awkwardly because before I kissed her I didn't believe one could kiss girls like Maggie.

I was puzzled. When I kissed, she kissed back. But what about the airman, her boyfriend?

When he took a furlough I avoided calling Maggie all that week.

My brother went into the airforce.

The evening he shipped out we all came home, and sat. My father was in a rocking chair. He rocked jerkily, a burst of short hither-and-thithers creaked anxiety through the dark house.

At one A.M., in total darkness, my father stopped rocking, snapped on a light, adjusted the large clock on top of the kitchen cabinet, waited for the chime of one. We scurried off to bed. He didn't wash up, nor did my mother.

Usually my father fell off to sleep quickly and breathed open-mouthed, loud and regular. My mother had a soft snoozing snore.

This night the house was silent.

My brother washed out of aircrew, but Johnny, who used to wad those damp newspapers and pitch them at palpitating park lovers, Johnny became a bombardier, his pilot Victor, who lived down the lane. The crew was all from our city, the eldest, Victor, twenty-two. They flew over Germany, dropped their load of bombs, picked their way through flak and German fighters, successful, victorious, lucky.

A British plane took off on the airfield just as they were landing.

Victor killed the motor, to lose altitude quickly, and duck a collision.

The plane wouldn't kick back to life soon enough, pancaked down, wheels badly bent, otherwise intact.

Everybody dead.

Nobody scratched.

Johnny's and Victor's doors marked with an "X."

We knew we should say something to comfort Johnny's mother. She looked like Mrs. Moroz, only finer, her hair a light brown; something of a girl was left in her, though she was fifty.

I was afraid to go.

She cried.

"I never told you, did I, sonny, how happy I was when you learned to walk?"

She had her apron in two hands.

"I came to tell you how sorry I was about Johnny."

"He was a nice kid. He played outside your window when you was in the cast. He wanted you to know what games were like. He didn't grow up. You notice how he runs?"

"He was a good friend."

She dropped her apron, smoothed it with both hands. Her hair had come down over her eyes. She made me sit close to her on the porch.

"In the army when they're dead, it's for sure. In the airforce when they say 'missing' there's still a chance. I have a friend whose boy is 'missing, presumed dead.' His ma knows he's alive. By rights Johnny's cable should have said that."

She grabbed at my hand.

"You think I hate you because you're here and Johnny's — nowhere?"

I shook my head.

She threw my hand away from her.

"I can't stand to see you. You're that time. Did you hear, sonny? Victor's mother feels better because he's without a scratch. Tell me, should I feel better? Tell me!"

"I don't know."

"It's worse. I want 'missing, presumed dead.' Sonny, go home. It didn't pass yet. I'll see you, I'll see Solly or my Paul or Lefty and it'll start again. I can't stand looking at you. When you were in the cast everybody said *you* would die."

She shoved me from her rudely. I stumbled, but didn't fall.

"Wait!"

I turned around.

"Does the airforce make mistakes sometimes?"

"I think it does."

"Did it make one this time?"

"No."

"Go die somewhere, you skunk of a kid! Who asked you to open that filthy mouth?"

Here let's tell his tale, civilian Bibul's, which, like Johnny's, like Mac's, and Wilkoh Joe's, and Grandfather's, ended in death. He fought the Depression battle, for real money, Bibul, like a Samurai, cracked-seam horsehide cap fiercely unsnapped at the visor, his blueblack beardshadow grained as emery cloth. He had tiny eyes tight with skepticism and disbelief, which broke in a tic-like blink from eye to eye, disconcerting semaphore.

Bibul was a peddler. A fulltime high-school kid, a fulltime peddler, both preparing to be a rabbi.

Surrounded by Stalinists and Leninists and Marxists, Bibul fought allout war with his haggling customers, and prayed. His faction was target, unifying symbol for all revolutionary parties. Kids who went to Socialist schools, Communist schools, Freethinker, atheist, half-day religious schools fought each other in the streets, scratched slogans on each other's walls, vandalized windows and all breakables, splattering paint, splintering wood. And knew solidarity only when Bibul's kind came on stage.

A Liberty Temple kid would see Bibul and aim a rattling kick at his shins.

"Bibul," I asked him, "why do you take it from the pig?"

"Aaaa," he made a sour face, his hand out as if he were throwing feed to chickens.

"A lot them kids know about life."

He had a wagon, and a horse, Malkeh, mare of buffed hide, etched rump, brownmaroonpurple, faded, like ancient sundrenched velvet. In profile fixed in permanent backbend, a depressed "U," her belly a Salvation Army sofa's stuffing. Her tail a Gibson Girl's featherboa picked clean by souvenir hunters, invitation to those horseflies with no sense of standards.

Her legs, droopily veined, were of different lengths, like a badly carpentered table. She moved sidewise in a sad shuffle, like two hobbled softshoe dancers. Her harness once belonged to a Czarist artillery horse, the collar triangular, yellow, lumped, ripped, showing some old relative's horsehair. To keep her from invidious self-comparison Bibul bought a pair of racehorse blinkers, black leather, shining with rivets, a snappy touch to Malkeh's decor, like a monocle in the eye of a Bowery bum.

For so mortal a horse Bibul had to have a disintegrating wagon. It listed to one side like a sinking ship, bare of paint, openpored, crackseamed, gapjointed, warped. Should Bibul renew its color when no spray or tint could bring mortal mare hide back from the dead?

"Giddyup you, dere, you Malkeh," Bibul shouted, and waved his whip far above her head.

Malkeh pulled with that old head down, her reins cracked and peeling, buckleworn belt of an old poor fat man. Slowly the wagon's squarish wheels turned on their worn rims. From his high perch Bibul surveyed crowds.

In school Bibul the rabbi tried to make it through the day, gentle Gersh his untiring ideological enemy.

"Hey," he asked me, "don't you get the urge to give Bibul a little hit?"

"What for?"

"Up at four, praying, buying fruit, praying. Just one little backhand? Phylacteries, every morning, with that stinking horse parked in front of the synagogue. This is the twentieth century. It's our *duty* to give that guy a little smash."

Lunchtime Gersh and Bitner and I sprawled on the lawn.

"Bibul," Bitner said, "let me fix you up with Lady Bigtits."

Bibul looked up from his memobook rich with the squash of red berries.

"Aaaa," he made that chickenfeed gesture.

He reached into a wrinkled paper bag for a chunk of salami, a few cherries, a very ripe tomato. He bit down with a juicy squirt, jumped back, not soon enough for his pants to escape a red shower of seeds.

"Slop," Gersh said. "See, doesn't that demand a belt?" he asked me.

"Bibul," Bitner said, "do you believe in free love?"

"Who's got time?"

"How much time," Gersh asked, "do you need to believe in free love?"

"You know books. You don't know the first thing about life."

"Books? I'll kill you, rabbi! Who prays out of books noon and night."

"I know by heart. I don't use books."

"Bragger!"

"Bibul," Bitner said, "what does the stuff you know by heart *mean?*"

"Who could tell you guys?"

"Did you try learning the *Manifesto* by heart? How much Marx did you read, rabbi Ben Jerk?"

"Marx don't know either about making a living."

"He's dead, you idiot."

"Aright, so Stalin. Or Trotsky."

"Did you say Trotsky? I'll pound you to a pulp like your tomatoes."

Bibul walked away.

"You should be in Latin class with him," Gersh said angrily. "When he translates Virgil he rocks back and forth like he was praying."

Women old, women worn out, women in nightgowns at four in the afternoon, hair uncombed, feet in their husbands' wide felt slippers, hands deep in pockets. Into their slums Malkeh dragged that creak of a wagon, in front of houses that sagged against each other, crazy-angled, insubstantial as playing cards. Gates listed at the angle of Bibul's wagon; dry, cracking wood fences leaned in quits toward the ground, begging like bent old men in sight of their graves to be allowed to fall the rest of the way. Windows were tarpaperpatched, like pirate's eyes.

The women waited behind doors.

"Apples, apples, ten pounds for a quarter," Bibul called out.

"Ebblz, ebblz, den bondz f'a kwodeh," the women heard.

Malkeh hauled the loaded wagon into ruts and frostheaves, back alley battleground.

"Whoa there, Malkeh. Back you."

The women stuck their pincurled heads out of screen doors. Bibul shined his reddest apple, held it up to the sun, cracked into it with a juicespraying burst. The women let that bait go by. Bibul swiveled, his elbow toppled a firm red pear off the wagon, to the ground.

The women charged.

A redhaired woman and her thinfaced daughter moved in, the old one snatching two-cent oranges and dropping them deftly into the one-cent box; before they stopped rolling, daughter snatched them up.

"Rabbi," she smiled, "your fruit today is lovely."

Bibul's tic-like blink snapped the coup.

"Give here back them oranges. Shame! Where's restraint?"

"Two cents for oranges that bats sucked dry on Arab trees?"

"One orange'll make two glasses juice."

"Perls the peddler gives off a couple coppers when we buy six — Perls who supports a sister in Poland — maybe two."

"Perls who gets oranges off fig trees deal with, missus."

"Blackhearted robber, you hold *me* up? My husband to make a dollar washes dead men!"

"So respect the rest, missus, and don't touch my fruit."

A whitehaired old lady crammed a cherry into her toothless mouth.

"That's a sin, lady, a big sin."

She spit half the cherry, all the pit, past Malkeh's patient head.

At the other end of the wagon a redhaired woman was busy splitting a melon.

"Busted, rabbi, so how much for started watermelon?"

"Cheaters, I don't know you? Kill my profits. Pay for what you wreck."

"Bibul, what's your pa, a mayor, a doctor?"

"He don't even have a pa."

"He never had one ever."

The whitehaired old lady reached for a fistful of cherries. Bibul's hand clamped on her wrist.

"I was sampling. God should strike me dead this minute if in my whole life I stole one thing!"

She moved a step closer to Bibul. A kid studying to be a rabbi might have all kinds of pull.

From the houses they came, an outpouring of women.

"Missus, my heart'll break better for your troubles if you don't steal plums while you cry."

"Rabbi darling. My daughter's third kid has a sty in the good eye now, big as an apricot — how much for half pound — might she'll have to take the eye out — ten cents —"

"Fifteen."

"Bibul, darling, you remember my cousin's wife with the hump. She's full by the belly, Gertie. Ain't you glad?"

High on that throne, manyhanded as Shiva, Bibul collected reluctantly released pennies, nickels, quarters, the odd graying dollar bill.

"You know what Party I belong to, Comrade Bibul? It's against my principles you should make on me a profit."

"Lady, go to fat Safeway and cheat yourself a capitalist."

While she tilted the tinscoop on the scales upward Bibul countered with his just thumb.

I'll stop the spool's spinning and turn back to me on that porch where, once walking, I slept on hot nights. And thought of Icarus released from a labyrinth and flying over the sun, unsinged. High-school, Depression, war, love, everything too fast. Huge ball of fate unwinding in its speedy roll down a hill, I in chase, my task hope-less — catch the ball, rewind it, come back to time's unwinding hill.

That ball's still unwinding, war and Bibul and the thronging world. Or, as if we watched a depth charge strike the calm of ocean, a boat beneath, heard the roar, water erupting, and the de-molished boat — this, our story — floats up to the surface, spar by spar.

On that verandah I was wakened by a dream, Proteus trying to live with freedom on Procrustes's bed.

A girl's voice was singing, with a child's range.

"Your pain will be as nothing."

"It's not my pain, it's the war."

"If I gave you Orpheus's power, would you sell me out?"

"Never."

"Even now that you walk?"

"Even now."

"Would you have sold your soul to the Devil for an unbroken hip?"

"I don't know."

"Do you know then that war is a wall."

"No."

"That violence is the shortest distance between two points?"

"I could not hear your lovely voice and not fall in love with you."

"What if I record what I say and give it to all the women of the world?"

We got off the bus, my father and I.

The hospital was once almost white, now grayed. Ugly, brick by brick, as the dull seminary across the road.

Gray-white walk, mammoth gray-white approach leading nowhere but inside. Whores in the isolation wards leaned out the upper windows, corkscrewcurled, shouting.

A brass-faced door, uneven tile on the floor, a dark elevator. I swell with fear and hatred for the helplessness I once felt here. I feel it again. Black elevator gates spill us into dinginess. Sunken eyes, bony faces, toothless mouths, hands knuckletaut on white iron bedsteads. A plasma bottle on a white stand, chipped black. A man with striped pajamatubes for legs, feet bony and darknailed. His hands, as if broken at the wrists, dangle over the side of the bed. A priest's palm darts over a face in profile.

My choking shadows and choking yawns are here. I feel them in my throat, see them in corners, under beds. My jaws are heavy. Shadows mount me, my riders.

But this is my mother's illness, and I must shake them off, as he tries, my father, who feels everything heaviest.

My mother looks up, tiny in her bed, sipping air through her small lips politely.

My father's face, dark as the day he smashed that alarm clock, stares. No words come. A nurse enters, shoos us out, closes the door. We walk into the air, my father and I. He runs ahead of me down the steps. A whore shouts, waves a come-on. Her sad hair is copper.

My father stumbles on the bottom step, his shadow dips long and pale on the concrete. I have to skip to catch him. Something inside him is flying apart. His breath explodes a creaking cry, a nightmare scream.

"Pa, let it go."

He cries as if he's been struck.

"Go on, papa. Don't hold back."

A cry breaks out of his restraint — another, another. I can't stand to see him convulsed with choked-off sobs.

"Pa, I'm here. Strong as an ox."

Tears burst from my eyes and choke my throat. I can't be hero before his crying.

My father weeps. And I weep with him a comfort which can't be heard. My father is a river broken out of its banks. His sobbing sweeps me under.

We stand by the water in afterlight's neon shimmer from the opposite bank.

"Look, pa."

A waterbird dips gently toward the river's trembling threads green and red and gold.

"Does it look as if I've been crying?"

"Here's my handkerchief."

"Have we been away long?"

"No more than two minutes."

"I feel cracked. Like my collarbone broke in my chest."

"Pa, it will mend."

"It can't."

"I did."

"Did you?"

I stare at his eyes. He doesn't mean to chill me. We have never mentioned imperfection before. I can't stand his words.

On those concrete plaza steps that nursery tale's truth fell, and we again were shattered.

And all the king's horses fell to it, to pull the vacuum-locked hemispheres apart. They churned the earth and foamed their hides. The king's men joined too, the wise men, the brave, the serious men, and their ladies full of warmth and delicacy.

Lazarus joined them, who should have known; Prince Charming did his best. Hercules, Bellerophon, Pervical, and even him, Moses, and Joseph, and Jason. And when they were all gone, and had not one prevailed, he, the king, himself came and took what had fallen and held it broken in his palm, spoke gloriously to it, unchanged, in his hand.

And my cousin Jimmy, who learned to love to fly, winged his way over Berlin, and searchlights found him out, in a crisscross, white "X." Two puffs, three, curled the dark air like char under paper, and he on his belly in a darkbird's tail, was unwinged, and plummeted.

That, too, love could not prevent.

His city, my city is set where two rivers meet. Its two main streets hug the rivers, one better than the other. Often they wander off, but in time remember, and not much is lost.

War liveried those wide streets. Lightstandards wound in bunting fly three different flags above airmen in smoky blue with strange shoulder patches and dark or yellow faces — Indians, New Zealanders, Aussies, Maori tribesmen, Australian bushmen, carved-faced men from Ceylon and Malaya, Bermuda, Jamaica. Beer parlors are khaki and navy blue set in airforce gunmetal. The city's accent, Scottish, Ukrainian, Polish, is now turning stage English, with the "sye," "wye," "hi," of Anzacs.

The city is a hospital flat, shifts moving in, shifts moving out. Things go badly across the widest water. These are the men who take up the bad places. Boys from St. John's High are among them, and boys out of the University. "X's" on doors where Johnny and Victor and Jimmy lived make ours a mourning city.

Johnny's mother doesn't come out anymore.

And Jimmy's father, shading his eyes from sunlight, and green grass, and airman striding, asked me "Is there a chance he didn't know what hit him?"

And this time I said "Yes."

Bitner, who used to bait Bibul, had an old car with hand throttle, and gas coupons, and a girl whose eyes glinted in moonlight. We joined him, Maggie and I, in hot August, when the war was phoniest, on a road which led out of the city beside the heavy-flowing river. The road shone straight in snowy moonlight. Bitner adjusted the hand throttle, left the car driverless, and climbed out on the hood, his feet crossed, his arms behind his head, feigning sleep.

The girl with glinting eyes said he was brave and never had she seen such daring. And Bitner, who too was 4-F, climbed back inside.

Our swifter river ran to a larger lake, with locks intervening, and islands Maggie and I came to that same August, when air was warm as a desert. In spray misting strung lights on shore I wandered with Maggie, the locks' roar stopping our shouts down to tiniest whisper.

Grass was soft, like camelbrush, the heatdried earth yielding. Waterfalls were shush as seashells to our ears. My mouth on Maggie's, her breasts against me, our bellies together on the dewless grass. Her tongue was soft and her thighs soft, her loosened breasts soapscented, soft, loving, warmer wet wild in a sky spun green, rainbowed and misting. Arms around, backs on grass, we watched the sky skim a graygold. All night we lay, till color spun back to our world.

Kneeling we kissed and thigh to thigh rose slow as morning.

At our feet on the drab dry grass two tiny crimson drops, imperceptible as tears, seemed suncaught drops of dew. Ineradicable in our eyes but, like us, doubtless gone by noon.

Bibul calls, Maggie must wait.

Darkcheeked Bibul joined his Elders in New York, and, after class, at a stall in the Essex Street Market took his worldly stand.

He wore a Williamsburg capote, wide flatbrimmed hat, two thick sidecurl springs which bounced with his tic — Bibul, Essex Street's fiercest puller.

"Grandmothers, oldies, goldies, by me iceberg lettuce is tight like a fist, like borscht cheap."

"Williamsburg he means. Rotten leaf lettuce he wraps around a stone."

"Grandmother, buy from me today and you guarantee to steal from me tomorrow."

"You swear iceberg?"

"If it ain't let's try again tomorrow."

Noon it hit a hundred, at sunup he prayed, since sunrise sold. His sidecurls flattened on his wet cheeks. Sweat ran in a steady stream off the tip of his nose. Every nervous blink sent spray off his eyelashes.

The market is a furnace. The world has lost its air. At five his head darkens. At six he stumbles into the hotter outside.

He passes a YMCA. "C." Bibul grimaces. But perspiration's reality has it over cool ideology. He walks in.

The pool is closing. A lone attendant is mopping up.

"Hey, rabbi, you're too late."

"I am dying, mister. Be a good sport."

"We're closed."

"One dip —"

"Alright, rabbi, while I wash it down. You guys should get permission to wear white in summer, like nuns."

Bibul puts on a onepiece cotton swimsuit. The attendant hides his laugh behind a mop. Doubled up he steals out of the pool area to fill his pail.

Bibul pads flatfooted on cement. The soggy sisal mat over the diving board seems unslippery. He always wanted to try, hands on his hips, smartly, like a pro.

The attendant comes back in. Bibul's arms make a church spire. The attendant rushes out to fill his pail.

Bibul checks his reflection in the water, a long way.

At the top of his jump Bibul recalls he cannot swim.

"Aaaa," he says to the water.

His knees bend, his hands aim at his reflected face. Speedily the gentle water rushes up to meet him. He grabs at it, wall floor cool but airless. Cried out with his waterfilled mouth.

The attendant swishing water loudly in his pail heard nothing.

Gersh, who never did belt Bibul, went into the army, bad eyes and all, and his mother gloried.

Gersh had a sister, sixteen, a singer like her mother.

Gersh's father was a poet. Wrote unfresh depressing lamentations. One unpublished essay, "What, Karl Marx, is the Communist Answer to Death?" he read aloud after every quarrel with his ideological wife. And, sometimes, during.

In Communist as in Catholic mixed marriages, children follow the religion of the mother. Gersh moved into a bourgeois house his mother scorned, but sanctified with a peeling bronze of Lenin.

Gersh went east with the army.

His mother went west for Soviet friendship.

And one night Gersh's sister, Evvie, called me on the phone, her voice dark and trembling.

"Daddy's having a heart attack. We're all alone. He's dying."

I raced over in a cab.

Gersh's father greeted me at the door.

"Shouldn't you be lying down?" I said.

"Me? I do nothing but laze around anyway. "Evvie," he called, "put on the kettle. Listen, my friend," he said, motioning me to sit down. "Do you and Gersh try to preserve an intellectual life now he's a soldier?"

"You made a fast recovery," I said.

Evvie passed by the open kitchen door.

"Talk to Evvie better," the old man said. "I'm maybe too old-fashioned for my kids."

Evvie shut the door behind me.

"Why did you tell me your father had a heart attack?"

"Because he did."

"He didn't."

"I saw him halfdead on the floor."

"Evvie, that's a pile."

"He follows me all day. I can't go to the bathroom. Stay on guard. Don't let him sneak up to the keyhole."

She grabbed my hand.

"You're Gersh's friend. Hide me till Gersh or Mommy gets back. I sleep all night in my clothes. He wants to hand me over to his cronies."

Gersh's father rapped on the door.

"Hey, how long does it take to make a pot of tea?"

"He sleeps with my garterbelt under his pillow," Evvie whispered.

Gersh's father shuffled away from the door.

"Pull at the door quickly," Evvie said. "He's listening!"

I opened the door. Evvie gasped.

"See how sly he is. He's gone."

She threw herself on the cement floor, screaming. Police rushed to cover her naked breasts.

"Must be West Indians," an old Scot whispered. "How did it happen, miss? Who did it?"

They woke Gersh's father out of deep sleep. Teddybear tow-seled, sitting on the edge of the bed.

A policeman's truncheon poked hard against his belly.

"You have to be pretty low, fellow."

Old man befuddled in the middle of the floor, trying to pull trousers on over his pyjamas. His suspenders hung down.

A policeman's stick rapped him hard on the shoulder.

"You ought to be hung, mister. It's the worst there is."

"What is it with Evvie?"

The stick snapped hard against his ribs.

"Evvie, we'll sure as hell show you Evvie."

The doctor's examination found specks of blue ink.

I called Gersh to come home.

She locked the door, stuffed the keyhole with Kleenex, shouldered a dresser against the knob, her bed against the dresser. Her preparedness heaped high: Gersh's celluloid T-square, the fireplace poker (which streaked her yellowing sheets charcoal) seven pairs of scissors — base of her metal sculpture — a protruding crowbar, two hammers, a hatchet, five weighted brass candlesticks. At the foot of the bed six glass paperweights were missiles readied for throwing.

I found Gersh's father kneeling at the door in his gymshirt. His skin, the color of what never sees sun, fell in wrinkled folds from his cheeks and neck.

"I leave her food," he whispered without turning, "at the door, like for a kitten."

I helped him to his feet, found a shirt he put on without knowing he did so. Glass smashed against glass behind the locked door. Bedsprings shifted. Something heavy clattered to the floor.

"I'll leave the house," he said, "maybe then she'll eat. I don't know what got into her mind. I was always friends with my children."

On the sidewalk he stood hesitating, trying to decide if he should go right or left.

I rapped at Evvie's door, called to her.

"I'm naked," she said in a voice I hadn't heard before.

"Put on a robe then," I said.

"Don't pretend you don't want to see me bare."

I waited.

"Tell me the truth," she said, "you're dying to see me all skin!"

"Right."

"Are you just saying that so I'll open the door? You've got him hiding behind you."

"I'm all alone, Evvie."

"And you want to see me — if I put on a robe you'll go out of your mind knowing what's underneath."

"Open, please."

Rollers squeaked, something skidded, caught, then scraped the floor. Her head poked out, bright red sausagecurls full of pins and rollers, her face smeared wide of her lips with a blue-red grease, her eyes black from brow to cheekbones.

"You're sure he's not here?"

"Come on out, Evvie."

"I thought you wanted to come in — look, I'll show you my sights."

She flashed her robe open. Closed it just as quickly.

"You think I'm a freak!"

"You're lovely."

"You hated what you saw!"

She slammed the door against me. The key turned. Her face hung on the white doorpaint like stared-at sun's afterglow. A mimeface, warmask, smeared palimpsest. Below that face, and below the one below, and below even that, the Evvie who was Gersh's kid sister, lovely as a medlar pear secret about what's hidden inside.

I knocked at the door, pounded with my fists calling — begging — her to come out. And, I think, to reverse. Pounded and prayed. Felt myself swallowed by a hideous reality. Not the world I didn't know when I was locked in plaster away from the world; something frightening — more frightening — a reality I stared at but did not *see*.

Archaeological subcity. Hellcity. My feet walked a modern street but my step might echo in a dark town totally hidden. Scrubbed of lipstick, rouge, and mascara, Evvie's face sent out no messages. Unchanged outside. Belowground cronecackle mocking my seeing eye, and my happy-ending vision. Turn one knob and everything reverses — Evvie is old Evvie, Gersh's baby sister Evvie; Gersh's father smiles and writes more unpublishable poems; the war ends and the dead return with peace.

Irreversibility.

I could not stand to think of it. But heard it in the clatter of metal and glass behind the door my fists pointlessly pounded.

Gersh and others were away, but that same fall the university opened, on its city site, World-War-I-temporary buildings never abandoned, low as an old fort, mean-windowed, low-ceilinged, trench-corridored. Hydrogen sulphide fumes almost a third of a century old lay under dry splitting linoleum. Air and light which seeped in years earlier had not yet found a way to seep out.

Our squat rootcellar faced the legislative buildings, wide of lawn, treed, avenued, boulevarded, formal with gardens, spacious with walks, high-pillared, balustraded, crested with Greek statuary, domed in gold. At its very top a lit-up golden boy ran the good up-and-doing race. He was the last one we saluted before disappearing into our dark academy.

The university I thought I would never reach.

We took our seats in a chemistry classroom our first university day, Maggie among the girls in new cashmeres, old pearls, their hair soft in pageboy, and in the topmost row, I, with the six or seven other men students. When the tiny windows were open the legislative buildings sat over our shoulders like a cameo.

We sat still. Uneasy. A door crashed open. A man enormously tall wheeled and vaulted onto the demonstration table, sat down quickly, crosslegged, grinning, a redhaired spectacled Buddha. His wrists stuck out of his too-tight rowing blazer, and, still further, his enormous freckled hands. His face was huge and long and lantern-jawed. Deep etched grief lines ran along his grinning cheeks. Bifocal glass turned his eyes into distorted concentric rings.

"Dearly beloved," he began — his voice was as high as Alfred Deller's — "and particularly you sweet things from Millionaire Crescent, I take it you will await the return of your war heroes in my chamber."

He leaped to his feet, gigantic over the bunsen burners and gas jets his striding feet skimmed. He paced out a rhythm Aeschylean, left step step, turn, right right turn again. His arms sawed the air. His eyes disappeared in a centrifuge of glass.

"I hear pater cooing. 'Certainly there's a war, daughter, but our family is not doing badly.' You, dears, are to be stored here. You will wrap little bandages, collect discarded unopened Book-of-the-Month volumes, visit the sick and the tastefully wounded."

Miller, who used to break Bibul's synagogue windows, clapped his hands silently.

"Look at Grover give it to those bitches!"

"I want a promise, sweet things, to pass my messages to momsie so she, in turn, can educate the garden club. 'Pammie has a queer chap teaching her at the university. It's the war, you know. He's the best we could get.' "

In the fall semester's last class he lolled full length on the chemistry table.

"Come in, come in, sweets. Christmastide is on us once again.

Daddy gets his bonus. Mummy has complained to Prexy only twice. Am I that tame?"

He dropped his legs down, swung before us sandaled feet.

"Swift, ladies and gentlemen, died lacerated by his own fury. He could not prevail. Your mummies and daddies would inherit the earth. And Christ's end too you've no doubt heard rumored. To die for a Fall had matter in it, sweet ladies. Bitter to be resurrected, and find the bourgeois still in their nests."

He lived behind high black wrought-iron gates and a thick graystone wall. Posh flagstone walks wound through rock gardens and snowcovered shrubbery. His flat was in a mansion broken into suites. Beamed, brown, Tudor. Leaded windows, handmade shimmering glass.

An old grayfaced housekeeper answered our ring. Grover stood lost in winetinted carpets leading up the stairs, his glasses frosted over, his face massively cavernous, sadder than ever.

Seven students stood politely in a row; only one, Christopher something, I saw frequently in the university halls.

Grover led us through a mildewed hall, into a room paneled in ancient oak, with bishop's chairs ceremoniously set at a long heavy monks' table. A sofa of peeled black leather, scrolled at one end, too hard and slippery for sitting, was lit by lamps with parchment shades of Oxford scenes which gave no light. A Holbein drawing of a child was half hidden in darkness. A grisly Bosch. A Klee drawing of a man under a black cloud, oblivious of a bolt of lightning aimed at his head.

Grover poured warmish beer into Oxford tankards. It tasted of metal.

"It was forbidden, absolutely, so our work was all *sub rosa*," Grover said to Christopher.

"By God, Ben," Christopher burst out, "I'd love to see it here."

"Parents would misunderstand. They say it's surrender of the will."

"Sir," a fat boy said softly, "if someone insinuates a naughty idea do you wake up immediately?"

"You merely fold your arms, Freddie. The way a reluctant young lady refuses to let you steal her panties."

Christopher let out a wild coughing laugh.

"By God, Freddie, let's start with you."

Freddie was a plump old man at seventeen. Prepschool gentle, mother-attired — flannels, black sweater, blazer.

"I wouldn't like to be first, sir," he said.

Grover whirled. A thin boy ducked his face into his tankard.

"Bellingham, you," Grover said in shrill falsetto, "I feel emanations. On the couch, sir."

Christopher snatched Bellingham's tankard.

"Give it back, Chris. I won't do it."

"By God, Bellingham, didn't you hear Ben say you have been called and chosen?"

He shoved Bellingham roughly, but laughing.

"My glasses, sir," Bellingham said weakly, "do I leave them on or off?"

"We must have you comfy," said Grover.

He tipped the dimmest lampshade down. The walls darkened. One small pool of yellow light fell in a circle on Grover's cheek. His glasses flattened, opaque rounds. His eyes were lost. He held a shining dime up to the light.

Freddie inched closer.

"I did not mean I would not participate, sir."

"Can it, Freddie," Christopher whispered. "We're not up to your sixty keens."

Grover's huge shoulders and bent back heaped over Bellingham, the dime turning slowly between forefinger and thumb. Bellingham licked his lips, blinked, rubbed the back of his head against the hard leather.

"Bellingham, look, so soft, so restful to your eyes. Relax. Your eyes will grow heavy. Stretch, luxuriate. Your eyelids want to close,

rest, sleep, a beautiful sleep, soft breasts, a beautiful woman crad-
ling your head, restful, soft, your eyes are heavy with sleep, gentle,
heavy sleep, so soft, so warm, sleep, sleep peacefully, rest your
heavy eyes in sleep, deep sleep, sleep, you're in a deep deep sleep, a
deep deep sleep."

Grover's cheeks were shining wet, perspiration rolled off the ear-
pieces of his glasses. His skin was gray. The bald spot behind his
stook of hair made him suddenly pathetic.

"Ben," Christopher whispered, "why don't you start by telling
him he's got a chance at Waterloo."

Grover bent closer to Bellingham's face. His hand waved above
Bellingham's eyes. He snapped his fingers. Bellingham lay back
rigid.

"You are in a desert," Grover said in a hollow voice, "The sun is
burning, no air, your clothes are choking you —"

Bellingham's face contorted, he grabbed at his tie and collar.

Grover turned to us, and grinned.

"Polar winds are blowing, it's icy, fifty below, you have no over-
coat, the wind slices into you —"

Bellingham wrapped his arms around himself, shuddering.

"Relax. It's a mild day. You love this weather."

Bellingham's arms flopped back on the leather.

"The strongest man in the universe is you. People over the world
want a look at your muscles. Flex them, Bellingham."

Bellingham's skinny arms and legs tensed, his hands locked, his
feet pushed hard against the floor. Christopher collapsed into an
overstuffed chair, laughing.

"Stand on one leg, Atlas," Grover said, "the world is on your
shoulders."

Bellingham swelled out his thin chest, perched birdlike on one
leg. His leg began to tremble, like a beginning ballet dancer too
long in arabesque.

"You can carry any weight, Bellingham. Nothing is too much for
your powerful frame."

Savagely, Grover threw himself, heads taller, tons heavier, on Bellingham's back. His feet swung free of the floor. The tremble in Bellingham's leg grew to a shaking shudder, snapping his knee back and forth, convulsing his body. His face was beatific.

Grover got down.

"Hold out your hand, Bellingham. I've laid a speck of dust on your palm. You can't bear the weight."

Bellingham's arm held out dropped swiftly slapping his sides.

"Sit down, Neddie," Grover said, "you are a powerful chap."

Bellingham sat, in Grover's shadow.

"You have a girl, Neddie?"

Bellingham smiled widely. Christopher stood above Grover, squinting, his mouth in an o.

"Your sweetheart is here, Neddie. You and she are alone."

Grover edged closer to Bellingham. Bellingham smiled, raised his arm slowly, put it around Grover. He kissed Grover shyly on the cheek.

We held the tankards like shields before our faces.

"Mommy says it's all right for us to do everything," Grover whispered. "Feel me. Be kind but be masterful, Neddie."

Bellingham's hand slid to Grover's knee.

"My bubbies, Neddie, don't you want to feel my bubbies?"

We stole into the shadows.

Christopher moved closer, breathing through his mouth. Bellingham slid his fingers over Grover's chest, undid a shirt button, slipped his hand inside.

"Oh, I love that, Neddie. Everything is yours, sweetheart," he said in his highest falsetto, "everything."

He steered Bellingham's other hand downward. Christopher's palm crashed down on Grover's shoulder.

"By God, Ben, that's enough of that."

Grover jumped to his feet.

"You're far too slow, Neddie. I'm going off with Christopher. He loves me more."

Bellingham felt around the leather, his face long, frightened, his hands flapping at the dark empty air.

"No use, Neddie."

Grover's face lost its grin.

"Your sweetie, Bellingham. *La vie!* She's false to you. When you wake you will hate her false tricks —"

Christopher leaned his face toward Grover's.

"Ben, what the hell are you up to? Posthypnotic suggesting?"

"You will wake at the count of three, Bellingham. Now, lie back —"

"Goddam it, Ben," Christopher pounded Grover's shoulder, "look at Bellingham. He's going to cry."

"Now, Bellingham. One two —"

Bellingham's eyes screwed tightly shut.

"Ben, stop!"

Grover waved his hand in front of Bellingham's face.

"Bellingham, that was our joke. You won't hate your sweetheart. Though she's false. I'll count three and you will wake, taste beer and find it foul. Spew it into the fire, Bellingham. At three, wake, and remember nothing. One, two, three."

Grover slapped his hands together, half turned to us, smiling. Bellingham didn't move.

Grover shook him.

"Bellingham, wake up. You've had a little nap. Wake up now. Quickly."

One hand on each shoulder shook. Bellingham would not wake.

"By God, Ben, get him the hell out of it, now!"

We moved back from Grover.

"Bellingham," he said loudly, "wake up now."

He slapped Bellingham on the cheek, grabbed a handful of hair, tugged.

"Lie back, relax, sleep, Bellingham, sleep, you're in a deep deep sleep."

Bellingham's arms flopped back.

"At three, Neddie, wake. There, now, gently, one — two — three —"

Bellingham's eyes opened. He sat up.

"How about you next, Freddie? Oh, my mouth's so dry. Who's got my beer?"

He put the tankard to his lips, filled his mouth, turned, cheeks swelled, leaped to the fireplace, spewed into the hissing embers.

"I don't think I will take my turn tonight, sir," Freddie whispered, and led the rush to the coats.

I cut through the parking lot, late for my appointment with the Professor of Orthopedics. We talked weekly, of books, and olden times, and while we talked measured the hip that would not heal. From its recalcitrance he drew philosophical conclusions, which led back to books.

Heavy footsteps sounded behind me. I turned, to see Grover, unshaved, his whiskers tipped silver, almost white. His hair was wetly combed. His navy blazer stained and dusty with cigarette ash. He looked like a derelict late let loose from the drunk tank.

"I'm out. Did you hear that?"

"We're all sorry, Ben."

"Did you communicate your pain to the President?"

He grabbed my arm.

"War is dreadful for the weak. Not one of my colleagues defended me. I'm far too left for Hottentot U. *My* students — intellectuals! You fail the cause every time!"

He fell into angry stride beside me.

"For days my ship has been sinking. I listen to the splash of fat rats."

"Ben —"

"Ishmael, doomed to wander the philistine earth. Is that too literary for you intellectuals?"

"You woke us up, Ben."

"Why should your growth comfort me?"

He cried his words over the parking lot, his hands thrown up above his head. A helpless big man.

"It was a vicious lynching — they rained lies on my head. Which of you hero intellectuals denounced them for saying I was queer?"

At the intersection he paid no attention to the stoplight. I held my hand up.

"You intellectuals knew I hate and detest all forms of sexual deviation. Fags and fairies distort the human process. If I've never said these things openly you were intelligent enough to deduce my point of view from everything else I stand for."

The light changed, Grover strode angrily past a row of stopped cars. On the sidewalk he sawed his hands through the air, shouting something starting buses drowned out. Two young girls leaned away from him, parting like skaters to avoid some obstacle in the ice.

"What will you do now," Grover shouted, "turn me into a myth, a martyr, Grover Agonistes, Jeremiah unheard?"

"Ben," I said, "you woke us all."

A wordless cry formed in his open mouth.

"Shall I take comfort from what I did for you? That's nothing to me, do you hear? It's bloody well not enough!"

This unwinding skein rolls out of my hands, too far from my gray mouse. Strands of Grover, strands of war all in a rush unrolling. I would play out each segment slowly, fingerwidth by fingerwidth: I tell this tale not to line gig lamps up symmetrically. I don't think of us as transparent envelopes on whom moments shower down. Nor do I want to open — willed or unwilled — hermetic jars which keep the past unstale.

I would merely lend you my partial eye.

Look with me out of this high window at a town not mine, on a river neither mine nor Hermes's. There's a beat-up old slum tar-paperpatched, tilting with broken TV aerials and slanty chimneys;

I look down on tarred roofs strewn with shale, pocked with last
week's rain stagnant in pools; wash flaps on rusted wire lines, casts
its undulant shadow on springsprung weeds. My tower stands between that slum and this lovely river bridged for walking. Trees at
the water's side are dark where shadows meet the ground, middle
green below the early summer sunfloat yellower than lemons. Off
the river, away from the sagging town, redwalls and white spires,
domes of copper's chalkygreen, and gold, and royal, and crimson.
Hours ring from temporal bells and holy towers, prayer chiming,
time telling.

A gull winds upward off the river, windlifted, airwafted, hover-
ing for an instant as if papier-maché and hung on puppetwire.
Shadows hide under its windblown wings, and dark red sinews; its
head is to the side. I see only one red eye, and that averted; white,
abstract and perfect, sunoutlined, sundrenched, flown by or blown
by this window, out of sight.

Back in my north city I saw a messenger once, real as this gull,
and think of him now this skein has momentarily stopped its fated
unrolling. Lights fall on space at special times. Divine sparks break
out of unsuspected stony places.

In the City Market I saw this old messenger in a tenting rain-
stained felt hat, faded cotton workcoat sizes too large for his tiny
body. Grains spilled out of buff burlap sacks at his feet; damp linen
coolly covered crocks of sour cream billowed snowblue. He stood at
his bare wood stall among women in babushkas and cotton skirts
hiding their ankles, and stubblechin farmers whose trousers gaped
away from their waists.

His huge hat like a nun's coif dwarfed his face. Pale, pointy-
chinned, he smiled at the even, widening streams his battered wa-
tering can aimed at his dusty tomatoes. The water fell like rain,
soft and silent, staining the bare wood dark, washing the skins of
bell tomatoes, cherry tomatoes, gathering in clear pools on the
greenfroth beefsteaks plumped out and bursting.

I stood watching. He looked up, smiled past me. His wide-brimmed hat dipped ceremoniously — it might have had nothing to do with me. His head turned to one side as if he were listening to the water drop softly over the stall.

Yeats once imagined himself a fisherman much like this messenger I was just lucky enough to see.

Swerved out of time's bend I saw that man in space.

But most of what we tell was seen while we're pulled along in time's gaggle. Time is terrifyingly insistent, a stampede we run to keep pace with since there's no other way to survive. Racing together in that one irreversible direction we give the impression of seeing while standing still.

An openshuttered camera records a thousand separate moments on a single plane of film: the developed picture gives the illusion it has captured the motion of an instant: so this eye, and this imagination, and these hands which try to frame images out of what is rushing by.

I look at Uncle Bim in this whirling room. A party wheels around him, men and women dancing, heads thrown back, arms and legs flashing. That mourning eagle's head slumps. This face a palimpsest, all the earlier images erased, blurred, or harshly scrawled over. That marbling on those chalky cheeks is purple now, almost black, as if my old map illustration's streams and rivers were drained of color, sad black-and-white. His face is eroded, hollow with deepening shadows. I look for the unmarred Uncle Bim, the face of a younger man, and the younger man below that. All his widely separated moments are etched on my eye in only his present image. A woman leans over his highbacked chair to kiss his dry cheeks. She can't possibly know those earlier selves. His hat tips forward over his closed eyes. Under his white brownstain moustache a dry flat smoked-out butt is hiding. The dancers are leaping. They shout and sing. Above them and their music I hear the slow flapping snap of an old eagle's wings the day the mountain seemed highest.

I woke him. Maggie whispered in his ear that we were going to be married. He rose to his feet, shook himself once, then again, a burst of energy such as the moribund hold in reserve to avoid depressing visitors who are young, or innocent.

Stooped, darksuited he pulled the party closer to him. The dancing stopped. He raised his long arms over the heads of the guests.

"A toast to all of us," Uncle Bim said, rocking back and forth on his heels, "and to the angel of death. Maybe I shouldn't tell you, but he looks just like the angels of life."

He put his head back and drained his glass.

Nobody drank with him.

Dancers clogged the doorway. Over their heads a tray of frosted glasses teetered. Turning, twisting, a girl's foot came through, a leg, an arm. I reached for the tray and someone cried "Thank God!" A second arm broke through, a heavy head of hair tunneled under the linked hands of watching dancers. A tall beautiful flashing-eyed girl took the tray from me, shook her dark hair free of the pressing crowd, laughing to herself with relief and gratitude. Her voice had a child's tinkle in it. She held her tray toward me.

"To the allies," she said, "belong the spoils."

I closed my hand on two cold glasses.

"Take them," she said, "and stop that foolish grinning."

"You're gorgeous," I said.

"That earns you double — say one more nice thing and you get the tray."

"You are — you're spectacular — unbelievable — please don't tell me we're blood relatives."

"I thought being blood relatives was a good thing —"

"Not when it's the boy and the girl —"

"I'll be no closer than your forty-second cousin Zora —"

"God, is your name Zora? That's gorgeous too!"

"O.K., that wins the tray!"

She still held it toward me. My hands hadn't moved. They felt numb from the glasses.

"I think I should win you," I said.

"I think you should win the tray."

"You're so much stuff —"

"You mean big?"

"Generous!"

"Does that mean fat?"

"That means the gorgeousest!"

"Illiterate!"

I turned her round and round. Over her shoulder I caught sight of Maggie pointing Uncle Bim my way. She smiled. I ran the drinks over. But turned quickly as Zora pushed by with her empty tray.

"Hey," I said, "let me carry that for you."

I followed her into the kitchen.

"Zora," I said, "I think I've fallen in love with you."

"Great!"

"Seriously."

"Oh you big drunk — you don't have to tell me it's serious!"

"Get your coat on."

"This heat shrank your brain, boy."

"Come outside — right now."

"Now I'm sure you're out of your mind — it's forty below —"

Cold air stung my eyes.

Tiny frost diamonds floated free of sidewalk cement. Heaped snowbanks shadowed the night in blue. A light fall had furred the lightpoles; snowstuck telephone cables looped over an icesheathed elm. Twigs cracked. In the cold clear air a freight shunting in the distant railyards sounded in the backyard.

I shook my head to clear it of the fumes of toasts I had answered on this, Maggie's engagement night. I shivered. Wind ran a dull music out of stiff branched trees. I was waiting for a blackhaired girl.

Who was Zora?

Why should I stand chattering for her in arctic air?

The sidedoor opened. I heard footsteps. I wanted them to be Maggie's.

Zora ran out in an otter coat.

"I must be awful and drunk to come out like this."

"I'm sober enough for two."

"You? You are skunkdrunk —"

I slid my hands under the fur of her collar, pulled her close. Cold air whistled between our foreheads. I kissed her. She shook me off.

"What are you, the criminal type?"

"Come into Dan's car."

"We're awful."

"Sit in the car with me."

"We'll freeze to death."

I opened the door, Zora slid in under the wheel. Two breaths and the car windows papered white. Deadair cold inside. My freezing hands felt wool, silk, cold taut elastic, her thighs shocking warm.

"Take your icy hands off me, lunatic!"

"I love you!"

"You're mad!"

I opened her coat.

"Cover me up, madman. If you have to, kiss."

"You're beautiful."

"What good will it do me when I'm found stiff in the morning?"

"Let's go someplace warm."

"You're drunk, I'm drunk. Sober we'd know this is mad."

She opened the door on her side, ran back into the house.

"Make your goodbyes short," I called after her.

My mother was waiting at the kitchen door.

"I was watching," she said. "You drank too fast on an empty stomach. Go lay down till your nausea wears off. I'll take good care of Maggie."

The hanging streetlamp swayed circling shadows on the sparkling street. Passing headlamps shone black light on unsanded ice.

My head was clearing.

Blearily I saw her, coat buttoned to the neck, dark hair long under a lightgreen angora tam.

"God, out in this again. I must have some real bitch in me. And you are a terrible bastard."

"Let's go quickly," I said.

"Where?"

"To your place."

"We're strangers. How do you know I have a place? All I want is hot coffee. Tons."

We ran arm in arm, and wind scooped cold air into our downturned faces. Zora's hair caught her eyes. I stopped to spin her around. Kissed her.

"Never mind kisses. Feed me. You think this stuff is great, sustain it."

"Right now I want it to sustain me."

"Romantic madman, I weigh one hundred and forty-six, every ounce earned."

On the corner a shack shrank lean lumber ribs from the cold. A couple of stringy blondes turned as we came in, found us uninteresting. Two bald countermen leaned over four tattooed arms. A New Zealand airman puckered for a girl with mascara smeared over one eye. Count Basie on the jukebox was skying *One O'Clock Jump*. One counterman slid Zora a mug of coffee. She buried her nose in crockery.

"We'll have adjoining rooms in the pneumonia ward or bughouse —"

"Saturday night don't tell me of Sunday."

"We ran off as if we would never see anybody at that party again. It's crazy. There has to be an accounting."

She lived in a redbrick apartment house with gold leaf on the doorglass, redbrown woodwork shining like treacle. Her front window looked out on the snowcovered playground the Bully terrorized.

She looked back, pressed her key to the lock. I put my hands on her shoulders.

"This is all wrong," she said.

I drew her dress off her shoulders, her long hair free, her breasts shivering lightly, Zora white, and black, her waist dipped in sensuously, legs shyly crisscrossed, great gorgeous girl, all in my arms.

"Who brought you home?"

"Not you."

"How was the party?"

"You mean after you left?"

"I'm sorry. I behaved like a bastard."

"I saw that girl in the bedroom. I knew exactly what was coming."

"I love you, Maggie."

"In your way."

"We're going to marry and leave this town."

"Why?"

I called on a public phone.

"Please, Zora. The library."

"We did a terrible thing."

"We?"

"To your girl."

"Let me come over now."

"Like hell."

"I love you —"

"Do you love her?"

"Yes."

"Didn't anyone ever tell you? You can't be in love with two women at once."

"Meet me at the library."

"You're going to marry her, what do you want with me?"

"I told you —"

"Why don't you ask her to join us?"

"Zora, I'm leaving now."

"Listen, you sonofabitch, I've fallen in love with you. Isn't that enough?"

"Meet me on the steps."

"You'll wreck me."

"Hurry."

"Promise never to see me again after tonight?"

"No."

"I'm not coming."

"Ten minutes."

"Listen, you bastard, I'm a female. I'm weak. You can stop this right now."

"Ten minutes, sweetheart."

She ran, face tucked in her fur collar, green angora tam gray in the evening light, looked straight ahead, as if I were a stranger.

"Does every girl body do exactly what you want her to?"

In the high-ceilinged library she pretended to be alone, awkward biggirl womanchild. Once she caught my eye, looked away shyly. When she spoke to the librarian I heard a whisper and a rush.

I pulled her into a corner of the stacks.

"Fiction reminds me," she said. "I'm unlucky at love."

"Check out your bloody books or I'll start undressing you in front of the chaste."

"Is this whole thing physical?"

"God yes!"

"You think I'll do any dumb thing you ask. You own me —"
"That's a gorgeous idea."
She stuffed her tam into her pocket.
"Own me, marry Maggie. Bastard!"

Snow fell in library lamplight, large wide flakes spinning lazily, free of gravity. Settling on Zora's long lashes. We walked with fresh footfalls, past the house of the girl with braces, her trapping stairs hidden by snow. Snow fell on my darkened porch roof, outside Maggie's window.

I kissed a flake off Zora's cheek.

"I loved three guys in my life," she said. "One was a bum. The other loved soldiering. Now, you."

"I don't love soldiering."

"He was killed."

"Oh — I'm sorry."

"He hurt me."

"I'm sorry about that, too."

"The other gave me this coat. He was a rich bum."

"You love him?"

"I *did*. I'm not you."

"I love you, Maggie."

"Then see me tomorrow night."

"Sonofabitch, let one of us be chaste?"

I kissed her.

"What did you do to my shoulders? Mark them up with ownership?"

"With emblems of love."

"You crazy cornball."

Her mother tiptoed in, let dawn light Zora curled in sleep.

"Zora," she cried out, and pointed at Zora's shoulders.

"You tramp!"
She slapped her big girl of a daughter across the mouth.

After the Christmas break she turned up in the seminar, dangling earrings, stylish in a black lowcut dress. Sixty pounds lighter she looked, Alvira, whose bangs used to hang over her hornrim glasses. Always angry, looking for a scrap. No lipstick, no powder. Heavy men's workshirts hanging out of paintspattered jeans. Her feet in scuffed cowboyboots. Flesh on her eyes like bruises. Fat shield, up against involvement in the boy-girl game.

Battling Alvira, girl intellectual.

Now smiling. Now dainty girl-girl.

"Eliot," she said, to conclude, "became prosy, poor man. Auden is so brilliant he writes poems to hear himself discuss. Spender? Well, we never really were serious, were we? That leaves only him, of course. A singer. Poetry hasn't had one since Hopkins."

She smiled. Christopher looked at me, his mouth in that o. He blinked at Phippsie.

Alvira the hostility package — where was she now?

She shook her head at the doughnuts Phippsie passed. She used to eat savagely, remorseless to the last crumb.

"By Jesus," Christopher whispered to me, "Santa Claus or some such surrogate has buttered Alvira's bun."

Alvira led the way outside. Three athletes in Eskimo sweaters barred her way.

"A kiss lets you by, sweetie."

She three times kissed the tips of her fingers. We winced thinking what old Alvira might have said.

"I loved that," she said as we passed them by. "I'm flying to Rome to have my ass pinched."

We stopped in at the bookstore across the bus stop. A gaunt boy in faded corduroy was slipping magazines into a rack.

"Damn it, Alvira, you look magnificent. I'm off in an hour. Let's start a party."

The manager waved at me.

"Tell that redhaired girl we have her copy of Rilke's *Journal*."

"I'll take it," I said.

"Are you higher on Rilke than Thomas?" Alvira asked.

"Not really."

"Who's the redhaired girl, your intended?"

"*Intended?* That sounds like 'loved one.'"

"You're engaged, I hear?"

A girl with long blonde hair was staring.

"Alvira? Did I hear Bob say Alvira? Alvira Drummond? Alvira the Great?"

Alvira bowed low.

"You're on a big Thomas thing, I hear."

"That's vulgar, girlie."

"Do I have to clear it with you or can I get into Phippsie's seminar on merit?"

Alvira flexed her fingers.

"*Ciao*, honey."

We hurried to catch our bus.

A business school professor came grinning toward us, elbows up like a charging lineman, hands met in matchstrike at his waiting cigar. Lit, he puffed joy our way. Beaver fur collar, smallbrim hat, fleecelined boots.

"Celibacy and a private income add up to a cloud of niceness," Alvira said, smiling. "He has a Bentley and gas coupons and will purr purr purr all the way home."

"While you and I remain loyal to the class struggle."

She laughed, locked arms with me.

"Treat this newborn gently. I was born two days ago, on a milk farm. Alvira in the rice padding. They found me buried under several tons of fat. God — do you know fat people are members of a

secret society? Like fairies, or lesbians. Fat women have no breasts
— they can't ever be sure."

"You look great."

"Thirty-six pounds in a month. Poof! Like that! A sullen bitch
was masking me, so I did her in. Two days old. Don't I speak well
for a baby?"

Hers was the last one-family house left on the treelined boulevard. She put the key in the lock without looking back.

"Where," I asked in the hallway, "are Phippsie, Christopher,
the rest of the guys?"

"They aren't coming."

"Oh, hey — I'll be going."

"You can't!"

She backed into me, let her coat slide loosely off her shoulders.

"Help me," she said in a thick voice.

"Perhaps you'd like animal imitations too?"

"Don't mock me. I told you — I'm two days old."

I threw her coat over the bannister post.

"I'll make tea," she said. "Go on in. I'll join you. One fast cup."

An ancestor glared down from the wall, forbidding fat man hid
in flesh.

Alvira saw me staring.

"That's Bulldog Drummond, my great-great-great fatty gene. He
married Alice Ben Bolt Broomstick — Drummonds always marry
wispy ladies — but what could prevail over his chromosomes? He
wrote sermons about measure and restraint, had umpteen kids, and
died, the story says, eating."

A huge fat man crouched over a roastboar above their dark
carved sideboard, the table sat round by skinny women and bloated
children. The room swam with fat. Fat's legend was on the dark
walls, on the high chandelier, wearing away the rich thick Persian
rug. Before an ornate gold-bird-framed eighteenth-century glass Alvira turned in profile.

"I need your touch to assure me it's all true."

"That mirror and I concur."

"Don't you love me like this?"

"You look great."

"I mean don't I get to you?"

I laughed.

"God, I'm buggering it all up. Listen, I purged myself of this hateful fat, ounce by ounce, for you!"

She unbuttoned her dress.

"Feel me. I wear a strapless bra. Feel me. Please."

"Alvira, for chrissakes —"

"I can't get through — you still see me fat —"

"I don't —"

"Then put your hands on me!"

"Alvira, come off it."

"I'm real. Please. I'm exploding. I'm exposed. I don't know what to say — I want your hands on me — touch me — what will it mean otherwise, to go through this untouched?"

I sank down beside her under Bulldog Drummond's jowls.

She stretched herself on the dark velvet couch, as if I were already gone. White in the darkness of the room, whiter in the dark mirror.

She sat up, suddenly shy, draped a pillow over her knees.

"I used to think I couldn't slim down lower than a Rubens. Look in that glass. That woman is a Modigliani?"

She let the pillow fall.

"Isn't it great, when everything's showing? Those attenuated odalisques. He'd know them pretty well, wouldn't he?"

I reached for my shoes.

"Did it surprise you, a big girl like me a virgin?"

She pointed her toe toward the glass, swung her leg in a graceful arc.

"You weren't just experimenting, were you? It wasn't just pity?

You love my body — I felt it. It's going to take a lot for me to forget I was a gross fat thing. Was it nice for you?"

"Lovely."

"You're not just being a gentleman?"

"God, no!"

"Then take me home after the seminar next week. I felt your lust. I got it up in you."

Maggie tried to pat a snowball between her blue angora mittens. The wind puffed the cold dry powder back to the ground.

"Where will you go when you leave tonight?"

My shoe squeaked on newfallen snow.

"Home."

"You won't. Why don't you stop all this, right now?"

I ran in front of her, turned, opened my arms, waiting. She did not slide to me.

"Any girl could get you. All she has to pretend is she's falling apart."

I threw a handful of fluffy snow in a shower over her head.

"Admit it. Didn't that Zora play dead?"

"I'll admit it."

"Don't. She wouldn't know how."

"I told Christopher all about us."

I sat up.

"What was it you had to tell?"

"How I used your name at the gynecologist's. He said you have at least two gynecological wives already."

"You're both full of high style."

She rolled out of bed, sat, her feet on the floor, patting herself.

"I think you knocked me up. I'm true to my diet but this tummy is definitely fuller."

I groaned.

"You're a romantic. What the hell do you care about diaphragms? What would you do if I were pregnant? Chris says you love a blackhaired wench. Did you tell her about me?"

"I've left the public relations job to you. And Christopher."

"Listen, lover man. I dieted to get you."

I pounded my palms together in applause.

"Tell those bitches you're screwing that they're in a tournament."

"Why this *True Romances* bullshit, bluestocking?"

"What else do I have to go on? Listen, I watched floozies at bus stops for years. I read *Fanny Hill*. I stole in to see feelthy movies. If I act stupidly, help me. I'm your — what do they call it in the magazines — cherry. Doesn't that make me special?"

Her heart was pulsing her soft damp breasts.

"How can you do this with another girl? I know you love me."

Her hair trailed over my face, shutting out the room. My lips settled between her breasts.

"What do you want that I can't give you?"

"Nothing."

"You said I was a huge girl. Test my quantities, Don Giovanni."

"I hear you're engaged to that blackhaired bitch."

"She's no bitch. And I'm not."

"Christopher said you were engaged."

"When," Maggie asked, "do you sleep?"

"You should leave this craziness. Let's run off together."

"Where?"

"I don't know — New York?"

"When?"

"Now. I'll dress, and pack."

"Wait till morning."

"Morning's too late. You want every girl's door open forever. Close somebody's. Doesn't she know?"

"Sure."

"At least there's no crumby deception."

"I love you."

"Take me to New York."

"O.K."

"You've promised to marry Maggie."

"I'll tell her."

"When?"

"It's three o'clock. Everyone's asleep."

"You won't be able to once the sun comes up."

"We'll go to New York. I promise you."

"The three of us?"

Tabaleh, the girl we ran into in the bookstore, sat like a princess, her hair in a chignon. Alvira glared. I talked to her, ignoring Tabaleh.

"In Bloomsbury his silliest words were heard with awe. They tittered at his *in* stuff. The boy from St. Looey played them, like a wind harp."

Alvira slammed her hand down on the table.

"That's muckraking. Get to his poetry!"

"That sonority on his record is Bloomsbury-bore sound. Wrap up in Edwardian draperies, top yourself with a bowler, pad on orient rugs. The old toff was right to have a fix on Tiresias, who couldn't see the historical world either."

Alvira guffawed.

"Is it our Eliot you are referring to with your liberal nonsense?"

Christopher fisted the air and cheered.

"Yours is stale leftwing bitchery," Alvira said with a shrug.

Tabaleh whispered.

"He *did* think Donne a greater poet than Milton."

"I," said Christopher, "would rather be than see Donne."

"There's no quarrel," I said, "with Eliot the critic. Just throw out everything he wrote after nineteen-twenty-eight —"

"Is it Eliot the Christian you can't abide?"

"Eliot the christly, I think."

"That's just smartass," Alvira said, and stood up.

Tabaleh walked beside Christopher. Alvira caught up to me trailing.

"Buy me a coffee."

"I have to rush home."

"Chores for mommy?"

Her eyes were on Tabaleh's calves, full against the dark snow.

"You like that?" she said.

"What?"

"You know damn well what."

"Are you going to start that spook routine again?"

"You'd better turn up one of these nights, buddy boy."

"I've been tied up with family matters."

"You are a sonofabitch. This little asswag, why do you think she joined the seminar?"

"To sit at the feet of Alvira the Great."

We stepped into the headlights of the idling bus. Tabaleh talked intimately with Christopher. I sat with Alvira.

"I'm going to phone your betrothed and spill the beans."

"My betrothed? What's the nineteenth-century —"

"Never mind my words — that Zora, I'll get to her one of these days too. We'll blow you out of the water."

"Alvira, do what you have to do."

"Scrap this diet and turn bubbly fat?"

"For chrissakes don't get fat."

In this world solutions come from specialists. So I went in search of him, my hero long before morningshift dayshift nightshift turned from metaphor to reality. I would never have known him had the natives not pointed. He looked ancient, Uncle Bim's grand-father, poor old man crippling his way along a walk. His teeth were bad. He was most unexpectedly ugly.

His starched shirt, an Eton schoolboy's, flowed a purple tie. The knees of his white satin breeches grass-stained, his long Spanish cloak uneven and piebald. The head of his cane was a version of the foxhead — a woman's face, her mouth a carved grinning slit, as on a shrunken head.

"Come," he croaked.

I followed him into a monastery with walls of sweating white tile. A massive Toledo ironwork lamp swung above our heads.

"My chamber," he said, and waved me through a doorway.

The room was dark. Pictures covered the wall, like posters plas-tered over posters in dark abandoned subway tunnels.

Every picture was of a woman.

Women slept in stone, sat in wood, cupped their breasts in fresco. The naked virgin's hand bumped against Eve's breasts. Seven Rubens nudes tumbled squarefleshed buttocks over the grin-ning face of him, younger Don Giovanni. Botticelli's women broke through stained glass, found fading Don Giovanni asleep: Goya's Maja in an obscene candid pose from behind, then scissoring her legs open. Eric Gill bellies and thighs tumbling like cotton quilting in a dryer. Nelson's Lady Hamilton held a lorgnette, naked from the waist down. Kitty O'Shea was Lady Godiva. Color photographs of Nell Gwynne, Medea, Moll Flanders, Helen of Troy being studded by a Trojan Horse. Nude portraits twenty feet high of Sophia Loren, Cleopatra, Marilyn Monroe, Queen Victoria, Theda Bara. Tacked over them tiny snapshots, etchings, watercolors.

Don Giovanni groaned up at the wall.

"Now I know only women in general. Women in general are like music in general."

"Sir," I said, "I did not associate time with you."

He tottered over to a low dark bench.

"Sit," he said. "Are you after my addressbook? Glorious! Different names, yes. They fell into categories. It made me into — excuse me, young man — nothing more than a curator of —"

His arthritic arm in a painful arc took in the entire wall.

"A curator. Not a savorer — that's what your kind won't understand. When I should have been witness to womankind, when I could have lived a pilgrim, a troubador, a canvasser, a pulse-taker, an idolater, a thwacker, a stirrer, a tit-developer, an eye-glistener —"

"Sir, I need advice. You're love's leading expert."

"That eunuch Leporello auctioned off *my* addressbook, which only a king or pope deserved to see."

He wheezed, fenced his cane against the air, tossed his cloak with a bullfighter's turn.

"Reminiscence is wrong for lovers. Photographs, drawing. My cock was once *my* pen. Now I have a disgusting harem — obscene, o filthy! My own wenches mock me: 'Hey, cocksman, when will it be?' Or 'Man, what else was cut with the prostate?' I have lumbago in my humper's back, droop in my testicles, wind in my gut, and o, rashes. Sometimes the old horniness comes, but nothing after."

"When you were a little boy, sir, did you want to kiss every beautiful woman you saw?"

"Don Giovanni a little boy! Was Oedipus ever a little boy? Faustus?"

"I mean how early did you discover you'd never pass a beautiful woman by?"

"I can't date it. I always had that."

"Sir, who is this Sophia Loren on the wall? And how come you have a photo of Marilyn Monroe?"

"Find better things to ask this old pro. O, I was a legend in my time."

"My trouble sir, has to do with women too."

"Naturally."

"I'm in love with two and sleep with three."

"Five? Only five. God, boy, would Bluebeard expect sympathy from Ghengis Khan?"

He walked over to the wall, his cane a pointer, tapping photographs and paintings, showing his kind of thigh, lip, breast.

"Behind that arras," he said with a sudden collapse, "are the fleshly thing. All the women a cocksman could wish for. Portraits are less demanding, and allow an old letch to catch his breath. Once I could recognize each of them by her loving scent. God, what I'd do at the whiff of hot snatch! Then they" — he pointed up at the sky — "took away my olfactories. I, who knew Anna in the dark because her thighs breathed out lemon — my first thousand had discreet signatures, you know. Now all women are gray in the dark."

My expert was no help.

I stood up, and Don Giovanni followed me past the flashy wall.

"Listen, son, one tip, not about those five women you're shagging. I mean me. Keep my story to yourself. Don't destroy masculine morale. Troilus is no better as an old man. Antony. Parnell. Take it from somebody who knows. They don't get their women confused, but time which ne'er spared the rod wilted it too. 'Screw my myth!' say I who know too late to opt for youth."

Maggie's cheeks were red with wind, her chin tucked down in her collar. I tilted her face my way.

"You're mad," she said. "Woman-mad. As if you were meeting the species for the first time. Let's go west. Haven't you always wanted to beachcomb?"

"Nobody beachcombs in wartime."

"What is it *you* are doing in wartime?"

I kissed her cold chin. She looked up.

"Do you really want to marry me — tell the truth now."

"Of course —"

"Her too?"

I kicked out at a crust of snow. Dusting it shattered the length of the sidewalk.

"You might some day fall in love a hundred times — it's only a matter of numbers available. You'd marry each and every one too."

"Poof," I said, and blew a handful of snow her way.

"Evader! Life deferring teen-ager — eternal loverboy! Can't you even see what you're doing?"

Christopher phoned, about the Dieppe returnees, and a party; I called Zora to meet me at the hotel, and came there to see wartime which I had all but forgotten.

Midtown swarmed with servicemen. A Ceylon airman with polished wood face shone under a flashing yellow safety light at my car stop. I got off the trolley, three Aussie airmen linked arms and swerved in front of the tram. The motorman clanged. A whitehelmeted head leaned out of an airforce patrol car to curse.

At the corner drunk sailors sank in snow. A Royal Navy hat lay upside down on a dirtcrust bank. Cockney voices shouted. Someone started a Maori warchant. Harsh laughing drowned it out.

Closer to the hotel I heard heavy boots crunch ice in rapid cracktroop beat, rattling manhole covers, scraping bare patches of cement. Gloved hands swinging, a sweep of maroon berets headed for the beerparlor, their high paratrooper boots shiny brown and wet.

Khaki uniforms flowed into the hotel, and out, on two conveyer belts, palefaces in, redskins out. Two sailors fenced in the middle of the street, clashing snowshovel on snowshovel.

Under the hotel canopy an elegantly dressed man shielded a whitegowned woman behind him while the doorman puffed his cheeks to whistle up a civvy cab.

Ginred Christopher opened the door. His eyes were bleary, his hair and lashes looked like canary-white stage make up. Behind him a squarejawed blonde lay sullen and casual, her skirt crept up, her shoes on. She flicked a long cigaretteholder to acknowledge the introduction.

"Here, are you 'eyeing Tish?" Christopher said. "You come wenchless and cast a lecherous eye on Tish — by God, have you no loyalty to Dieppe, you bastard? Aren't you ashamed you didn't turn over for this night the six or seven beauties you are shagging? Hah, Tish, that interests you, doesn't it? But we'll not share these pectorals tonight. Graham, pick your head up you drunken misconception — meet a friend — and turn your back, both of you, for I seem to have misplaced Tishie's breasts."

Tish's husband Graham smiled, his lower teeth scraped scratchily at his soggy RAF moustache. He pointed to another airforce officer slumped on the floor.

"Graham's trying to introduce you," Christopher said. "He is middlephase paralytic, tertiary sclerotic, suffering from alcoholic aphasia; look closely at the sonofabitch's chin and you'll see the will is there, but not the way. In short, in fine — keep still, Tish, I've bloody well lost your swingers again."

Tish pushed his hands away wearily.

"That man on the floor is an ace," Christopher said, "eleven nahsty nahzies he shot out of the sky at a rough cost of two hundred thousand per to Adolf. We call him Eleven — Lord Eleven. When we know him better we shall refer to him by his serial number."

Graham crawled along the floor, fished a worn deck of playing cards from under the bed.

"We're not going to spend your bloody leave the usual way, Graham," Tish said, shaking free of Christopher. "You're just not going to play poker till you fall in a drunk faint."

"Goddam it, Tish," Christopher said, "don't you speak to warring types every minute out on those bloody posts? I'm offering you an evening at strictly civilian pursuits."

Graham raised his eyes to the ceiling, began counting cards, slowly, audibly. Cards dropped. He swept them up and began his count again.

"Put those stupid cards down," Tish said. "Keep an illusion going, Graham. That I am married to a man."

Drool and porter wet the corners of Graham's moustache. He grinned.

"Twenty-six," he muttered. "Half a pack. Not bad for a start."

"Tishie," Christopher tugged at her from behind, "I am having the goddamdest time with your brassiere catch. Look at that husband of yours! Graham, you ill-mannered shit! How can you see me struggling thus and make no move to help?"

Tish pulled her sweater down fiercely. Her upperlip was bleached, and tiny beads gathered in a line above her lipstick. Her shoulders were wide — tennis shoulders, swimmer shoulders. All of her tanned, even in winter. Hair just done. Bleached, set. Girl who didn't quite make femme fatale.

"I am beginning to feel rejected," Christopher whimpered.

"You stink as a poker player, Graham," Tish said shrilly. "You bluff every hand. Every airforce moron from coast to coast knows you bluff every hand."

Graham nodded, sat down on the floor. His hand reached under the bed again, came out with an unopened bottle of gin.

"Tish," said Christopher, "I think it better to tell these interlopers to wait out in the hall while we go to our buttockbanging. The primal act has been known to scar witnesses, and, some say, maim husbands."

"For the last time, Graham — get to your bloody feet! I want out of here!"

Fists and boots rained knocks on the door. Three ragtag soldiers bulled their way past Christopher, made a rush at Tish. Chris barred the way, laughing. One soldier's hands were curled, like a boxer's bandaged. He held them out before him, as if for inspection.

All three sagged in their bagged-out uniforms. The man with
bad hands held his head tilted like a doll badly repaired.

"Nurses," he said.

His voicebox hummed some electronic device. He burped up his
words. His throat had a deep scar. His face was a tangle of healing.

"Tish, sweet," Chris said, "we will defer sporting. Store my
pleasure in moist warmth."

"Nurses," the soldier said.

"Jesus, Montie, a little style, please. Those goddam Nazis shot
taste away with your throatbox. You dumb sonofabitch — nurse
isn't the language's only synonym for woman."

"Where are they?"

Graham staggered toward the soldiers, three brimming glasses
clutched in his hands.

"Mont old man — gin and porter — pencil lead — nursies will
thank us all."

Montie took his drink, left hand, elbow hugging his rib cage; he
pushed the glass between the heel of his palm and his body, lifted
it toward his mouth, buckled, threw back his head, drank.

"Graham," Tish whispered loudly, "I can't believe a man who
flies can think of a bloody poker game."

"Montie, you bastard," Christopher said, "I had Tish by the
flipperflap, and you come growling abstract things like nurses. No
wonder those krauts blasted us out of the water. What has happened to our taste and timing?"

Tish slapped at the cards in Graham's hand.

"Graham, you pig! Did we leave Halifax for this?"

"Mont, old man," Graham said, "fifty-cent limit — are you in?"

"Christopher, let me out," Tish said loudly.

"Tishie, wait!"

She grabbed her coat, slammed out the door.

Graham smiled sickly.

"She'll be back."

He looked at his cards.

"I can't open."

Montie bent forward, freed the small finger on his left hand, swept the dealt cards up, jammed them against his chest. One of his friends separated the backs of the cards.

"The shore batteries, right?" Graham said.

"Right," Montie said in a hoarse whisper. "Lobbed in. A skeet shoot. The krauts didn't need guns. Somebody fucked up. We died."

"Never mind the morbidity, Montie," Christopher said, "Graham, how did you dull your wife's lust? She used to burn for my embraces."

Graham sucked porter off his moustache, pensive, forehead wrinkled.

"Can't anyone open?"

Montie held up his little finger.

"I worked eight months with a hairylip therapist, to get this trigger-finger in shape. I'll find the bastard. Whoever it was."

He fished a cigarette out of his tunic pocket, angled it into his mouth. The heel of his hand pressed a pack of matches against his knee. His one good finger tore loose a match.

"A cabinet minister. I'll settle for a civvy in command."

He threw one match aside, struck and lit another.

"Right, Mont old man," Graham said, "criminal. Don't have the right planes. No cruising range. Go out. Can't get back."

"Oh Jesus," Christopher broke in, "this shot-up neanderthal and you, Graham, usurping my territory."

"We could have gotten larger planes from the Yanks —"

"And fucked up the exchange rate."

"We could have saved lives."

"God, Graham, you're not so bloody naïve to think a few airforce lives are more important than the exchange rate?"

Graham muttered an answer, Montie growled into his chest.

"Nurses," said another soldier, "where the hell are they?"

A foot kicked against the door. Two grinning sailors waved at Christopher.

"Suds, God, you're still the ugliest sonofabitch in the world — didn't mother knit you a masking afghan?

Sud's front teeth were missing. His broken nose badly repaired. He had a hairlip, was bald at twenty.

"Thank God you didn't get killed on the seas, Suds. Mother says I'm the ugliest till I remind her of you."

"Where are nurses?"

"On the way. Not those in their menses are exempt. I swore to Mother Superior our heroes would never notice."

The doorbell rang.

Christopher threw his cards in the air.

But it was Zora.

"One nurse? By God, most gorgeous black and white nurse, let's go it alone, at least till reinforcements arrive. These animals will divide you unevenly."

He stepped back and gave Zora exaggerated clearance. I took her by the hand.

"My God, Rebecca at the well!" Christopher said. "May I be a pilgrim, lady?"

Zora slapped his hand away.

"Lady, if you must deny me, deny this sonofabitch too, and cover thy amples wisely with orchids."

He pressed a wad of paper towels over her breasts.

"Nurses," Montie whispered.

"Without you, black loveliness," Christopher said, "the heroes might have overlooked the absence of females."

He steered Zora into a corner.

"How will it fare, lady of the urns?"

She arched her eyebrows up.

"King Solomon's solution, lady. Split the sonofabitch one part east, one part west, luckiest the lady under the cuckoo's nest."

Zora shrugged.

"If one sensible bone hides under this lovely flesh, black one, desist. This dark conductor loves all womankind."

"Nurses," Montie said, and beat his good fist against his knee.

"God, Graham," Christopher said, "if Tish were here, we could throw her to the wolves."

In the hall the nurses were an army storming a palace. A press on the doorbell and the men around us charged. Women poured into the room.

Christopher tried to shout. Two uniformed bodies belted him from behind. Suds grabbed silk, winched it in his hands, reeled a nurse in. A blonde tried to connect a portable radio and two hands caught the flesh her bending flashed. Montie broke for a nurse, hoisted her up, his arms stiff against his chest, over his head. She screamed. He spun her, round and round, her legs locked, her skirt flying. Faster Montie whirled her, knees quivering, hair streaming, her face running tears and saliva.

"Montie," I shouted, "put her down. She's scared to death!"

He poled her by the feet, into the center of the bed, between two squirming couples fully clothed. Her face was white, the front of her dress darkly wet. Two steps Montie took, hoisted her on his shoulders, shirt blown over his face. Every time her spinning thighs whirled by, Suds saluted.

"Montie, for chrissakes," I shouted.

A redhaired nurse pulled at me from behind.

"Honey, where did it happen? Show me. Mommy kiss."

An airman and a nurse danced on their knees, faces locked in a kiss.

"Montie," I said, grabbing him by the arm, "she's terrified."

"Hey," Suds said, "salute the cheeks of the fair."

The redhaired nurse pulled me back from Montie.

"Did they amputate, honey?"

Montie's arms were wood. The girl's head hung down, her mouth open. Saliva ran in a whipping stream.

I pushed Montie, spilled him on the bed of arms and legs. His chin dug into the limp nurse's belly.

The redhaired nurse hung on.

"You aren't going to claim this man all night?" she said to Zora. Zora smiled politely.

"Christopher said it was wide open. No previous pairing."

Suds from behind jerked her off her feet, dragged her to the squirming pile on the bed.

A blonde grabbed my hand.

"Airforce, right? Flak? Sink down on the rug, flierboy, and act out the story of your life."

Zora backed away.

"We shouldn't be here," she said.

"These guys haven't seen a woman in years."

"I don't mean that."

A soldier and a nurse rolled at our feet.

"Turn out the goddam lights," Suds shouted.

"Lights," Montie growled.

"Never," shouted Christopher, "light is all between us and pre-creation chaos."

A soldier jabbed at a light switch, Christopher quickly turned on a lamp. Suds kicked out with his stockinged feet. An empty porter bottle smashed the ceiling fixture.

Montie knelt at his nurse's side, Sud's sailor friend reached over one girl to undo the bra of another. The redhaired nurse leaned down from the bed to kiss Graham on his open mouth.

Somebody stood in the doorway, laughing. Two people. Tish. Behind her a big girl. Alvira.

A soldier dived for the light switch, but Tish ground her body against him.

"Kiss harder, Nellie," she said to the redhead with Graham, "there's bounty for anyone who finds wolf on my property."

Christopher pulled her away.

"We aristocrats must stick together, Tishie," he said, and slid his hand down her dress.

Alvira stared at me. Light from the corridor framed her. Christopher's idea, I was sure. Michin malicho. To see what could be stirred up quickly.

"Who are *you?*" she shouted.

"Zora."

A soldier grabbed at Zora, she dodged, he fell into Tish and Christopher.

"Does he recite Dylan Thomas on your breasts?" Alvira said.

"Alvira," I said, "you're drunk."

"Did he tell you about me? You're so intimate — tell me, did he even mention my name?"

I stepped between them.

Alvira drummed her fists on my shoulders.

"You're taking her side, you bastard."

The redhaired nurse sneaked up behind me.

"Who's the angry one? God, can we all fight for what we want?"

"You bastard," Alvira shrieked, "you bastard — turning me into a fat freak!"

Her hand grabbed a handful of Zora's hair.

"Go at her, fatty," the redhaired nurse shouted.

Alvira's hand wound Zora's hair tight.

"On your knees. Beg forgiveness, for shaming me, you whore."

I shook off the redhaired nurse, smashed at Alvira's wrist. Zora fell forward, her hair streaming over the rug.

Alvira turned her back on us.

"Don't you comfort her — stay away from each other. Leave me one touch of dignity."

A soldier grabbed her breasts. She screamed, backing out the door. Her hand was dark with Zora's hair.

Zora raised her head.

"You bastard!"

I helped her to her feet.

"Name them," she said, "I should have known — thirty, a hundred."

"Soldier boy," the redhead whispered, "I wouldn't yell at you. I'd never get sore. Only where you'd make me sore."

Zora's eyes in hallway light were dark, and glinting. I put my arms around her. She slid her hands inside my shirt.

"Sweetheart," I whispered.

"You fucker!"

Her nails dug into my chest, searing ripping burning, like adhesive tearing. Choked my breath. I pushed her away. She stumbled back, her nails clotted.

"Jesus, look," the redhaired nurse mumbled, "O Jesus, look!"

Christopher wrestled by with Tish. Her dress was up over her tanned hips.

"Close that goddam door," he shouted. "And turn out the light."

I ran out after Zora.

"Soldier boy, don't leave me," the nurse called into the hall, "I've got salve here for all your wounds."

My chest was burning. I held my head low, my face in a cold sweat, my heart pounding.

"You crazy crazy murderous bitch!"

The cab sped through bare snowcovered streets, up the bridge over the railroad yards. I pressed my forehead against cold carwindow glass.

The cab braked.

"Are you coming in?" Zora whispered.

"You've got to be kidding."

"That's it?"

"It."

The driver looked around, crawled out grudgingly, opened the door. Zora backed out.

"What if I said I'm sorry?"

"I'd tell you to fuck yourself."

The driver gasped.

She crossed the street, paused, stepped up the curb, quickened her step, disappeared.

The driver sat still.

"Sonny I'm older than you. You're a paying customer. But it ain't right, what you said to a beautiful girl."

I frame this now, Zora with one foot on the curb, fur coat swinging, her long hair lifted by the wind. Now my hands make the same frame, but nobody's in it.

I ran for the bus, saw the black ice, felt air beneath me, then the crash, my ankle under all my weight. A fruitstore man threw a fuzzy red blanket over me as I lay on ice. Snow between my neck and my collar burned my skin. I was grateful it wasn't my hip again.

I refused to be thrown back on the inner life. I didn't want to look out the window, or start my old transcribing. To hell with passing cars, and mailmen, and singing birds!

I thought I heard that girl in braces, tongue thick between her teeth.

"See, Mister," she said, "run with all your might and you still swing on my scroll gate."

The doorbell froze them. It always did. The telegraph boy who told of death passed frequently on his bike. He wore a uniform of charcoal, with shiny belted leather gaiters, and whistled tunelessly.

My father opened the door. But came in with Zora. My father stared at her, my mother stared at Maggie.

Maggie stood up.

"Didn't I challenge you two," she said, "to a game of casino?"

"You look lovely, Zora," said my mother as they left the room.

Zora sat on the bed, in big black and white checks, black hat. Her eyes were darker, or shadows made them seem so.

"Black," I whispered, "you are beautiful."

"I brought you a present. A handkerchief."

"Come closer."

"You mean under the covers."

"Right."

"O.K."

She kicked her shoes off noiselessly, slid quickly under the sheets, in her coat and hat.

Cards shuffled loudly in the dining room, voices sounded far off, strained.

"Black, oh how I would love to."

"Shame on you."

"I love you, Black."

A card slapped a tabletop. A chair scraped the floor. Zora slipped out of bed quickly, stepped back into her shoes.

"You're terrible!! We're both terrible."

"Come back in here."

"Don't kick over my building blocks. I'm constructing a new life."

"O.K."

"Maggie's very pretty, she's got style. She loves you, bastard."

A chair pulled back raspingly, my mother stood in the doorway like a head nurse calling an end to visiting hours.

"What do you think of this guy breaking an ankle?"

"He looks to me," said Zora, "like a person who will recover."

"Will you live in New York from now on?"

"I think so."

My mother blocked her off in the doorway.

Black hat dark flower, coat alabaster and basalt. One microsecond my eye held her, out of time, framed in space.

Then gone.

In darkness's timeless orbit I tumbled, and landed outside a massive wall. A woman sat mourning a length of thread in her hand.

I spoke to Ariadne, and heard a reconstructed tale.

In the heart of that stone labyrinth her man Theseus finally met his Minotaur brow to brow. Theseus, his sword upraised, wrist turning downward. The poor Minotaur — as aware as Theseus of his role in the myth — played out his part — snorted, stamped, cowered. Theseus was, after all, Theseus, which meant the Minotaur was as good as dead (the Minotaur was a true believer).

That sword hung in the air an instant too long, the length of a second thought. The literalist Minotaur missed the pause, assumed the worst, and fell. But Theseus wasn't thinking about Minotaurs. Ariadne's thread — a woman's thread — to lead him, a hero, back out of the maze? Shared billing was no hero's stuff.

"Did Hercules need a woman's help?" Theseus cried hollow-voiced to the walls. "Bellerophon — who?"

He ran rapidly through the hero rolls and found each did his solo singular.

His wrist turned again, just as the confused Minotaur was reviving. It heard that sword cut through the air and, for the second time, died, though untouched.

Because Theseus's blade cut Ariadne's deheroizing thread, clean through. The Minotaur revived once more, saw, and understood that terrible sundering. This time he merely fainted. Outside, faithful Ariadne felt the sharp tug and, heartleaping, reeled her hero quickly in.

The Minotaur revived for his last time, wordless and weeping. Poor Theseus misunderstood it for a coward's cry. Down came his disgusted sword, off rolled the pitying Minotaur's head.

Theseus was ready now to leave. Of course he encountered a blank wall. And another. And knew almost instantly what the Minotaur had no chance to tell him.

Ariadne on watch at the wall knew something had gone wrong. But not what. Her happy-ending legend did not mention a severed thread.

Though nobody was with Theseus at the very end it doesn't take much imagining to know that the properly slain Minotaur was little consolation.

Her hair fell over her knee of rayon. Mother's gift, who herself tonight wears nylons. If Mother did it willfully Maggie might sustain such a slight.

Mother, a depressing word. Breathing out. In her slip. Depressing cadence. Blow out out out — ash long — soon it falls. Mother absently brushed that gray ash off her white satin. Crushed ash. All over the house. Dead ash.

No thought for a bride on her wedding day. Oh! A great building, about to be topped-off, collapses. Dirt puffs up slowly, like smoke in disaster's slow motion.

Nicer start to a wedding day. Like. *Once upon a time a beautiful girl named Maggie* — bad Sybil's leaves. Bad Sybil, black hair, bursting with life, no man could fail to recognize her. Innocent, in her way. In her way more murderous.

How did Rosalind feel? Romeo went to the party in love with Rosalind. Saw Juliet. Never another Rosalind thought.

Poor Rosalind.

Once upon a time a great gorgeous girl named Maggie went to a party and there she met a young man all dressed in leather who seized her by the left leg and threw her downstairs.

Marry.

In fear.

Repent.

At your leisure.

Once upon a time there was.

Fairy godmother sat yoga on the window sill.

"Fairy godmother, let's make it a smashing wedding —"

"Ah — fluttering streamers — white and — yes, blue — spring flowers — we'll build a yellow flower tower —"

"I'm sorry — the money went to the Red Cross — mother said flowers in wartime are tasteless —"

"Ah well — waft down the staircase slowly, your bridegroom's white dream —"

"Fairy godmother — I let myself be talked into a sensible dress —"

"Mere externals, sweetheart — your bridegroom will crush you to his chest — full of ardor and a lover's flame —"

"Perhaps forget, and murmur another name —"

"I beg your pardon, dear?"

"A foolish bitter rhyme."

"A joke? See, we jollied ourselves out of gloom."

Zip.

Oops. That long ash shattering. Gray on a bride's slippers. Get that goddam cigarette out of your mouth long enough to do one thing and one thing only — Mother!

Mother's slutshuffle. Backless mules. Depressing. Those mules could send anybody under for a week. Mother butting her butt. Twisting, grind against glass, hideous, squeak, a screech to obliterate bride Maggie.

Her hair brush softly, gently. One hour. Turn into somebody else. Everything new. Voice. Walk. Conversation. Touch everybody — grab every male — hand, arm, smile, touch cheeks. Great. At home with everyman.

Tough on poor Zora.

"Zip me up, honey. Don't I look great in white?"

Maggie winced.

"It's a little formal for this occasion, honey, but I'll get a lot of use out of it later. You won't entertain much in California."

She stood in profile.

"Pretty slim for an old bag, eh?"

Maggie nodded.

"Come on, Maggie, zip me up. Spare a minute's thought? We'll be fussing over you the rest of this wonderful day."

Out the corner of my eye I saw the ivory lace and moved over to leave room for Maggie.

Her mother passed by.

Maggie wore gray.

The piled rug woven with a gold and royal blue eagle lay under our fourposter, manypillowed, with small oak steps at one side. Liveried waiters rolled champagne in on a damask-spread cart, pretending no bride was behind the closed door. Silently they withdrew, and Maggie came out. In white at last.

"Look at me," she said, "I'm trembling."

"Me too."

"Why should it be?"

"We've never been married before."

"I don't understand."

"It's a mystery."

"Do I excite you?" Maggie whispered to my ear.

"God yes."

"I'm shivering."

"The champagne's cold."

"Love me now, fiercely, as if no other person lives in our world."

On the platform I stared at the iron net of rails jeweled with signal lights. Steam hung in light-spotted puffs over a battlefield of dustmoted cones flashing in darkness below crowsnest switchmen perched in yellow squares. All around us shunting freightcars coupling crashed, brakescreech belltoll dying dying whistles. All this I first heard long ago, when imagination built metal bodies and wooden boxes on sound's phantom frame.

My mother's glasses steamed away her eyes. My father's lashes wet in those spears. Uncle Bim stood above them, his fingers spread like two gnarled crowns.

High above every other sound, his voice, though he spoke no louder than a whisper. They looked up, my father sagged in the shoulders, my mother with her glasses pushed up, Uncle Bim fierce mourning bird. Fierce falconer. Three falconers, none fierce, hands in a releasing motion returning their birds to a green world, watching numbly as their falcons spring and soar, higher and wider, into a green sky.

I conquered my fear of presumption, because only he could know.

"I'm ashamed to speak, father Abraham," I said.

"What is it?"

"I now think — the worst time was not when you put that knife to Isaac's throat."

"You have left the house of your father."

"Was it sad for you?"

"Sad, and bleak, and lonely."

"With God's voice in your ear."

"I missed my father."

"Who worshipped idols."

"I missed my father's idols."

WEST

sand signatures

T<small>HE</small> black foamy soil faded, grayed, grew sandy. Oaks changed to oily-leaved orangetrees, elms to coconut palms gray and wrinkled as an elephant's leg. Royal palms crowded in, common as maples, with sculptured brown pineapples for trunks. Ice was gone, and swooping snowbanks, trapping walks. The train cut through black-green walnutgroves, peppertrees with blackgreen pompoms.

Rough whitewash walls met our eye, red tile, bakedclay, wrought iron in twists and spears and circles.

We dragged our bags off the racks.

"I'm frightened," Maggie said.

The train stopped among roses, camellias, a magnolia tree with petals like small oars.

We leaped off the train into warm moist air. It was a release. Like the end of war.

Hand in hand we hurried the station's long passageway. I listened to our footsteps distinct in a flowing crowd, sharply loud in new space. Behind us, unreal, held like statuary, my mother and father and Uncle Bim in that gesture of release; beyond them, a wintry backdrop, and that dreamed world's snow and ice.

Uncle Baer was a powerful man.

He shook hands with a crush, walked on his heels, talked with a jerk of his arms outward, as if tearing at resistant leather. His face was red, his small dark eyes lost behind thick glasses, his thinning hair in a reddish scroll, an infinity sign rolling across his head from one ear to the other. He spoke standing at attention, like a small boy at a small boy's congress. He tuned out like a small boy, too, suddenly, his large face twisted, ready to cry. His tuning-out was dangerous. Several times he walked into an oncoming car.

Uncle Baer was a big man, and only slightly shrunken.

In front of a great green tree he spread his powerful arms, grabbed Maggie up, lifted her high off the ground, hugged us both, covering us with kisses, mumbling "lovelovelovelovelovelovelove-love."

He had no children.

Aunt Teena was a powerful woman.

Her skin was pale white, her cheeks heavily powdered, dry to my lips. She looked asleep, her eyes closed behind glasses thick as Uncle Baer's. She stood beside Uncle Baer, smiling, her hands locked together to support a large black leather handbag. Her hair was tinted a pale purple. She wore a silver coat, one glittering shade darker than her hair.

"Look at my wife," Uncle Baer cried to the redbarked manzanita bush, "she is a princess!"

He didn't pause to let her say he was a prince.

"This is my sweetheart," he called up to the pale sky, "was there ever in this whole world a woman half so beautiful?"

Aunt Teena walked with her feet turned out, and took even steps.

"Four times I was a millionaire," Uncle Baer whispered into the palms of his hands, "ten times I went bust. She kept me living! She is an angel! She brings love to me from heaven!"

Aunt Teena turned to me. She was my father's stepsister.

"You are my son," she said, and laid the hand free of the bag on my shoulder.

Maggie waited.

"I don't care where you go," Uncle Baer said to the windshield of his Packard, "you can go all over the world, but you'll never find a couple so happy, so in love, so devoted as your aunty and me."

"*He* can't have children," Aunt Teena said suddenly one day, savagely.

Much later.

That ocean, the Pacific.

Blue, and vast, a watery sky such as I imagined when I escaped my plaster to orbit the world. Powerful heaves of water breaking the surface, rising slowly, foamed, crested white and green, sweeping with a crash of spray in ragged-edge scrolls to a trough of water bubbling with sand. Line after line, now higher, now smoother, cavalry in even charge across water.

I wanted to drink it down.

Aunt Teena sat up on a bluff in the car, its door open. We walked the hot soft fine sand, dipping down among dunes, three pairs of footsteps leading back to Aunt Teena's glasses glinting behind the windshield.

Uncle Baer stopped, turned, shaded his eyes.

"I'd better turn around now, kids, and sit with aunty. She is making a sacrifice coming out here. She hates the sun."

He backed away.

"Don't you forgety it," he said, "just don't you forgety it. She is a person of sacrifices. I honor her the way I honored my mother and would honor God if I wasn't already a atheist."

We left him and ran hand in hand over the spray-cooled shore. Waves pitched pebbles like stinging insects at our feet. Wading with knees high like hurdlers who catch the wood we dove into the break of a wave.

Salt.

My eyes stung, my mouth hated the taste.

The salt sea was salty.

We came alone to the dunes, Maggie and I, and stretched ourselves by the sea on sand under that sky.

"What is snow?" I asked her.

"Never heard of it."

"Where are you?"

"On the moon."

"What has all this warmth and loveliness to do with life?"

"Tell me."

"Everything!"

The sun bleached Maggie's hair and freckled her nose. Tan brought new rich brown to her eyes. She stood with her toes in the foam, stretched her arms, her feet wide apart.

"Aunt Teena —" I began.

Her head dropped quickly.

"She doesn't approve of me. She has her own secret ideas of the right kind of girl for her 'son.' "

"She just doesn't hand out walks, sweetheart. Hang in."

"The first time she tells Uncle Baer he did something nice he'll turn into the Frog Prince."

"She's from the school of tough and grudging."

"A mother from that school is enough."

Along the sand a bather shouted. Screams. A gathering crowd. In a circle. Something lay on the shore.

It flashed silver and red, twisting, writhing, flashing sun and streams of blood. A sandshark, mouth ripped, gills torn, stiff fins silver smeared red. A fat bald man in satin trunks toed it with his foot. Its tail lashed the air, swept in flicking broomstrokes a swath in sand. The fat man rolled the shark with a quick jab of his heel. Tailfins slashed wet sand, churning pebbles. In water that power would be driving flight. In sand each thrust sent it further up the shore. The fat man's heel gave it another buffet.

A woman cried out:

"You're torturing it! Put it back in the water!"

"Lady," the fat man said seriously, "this here is a shark. A killer. He is wounded. He could kill somebody. Maybe your own kid."

"It's a beautiful fish!"

"It's a beautiful half-dead murderer what maybe ate half the thing that give it the bloody mouth."

"Then stop toying with it! Kill it and be done with it!"

The man looked at her dumbly.

"Go on, do something," the woman said.

He stooped to pick the shark up with his bare hand. The fin flashed out. The man screamed, fell back, holding his wrist. Blood streamed from it.

"You crazy dame, see what you done! You done that to me!"

He kicked at the shark with one heel, then the other. The fish leaped in a lurch. Something fell from it.

"Holy Mary," the man said, and let go his bleeding wrist, "a baby, in there — this here is a mother shark, lady — a baby, with a cord or what, and like cellophane, look, lady, Holy Jesus, just look!"

The woman crouched beside him.

Swiftly he snatched the tiny fish clear of the writhing shark, turned, running, the fish held palm up. He waded in, jumping waves, his red hand high above his head. Water churned against his chest. Gently, like a small boy floating a toy boat in choppy waters, he lay the baby shark into the foam, released it with a pushing motion toward the open sea.

The mother shark was almost dead.

Holding his bloody hand he passed it by without a look.

On the mantel, among the paper roses, the waxed orangeblossoms, the dried daisies and plastic lemonleaves, a large tinted photograph, framed in shined silver, Aunt Teena in an armchair, legs apart, leaned forward, solid as Gertrude Stein, behind her Uncle Baer, his hair wild, curly, rising high to one side like a leaning appletree. Beside him stood a girl with short dark hair, dressed in white, smiling, perky.

"That's my cousin Tamara," I told Maggie.

Aunt Teena looked into my mouth, as if she were counting teeth.

"Tamara is dead," she said.

Uncle Baer nodded his head violently.

"Tamara is not dead," I insisted.

Uncle Baer turned the photograph to the wall.

"Tamara is *daff*-initely dead," he said angrily.

Aunt Teena put herself between me and the photograph.

"She weighs two hundred and fifty pounds, she won't comb her hair, she tries to kill herownself or somebody at least once a week. You want to call a person like that 'Tamara'? Call her Mrs. Lump-of-dough. Call her Mrs. Cement, Mrs. Ghost. Did *you* have to sit beside her bed and look at that fat back for an hour?"

She turned the picture face out, put her arm out stiffly, like a ringmaster announcing the night's star attraction.

"Now," she said, "you want to see Tamara, look. This is who you mean when you say Tamara."

Tamara is a nightmare.

Tamara is the first etching on the palimpsest, which then was Aunt Reva, then was Evvie. Etched stone, on which beautiful image after beautiful image was scratched. One only was male, Bobby Cook, Aunt Reva's son, his face darkened by an intervening screen door, a good face, sensitive, handsome, with doll-blue eyes behind the screen, and a torn tweed cap pulled over to one side like The Kid's.

In time palimpsests surround us.

On this one, *those who died soon after*.

Mac, his light, his eyes, his words rolling in a chamber, and years later, paused outside a newspaper store, Jack Roberts, mopping at his brow, his left hand hanging on to a no-parking standard, "This heat is more than a man should stand. I'm all wrung-out," and next day dying, among Wilkoh's shadows in the darkened shed, and that darker car with posts twisted like the legs of the diningroom table. And the loud dark flap of wings, that old beaked face in pain, for he too died, Uncle Bim, whom I saw in an Old Folk's Home, years later, his face brown with age, his arms spreadeagled on a blue coverlet, his tobacco-browned white moustache smouldering a butt. I called his name, roused him even as he did me, and his hat came off his eyes, as if he were shaking himself out of a dream. He reached two stringveined hands to my shoulders.

"I am tired."

His voice was strained to a whisper.

"But you," he said, and tried to swing his feet off the bed, "remember! Remember!"

Maggie wanted to know more. In Aunt Teena's room another picture hung on a wall of pink roses, Tamara staring.

"It's spooky," Maggie whispered, "like those crazy Gothic movies with women running through gardens chased by wild organ music."

Aunt Teena shined the silver frames Fridays at three, sinking deep in the billowed-out-pillows of her couch. In the pictures Tamara was sixteen or seventeen. The Tamara I remembered, who knelt down when my mother introduced us, a lovely friendly girl with a soft voice, California tan, wearing a white headband.

I fell in love with her. She didn't know Aunt Teena *wasn't* her mother.

When Tamara's name was mentioned Uncle Baer and Aunt Teena fell into a crouch.

"*He* can't have children," Aunt Teena shrieked.

"What's bad is in *your* blood!" Uncle Baer shouted. "Your sister and Tamara, I see the same in you!"

"I wouldn't want a child with a man so ugly!"

"God wouldn't allow a woman with your black heart to be a mother!"

"Then how come you *couldn't —*"

"With you, only with you!"

"Hero, why didn't you go get a child on a stranger?"

"Because you're my princess, that's why!"

"Because you are hollow, and stale air, that's why!"

But then there was Tamara, as I saw her last, old woman with colorless lips and colorless gums, hair pinned in a wad, her body wide and huge and shapeless.

And this time Tamara didn't even turn toward me, stared at the blank wall. Her ears were full of wax.

It may not have been a brave new world. All of it was new to me.

Olivera Street, with cracked walks tipping, broken Spanish walls gaping brick and smeared cement. Blue, gold wooden saints with sunburst haloes swooned in brown shrines under carved balconies trailing trumpeter roses. A rubber tree with waxen leaves hid a sandalmaker, gray face, grayer hands, who tossed pungent leathers into the mix of perfumed candles, sprayed flowers, hot tamales. A huge rusted cauldron, mudcaked, a glassblower wringing wrists and bellowed cheeks, an old wooden cart with almost square wheels. A low roof, baked pottery in halves, like red shinguards row upon row. And the shop ceiling floating piñatas, tiny yellow-magenta-emerald, ruffled-paper bulls, strawcolored donkeys with orange legs and purple heads, goats wedding-white, sheep all black except their pleading eyes.

There were messages here, too.

The land.

Where I was born the earth was flat, and meaning came down from the sky. It spoke out of hail and rain and lightning, the snow and wind which alone tranfigured flatness. Summer was a passive time, when the land murmured.

Through Malibu Canyon rock thrust high for ocean winds to scar, and rain and water score. On my flatland dialogue had to be imagined; here messages were shouted by a root bared and dry where protecting rock wore away. Cracks wide and jagged said here earth tremored or wind found fault. East of the ocean golden grass hid a battlefield, gentle hills dappled, dimpled, camelhump and dinosaurback, feminine rise and feminine fall. Stripping shredded eucalyptus and shedding sycamore, bare of bark, making like ragged beggarwomen a last-ditch show of modesty. Higher up, rock broke through in tiers and shelves, grass tried to cling, and scraggly bushes, and leaning trees. The ocean looked tipped. Mounted on the sky. Whitecaps like clouds, clouds like whitecaps.

I walked toward the sea with Maggie, my feet slapping the soggy margin, rocked into a rut foothold as waves broke and foamed and riptides pulled out to sea. My legs were like snags the waters rushed by, threatening to tear my feet loose of their anchoring holes.

I ran with the riptide to where it crashed like the clap of hands against a breaking wave. Dived through, into another wave, and bubbling surf. Eyes shut, arms behind my back, I made my will the water's, which threw me forward and pulled me back, closer to shore, then out to sea.

I swam, struggled with the waves behind, the tugging tides all around. Left to its own, the ocean would not deliver me back to the shore.

That was a scary message. But it saved hours and hours of pastoral sentimentality.

Sun sank quickly. As if on the count of three. A bright red band unbonded ocean and sky. Sandpipers ran their silly broken-field paths like old ladies shying clear of pools and puddles. Gulls with a hungry cry mounted the dusk. The pigeons wheeled for the red cliffs across the highway.

Night came. We lay on our blanket under the near stars, slept the night arms around, and kissing, till gray light seeped over the pigeons' cliffs, and the sun changed the gliding gulls to metal.

We stood up with the sun, turned our backs on the ocean, took ourselves back to the city.

Uncle Baer had a nephew, Dan, short and tough, with huge RAF moustache, Winston Churchill siren suits of Italian corduroy easier to come by now (for did I tell you?) the war was over. He was a studio writer, with a Frank Lloyd Wright house, a swimming pool, three unfinished novels, a starlet wife, two Dalmatians, a Ferrari, a Lincoln Continental, and executive membership in the American Veterans Committee.

His house was on an eroding cliff, where Australian spruces joined with Japanese bamboo in defensive conservation stand. Huge acacias flowered powdery yellow, like forsythia blooms run wild. Along his quiet driveway torches flamed trailing tails of wispy black smoke. Around the pool a magenta canopy hung with Japanese lanterns. Aalto chairs and Mies lounges; metal sculptures of roosters rusting, their tailfeathers silver. A woman nude with breasts of battered fenders, arms curved tailpipes, head an inverted country telephone, with two dials for eyes.

It was Gatsby gorgeous.

A lovely girl stood on the diving board this party night, stretched her long brown arms over her head, lifted herself into the air and dropped with no splash, her brown legs glowing in underwater pool lamps.

A man slid into a chair beside Maggie. He needed a shave, his shirtcollar was a hoop of sweat.

"Kazzy, we missed you," a voice called out of the dark, man or woman.

"O.K., here I go," the man growled to Maggie.

He moved his shoulders back and forth like a weathervane, turned his shoes pigeon-toe, his right hand wigwagging. A giggle came from his throat, a lisp answered by laughter in the shadows.

"Will you do Hedda tonight, Kazzy — for us?"

Kazzy snatched someone's hat, jammed it white and broad-brimmed on his head, gyrating, his hands hooked in front of him.

Laughter tumbled out of the darkness. Kazzy parted his hands, held them out daintily, stumbling pigeon-toed the length of the pool. A man with flat freckles applauded; a Princeton boy threw his head back and laughed.

"Kazzy," another voice said out of the shadows, "sing like Marlene."

"Yes, yes," said the old man with freckles, "Kazzy must do 'See What the Boys in the Backroom Will Have.' "

The laughter was loud.

Kazzy stopped suddenly.

"I'm tired," he said in a flat voice.

"Take a drink — but you *must* do Marlene."

Kazzy fell into his director's chair. His hand dropped onto Maggie's bare knee.

"Nothing personal, Mac," he said to me, "I'm just touching bases."

A Hawaiian girl stopped at the table with a tray of drinks. Kazzy took one for each hand.

"What do I do to show I'm no fag?"

"Don't worry if I stare at you," Maggie said. "I'm blind not wearing glasses."

"You trying to bust into film?"

I shook my head.

"It'll get to you, stay long enough. Fifteen hundred fish a week. Cough at that!"

The voice called out of the shadows.

"Don't get tired resting, Kazzy."

"Thmartie!" Kazzy sang out.

The shadows filled with laughter.

"Worst thing is two queens in competition," Kazzy growled. "The old queen has a house full of incunabula and young boys. The one over there is like the Garbo."

"You do Garbo after Dietrich?"

"Naturally. You don't get it? Art is feminine, a guy who's sensitive is feminine; so he's feminine, so he's an artist, so he has a place. Fifteen hundred simoleons — I already made my point."

Dan wrapped a long heavy terrytowel robe round the girl, put his hands into the front opening, helped her out of her wet bathingsuit.

"Boy, would I love that!" Kazzy said. "One look — never mind the follow-up — and I'm a dead duck."

The girl's suit dropped with a splat on cement. Kazzy gasped as if he were choking.

"You kids wanna know why I was late? Not only the sick kid. The other game I play. 'Integrity.' He's a great guy, Dan. We belong to the same AVC chapter. You don't know 'Integrity'? I make people think I'm a Stalinist, that's integrity. For them I do toughguy long-hard-look scripts. My wife calls out when I'm leaving, 'Don't forget where to be red and where to be kewpie doll!' "

Maggie and I broke up.

"Now I *need* the goddam fifteen hundred — five-day-a-week analysis. Basic insecurity, what happens to immigrant kids. Status — you know the schmeer. Two more years and I'm off the couch. If my analyst is wrong I'll have logged so much time as Dietrich and Garbo I'll do my act at a fag club."

The war: I did tell you, didn't I, that it was over? My brother came to California, and found a wife. And Bitner came. And Gersh. And Christopher, who was in his way in love with a Nevada Indian girl, Sammie, beautiful, pregnant with another man's child. She didn't say whose, and Christopher didn't ask.

Just narrowed those white lashes, his head to one side. Contemplating her belly. His mouth in an o.

She had black eyes, and black hair she wore in two thick braids circled with turquoise beads in rows. She had black freckles on her tiny nose, half a dozen on each round full cheek. The belly Christopher contemplated was terribly full for such thin legs and slim arms.

"The West," she said, "keeps men baked, and prevents looking like uncooked pork."

"By Jesus, Indian bitch," Christopher laughed, "I'm the palest paleface that ever was."

In fall, a hot hot summer, I gave up on beachcombing, and entered the university. A Lombard building, azuremauve brick which at dusk disappeared into the azuremauve sky. Traffic flowing over Sunset Boulevard joined planes fading in and out of the continuous automobile roar.

In those Lombard buildings I heard gossip, measurement, tillyvally, knew of sand and gravel under Shakespeare's shoes, and nothing of his feet. There, in a cubicle, behind a beautiful girl — alas! — I tried with Astrophel to win Stella, and sang soft songs to Laura. In a gray mausoleum on green irrigated sand I held in my hands the books of messengers. Keats said *get your eye as close to the flower as the dew allows*. Hopkins showed me messages in tree and sky. I mourned for Maude Gonne and regretted never knowing Nell. Heard the clamor of old bishops, and new lamenting preachers. And knew Antigone was a lovely young Greek girl, in great trouble. And would have told Desdemona not to listen.

And coming back at night saw Uncle Baer stooped over a lemon tree, fingering its leaves.

"She's gonny bloom some day, this tree of ours," he said. "She's gonny grow a hundred yeloo lemyons. It already-a smells like paradise here but when this sugar tree blooms we will carry sun into the house in handyfuls."

My brother Gad's mother-in-law was a beautiful woman, Hettie Karousel, who had seven children, and a tiny husband, Levitt, who contemplated the part in his hair before mirrors, and loved his aquiline nose. Levitt could have been a jockey, his shoulders narrow, hands large and strong, no hips, just bandy bowlegs.

Hettie Karousel was very large, and very sick, arms pocked and blotched from insulin injections. Years earlier she ran away from home, riding the Trans-Siberian rods, lone female stowaway on a Japanese freighter. What happened during her seven weeks on the boat nobody ever asked.

Her face was very wide, with open pores on her great nose. Her eyes the lightest blue, her cheeks veined like Uncle Bim's. Her mouth was small and easy, her voice terribly shrill, rising like a rooster crow.

She eyed Aunt Teena, swung a bag from her wrist, let it bang up against her like the brush of a kilted chieftain.

"You are older than I thought," Hettie said to Aunt Teena.

"And you," said Aunt Teena, "are larger."

"Levitt, we must go," said Hettie Karousel, and crippled her way down Uncle Baer's steps, that bag swinging.

Levitt sat in the driver's seat, Hettie in back, fanning herself with a drive-in menu, her view of both sides of the street unimpeded. Hettie bought apartment blocks the way some bought coins.

"Drive, Levitt!"

"Hyokay!"

Hettie fanned herself slowly, then faster.

"Levitt, stop!"

Levitt applied the brakes.

"Wait," Hettie ordered, and rolled her painful legs out of the car unassisted.

Levitt turned on a rock 'n' roll station, and dozed.

Diabetes did in Hettie's eyes. She shuffled with difficulty close to a brick wall.

"Seems they once had a fire," she said to herself, and sniffed the doorway.

The superintendent said the owner would not sell.

"He will sell," said Hettie, and withdrew.

"Levitt," she said, settled against the back cushions, "go!"

The owner was adamant.

"Never," he said.

"What premiooms are you paying on your firetrap, mister?"

"It is a safe building."

"Somebody set fires here for fun?"

"The fire department put them out, without no damage."

"Ain't you heard, mister, sparks sat in walls for years, till firemen snored and the building went up like toilet paper?"

"I have heard, what in my case don't apply."

"Sleep on it," Hettie said.

Levitt saw her approach, and punched the Mantovani pushbutton.

"Where to now, dolling?"

"Sit, Levitt. Run the motor. Only the strongest can think fire and not fall on their knees. He is not from the strongest."

One Strauss waltz and two Welk records later the owner sold. From that bag Hettie took out cash.

"Steady human nature and you are half a success," Hettie told herself, and Levitt if he was listening, then snapped her bag shut with a ten-gun salute.

Hettie had two brothers, one older, one younger, and the older, Shimmy, lived in an oil millionaire's mansion, high in Bel Aire, sat, tiny Shimmy, in the middle of a twelve-foot Italian brocade couch, his English flannels rolled to his thighs, his legs covered by fleece-lined underwear.

"My knee-ehs, it is oompossible the poison painss I got in my knee-ehs," Shimmy said to his broker who had a hot line to Wall Street.

Shimmy had nine children, seven boys and two girls in a froth over money. What Hettie made, her kids turned to dust; what Shimmy made, his kids increased and multiplied.

Like a Renaissance prince Shimmy built memorials over the city. For his kids three-floor walk-ups called "The Jenny," "The Ephraim," "The Isadore"; his grandchildren had five-story blocks, "The Sheldon," "The Lee," "The Linda." Two greatgrandchildren had high-rise apartments on Wilshire, "The Penelope," "The Aubrey."

"IBM is up four, sir," Shimmy's broker said.

"Keep buying — I think so there's a bad vein in this worst knee-eh, Malone."

Isadore ran into the room, with three of Shimmy's younger sons.

"It's up six, sir," Malone whispered.

Isadore rolled down his father's pantlegs, straightened his tie, caught him up on his huge arms like a rag doll, sat him carefully in his wheelchair.

"We've got a board meeting, Malone."

The four sons fell into a trot behind Shimmy's wheelchair, infantrymen following a three-star general's tank.

Then there was Hettie's younger brother.

Percy.

Who had a bad heart but a good insurance policy.

A huge man, Percy, with a broad round red face, and bubbling voice, and tearing eyes, and a way of charging into the middle of things.

"You seen this L.A., it's not a city, it's a package, a gift box, and Freeways and Expressways all one ribbon tie in a bow the Figueroa Cloverleaf."

At six A.M., when smog still could sneak through to throw a few fast beams his way, Percy got up. His wife Alison, American-born, slept under what she'd packed away in a midnight snack. Six A.M. was Percy and L.A.'s finest hour. Percy contemplated the big mystery, brotherhood, oneness. In this town a guy brushed his teeth and shaved to one single idea — how to make a million bucks, fast.

Tiptoeing by Alison, Percy aimed a kiss at Alison's forehead. Missed. Percy hadn't tried too hard to hit.

Two driveways were already empty. What a system! Guys off and running for the buck. In America this guy screwed that guy, that guy screwed the next, the next screwed his brother! And it added up to the highest standard of living in the world!

Like an airplane pilot Percy slipped his dark goggles in place, jumped into the bucket seat of his custom Imperial convertible. Gunned the motor, took off, screeching into the fast lane, off the Cloverleaf, on to the Freeways.

Democracy! A Mex in a lousy jalop rammed a Caddie in the back. A movieguy in a white sports car rode a Japanese gardener off who wanted on. Money, being crazy for money, made everybody equal.

Percy by himself was an industry. His moulded shoes cost seventy-five bucks, his Cassini shirt thirty, his Daks another thirty, his lisles three-and-a-half a pair, boxer shorts four, gym shirt three, his watch five bills (a little hot). How many guys lived off Percy? All the ones who wanted and shouldn't. While the one who should didn't.

Stacey.

Percy's only born. Handsome guy, junior Phi Bete, hundreds tanned tall long-blonde-haired California girls crazy for him. What couldn't Stacey be! Everything but what he was!

Percy could feel a pain in his throat, a pang like a small sunburst. A memory. It started in the throat, under the tongue, and broke inside the chest, like a skyrocket.

He put his Corona-Corona fingers over his chest. You could never tell. Doc Schiff said *never alone in the car*. And on a Freeway yet, doing eighty-five.

How could Shimmy have so many sons all crazy for money? Hettie's lousy kids had proper American respect for millionaires. Without respect the system was a goner. What if Coca-Cola's kid said

"Pa, I don't want the Coke formula"? Or Ford's kid had a block about money?

Percy wagged his huge finger at the empty seat.

"Stacey, you loving keed, aren't you glad you took time to go to Bakersfield with your ignorant old man? I'll teach you. One afternoon a week. Buying, selling; the biggest game there is, keed."

Stacey — pretend-Stacey — reached over to ruffle the few hairs on his old man's big balding head. Percy gave him a playful punch on the arm.

"You may be a lousy intellectual, keed, but I love you!"

Percy felt terrific. Sun warmed one side of his face. He accelerated, zoomed by six or seven cars, glided back into the cruising lane. The other guys were in a big hurry to make their million. Percy already made his million.

"For you, you lousy intellectual," he told the cool leather beside him. "Not just because Doc Schiff gave orders I don't go alone. Education. How come when you feel ignorant about Hindus and Chinamen you learn a little something, but when you're ignorant about money you ain't bothered? Ignorance makes trouble in the world — war even. And the worst ignorance, keed, is a person who don't know money."

A gunmetal Rolls Royce pulled even with Percy's Imperial. The chauffeur wore dark gray buttoned tight at the neck.

"Go 'head," Percy hollered, and waved the Rolls by.

The chauffeur saluted. A skinny old guy in the back seat turned his face away, held up a screen of *Wall Street Journal*.

That, Percy could see right off, was a *big* millionaire — a Huntington, a Mellon, a Rockefeller maybe.

"You tell me I don't read, Stacey. When you give me that *Great American Fortunes* didn't I try — what beautiful stories, and sad. Those guys made senators run errands, congressmen shine their shoes. But if their kids didn't want to get out of bed in the morning, they were finished. Guys crazy for the buck And their kids play tennis in Egypt, go sail on the Isle of Capri."

That's maybe what made the old guy in the Rolls pinched and blue.

No kids. Or the wrong kind. What was the point of making then? Money, by itself, was dead gravel.

The car swayed in the cruising lane, the needle touched 80. Percy pulled his moulded off the gas. Baer and Teena, no kids. Tamara in that place.

Stacey was the best loving kid in the world. Never embarrassed by his crazy old man.

"Gun it, fats. Come on, drag, huh? You in the ten-G heap and this little ol' 'M'."

A jalop was beside him, the roof cut off. Percy smiled at the driver, waved his hand to charge him through.

"Come on, don't slow it, lardass. G'wan, get in front. Let's see your tub go."

The kid bore in close to Percy's lane, clutch part way in, gunning. Greenish skin, hair in ringlets, mouth open, cigarette hanging down. Mercury without fenders, two aerials, announcers screeching, echo chamber, a loud guitar.

"Pass, sonny," Percy said wearily.

"You got better'n four hundred horses going for you, man. You can beat this little ol' wreck. Gun out, fats. Go on, go on, I dare ya."

Percy slowed down, 65, 55, 40. The Mercury braked, swerving.

"Shit on you, fat ass!"

The kid gunned the car, drew away, braked again, cut in, still braking. Percy jammed his foot on the pedal, his chest slammed the steering wheel. The kid screeched tires, disappeared in a mufflerless roar and cloud of burning oil.

Percy fought the wheel, tried to catch his breath. He should chase the little bastard and give him a good lickin'. If Stacey were in the car that kid wouldn't try anything. Savages! Killers! Roaring around on motorcycles, hundreds of them, goggles, back level with the ground, zooming. Zipguns, switchblades, garrison belts, jagged glass and beercans, chains, whips, those sideburns, Nazi caps and Nazi boots and Nazi wings on black jackets.

His heart stopped pounding. He felt thirsty. Up ahead was that lousy desert.

Everything in Southern Cal Percy loved.

Except desert.

In the Biltmore Health Club, when men in the steam room complained, Percy pretended his kid was a motorcycle.

"He runs with Okies and Arkies. He was a drop-out at twelve, my son the delinquent."

The old men, huddled like Roman senators under their heaped-up sheets, marveled.

"He banged up six cars."

The men like a Greek chorus groaned, shifted their seats, hung their limp wrists in pails of cold water.

"He knocked up a Mex waitress I sent to Japan for that operation."

The men flapped their sheets and keened like banshees.

"Any time I don't see the kid for two hours I gotta figure he's in Vegas playing chemin de fer."

"Hard lines, hard lines, Percy," the old men croaked, "you gotta be the unluckiest guy in the world."

Should Percy tell these old geezers the truth which made his face flame! That his handsome Phi Bete of a kid was a lousy *school-teacher*, of fourth grade!

"Nine-year-olds you'll teach! Stacey, lay down with peegs and you'll turn into a peeg yourownself!"

The words got fainter and fainter, as if he was falling over a cliff.

The Mohave. Percy wished he had a special pair of goggles to show only road and never that wasted sand. Nothing growing. No action. Everything that lousy smog color. Smog sky, smog rocks, smog sand. One color — red — animal guts. Losers. Couldn't make it across the road.

A flock of black desert birds picked at entrails with their sharp beaks.

"G'wan away from that, animals you!"

Percy aimed the Imperial at them.

They lifted up slowly, lazily, right over his ducking head, wings flapping with a scary whipcrack.

In his rear view mirror he saw them settle back like a dark sailed-out blanket.

Because it was natural didn't mean Percy liked it.

When Bugsy was still alive, before that lousy guy got him with a rifle, Percy asked his advice. Bugsy knew the ropes. At Santa Anita, dressed like the Duke of Windsor, Bugsy with a stop watch and three bodyguards. Class. All the big gangsters tried to dress like Bugsy.

"So Bugsy, what do I do now? 'Go back, keed,' I told him, 'lose your deposit, whatever. But tell the Principal it's a mistake.' Bugsy, he don't have ambition? Aright, if he's gonna teach, teach. But tell them the eighth grade. O.K., settle for seven. But fourth! It's a scandal, Bugsy."

"I got a nephew with colorblindness, Perk. What are you gonna do? A kid gets dealt crooked from the genetic deck."

"So what's education for, Bugsy? I could have been like my pa, sleeping on flour sacks and reading and praying while ma was a store, a postoffice, a marriage broker."

"You got a problem, Perk. But no human being can live in L.A. and not get the money bug. Give him time."

A kid American-born, with every gift, and gorgeous tanned girls all around, married a refugee who don't speak English half as good as Percy! And her old man has to have a art gallery and sell books and encourage Stacey's sickness.

What would it have hurt to have a California wedding, like Baer's nephew, Dan? By a swimming pool and beautiful brides-maids in yellow and red, and a tanned bride, and a red-and-yellow canopy like a circus tent, and the bride and groom get tossed in a swimming pool, and everybody jumps in, top hats and tails, and then soaking wet around the pool dancing in one circle, grand-mothers, parents, and bride and groom, kids, everybody high and eating salami.

Percy gunned the car clear of the Tehachapis.

Better.

The desert made the bitter thoughts.

Bakersfield broke on Percy like Jerusalem. Buildings of white rock. He swung the car into the right turn lane.

"You cuttin' in, fatguts?"

It was the same kid! No.

"Sorry, sonny," Percy said with a friendly wave.

"You own the road, creep-o? You payin' taxes curb-to-curb?"

Percy felt gloomy.

"Ah, come on, keed," he said with a swing of his hand, "it's too beautiful a day."

The kid brought his left arm up, hit the muscle with his right. His face was twisted.

"Shame on you," Percy roared, "I'm old enough to be your father!"

The arm came up deliberately, in slow motion.

The light turned green. Cars and trucks honked behind.

Percy gasped. That shirt! It was a girl!

"You — a girl! Double shame —"

"Fatass, my eyes are dripping!"

"Get 'er the hell out of there," a cop hollered from the sidewalk.

With rockets exploding the car took off.

Percy slumped back in his seat, sure the prickles in the chest would turn into a sunburst.

He needed a Bromo, bad.

A sun in his chest, yellow flames in the center.

Terrible. It could wreck Stacey's life. Lawyer Flomm would rub it in. Doc Schiff would holler.

Percy wanted to talk deal with God. Let him make it back to L.A., to the bed, then O.K., *pack me off.*

He raised one sweating eyebrow.

"If this is only a false alarm, remember, God, it's no deal."

He pulled into a parking spot, and dozed. Foul mouth sour. Cassini soaking. The pain. Gone. Maybe.

A good thing God was honorable.

Percy pulled into traffic.

In front of the restaurant he ran out, doubled up, his flabby chest bouncing.

"Foonya," he shouted, "a Bromo!"

He peppered Foonya's gray head with kisses, grabbed him up in his arms.

"Whatsamatter, Perk, you nuts? You ain't supposed to lift things!"

A guy stopped sipping his coffee.

"We're pals from a thousand years," Percy said.

"You must be foreigners," said the man. "I mean Americans ain't usually that glad to see anybody."

He smiled, put down some change, left.

Foonya ran up with the stuff bubbling.

"An attack, kid, is that what this is? I'll call Bessie."

"Not Bessie," Percy coughed through his full mouth.

"A stress reaction," Foonya said. "I seen all about that on TV."

"No *Reader's Digest* medicine, Foonya. Not till *after* the burp."

The belch seemed to mash the sunburst.

"Foonya, back to the city, immediately."

Not till the corner of Stacey's school did he know where he was or what he was doing. He muttered something to Foonya, jumped out of the car, running.

Two kids dodged past him, playing tag. Percy slowed. A big man running. Scare the kids. No tie. No jacket. A teacher's pa.

Near the main entrance he stopped. Stacey on the stone steps. His wedding suit. A man in a straw hat. Maybe his boss. Stacey looked his way. Percy broke into a run.

"Stacey, keed," he mumbled, and kissed Stacey smack on the cheek.

A little kid looked up and gasped.

"Shut up, you peeg," Percy said to himself, "you don't know what trouble you lousy nine-year-olds made for me already!"

"Dad," Stacey took Percy's arm, "I want you to meet my principal, Mr. Granger."

"How you like this keed, Principal?" Percy growled.

He threw his arms around Stacey with a bear hug.

"I think Stacey is wonderful," Mr. Granger said. "I've wanted to meet the father of this boy. In these days, to let a brilliant guy go into teaching."

"Principal, tell me something, you got keeds?"

"Yes."

"Then *you* know. I don't have to tell you."

Percy grabbed the Principal's small white hand in a crush.

"Excuse me I didn't wear a suit and a fedora," Percy said.

The Principal smiled and took back his hand. He walked into the building.

"Boy, you got a nice boss. I'm so glad, you lousy intellectual."

Stacey grinned, put his arm around Percy's shoulder.

"Who've you been trimming so early in the day? That's Foonya in the car. You've been to Bakersfield already, eh, Chichikov?"

"I would like you to go next time. How's Saturday?"

"Joanna has to —"

"O.K., keed. Next Saturday, then."

"We'll see, Pa."

Percy wanted more. Fall on his knees. Tell Stacey. I'm dumb, I know only money. I gotta stay in the moola game. Keep me living.

He rubbed his eyes. A stone lion on the steps made a big pool of shadow in the noon sun.

"O.K., Stace. I know you gotta go back in. I just wanted to see your handsome kisser."

"I love seeing yours, Pa. Do this more."

"Those insurance snoopers will be after me I don't get back and start groaning."

"Did you want anything in particular, Pa?"

"Nah."

Percy shaded his eyes. Foonya was sitting straight up in the convert, still in his white restaurant outfit, like an orderly.

Gad led him into the room.

"Maybe you could talk to Stacey.. School. Books. You got the same stuff going."

Gad whispered something. His Uncle Percy gave him a hug.

"What would you want me to tell him?" I asked.

"Telly him how his father has a bad heart and needs help," Uncle Baer said. "Telly him it's a matter of life and death."

"Nah," Uncle Percy growled, "it has to be some other way."

"Tell him he has a responsibility to his father," said Aunt Teena.

"That's out," Uncle Percy said. "That's the most responsible kid in the world. Listen, I got an idea. Let's not tell him anything."

"Right," Gad said, "Stacey will come to it himself."

"Ask him only if he would like to come see Man O' War at the stud farm. 'Big Red.' That ask him. For Sunday. Or the week after."

Dobrushyn in my cold north city lay dying.

Propped up on velvet pillows, under the wine velvet canopy of the fourposter he himself designed. A scarlet embroidered coverlet fell in soft drape to the floor. Dobrushyn's small yellow face wrinkled above black silk Russian-collared pyjamas.

I.D. his lawyer sat at his side, his hearing aid turned Dobrushyn's way, his eyes failing. He had had a stroke. His speech was muffled.

Leeba sat on the other side of Dobrushyn's bed, and at the foot, his sons. And Ziff, his mouth open, his face a blank.

"I.D., they will turn my money to piss, which you will prevent," Dobrushyn said weakly, and I.D. scrawled in shaky handwriting a new note, two words to the line.

"I want at least six executors. Bankers. The worst. The toughest. Let them crawl to each and explain."

"What do I do if I got a deal in a mine up north and need three grand today?" Morrie, the youngest, said.

"Today I am alive. Today you get zero. I am making a will, not being your banker. You will find some other way to pay a whore than with my estate. Him, I.D., make a extra clause. Once more clap and he's out. I don't mind the whores. It's a kid who don't learn from experience."

He struggled to raise his head.

"If I get weak, and they try to pack me off to the Old Folks' Home, cut them all out. I stay here. Let them carry from me. Let me be in their nostrils what they are in mine."

I.D. shakily turned a page in his notebook.

"In case you have dreams," Dobrushyn said weakly, "that I'll die and you'll roll in gold and piss away in two months all I made, hear what won't be."

Next door to Uncle Baer, in a mansion guarded by three boxers, the Pinkerton Agency, and the L.A. police, lived a blonde lady who drove a brand-new white convertible Cadillac with a top which had never been down. She spent three hours every other day with a hairstylist called Cam, who took out the color of her hair, and gave back something wispy yellow and perishable. She was a large lady, with high bosoms she pushed out higher. She wore only real jewelry, and had it in profusion. Drawers of diamonds and boxes of emeralds and bags of rubies. Which alone did not account for the dogs and the police and the security men.

Her name was Lila, and she had a special room in the basement to hang her furs. Her furs were of all lengths and all colors and all countries of origin. Some went with ruby rings, and some with diamond-flaked watches, and some hung on her great bare shoulders and bosom in that chill air-conditioned Cadillac when the temperature outside neared one hundred.

And Lila looked out from her second-floor patio, her head free of a drier, and spied Maggie by the lemon tree, alone, her long red hair wet in the sun and drying. Called her up, Lila did, to dry her hair in Lila's machine, and drink coffee, and explain why she looked sad.

Lila's face was full and round, her eyelashes beaded with mascara, her eyelids silvery blue; she had a straight nose, and full lips, the lower pouted, always holding a custom cigarette rolled with black paper. She had only one dimple, which she used well. And fine even teeth. And legs she disapproved of. So she wore her skirts long.

Everything she admired she coveted.

And made her husband Nate buy her.

Then coveted no more.

Nate it was whose life was in danger, which endangered Lila, and their three children. Nate was in the mob, but not of it, and though the difference was but a thread, such was the thread Nate's life hung on. He made flashy deals, knowing each might be his last. Pretended he had never known Bugsy, who was shot from behind equally fashionable shrubbery. And mourned for "Hooky" Rothman, and "Bennie the Meatball," who lost their nerve first, and shortly after, their lives. Nate too drove an air-conditioned Cadillac, with license plates he changed every other week, with windows that stayed up, thick, built by the glazier who looked after kings and emperors.

Nate once was very poor.

And so was Lila.

The mansion told of Nate's joyous transition. A Bengal tiger in a rumpus room, dead to the world, its glass eyes on a line with a polar bear who'd fared no better. On its white back a marble coffee table the mob gave Nate and Lila for their anniversary, which, luckily, proved not their last.

One room had a pooltable, another a sauna, still another a thirty-foot bar and stools haggled away from unideological Arabs. Chairs everywhere were low, because Nate was quite short, but padded with quantities of foam rubber, because Nate was quite round.

The upstairs was carpeting and chandeliers and sofas silk and tasseled and sheathed in sensible plastic, for Lila was a Chicago girl. Every room had a stone fireplace, wired electric. One bathroom was candy-striped, another polka-dot tile (for the children). Lila's own patio was on that second floor, and from there she saw Maggie drying her hair, and called to her, in a voice tough and tight as Ida Lupino's.

Maggie had already seen three or four hundred Lila's in L.A.

She looked up from under the lemon tree at the woman holding *Redbook* on her blue silk nightgowned lap.

"You look miserable," Lila called without taking the cigarette out of her mouth, "come on up and I'll put my arms around you."

"Can I be frank," Lila said through smoke curling into one half-closed eye, "when I looked at you I knew your mother."

A maid brought coffee and cakes, and left.

"You're a beautiful girl, and young, so what's tying you in knots? Your Aunt Teena is a killer type. That's all you have to know."

Maggie laughed.

"Are you a good lay?"

"What?"

"I know. *You* can't talk about such things. You don't know me, so be free, for godssake!"

Lila laughed under the drier, and Maggie laughed with her.

"Before I got married my ma said, 'Lila, throw everything into it. Everything, you hear me?' I heard her."

Nate reclined on his vibrating lounger, and dozed. Two boxers crouched on either side of his slippered feet. Every time Maggie or I moved, the dogs growled business growls.

"Nate's worn out. I did that," Lila said. "A four-hour go last night. He cut back and cut back. Now it's only once a week. But we make L.A. shake."

She was in an Italian silk slack-suit, royal blue and sunflowers, with a matching hairband, and earrings spun sunflowers, and a sunburst watch.

"I'm the best lay there is," she said seriously. "I try to think how anybody could possibly be better. Look, the guy's out. From pure pleasure."

Nate's belly heaved in polite snoring, draped in cream gabardine.

"Years ago he was the kid whose ass you kicked everytime he stepped outside. 'Nate the Freight.' Kids knock the shit out of anyone they know won't make a good lover."

The boxers held their ears up.

"At thirty he hadn't made it with anyone. Can you imagine? He was an orphan, otherwise a shrink could pin it on his ma. My girl friend fobbed him off on me, quick switch on a double date."

Lila walked to her Florentine mirror, stood in profile, tried to pull her full tummy in, and arch up her great breasts. I thought of Alvira.

"This stuff," she said, and gave her belly a pat, "what's the point if something great ain't made with it? Kids. A life. What would Nate have been without my ass? I said to him, on the third or fourth date:

" 'When are you going to try something?'

"He gave me some jazzy answer.

" 'Get your clothes off,' I said. 'Right now.'

"He was too shy, he wouldn't.

" 'Take them off or I'll pull every stitch off your back. What is it, I'm not attractive enough? Four times together and you still aren't interested in the color of my money!' "

Lila tiptoed to where Nate's head rested on a tiny foamrubber pillow. The dogs nestled their heads on their forepaws.

"It wouldn't stand for him. Naturally. A big-titted aggressive girl like me would frighten anybody.

" 'Nate,' I told him, 'I don't go for this impotent stuff. Every guy can get it up somehow. And you are going to get it up now. Your troubles are over, Nathan. I will make you a great fucker.'

" 'How come you're so sure?' he said. 'Are you that experienced?'

" 'Let's get it up first, Natie. Here, see, everything is yours. I will lay like this one thousand and one nights if I have to, and your cock will start up like the Tower of Pisa and never look back."

Maggie's face was bright red.

"I did not need the one thousand nights," Lila said, and stooped to kiss Nathan's brow.

He stirred, but did not wake. The boxers closed their eyes. Maggie opened hers.

"That's how come he can deal with the mob. He thinks of himself as the best lover that ever was, and if they make him doubt the rest, he's got me waiting, and ready. Together we could take on czars and army chiefs."

Uncle Baer wanted a trip to the northwest country. Late in October he and Maggie and I flew into Seattle over Mount Rainier. Winding black clouds scarved its base, black streaks on its snow top; a buff-black band of slash fire smoke curled up from its black evergreen depths.

Uncle Baer looked out.

"See through this windor, waste. The lumber intyrests don't love the land."

When he was asleep Maggie and I stood on Crystal Mountain, our frosty breath puffed up to stars almost touching our heads. Pines smelled cold. Freshly cut-down, raw.

I kissed Maggie's chilled lips.

"You're excited?"

"Sure!" I said.

"By the night?"

"By everything!"

"By me?"

"By you!"

We woke in mountain mist rising, storm clouds swooping a belt from peak to peak.

"I would sit and looky at nature for the rest of my life," Uncle Baer said, "but your auntie is alone and we have taken enough advantage of her good nature."

I drove down the mountain with those black clouds pursuing, a rut of a road falling to a wilderness of evergreens. Our own swirling dust we met again in hairpin turns down, down, into the darkest forest of seventy-foot trees.

Great trees, felled, snapped like riflefire in the clear air. A crack, a topple, a scrape of needles on needles, fir after fir, rumbling the earth. Waters choked with stripped trees made a maze like match-

sticks. Trunks hung rotting on rocks. Waterlogged, barkstripped
boughs wedged among stones, vibrating like a pilgrim's staff. The
road plunged and streams climbed. The road rose and waters fell
away.

Ahead, on a bridge, a crowd gathered.

"An accydent," Uncle Baer said sadly.

But there was no car.

"Men must be fishing," Uncle Baer corrected.

They held no poles.

"Let's looky at what they are lookying at," said Uncle Baer. "We
won't miss our plane."

Fish, hundreds upon hundreds, fin to fin and mouth to tail,
sockeye salmon the color of raspberry, with heads a greengold, and
yellowed fins, scaly with chainmail old, and greenish. Bodies ripped
and scarred, like a thousand bent-back sowers seen from above,
unsuspecting. The Cedar River flowed cold and clear, with riffles
almost invisible, smooth, seen only where the whitish oldest
salmon heads broke in two planes moving in, and aside, swishing
tails and disturbing silt, dodged into by female fish who laid their
eggs for males who covered eggs with milt. And then it was over.

Downstream redder fish jumped clear, splashed back, but tattered tails swung them aside, torn old heads pushed further against
the current. A dying fish tumbled, tail over head, like a sheet of
paper under water, brushing rocks, sticks, sunken logs, stuck dead
fish.

The dirt riverbottom was mosaic with round, small, rust, moss-
green stones, into which, as if worked by a silversmith, three dead
fish shone dull as pewter, two-dimensional abstractions of the fish
powering forward, dying, tumbling backwards, dead. Red turned
gold and gold turned green and green faded. Salmon-death-silver.

And still the young leaped in tag, while the old burrowed their
heads and swung their tails and ignored the dead. Water whirled
light over their raspberry backs and the patterned stones.

The river boiled with fish. Blue and orange and the sparkle of water. A fish struck a stick, folded in half, both tail and head pointing downstream. One with markings like a calf, hung on a snag, then, dead, itself a snag, was swept away by the current, ignored by hundreds and hundreds of struggling salmon, their tails weakly waving.

In that cubicle in the library, as I raised my eyes from a Coleridge page, was a girl's white shoulders. Her head made a lovely turn from book to notebook.

On the days she wasn't there my reading grew flat. Silence was warm and intimate only when she bunched her back and laughed. Metal-green shelves made a fine backdrop for her white skin.

She had sturdy legs and solid hips, stood with her sandaled feet wide apart, head tucked low, at the stacks, reading. Once she wore her hair up, wound and twisted to a crown, her neck long and soft. Caught me staring, and smiled, not at me, but outward, taking in everybody.

And began to wear flowers in her hair.

Gardenias, with large damp flapping petals, brown on the edges as the day wore on, charred, like smoke-blown nicotine stains on linen.

I knew I would try to leap that fence again, the one I did not get over.

"You keep staring at me. Is anything wrong?"

She spoke with a faint Russian accent, furrowed brow, scolding.

"You are beautiful. You are wrecking my work."

"Perhaps we should study on separate floors?"

She stood above my table, looked down at my reading.

"Why don't you read Russian? In the old tongue, I mean."

"Will you teach me?"

"Of course not, silly. I can see what kind of pupil you would make."

"Apt, and, I think, adoring."

"Educationally your attitudes are unfeasible."

"I never learned half so well as when I was secretly in love with my teacher."

She blushed. The flush sent firefreckles to her cheeks.

"Probably you would want to learn sovietized Russian. They stole from the language its nicest letters."

"For you I would be a staunch Czarist."

"You are making fun of me. So I will return to work."

Coleridge seemed irrelevantly abstract. Get the damsel with the dulcimer in your arms, bug-eyes! Lay down laudanum, bow to your lady! No wonder Long Willie made time with Sara. And Annette Vallon, too! The diff between imagination and fancy, Sammy, is imagination insists on making dreams real!

I stood over her at work, as she had over me.

"Is your name Natasha?"

"No."

"A pity. Is it Grushenka?"

"I can see how predictable your familiarity with our literature is."

"Masha? Pasha? Basha? Sasha?"

"No no no no."

"Liseveta? Svetlana? Ekaterina?"

"Still no."

"Fanya? Marusha? Katya? Lubka?"

"Never."

"What then?"

"Nina — Neeeeeeeeena."

"That's gorgeous!"

"And more common, I should tell you, than the other names put together, *po-et*."

"Nina. Come have coffee with me, Nina."

"I am a married woman."

"I am a married man."

"I'm not sure our exchange of information is reassuring."

"Let's debate over coffee cups."

"Thirty minutes, including traveling time, the coffee house portal-to-portal, *po-et*."

"A deal."

She lit a cigarette, half her face under a table umbrella, half in the sun, and grinned, her mouth wide, her great green eyes crinkly. Her coffee mug was resting on her lap, her legs crossed, her toes on one foot pointing to mine.

"Neeenitchka," I said.

She reached for the wilted gardenia in her hair, pulled it free, placed it between us on the table. Dark long hair clung to the browning petals.

"May I have this?" I said.

"Promise not to give it to a witch?"

"A witch?"

"To make me do your will."

"Isn't there a less ominous way to get me in touch with you?"

"What would you want me to do — if you had your way, *po-et?*"

"Go out to the ocean — right now — to hell with books, to hell with classes."

"O.K."

"O.K?"

"O.K."

She butted her cigarette, and gave me her hand.

I drove with her thigh against mine. Strange shutter-closings in my eyes blinked away the highway. We leaned far forward.

The sun was a circle of suddenly gathered red light. Clifftops reached high enough to be touched by color, and the uppermost branches of hill trees. Below, shadows grew smoky. The stipple in the mountains deepened.

I raced the car over the winding roads, oblivious of traffic.

"I think I should unjumble my morals, what do you say, *po-et*?"

"If the unjumbling has good consequences."

"A car is bad for clear thinking."

"If you lean a bit closer I will kiss your beautiful mouth —"

"Will that improve my thinking? Or my jumbled morals?"

"Yes."

"Then I will do it."

She turned in the seat, kneeling, her back to the windshield; put her open mouth on mine a long long second, lips and tongue and dark moist wonder.

"Now, *po-et*, drive quickly, and safe." She sat face forward again, but closer. "My thinking is improved. My morals are gone. Like a migraine."

"Good."

"Perhaps good."

"I love your mouth. I would like the rest of you like that — right now —"

"O.K."

"We would be arrested."

"Beware, *po-et*, of asking me what you don't really want."

"I want."

"Take."

"Soon."

"Why not wait to ask till you are ready to take?"

"O.K."

"You *are* a willing pupil."

Her head was on my thighs, right under the steering wheel. Lights reflected flitted over her face, red in shadow. Her dark eyes stared up as I slid her sundress off one shoulder, her breast in my hand, a dark pucker around her nipple, firm and soft.

"Nina, you're beautiful."

"What woman wouldn't look beautiful like this?"

She nuzzled her nose at my belt buckle. The road seemed to be hurtling toward me, over me; I pressed her breast and her hand slid swiftly over mine.

Dan's Malibu place.

I raced the car, feeling her hand, her cheek on my lap. Red blotches, blue spears blinded my eyes as if they were shut a long time, and too suddenly opened. Every movement of her fingers sent a pulse exploding.

Somewhere, as if hidden under bales of cotton wadding, my ears recalled Dan saying the key was on a post, or under a horseshoe. I pressed Nina's breast back into her dress, jumped out of the car, running with her, my hands shaking. The key dropped. Picked up, dropped, picked up by her. I opened the door.

The room was full of windblown sand.

I shook a rug, in one motion pressed Nina down, her dress up, off, her hands as quickly tugging my shirt over my head. My mouth found her, my hands freed her hair, long, in a black lovely wash over her breasts.

"I want your lips, your tits, your cunt, everything, all together, at once, for my cock, my hands, my mouth —"

"If you can do it, do it."

She tasted of heat, toasted sesame, love's spittle; smelled the way she felt, warm and secret and dark, her tongue so soft. A hot wave. My hands turned her legs up, arched, high, higher, her breasts swelling, nipples saluting, open, all open with frankness, her chin wet and her cheeks and her hair as I kissed her, my balls suffused, hot looping waves, moving, hurtled, stood together, sat together, sand on our bodies, sand in our eyes, rolled off the rug, falling forward, her breasts swinging softness, hands on my head, my lips on her shoulder, moaning, dark, low, halfhurled the earth, catching the room and the sand and the sky and the sea in one final whooping swoop and cry together to fall back together on the wet twisted rug, pulsating, all lovely together.

Passing boats winked red wrinkles off the smooth dark ocean. Waves crashed a seashell roar. My lips rested on the hollow between her breasts. Damp and warm on my cheeks. A lamp from a beachhouse made weak blue light which her dark hair ended and blue-white face began. One leg stretched under me, the other curled saucily round my back. That great hot toasted sesame smell on her breasts and on her face. She was unresisting as air. A move of finger or tongue was a snugging down, an opening of what was hidden. I kissed my way up her softness and secret smoothness, damp thighs and the soft roughness between.

"I am tongue-drawing a treasure map."

"Are you afraid you won't find this again?"

"It's my miserly instinct. I not only want you but want you engraved. Imperialism of this gorgeous flesh."

"Do you lay claim to other territories in your domain?"

"The metaphor has just outlived its sweetness. I mean I want this stuff all the time. Forever."

"Now you speak as *po-et*. Outside the window is the dark and sand and water. That is no reality. Behind the garage is reality. Where I have a husband and you have a wife, and a graduate school, and wages and hours. To stay here forever would be splendid. You think our bodies, even after this, live with love and a romantic's vision, forsaking nourishment and all confrontation? Never. So we take our stuff back to the world and cherish it, in stealth."

"Life is easy, Nina."

"I don't know we can make this conclusion so soon."

"No strain. Continuous."

"Because we are naked, *po-et*. Naked is unreal, and was in primitive times too."

"No. Life *is* easy. Here, now, I know it and feel it."

"But what when we reverse the voyage, and return to the library cubicle — tell me, do you love your wife desperately? No. Don't tell me. I don't want to know you have a wife."

"You sound sad."

"Only because you had to say 'forever.' Why not make love in darkness, or in sun, and not lay claim to anything?"

"Would that be real?"

"Did you ask me to the ocean because anything was real? I came because I felt a magic."

"Your tits are real."

"As flesh they are real, but at love —"

"Magic! It's all one."

"Except that I am terribly hungry, and dry, and covered with sand. Our magic love chafed our real bodies raw."

"Let's make love in the ocean."

"Romantic madman."

"Compromise. In the shower."

"I said you were a romantic madman. Did I reject the ocean?"

"Let's fox the neighbor with the light on his porch. We'll drop our robes at the water's edge."

"I will smell of ocean brine. It is I suppose to be preferred."

The sand was cold. Wind whipped its powdery fineness. Hand in hand we ran to the water sweeping high up the shore, tide swish and dart, icy cold, our backs bent, then arms around, like two reapers into waved wheat in high wind. Swirled-up foam drove us back to the shore, pulled at us, smashed us back till, letting go, we dived into the water, breasting it under the surface, coming up beyond the line of wave-rise, bobbing as the ocean heaved and tipped.

Her breasts in water were smooth and larger and teasingly slippery, till I ducked down, and gently bit her, her hand on my hair, yanking me up, our faces streaming, sputtering laughter into the vast night. Every drop's tinkle rattled on glass.

"Let me tow you."

"Ask no permission, lady."

Faces buried in each other we tumbled in slow belly-lurching somersault, backs bent to join in ferriswheel.

"God," I shouted as we came up for air, "it's right. What a way to go it would be!"

"*Po-et*, in the midst of this much life, why death?"

"A passing thought, mermaid."

"Then it's time to go."

She stood at Dan's stove, a tiny frill of apron tied like a tu-tu round her waist, her hair dripping pools on the dark red wood. Held a skillet away from her naked body, forkwhipping eggs.

"We will feed ourselves tinctured reality in easy stages, like that king — what was his name? — 'he dies old.' *Ab ova, po-et*, where else should lovers nestle white and yolk?"

"Mithridates. And nowhere else, you gorgeous lay."

We heard the sand sifting into the room, and felt it, sadly, as if it ran through an hourglass. My chest was wet where her breasts rested during short sleep. Her damp hair was cool and silken on my face.

"*Po-et*, tell me, did you intend to knock me up?"

"Never."

"Idiot boy, did you even ask? I'm a married woman. Was that sufficient information?"

"I would have fucked you, sweetheart, no matter what."

"I am not complaining of devotion, darling. It has to do with reality. You are a wildman. Why did you not ask about diaphragms?"

"I didn't have that kind of time."

"What if I am knocked up? What if my husband is in the Arctic? Or is older than Methuselah? Would you play madman's roulette? One day a week I perhaps come to school wearing my diaphragm. How do you know this is the day?"

"Maybe it was in the way you said 'O.K.' "

"That told you I was wearing a diaphragm?"

"I would have said so then. I know better now."

"You, an empirical people. If you found I had no diaphragm why were you not stricken? Who are you to knock me up?"

"Someone who loves your hair and your eyes and your tits and your tongue and your everything."

"Shame on you for evading. You think there are romantic sperm who bow and do not enter?"

"Hey, that's a great notion!"

"You are incapable of answering to the point! I say again, *po-et*, what if I am pregnant?"

"Let's not hang on an 'if,' sweet."

"I agree with you. That's silly. But the point is not. Pleasure principles you understand, but a pleasure principle tied up with a reality principle — idiot, I am lecturing, and you spread my thighs? If you did not knock me up these other times for sure you will now!"

"Sweetheart, would you argue with the tide?"

"I would not argue with the tide. I would move back out of its range."

"There was never a tide so willful, with hands to lock behind your knees."

"In the metaphor, *po-et*, that to which the tide ran would not be a naked woman, as in this case you come to pursue, but the shore, and it would know it could not run —"

"And then, perhaps, would spread itself to receive the waters —"

"Perhaps. And tiny cells, several million, would strike that shore and even one take root. The sand would cry to the sea, 'Did you intend to knock me up?'"

"In the crash of the sea's breakers it would be hard to hear the answer —"

Every car but Nina's was gone from the parking lot.

I led her by the hand, small hand, familiar. I could not believe we hadn't walked like this a hundred times before. She let her head rest on my shoulder, light, snuggled.

"If you did knock me up I would be very curious about our child."

"She would be a girl and have a Russian accent."

"Oh, I feel heavy. It is delicious. I shall go to bed after a shower which removes advertising but keeps you hugged deep inside."

"I love you, Nina."

"How can you say that?"

"I say it softly."

"It's the love you felt when you looked at me in your lap. Just a word, escaped from the passionate throat. Gurgle, when waves come over our heads. I babble. Do you know I sometimes babble? Lecture, *moralisé*, my form. Babble, too, speaks love, *po-et*."

Distant lights filtered the parking lot, the overhanging trees silver blue. Darkness drained fire from her freckles, shadowed her shoulders.

"Yesterday, Nina, I didn't know you."

"You didn't?"

"I was just aware of this beautiful girl."

"Shame on you for abstractions."

"Babbler, I'm thanking you. Telling you how grateful I am. You magnificent gift."

"Enough, *po-et*. Kiss me away. When I turn on the ignition we will be pumkins — no. Only I will be pumkin."

"The minimum number of pumpkins you can be is two, four, five, six!"

"I am huge?"

"You are gorgeous. And I want all that tomorow."

"With or without a diaphragm?"

"With or without."

She looped her car away, the red of her brake lights glowed, the beam of her back-up lights cut through the gray mist settling over the lot. She stopped with her front door even with mine, wound

down her window. The lights from her instrument panel caught
her lovely cheeks and throat.

"*Po-et*, do you know you have made me an adultress."

"And you have made me an adulterer."

"Ah."

"Are you sorry?"

"I am not sorry. But I do not like being an adultress. I am too
serious a person. Goodnight, *po-et*."

"Goodnight, my love."

"Ah. Love, *perhaps*, will balance what's adulterous."

Mist speckled the hood of the car, a million light-reflecting drop-
lets usually cold and shivery. Nina was a wandsweep. Neon signs
picked up by chrome and metal striated colors, lovely alchemy, all
that unbeautiful Los Angeles junkiness absorbed, transformed.

I heard every dry palm leaf click, watched the wind ruffle
through eucalyptus and peppertree. I smelled Nina in every breath,
her sesame taste burnt on my lips.

I tiptoed into the house, up the stairs.

"Sweetheart, I've been waiting all evening," Maggie called
cheerily. "The men pick up tomorrow. Be a good husband and take
the wastebaskets down."

I broke out.

Not that fleshly love alone.

Broke *out*.

Smashed the window of that porch to bits of multicolored glass.
My privacy, my secret storing places. Smashed. Blood and darkness
and anger and fright. Every held-back cry, or bird who dented
memory with a clawfall.

A bust-out.

Nina.

Who broke the wall with a shatter of glass.

When you can not *tell*, you do not *see*. I could imagine a love, and a love's ear. And for her stored every detail, every nuance resisting boredom, nothingness, death.

That mouse, and Uncle Bim, made me *take* messages, and hug them to me.

Nina made me sing them out. I ran, like a delighted squirrel who now knows the meaning of his hoard, to savor each acorn bump and discolored dent.

Perhaps I blamed Coleridge too much.

I wanted to turn a page and find him in loving business. He was brilliant seeing the sour.

My attention could only be partial, tuned to my lady's sandal slap. What to me now was the sweet smell of beanfields? Every book of messages I tossed aside the second that cotton swish reached my ears. Or Nina's voice.

"First we must work. I sit with Chekhov, and you with that Englishman. I will only settle for brilliance, *po-et*. You would not expect low standards."

"Let me sit with you and Chekhov."

"You do not sit. Therefore stay in your cell till two hours have passed."

"O.K."

"My God! Your ardor cooled overnight."

"We'll go out to Dan's —"

"Is it possible to make love without sand?"

"Where?"

"My place."

"Your husband?"

"He is not there."

"When does he get back?"

"Isn't enough, *po-et*, that he is not there?"

"Let's go."

"Two hours. From the moment we settle down and work."

Samuel Taylor, cursed with the same initials as the *Short Title*

Catalogue, how would you sound in a Russian accent? *A domsell vid a dolceemer eeen a weesion* — great!

Nina turned round suddenly, caught me staring. Her scolding finger waved me back to STC.

"Ten extra minutes, *po-et,* because you cheated!"

"Looking at your back doesn't count."

"Your face had no expression I can connect with backs."

"Think a bit, sweetheart."

"Shame on you! Work!"

I switched from old Coleridge to young Donne.

Her house was redwood, on a high bluff, a hundred-foot drop to the Pacific Coast Highway, the sand, the ocean. Built into the hill, wood and glass, California as her sandals.

I parked beside her car she sat in, waiting.

"Welcome, *po-et.*"

"Thank you, princess."

"You think this is a castle? I think it is too."

A cement workroom, powertools, lumber, shavings on the floor, fresh-white, new. A redwood staircase she started up.

"I know you, *po-et.* My thighs are tight together. I must be allowed to climb these stairs without you."

"If we miss this sensual touch, princess, how will we explain it to Eros on his Day? He will charge me with this omission, that you preceded me on these stairs and I, a recalcitrant, walked like a holy clerk whose devout hands interlock behind his back."

"I would not lead you to damnation, *po-et.*"

Together we rose into a room all beige and brown and black and rust. Over Nina's bare shoulder a wide bed covered in dark brown satin.

"Never, *po-et.* That would make adultery aggressive."

"The yearning was practical, not political, princess."

"Won't my secondbest bed suit you, darling?"

"Even your thirdbest rug."

My heel bounced brown bolsters off a low bed hot with noon sun. That toasted sesame smell rose from Nina's breasts, and, blinded, I slid my tongue up her belly, between her breasts, to her mouth, my eyes closed to the dazzle the rocketing reflecting love-spotting sun.

And there, wrapped round, legs and arms, I whispered on Nina's wet sundrenched breasts the dark things the years stored.

I was in love.

My body churned with hers, and my soul soared through clear reaches. The room was suffused with heat and loving.

"Perhaps, *po-et*, I am not as enamored of toasted sesame as you."

"I loved it even when I didn't know why."

"I love you, *po-et*."

I looked at her face, forehead smooth and golden, jaw firm, queenly, her beautiful nose dipped saucily at the bridge, and those dark green eyes sun and love made glassy.

Everything else in life seemed trivial. Nina's green eyes. Frank, wide wide awake.

"Sweet, you are a success."

"I am glad you are here, *po-et*."

"I've been reading you in your drapes and rugs and colors and woods. Nothing surprises me. Only this pink is unrepresented. The other colors mimic your hair and your eyes and your aureole —"

"Aureole — ugh, I hope I do not have an aureole."

"Your tit-tints, princess, which deepen your kissed fleshly message. These fine dark ringlets, love's garland."

"You are making me very hot in the deepest hiding places."

"I believe you but still prefer investigation — with a practical touch, princess."

"Your practical touch has permission to discover if this deep blush is true, or false."

"I will not cease till success is ours. How long may I search, princess?"

"By the sun, explorer, I would say two hours. I know it will take less. But by then I may want you to check a dark cascade, and claim it."

"I do."

As if I stared into the sun, then closed my eyes, colors swept off my lids to cover the room, and Nina. Hot flapping motions darkened those colors, dizzying, soft, sweet, gentle as a whisper, love's secret music, sticky, cool, and drenching hot, softer than our kissing mouths till our bodies came together faster faster, like shuddering handclaps, the couch lurched against the wall, crashing away all gentle music, and Nina in Russian cried out.

Aunt Teena stared at the salad bowl.

"It's not that it makes a difference to me, dear."

Her cheeks were heavy with a perfumed powder.

"You will become a hostess in your own home, and have to entertain your husband's associates. So why not learn to do a salad right, dear? The radishes are chunks for a peasant. Your onions lack delicacy. You have big hands, Maggie, but with concentration you could learn to use them in a feminine way. I'll fish out the oversize radish pieces, and this time make it perfect."

Uncle Baer had his arm in a sling.

He had fallen off his horse.

His face was screwed up, puzzled.

"So I said to my horse, 'Girlie, you are gonny have to do it all yourself. You are gonny take boddy of us back to the stables.' And she turned and looked at me with her big brown eyes. 'That's right, Tango,' I said, 'it's all in your hands now. I'm depending on you to get us back.' And she walked gentle as an angel, like she was floating me back to the stables."

Aunt Teena shrugged.

"He imagined the whole thing."

"Dear," Uncle Baer said in alarm, "are you doubting my words and horse?"

"You didn't say a thing. You have to make up a story about everything."

"Dear, you are wrong, do you know that, dear? Without that conversation I couldy been left in the woods and my arm get wrecked by the night cold and they'd have to amputaty it right off —"

Aunt Teena looked at us.

And shrugged again.

"See?"

I did not believe what I had heard.

"Sweetheart, you've got to be joking."

A mockingbird, whom I would have tuned with her, lost its nightingale tone, turned mocking clown. Malibu seemed a desert, sand metamorphosed into drifts to whirl a wall around travelers.

"Nina, you can't mean it."

"Oh, it's now I know I come from an old civilization, and you from this new. I must, *po-et*, must. You are properly apolitic. Romantic. What I must do is tied up with Europe and the war and Dachau and rescue and heroic people who are alive who might be dead. Old World, embarrassing to me when I'm not in your arms, who have lived these months a new world young life. I told you I would not talk to you about my husband, and will not. Or debate. Or regret a second of this loveliness, *po-et*. Or apologize for not preparing you before. Or stop being yours."

"When you're a thousand miles away what will it mean to be mine?"

"That there is a spot here and here and here and here, your spot, and nothing will touch it ever —"

"That's sentimental, sweetheart. I would have you in my arms not my memory —"

"And I, were it a choice, would stay in this loveworld forever."

"This is crazy, Nina."

"It is crazy, and real. I thought I was going for a time, but we will never see each other again. I won't ever be back in the cubicle."

"What will happen to space, Nina?"

"I am too arrogant to say 'nothing.' "

"Oh, I wish I had knocked you up."

"That would have changed nothing, *po-et*."

"I don't mean only to hold you here. A child would be proof that one and one once made three."

"I would have liked your child, *po-et*."

"Nina, if something happens —"

"You mean if my husband dies?"

"Anything. Will you look for me?"

"My obligations are for seven or eight lifetimes, darling. When I go, I go."

"Is our love that weak?"

"I could answer it is very strong. Otherwise I might not be able to lay with you here, under sky we love, cool ground, feel you in me, and know it won't be tomorrow."

"Couldn't our love embrace all obligations and duties — everything, Nina —"

"No."

"I am sure it could, and can."

"I have thousands of Europe's sad years to say it couldn't, and can't."

"This must be?"

"Must."

"There's nobody we could plead before, or pray to, or fight, or scare —"

"Nobody."

"That's it?"

"That."

"What if I refuse to let you up? What if I lay claim on this my territory forever?"

"You would be foolish to claim what was never denied as yours."

"I won't let go."

"Even there, *po-et*, reality has you."

"Eros will charge me in perpetuity and stand for what is right —"

"Now kiss me, darling, and I will go."

"How will my mouth let go?"

"With the same inevitability all of you just learned."

"Nina, I *love* you!"

I heard my words in the darkness like the cry of a man diving from a bridge. Echo upon echo. In the canyons, brushed against trees, floated to the sky and over the waters, away, and fainter.

I wanted to shout out to Romeo and Tristan and Troilus, to see if anything has been missed, or found, the right word, the right act, to change this terrible bleakness. As if the color and the shrieking joy only gamed me into thinking that porch were gone and my prison window truly broken.

"Help me with my brassiere strap, darling. This is reality, you see? A safety pin."

My hands brushed the silky cotton tightly binding her heavy breasts.

"Can you leave these behind? That, at least?"

"I would like to fold me in a sweet package, *po-et*, and leave me with you as a parting gift."

"Here, is your brassiere strap O.K. now?"

"Almost perfect."

"Mine own executioner."

"Breathe a kiss inside, between me and the cotton."

"Two kisses. I would not have my love go round the world on a tilt."

"Two kisses."

"Three."

"Ah. Three."

"And your mouth."

"Four."

"Nina, I know why Adam ate that apple. Otherwise he would have stood at Eden's gate and watched Eve go. And lay down in Paradise all all alone. Couldn't I be a camp follower and live on the edge of your obligations? Late at night, when all but you and I were asleep, you'd steal outside like a gypsy and I would love you like a phantom."

"Now who babbles?"

"Somebody who can't stand this — not for a second."

"Put your hands on me — everywhere — press, so I'll have the strength tomorrow . . . "

"Love shouldn't have to end like this."

"Love isn't ending —"

"We are. Which is worse."

I drove in darkness expanded, black universe flaming with lightless meteors. I had been allowed to reach the forbidden castle, and consider the quest at an end, to find I did not understand the rules of the world. Dark space between the castle and my feet unrolled like the black skein I saw in dreams. I heard mountains shatter. Sequoias split, lightning-riven, trees once as set and certain as granite.

And she came to him in the night, the Carthaginian Queen, after he had chosen to give up the world and forget the gods and their demanded destiny, and she told him what he had refused to tell her, that as a woman of a world she would have to return to her queenly role, alone, as befitted her heroic tale. And would he not throw himself on a pyre in Carthage style, but pass on to great tasks in his own world. The one he had once foolishly rejected as stale.

Aeneas went.

Dido let Carthage know she was returning, their Queen. The tale she burned herself in sorrow is false. Like Aeneas, Dido was, on the contrary, heroic and successful.

Time has no stop for lamentation or mourning.

Millions of tiny strings tug and pull. As history doesn't ask permission to declare war and lasso lives up to that moment set on some dedicated path. So birth and death and accident, like a child crying in the night, impress with logic all their own. The single lament, like a floe in the rush of time's waters, is shattered, or casually tossed high on a sunhot bank.

Some thought I was ill, and some merely worried. And counselled joy and sunshine and a fling out of routine.

My lady was departed.

Gad's Uncle Percy had a heart attack. Tricking insurance detectives, playing games with Stacey's shadow, Percy fell low. Was carried on a litter, on the shoulders of four huge whitecoated men, into an oxygen tent, to which we came, Gad and I, and Hettie Karousel, and Levitt.

A huge red NO SMOKING sign, ominous as an air-raid warning, and a black QUIET hung above Percy's door.

From inside, Percy's bubbling voice, echo of an echo of an echo, was roaring. The oxygen tent was withdrawn. Three doctors came rushing out, redfaced, heads together.

"You think I'm crazy to live closed from sunshine and faces," Percy was hollering. "What good it'll be to save my life if I end up worse than dying! You don't know what's worse? Living dead — that's worse."

His wife Alison at the foot of his bed, chewed gum, pensive.

"Percival, don't tire yourself."

He saw us through the open door.

"Come inside," he roared. "She wants me to lay back like I was already in a coffin."

"Where's Stacey, Uncle Percy?" Gad asked.

"Gad, you see what it is: he's working pretty hard, Stacey, and stays in school long hours, and his wife is afraid to be alone. So if her mother ain't around Stacey stays with her."

Hettie Karousel swung her handbag in disgust. Levitt found one tiny mirror and began to contemplate the part in his hair.

"Levitt, just the other day," Percy said, rising up on his elbows, "I was thinking about you. I was gonna call you up and make you the deal the cemetery is making me."

Levitt turned his face away, closed his eyes.

"Look how scared he is if somebody says a word about death," Percy roared to the wall marked ABSOLUTE SILENCE.

Levitt's face was a bright red. Hettie Karousel and Alison tried to calm Percy.

"I went like you go and pick out a car. They give me a salesman, I walk from box to box. That's when I thought about you, Levitt. They had a special deal, but it had to be one family only. Six hundred smackers off if we order two boxes."

Levitt shuddering shook his head.

"If I leave it up to Alison she'll send me in a shoebox. I don't want guys going after Stacey for flowers and family cars and crap. I seen enough in my day. They gonna lay me on a shelf. I said, 'Here, you guys, put my name up on the mausoleum wall, and under it, from an old moo'im picture, get a sign what says COMING SOON.' I put tips in a sealed envelope. So much for the guy what sings over me and so much — double — for the guy what prays. And the diggers get nothing, because I ain't gonna get buried. A whole new wall they opened up, Levitt. We could corner it. Look how he's superstitious, the guy. Come on, Levitt. He's gonna bust out crying. You gonna die sooner because you look it straight in the eye? Nossir. I got three Rolls Royces in my procession. One for Alison and Stacey. One for you, Hettie, and my brother, and you — if you're still alive, Levitt. And you, Gad, and the wife, and your kid brother, in the third car."

"What about Stacey's wife?" Gad said.

"I'm trying to dig up in Hollywood a Model T, or a German car what'll creak and fart, so everybody will know in the long run Germans got lousy manners. If her old lady who's sixty wears braids to my funeral, they don't let her in. Levitt, if you outlive me, I'm gonna make an executive position for you."

Levitt opened his eyes.

"What's kind position, executive?"

"Inspector. To check on what's called perpetual care; they keep my name shined up in case a visitor wants to see where Percy got packed away. I already got a receipt. It ain't tax-deductible — it's my only complaint. Now I lay back on this pillow with a peace you couldn't imagine. Levitt, think it over. I'll treat you, how's that? So soon as I get out."

My body couldn't bear the disappearance of Nina.

Between my shoulder and collarbone was her rest and nestling. I tried not to resent Maggie's innocent, unknowing intrusion. A rage got to me if her wifely head touched that spot for Nina's hair. My chest wanted the press of Nina's soft hot breasts.

On the campus every longhaired girl reminded me Nina was gone. And the sandaled feet on stone. And any accent. A sundress against the azuremauve of those Lombard buildings. I shuffled through letters and notes and junk mail, hoping I'd see that hand feathered out, broad, regular at the top of a notebook page, picking up excitement, a wild scrawl at the bottom. I searched the stacks for books Nina signed out. Her signature sent chills through me. A presence in that hurried signing. I pulled down Russian books and looked through volume after volume for some small message.

A lanternjawed Icelander took over Nina's cubicle.

I let a Burmese take mine.

Her house had a realtor's name pasted over the front door. Dan sold his place in Malibu.

Erased.

The palimpsest of failed lovers.

A shirt would tease with a faint memory of toasted sesame. But time tamed even that.

With Nina gone the world came back.

In those same Lombard buildings.

Danvers, who wore his shortsleeves rolled high on his shoulders, carried cottage cheese and vegetables in a workman's lunchbucket, afraid his hosts would have only meat. He went through the war a vegetarian, ate peach melba and cherries jubilee out of officers' stores. All his life he walked martyr, pilgrim, through meateaters and meatservers, swinging like a censer his tiny wax carton by its unsubstantial silver wire handle.

He hated Kettrick who was rich, and fawning, and an actor, with a pregnant wife Kettrick let pick up books that slid to the floor off her heaved-up belly. A sweet quiet girl whom Danvers helped up steps, and down. Kettrick lived in a house behind a huge wall. A large chain across its Arc de Triomphe entrance. Kettrick and his wife had six children but lived in separate wings and spoke to each other through an intercom.

Danvers didn't believe anything in this world could get to Kettrick. But Kettrick and his wife, after the sixth child was delivered, quarreled over the intercom, and she switched it off. And Kettrick shot himself in the head.

Danvers only swung his wax carton by its thin wire handle, and said:

"I'm glad he's found *someone* he could die for."
I told him he was a shit.

Semester's end. Trudy, who thirty years later turned from Bryn Mawr to try her luck at the university, gave the party, around her pool, on a day exams let out.

Three Negro barmen in red jackets and gray shorts tended bar. Trudy's husband, Van, redfaced from bourbon and fire, cooked chickens on a huge open pit, and Danvers, his nose in disgusted retreat, stood as far away as possible, swinging that wax carton.

Trudy had a Cape Cod face, skin stretched tight over her sharp nose, weatherburnt cheeks. Her neck was long and thin, with great hollows over her chest, and only the slightest swell of a bosom. She walked like a young girl, swinging arms, great joyful strides, and spoke generously of books and ideas.

Guests teetered at the water's edge, were pushed, or jumped. Scrambled out, drank mightily, fell back in. The pool heaved with drunken splashing. Girls were pawed, men scratched. One girl's suit top sailed through the air.

She herself threw the bottom.

Carson had been in the artillery. He usually sat between Danvers and Kettrick, a peacemaker. He spoke falteringly, as if he had corrected a terrible stammer and feared someone would try to finish his every sentence. He stared down at the ground, said "Sir" to all instructors and "Ma'am" to all their wives. Imogen, his wife, whose hair was the color of reddened straw, stood flatfooted in handmade sandals, and rarely left Carson's side.

Someone doused a camphorcandle. Then another. Couples lay over the dry grass, under beachtowels. The barmen served with the merest tinkling of ice on glass.

A mockingbird sang in blackness, fading in, fading out.

Someone was crying softly. A man. Quietly, wearily, private, voiceless.

"What is it, darling?" I heard Imogen say.

And Trudy's concerned murmur.

"Carson, would you like to rest in the house?"

I walked toward the struggling sounds of Carson's voice. Words escaped his weeping.

"Let it go, dear," Imogen whispered. "Let it go."

A camphorflame flickered over his face. Spittle ran from the side of his mouth. His glasses hung from one ear.

"Hit. Everyone. Every one."

He coughed out a shrieking cry.

"Every every every, but me. Me. Me."

Somebody in the dark grass laughed.

"Canarybirds, crazy canarybirds," Carson shouted, "crazy crazy canarybirds, will they ever know?"

"Sweetheart," Imogen said softly, "what was hit?"

"IQ's were hit. Genius. Wit. That far from me, Ed. His head tucked in, writing. Then gone. MIT. Gone. No face. No dog tags. Gone. Back front sides. Every every every one. Officers. Ed's head and legs. Me! Me! Only me! Why not my head? Brighter. Ken. Ed. Brighter. Run faster. Think, head tucked down. Writing. Dougie in back of him, gone. Rhodes. Dougie and Ed. Just gone. Never. When I woke. Gone. Never found. Just that far from me. And why not me who never had it, won't ever. Ken with straight back. Looking up. Gone. Writerdoctorpainterinventorcongressmangenius gone, all together gone, all, together. Best brains gone. Highest IQ's gone. Best fists. Faces. Jud. Dougie. What was saved? Nothing. No trace. Gone. Ed Greek two months. Self. Greek. Two months. Gone. Company picture. X out. X out. X out. All X. All. One in glasses left. X him too! X him out. Average, glasses, never be near. A hundred him to make an Ed or Jud. Why him missed? Why?"

"Because you were a father and had three children waiting —"

"Dougie two and Ed four and Jud two and carrying. And Ken girl. Oxford with Dougie. Save us. Could. Won't. Gone. Best,

gone. In rain. From sky. Helmets, a hand, whose hand, a hand,
raining, helmets, hail, hailing helmets, hands — that light — whit-
est — Ed's head tucked down — gone, and hail and hit by hands
and helmets and out. Crawling in darkness. Who? Who? Not one?
Not even one? Only? Only only only! Joke. One joke. Who? The
not X. Always be. Glasses. All X. Glasses. Justify! Haven't got it!
Jud, if, could. Dougie. Ed. Sum up. Make up. Even off. Not him in
glasses. Never! A thousand, a million him's and no Ed. Unfittest
war's joke. Unfittest. Race depends. Unfittest. Survived. That one.
Fittest rained. Helmets, hands. Fittest. Gone. X out. Jud here,
glasses there. Ed, move. Dougie. Him X out. Right. Right. Inherit
the earth, Dougie. Ed. Him? Glasses? Earth? Joke. Joke inherits.
Poor poor earth. Joke. Poor poor earth."

Carson fell ill with lumbar polio, and when the doctor was listening to that cry-wrecked gasp, those who were there swore a
beatific look came over Carson's face. Which I myself saw days
after. Now Carson in his wheelchair traverses mere land; peaceful
he mounts his chrome braces and chrome-and-leather crutches,
drags himself to his work. He holds his head high as polio allows;
his eyes study the ground.

Berenson was a rarity. An intellectual on a university campus,
plying highbrow business in the midst of philistine trades. His lec-
tures played to standing room. His seminars were as carefully selected as a blue ribbon jury. His wit and sharpness fenced with
Sidney Hook in the *Partisan Review*, engaged in colloquy with
Malraux in French journals. Beryl Berenson to us was *the* Berenson. Our Berenson.

His clothes were relentlessly casual. Tapered sleeves. Edwardian
trousers, cuffless, shin-tight. Vests with lapels and oddly shaped
flaps. He wore mostly gray, almost always the same tone, to match
his hair. His shirts had long pointed collars, with three or four

inches of cuff starchily showing. Italian shoes. And belts of a pirate chief's thickness. He read with pince-nez he pulled out of a fine sealskin case and held with no self-consciousness on the bridge of his nose.

His hands shook continuously. And went with an appeal in the eyes. You were asked to do something, feel something, know something. Not be taken in by the clothes and the brilliance and the ease. To see pain. Acknowledge it. Not ask, not pry. *See.*

Then the coldness in his hooded eyes might die. Like a Fisher King in thrall, he came begging, but not openly, which ritual forbade.

He could never turn his back on anyone. Not even for a second to pour a drink. Or have a window behind him. He looked back over his shoulder, or sidewise, and his eyes died colder, his whole face snaky. All disappeared when he turned his head charmingly to one side, or held his hands out, smiling.

He hated imperfection. When we met he stared at me walking, and tried not to wince.

His tales picked on maim or amputation or twist. He said "crutches" with a peculiar violence, "wheelchair," and "cripple." Then his eyes grew coldest. Two hours a day he hung in neck harness from a bar in his basement. To stay in straight shape, he explained. Then tightened the pirate belt, tied a Countess Mara, and went forth.

To talk.

All his talk hinted at great victories in battles present and past. We marveled.

And wished him a greater role in history. Berenson had no power, though we were all on his side. He was Noah, Abraham, who had never been called, nor ever would be. The plea was we should know, and recognize that if he had been called and chosen, he would have become what his intelligence, sensibility, and wit merited.

We believed it.

He could not imagine a bad press for himself.

If Berenson had been Napoleon, and come back from Waterloo, the world's only reporter of what happened there, we might hardly have known. He would have said:

"I had a fairly nice afternoon with the Duke of Wellington. Everything was straight and aboveboard. I said, 'Listen, Duke, did it ever occur to you that things weren't really that different at Thermopylae or Agincourt?' And the Duke said, 'You know, Napoleon, you're right.' So I said 'After all, it's the only way to look at it.' And he shook my hand warmly, and agreed."

Rumor said he had once been Marlene Dietrich's lover. We wanted to believe that. History is touchable in mysterious ways.

The girls in the seminar vied to be Beryl's salvation. But one, Helena, did far more. Helena begged to be told about Chrétien de Troyes, asked Beryl over coffee to tell of the *Mabinogion*, and, later, to show her his reproduction of the *Book of Kells*.

Helena was a tall tanned California surfgirl with long white hair and gorgeous breasts. She always wore men's shirts rolled casually to the elbow, three buttons open down from her lovely throat. Looked through the *Book of Kells*, each and every page. And then lay down, while Beryl spoke rapidly, explaining.

Her tan faded.

Her eyebrows thinned.

Her lower lip which once could hold a wet cigarette tip dangling in standard surfgirl cornball kick, grew thin and flat against her teeth. She and Beryl had matching cigarette holders. Her men's shirts were replaced by brocaded blouses. Her oriental skirts were slit a cigaretteholder length on the sides.

Her voice grew throaty, metallic.

She smiled slowly, or not at all. Rarely showed her teeth, never laughed with open mouth. Her full lips flattened. Her breasts too. Deep hollows caved in her cheeks. Her eyes became veiled.

She swore no more. Didn't make hideous faces talking about creeps. Never snorted or slapped a back, or ran, or skipped, or went to a drive-in, or a drive-in movie. Never wagged her head from side to side. Never more sat on a motorcycle, or hitched a ride in a sportscar, or sang with the radio, or shimmied to rock 'n' roll. Gave up the ocean, and the ski-run mountains. Never soaked in the sun, or spread her hair on green grass.

Deep furrows grew in her brow.

Beryl watched.

His elbow on the mantel, drink in hand. Helena his hostess, dressed in long black. Silver Iranian earrings, silver old French bracelet. Her hair up in a high chignon, her neck queen stiff, her body tense enough for mounting.

Galatea.

With reverse run reel.

Berenson had an old girl friend who during sadder days encouraged him to cry on her white bosom the long tearful night. Altruistic Mitzi approved of Helena, and was unselfishly happy for Beryl. But needed his familiar head on her now-puckering bosom. And Beryl, loyal to his past, went.

Helena, almost an armature of loveliness sculpted, shook a fleshy tremor through her ivory brocade.

"Buddy boy," she told Beryl in pre-Beryl voice, "don't save that sad sack Mitzi with your pitying prick. Or this your ass will pass around town on our newest brass platter."

Helena. Who then put her foot back on the pedestal.

It's said when Galatea was brought to life she looked into Pygmalion's eyes and whispered.

"O.K. Now you."

Gersh and Christopher and Bitner came to dinner in our north-land foothold on California sand. Sammie came too, with her infant son, who had bright red hair, and might have been Christopher's child. Sammie in black velvet, her hair in a single braid, her face darkly freckled, held her son over her head, dancing, skipping up to Christopher, and away.

Maggie was making a salad.

"Maggie," Sammie said, panting, "fuck the victuals. Let's shake life into these dull buggers."

"Dull buggers!" Christopher said. "I'll show you a paleface dance tit-toss, crisscross, overtheshoulder."

Gersh hung over Maggie's shoulder.

"God, Mag, it's great. You a wife and look, in that apron."

"Maggie," Sammie shouted, dancing, "you know what a terrible time I've had with white men. Come help me."

"Let me do the vegetables," Gersh said, and took Maggie's apron.

"Here, take the kid," Sammie panted, "dance him around."

"What the hell is this," Christopher said, "a redskin initiation?"

"Oh fuck off, Pinky!"

"Don't do it, Maggie. I've been laboring the Indian vineyard, but you still are my first love —"

"It's only a dance, you shit."

"I've seen your dances clamp white men and white women pelvises in triple-bonding glue."

Sammie lay her son in Maggie's terrified arms.

"Dance!"

Maggie held one hand behind the baby's head, unmoving. Sammie whirled round and round Maggie flatfooted, paralyzed.

"Dance, idiot girl Maggie."

"Stop your lunatic rituals," Christopher hollered, "you bloody Indian bitch!"

Sammie slammed against him.

"You want to scalp me, whore?"

"Did you call me a 'bloody Indian bitch'?"

"That pastoral crap about sun and stars and the sea — as if you Indians have a bloody monopoly! Lay off Maggie!"

"Fucking whiteskins, hang together like whorehouse alumni!"

"You're as much whiteskin as I am. Don't pull this primitive shit. Sour white women's milk and wilt white men's cocks."

"Give me the kid!"

"*He*'s white enough, I'd say."

Gersh stopped chopping celery. Maggie remained fixed in the middle of the floor.

"You miserable fucker!"

Sammie swung her fist at Christopher's face. He blocked the punch with his elbows, the baby out of her reach.

"I love you, you whore!"

"And I love you, you bastard!"

"I care what color your bloody skin is. I have it."

"There, again! 'Have.' "

"Kiss me, you Indian bitch."

"If you join the dance."

"Promise not to turn my ballock aquamarine?"

"Promise."

Maggie lay too still.

"I *should* have danced. Christopher was wrong. Sammie wanted me with it. She believed she had the power. That child in my arms and I would kick my fixes."

"You'll pick the dance up tomorrow."

"I'll never ever make it."

Hettie Karousel woke early on a damp warm morning, and knew this was a day to buy a block. She showered and dried, dried and powdered, tucked a Russian-embroidered handkerchief into her bosom, and called for Levitt, who was still snoozing.

Her handbag was crammed solid as the rocks her forefathers once used as pillow. It descended with her down a narrow staircase to the garage, step by step, like a bucket lowered carefully down a deep well.

Perspiration poured from Hettie's brow. Her hands left finger-marks on the cement she pushed against for support.

Levitt was already in the driver's seat, so quick to do what was needed, Levitt, checking himself in the rearview mirror. Released the handbrake, just as his rock 'n' roll station came on loudly, and did not hear Hettie cry out, or see her behind his handsome image in the mirror. Till he felt a lurch, hit the brake, and came out.

Hettie lay on cement, her hair dark with oil.

And still did not know, Levitt, that the car had killed her, which was never his intent. And cried out:

"Foolish woman, foolish foolish woman, you couldn't watch? Look what came from that!"

Levitt in his mourning eyed the longest black car, Levitt who had never been in the rear of a car before. He patted his children far back in their seats so his view would be unobstructed.

"She must have at least twelve cylinders, this buggy, Gad," Levitt whispered from behind a neat dry handkerchief.

Shimmy was lifted from his wheelchair into the second Rolls, hospital cushions tastefully draped in gray sheeting, his knees wrapped in foam rubber for this trip. Beside him rode his baby brother Percy, released from the hospital just for the funeral, his huge tears splattering his stiff silk black Italian suit. And with Percy, finally, was his son Stacey. Holding his father's arm.

Shimmy clasped his worse knee with small bony hands, and wept.

"We are a family of hard luck, Percy you poor keed. The Devil drags after us. It wasn't enough Hettie married Levitt. Death too had to happen."

"She couldn't even have a last wish, Shimmy. I made her a promise. 'When I'm dying, Percy, sneak me in a corn' beef with hot mustard so the Angel of Death should know from my smell he didn't win over a dead one.'"

"You and me was so busy preparing to die, Percy, we didn't even get a place on our wall for our baby sister."

With a soft turn of pulleys, four openthroated gravediggers let Hettie's bronze coffin down. Her children and her husband and her brothers filled her grave with tears and spaded dirt.

Levitt led the way back. Held up by a son and Gad.

And Shimmy wheeled by his four sons crowded together, each with a hand on his father's chair. And weak and weeping Percy, held up by Stacey, with Doctor Schiff and Lawyer Fromm quite close behind.

Levitt tried to get into the driver's seat, understandable error.

Swiftly, without police escort, the black cars left the funeral gates.

Bitner turned up with her on an evening, Fran, who spoke with a western drawl and walked like a cowgirl, wore frilly blouses, her short pale brown lashes drawn in black beads. Her upper lip was tight against her teeth in a snarl, but she spoke softly, smiled much Bitner's way. And got Bitner's heavyhaired quick nod in return.

She asked me if we had ever met before, and dropped her eyes when I said no.

Her father was a postal clerk. Bothered nobody, Democrat nor Republican, keeping his job through every change of administration. One paint-peeled picture frame held a thick wad of his Presidents: Coolidge, Hoover, Roosevelt, Truman. The town wanted him honored, one of their few war veterans. Gassed a little, by a leaky American cylinder.

He failed at starting a Legion post in the town. But always carried the flag Memorial Day.

Her mother believed the Good were born to suffer. Her own bones were porcelain, her lungs porous, full of that damp foulness, groinoriginating evil. She let her husband lawfully enter her womb, but not grow lustful over her bosom. Or kiss her lips. Or raise up that porcelain which was femur.

Once, when her breasts had risen, and her belly filled, her husband pursued by the devil came at her. She did not turn him aside. But later, when he again was for Satan, the Lord smote him. He approached not again.

Thus they lived ever after.

She found a crystal set, and the air full of other suffering Good. Sat like Whistler's mother with a headset on her pale brown hair.

Fran poured milk into a blue glass. Liquid Noxzema. Everything in the house smelled Noxzema.

"I'm glad you're regular with milk, Frances," her mother said, "we have a vulnerability in our chests. Shhhh. Claudia — see, Frances, Claudia is asking Clifford what's troublin'. He don't want to tell. Sometimes folks say they don't want to say when they do want to say. I wish you had her voice. Think you could sound like that?"

Mother held out the earphones. Arched back to get her body out of the way.

"Hug me, Ma. I'm cold."

Kittens? Everything their own way. All round. Round asses, calves, busts. Even their faces, cheeks. Lean on boys. Never afraid.

Have the stuff. Even ninth and tenth graders. Faces turned up.
Who will kiss me first? Pudgies. Them too. The pudgy with pigtails. Ass on her like Dan Patch.

Fran stopped at her locker.

"Hey, Frankie."

"My name is Fran."

"You look like a Frankie. I been observin' you."

Tall. Pigeyes. Room for a goober, those teeth. Wrists ten miles
long.

"You never look at guys, do you?"

Fran fumbled with the combination on her lock. Standing over
her. Not horsepiss or cowpiss or dogpiss or catpiss or even human.
Sour.

"Turn around, I'm talking to ya."

She shook him off.

"Maybe you can't stand to be touched by a guy neither?"

She jammed her books into the locker.

"Look this way, goddam ya!"

He spun her around. She slammed her elbow into his belly. He
oofed.

"Goddam ya. You're no girl. I ought ta be allowed to swat ya."

"Go on. Swat me."

"Nah. Back off. You're a leb — a lesb."

"A what?"

"A lesby ann. I seen ya gawkin' at the pretty girls. Look at ya.
Flat everywhere. A lesby ann. No guy who ain't a homo is gonna
look at you, Frankie."

He trundled up the steps, laughing.

Lesby ann. Homo.

What was that?

Homo sapiens.

Homo ludens.

Man something. She was a man?

Homo genius.

Same. Same sex? Girls like girls? Boys like boys? Are there such?
Lesby ann.

Lesby. Dumb geek. Leslie Anne? A movie star who looked like a
boy? *Flat everywhere*. How could he be sure?

Kittens weren't flat anywhere. Ma was right. Drink milk. Put
pounds on. Eat yeast. Kittens ate yeast in milk for breakfast. *Then
I put on pounds. Boys flocked around me in the halls.*

Silly. *Two* girls? *Two* boys?

How?

Shoulders. Not wide. Couldn't be a boy.

Upper lip. Sixteen-year-old *boys* shaved.

Hips. Right, that geek. Flat. She tried to curve her hips to one
side. Flanks flat. Kittens don't have flanks. She tried to pinch her
thighs. Walking on rocks. Riding. Where pounds should go. Nice
to will it. Eight pounds for my ass, three — was that right? — for
each of my bosoms. Two for each thigh, three-quarters for each
calf. Four ounces on each cheek, two below my chin.

There!

Oh. Bad color hair. Flaming red or raven black. Twine it around.
Not this friz, Mother's hair. Wouldn't it be great! Dark nipples,
long hair, round belly. Oh, forgot to ask pounds for belly.

At least six. Let's see. Grand total — twenty-six, make it an even
thirty. Become one of those fat flouncy ones. Pink organdy, brassiere straps. Transparent peepshows.

Don't know who Savonarola was.

Go to New York, diet. No. Go on a diet. Put on twenty. *Then*
go to New York, L.A., Tokyo. Frilly clothes. Higher voice. Elec-
trolysis removes unsightly hair. Padded bra while building up. Padded girdle.

Joining was worse than fighting.

But Prince Charming comes into the kitchen: "My God, what's

a young girl doing with *Either/Or?* I will take you to Switzerland: wanted to visit Jung this summer anyway."

Trunkful of Lanz dresses. Every one white eyelet.

On plane eat like horse. Round assed by the time land in Switzerland.

"He is our President," Pa said, "and did it to save American boys. Jap too. If we'd gone on fightin', God knows how many more Jap we'd 'a' killed."

"Children," Fran muttered.

"Had to be."

"Why on a city?"

"Show him what it was."

"Who?"

"Hirohito."

"Why drop it again?"

"Jap didn't get the message, I suppose. Thought we were kiddin' maybe."

"Truman is an ugly old fart."

Mother gasped.

"Frances," Pa said, "get out of this house this minute."

"I'm going."

"When you can speak civil of our President — " said mother.

"Pro-Jap don't make sense, Frances."

"He's a murderous old fool. He wanted to drop that bomb on black men too, I bet."

"Out!"

Pa had his silly weak hand raised. Mother sniveling into her balled-up hankie. Over Harry Truman! Sweet old grandpop wants to vaporize dirty little yellow men.

Maybe not.

She didn't feel like going home.

At MacFetridge ranch, cook and have ass pinched. Bald guy who felt her up. Face dropped. *Give me a chance to fill out, Baldy.* Swinging udders guaranteed six months from some Wednesday.

"Jesus, you should see the the boobs on that Frannie!"

Her fate, Tommy MacFetridge, who never felt anything on anybody. Books under bunk. Bounced out of A & M for Red sympathies. Some story. Slow. Poems about shading your eyes and looking westward. Done up brown by all the near-poets. Frost did a small world. A barn, a horse, then trees cut endlessness off. West too much — open up, open out. Infinity everywhere and not a drop for ink.

Slow poems by slow Tom.

"Ma, I have something wrong."

"It's the sick."

"Sick."

"In women's ways."

"Ma, something is coming —"

"Never mind."

Stay windside of daddy, dear, and don't go near the water.

Tommy's hair thinning. Tanned. Scholarly forehead. Tough jaw. Wags when he talks. Massive chin compared to this v. How the West began. Some cowgirl took off her jeans.

Tommy too depressed to be a revolutionary leader. Depressed ones help the guys who breathe fire. Lenin said O.K. to screw as long as you take a cold drink of water after. Stalin probably put it to you out behind the Kremlin, then shoot you.

"Tommy, let's walk."

"Want to go down to the library?"

"Nah."

"I can saddle up a couple horses."

"Where would they take us?"

"Oh I don't know. Around, and back."

Waft something his way. Egyptians. Rapture out of a nightingale's droppings. *Tommy, I am nineteen and yet a maid.*

Where is dirty Baldy tonight? Choice of bunks. Big mattress left on the floor. To air. Is human. To use, divine.

Read Chaucer he'd know. Grab by the. Never mind hors d'oeuvres. Should all have lapel buttons. 'Ask me.' Waste ten lives wondering. Poor Frannie. Nobody to break, nobody to enter.

She turned toward the bunkhouse.

Nasty old buggers like Baldy always make out. Clothes off, legs up. No great pleasure, no depressing project. Rape simplest? All dark, someone never see again. Should have bureau. Will be at the corner of x and y at z. Wearing pink. If good put in a repeat order.

"Tommy —"

"Fran. I've had bad times with women."

A ton on her ribs. Getting heavier. Nailed down to the mildew mattress.

"Relax, Tommy."

"I'm not unrelaxed."

"I'm here, all of me, Tommy."

Should have borrowed somebody's something.

"Hold still, Fran."

Batted one eyelash. Otherwise no motion. What's happening down there, captain? No tits to zip him on. If face close enough, hot kiss.

Oh, trying to put one on. Poor guy. Should let him slumber chaste one night.

"Tommy," she whispered.

"I'm sorry, Fran."

"Shshshshsh. You're sweet —"

"The man isn't supposed to be sweet."

"You're powerful. I can feel your strength all over me."

Just a little skinny girl, buddy. Mashed. *My Frances, all I have.* Poor he.

Poor me.

"Fran, raise your legs, quick, Fran, Oh Oh, no don't move, hold still, your *other* leg, Fran, slow — one, not that — don't move, Oh you moved you moved you moved!"

Wet warmish on me in me — Oh for godssake without that — wouldn't it be ducky, still a virgin, still immaculate, but conceived.

"This time wait."

"Don't worry, Tommy."

"Hold still."

Impotentogenic? Wiltogenic? Fizzlogenic? It might have been but fizzle fizzle and blah bloo blub.

"Oh — you moved again!"

Any less motion makes our love necrophilia.

Fran looked pleadingly at Bitner, twitched a reddish tweed cape snug around her shoulders. Be a witness, her gesture said.

"I really think," she whispered to me, "we've met many times before."

I smiled. I knew it was not so.

The fifth month she told Tommy. Which caused him to disappear.

Tommy's mother, knowing her Tommy, nominated a fitter patriarchy of fathers: the last father was a flat five hundred, to be paid by a bank one thousand miles from Tommy's town.

No room at that inn. Or any other. And tearful Mother wore earphones over her eyes. Fran wanted to push her full belly forward, cause great outcry, but took the five hundred dollars to Los Angeles, quietly, and joined a houseful of pregnant kittens. Hollywood Bunkhouse of Bagged Bitches.

Who knew she knew Kierkegaard?

She steered the Hoover over Charlene's blue flowered rug. Took in weekends by nice folks. Introduced to kind friends. Green candy wedding ring Mrs.

Two days in sanityland then back to Bitch Barracks. Three knocked up by same producer. Sistered under the skin. Speech teacher fit the diaphragms. *Speak your lines natural, Mabel, and do not saw the air with your lower limbs.*

The Hoover buzzed over the bare floor.

Growl growl growl. Aloneness crying out. Mumsy will come as soon as Mary Noble is over. If the Hoover were a coping saw? Look through. *Hi there.* Wave. Hard to upset liberals. Understand you up to the ninth month. Insofar as we are animals we get knocked up. Never weep, never wail. Quietly understand.

The spirit in my circle raised a round hectic. God! *Nothing* was raised. Did any Roman matron carry one inverted to commemorate poor Tommy?

Soon weekend over. Fear returning. *Give up all last names ye who enter here.* Can always go back to mother. Vision. One earphone apiece.

Tough tough Frankie not tough enough.

Party sounds. Community or society? Something to make somebody feel *in.*

Cry help? Let tough Frankie *in!*

Fear rose undammed, like water. Irony no defense. Stuff to do it with somewhere. Like Juliet, but revived, with happy ending. *We didn't know you were in trouble, dear.* You mean you didn't notice? *Oh but that could have been just a lovely roll in the hay.* It warn't, ma'am.

Hollywood popcorn. Not a girl who didn't gobble. Pills to light her flare. Mixed met. Controlled experiment. Call med school. Hello, how many sleep p's to blackout, crash gently? Empty bottle. Simple. Flush most down. Death or salvation. The middle course — stomach pumped, Kierkegaard.

She filled her hand with capsules.

Positioned over the bar. A body crash even liberalism can't deny.

No water. A person playing at serious suicide should be able to swallow pills without mechanical aids like water. God! You could choke to death.

She woke in a stranger bed. Charlene's voice. Oriental way: *saved my life, stuck with me in perpetuity.*

How did you meet her, Charlene? She landed overhead. What conveyance used? Round sleeping pills. Name? Frances Blank, filled out because mother never filled her in.

Room at *this* inn. Nothing to pay, just leave us your child.

Charlene at the fruitwood frame, hooking. In Bitch Barracks the other kind of hooker.

Rug, two golden birds on brown with green leaves; orange berries hang from bird beak. Perfect.

Charlene kitten. Walks and world applauds. Right schools right everythings. Sings sews plays flute dances swinger in bed poems by heart bakes bread cooks French.

And stamps me under with soft reason.

"I can go away for a while. Say the father was killed in Korea."

"That's a poor way to start, with a lie, Fran."

"This is *my* living child in *my* belly."

"Your belly is not the world, Fran."

Head beautiful over that frame.

"What if I found someone to marry?"

"That *would* be different."

Whipped cream, cement core. A winner's head. Drape her with roses, black-eyed Susans.

"What is your opinion, Fran?"

"That you are *absolutely* right."

Maggie's brush searched and found snarls.

Hard short strokes. A cox would have seen the sculling in it. Hup-hup-hup, thirty-six, thirty-eight, hup-hup.

"That is a slut."

"That?"

"Fran. Bitner could have found something as feminine on Skid Row."

"Charlene told you her story."

"Sob stuff. That dike type gets to softies like Charlene."

Her face in the mirror. Head ducked to one side.

"Shall we forbid her access to our grounds?" I said.

"You dumb hyperboreans always get taken in! Fran of the Frontier. A goony girl gets bagged to pump up her hormones. God, I can't get this brush through my hair. Do something!"

I put my hands on her bare shoulders.

"Why are you guys interested in that nothing girl?"

"Why are you letting a nothing girl upset you?"

"Because you aren't brushing my hair."

"So give up your murderous brush."

She sighed, leaned her head back.

"Tell me, did you ever see a less attractive girl than that Fran?"

"Yes."

"The pat response is 'no.'"

"The pat question is 'Did you ever brush lovelier hair than mine?'"

"And what is the pat answer?"

I carried my coffee to a patio table in the sun. Classes had broken. Students traded spaces in and out of buildings. A heavy bookbag sagged into the seat beside me, then Fran, in a Russian peasant blouse.

"I'm flattered you recognize me."

"This ploy I don't understand."

"It's no ploy."

Her lashes, no color. Lids reddish. Rabbit eyes. Face recently washed. Damp at the hairline. Today she did not love herself.

"You didn't always know me."

"True."

"At your place I asked if you had ever seen me before?"

"And I hadn't."

"We *three* had a carrel on the same stack level."

She lit a cigarette. Blew smoke out at the corner of her mouth. Downjet. Snarling o.

"You stared right through me. Four months, more, five."

"I apologize for my bad manners."

"Oh, your manners were O.K."

Her fingers bunched a knot above her eyes.

"I admired your taste," she said. "Should I describe your type? — long dark hair, creamy skin, a touch of accent, wide smile, legs bare in sandals — isn't this a perfect description of your wife?"

"Why are you being so miserable?"

"I don't like being stared through."

"I didn't even know you were there."

"That's even worse."

"I really have to go now —"

I slammed away my chair.

"Oh God — listen," Fran cried, "I'm just coming from the shrink. A girl who reaches mother isn't responsible for her bitchiness, is she? Don't go. It was gratuitously ugly. I know you two were in love."

"Let the subject go!"

"I can't stop saying wrong things. I idolized you two — God, I'm doing it again. Help me, please! I've got a lump in my middle. Sit with me. Let's talk about other things. I'm not a killer bitch."

I looked at her pleading. Wanted to say something forgiving.

I had my own lump in my middle.

I walked off.

A bitter girl beat me flat.

I was rearranging space, packing that void. Fran tore everything open.

My hand passed through soft warm air. Now, nothing. Then it hummed. Spun when Nina tossed her long dark hair. Space alove. Space alive. On my cheeks like saltspray.

A sudden bombball and my universe lay flat. This breast bone once nestled her beautiful head. Softness burning my ribcage. A touch a kiss a surging soaring plunging hot wild wet loving.

I stamped my foot on the grassy ground. Pick up my vibration. Message from the front. Part is lust, all is love. Awash in each-other's wake. My love and I rode the jetstream.

Lost now. By earth's own murderous revolution.

At our table Fran sat. There's fine revolution for you.

Homeopathic remedies. Fran who smashed this space, this space repair.

Forgive one more wrecker. Hear that sinner confess! After I was nasty Jeeziebooda forgave. For him this shimmering tambourine. Rattle shake countcoins! Between Boodajeezie my shrink and Jeeziebooda my bloodbrudda I am returned to society a better poison than when I was only a borgiabitch.

Learn off me, ye piranhas.

We bartered at that patio table, a link with the outside world for her, a warming windswept memory for me.

Her analyst ventured I was friendly.

"Charlene," Fran said, "so impressed good sense on me I gave up my baby. Kierkegaard fulltime came next. I fulfilled the abstract leaning I showed by giving up a living child. I do right by Kierky and Nietsch, neither of whom starred in the boy-girl Olympics. My analyst tells me my redeemer liveth."

"It is so?"

"And yours too. A grownup girl with swimming eyes —"

"You want to madam for me?"

"I'm sure you've spotted her already."

"This is twentieth-century America, Frances. Democracy, equality. If you madam me up a dark-haired girl, you must find my wife a date."

My father came to California for the first time, like a little boy. Came on a bus, his face pressed against window glass, living with the expectation the sun would never set, knowing it would and did. Long ago the doubleness began, a spring in his step, but also fall. I wished then I could free him from inevitabilities.

On that bus he watched mountains come true, men on horseback, minemouths in hillsides, evergreens spearing upward like linked arrowheads. At every stop he inhaled pines or coffee brewing or new-mown grass or burnt onions. Marveled at matchbox covers and sugar-cube wrappings and WANTED signs, read signatures in pantlengths and bootheels and swaggering walks. Everything sprang to proper attention. Divine sparks swept up by the handful.

Gad and I spotted him as the bus rolled into the station, excited at the door, eyes wide and shining. Child lost in the woods come to tell only the wonders of flowers and sweet berries. He carried a holiday world with him. Bubbles from Yellowstone's azure pool, spray specks from its blowing geyser.

I loved his tweed sportcoat (later, not later enough, I hated that coat) and the rusty sportshirt open at his thin throat. He had shaved at the last stop, two red nicks on his chin, a missed spot, gray stubble peppered dark.

He cried, grown man, as he cried that lost-ago day by the river. But we walked him into the palm tree world, and it woke his wonder.

Let me frame him once more, broken man praising the world he has passed through. His mouth is drawn to one side. His arms move, gathering in, pulling space toward himself as a weakening swimmer, swept out to sea by the strongest current, tries to hug the receding land.

Marred man. Uncle Bim's palimpsest of a face I looked at long ago, to find the earlier Bim faces I myself had never seen. Timework. My father's face is marred by more than time. Men's pictures in posters are scrawled over with words and moustaches and slashes, but those with style still come through recognizable, definite. I read a message on my father's face: "Conclude nothing depressing from what you see. Life is more important than my defeats or victories."

News he brought.

Of Gersh's sister Evvie. And her hallucinatory relatives. Her familiars, her very own dramatis personae who, though they terrified her, could always be relied upon to be there. Not good company but company. Ugly enemies a last link with the outside world — like death-house guards. Daylight chairs turned into their shoulders and humped heads. The smallest ones huddled sneakily in fruitbowls. They talked to the wind and passing car tires. Dirty smelly ssssss things. Once they sprang all at once out of one closet. Evvie screamed and screamed. On the train in a locked room her mother and father couldn't stop that screaming. And in the barber chair tranquilizers couldn't stop it, and not even gas, and the man from the south did it quickly, a probe, a flick, leaving only a faint black eye to show she had had lobotomy.

In less than a week she bore no sign at all.

When she came back, they were waiting.

"I had a holiday," Evvie pretended.

"You plotted to kill us."

Paranoid hallucinates. Once they whispered, now they shrieked.

A man took Evvie to a red brick building on flat blackloamed ground. Her familiars followed like mourners behind a hearse, speeding up when her car speeded up, slowing when it slowed.

And like her became permanent residents of the red brick building.

When they recognized this was not his monthly performance, they did as they were told, and left him, all but I.D., whose beautiful wife wheeled him in, staring with fixed eyes, his head and hands in a terrible palsy, a ruled yellow legal pad on his quivering knees, blank, to remain blank. I.D. could not write now, nor speak, nor, perhaps, hear.

Dobrushyn's hand pounded air, draining his last small store of energy much as an alcoholic doesn't throw aside a bottle till it is dry.

"At night," he said, "I listen to it crackle. Their hatred. It should by rights light bulbs for the whole city. I.D., guess how many times I did like Samson, told the whole secret? Just be men and tell your father to go plump to hell with his money! I made this house a infirmary. I forced they should carry from me like Japanese. In the dark I hear their hatred, but I don't see one single sign of guts.

"And him, pushed into the old folks' home. Big hero! His kids threw him aside like a wore-out shoe! I won by a technical K.O., I.D. Nobody can feud with a man in the old folks' home! But he didn't have the brains to know I won! He died proud! He died winners! Those same kids carry his face. Stuckup queens and handsome princes. When it's down to the thousandth generation they'll still hold their beautiful heads high and walk through the world as if Bim was the king who marched slaves out of Egypt. Their noses will be his, and their hands, and his voice will make a king's sound in a hundred hundred people.

"And me, I.D. The years found me out already. These lousy snivelers will cry for my money you will wave under their noses, I.D. Thirsty men, chained by me two feet from fresh cold water. I'll lie — not to you — but I'll lie, and brag. To the devil and his imps I'll brag — how I died like a emperor in my palace, and him like a dog in the mountains."

Dobrushyn raised himself on one elbow.

"Idiots," he called to the closed door, "come in this second, idiots, and hear what I.D. has to say."

We walked on the sand.

"Pa," I shouted, "face the waves."

He shaded his eyes.

I led him to the water's edge. A wave ran up and over his feet. He shivered.

"How do men forget this?" he said.

I ducked into a wave, dove, up again, watching him tramp into the water, shoulders hunched, trailing his wrists in the foam. Like a cardboard calendar leaf coming down, a wave stood flat, dropped, crashing water at his feet, upended him, arms and legs thrashing, a clumsy cartwheel tumbled on the pebble shore.

I charged out of the water. He lay, scrape-faced, eyes and hair powdered with sand.

"I did a dumb thing," he said, "what you told me not to. Exactly."

I rubbed white sand off his face. He opened his eyes.

"I was dead one split second, facing the sun. The beach was burning light."

He brushed his hair hard. Sand showered in pepper specks.

"For one second. Look at me now. Silly old guy who turned his back on a wave, and got ducked."

I wanted to tell him about Nina then.

I'm sorry I didn't blurt it out, take a chance and shatter our separated moralities. I would not bet on the trading currency of our languages. Nor intrude my generation on his. So the moment passed into a planemotor roar and a disappearing speck in the north sky.

A paper coffee cup settled on the metal mesh tabletop.

"Do you mind?"

A floppy orange beach hat and dark glasses hid a girl's face.

"We could have been introduced," she said, and a pretty mouth smiled, "long ago, by our mutual friend, Frances. Her mother has died. She is home."

I couldn't place her accent. Bulgarian. Rumanian. Perhaps Israeli.

"My name is Gyla. With a 'y' if you would bill me."

I held out my hand.

"You were shining red and smiling as I came up. What could give such extreme pleasure in the mind?"

"Daydreams."

"Excuse me. I did not mean to make small talk. Frances was very upset by death. She wanted you to know —"

"Why?"

"She thinks of you as a close friend."

"She doesn't need my permission to think that."

"Why did you say something ugly?"

"I'm sorry."

"You are irritated. I broke your beautiful mood. Would you like me to move?"

"Of course not. I apologize."

"We had another mutual friend. A very special one."

"Do me a favor? Take off those goggles and that hat."

"You want to scrutinize me?"

She drew her hat up at a stripper's pace, held it poised above her head, let it drop, undid one earpiece of her glasses, pretended to fumble with a catch in back of her head. The glasses fell into the hat.

I applauded.

Her hair was a dark brown, wavy, lighter where she parted it on the side. Her brows and lashes were almost black, her eyes deepset, nose thin and humped, flushed and weatherheightened as her cheeks. She wore no make-up.

As I looked, a flush reddened her throat.

"It is not nice of you to take so long."

"You're beautiful. You didn't need me to tell you."

"You are not letting me in."

"In?"

"That mutual friend."

"Can you tell me our mutual friend will be at this table later today?"

"I'm sorry. I can't do that. Nobody can."

"How do you know Fran?"

"Ha. The gentleman wants the subject changed."

"Will the lady oblige?"

"*Ladies* always oblige."

"I'm glad you sat here."

"Are you making love to me, or loneliness?" Her blush heightened. "Knowing what I know I would have to think myself secondbest."

"We could talk intimately, and dispense with ratings."

"Are you of Spartan stuff?"

"Probably not. You are a very beautiful girl."

"When I sat, I had no notion we would soon be talking so. I know a lot about you."

"And you? That ring?"

"My husband is my father's venturesome business partner."

"What do *you* do on a campus?"

"Teach languages. Ten. A dozen."

"Then go home to your husband?"

"Eventually."

I slid her glasses back onto her face.

"You hate my eyes?"

"Like them too well, too soon."

I took her hand off the coffee cup.

"Gyla."

"You say my name gently."

"Beautiful women always have beautiful names."

"Thank you, though I don't appreciate the populated category."

"We've been acting like penpals."

"I have a Westwood apartment. I tutor there. Tell me, young gentleman, is your heart ready for a ride?"

"I don't know."

"Thank you, at least, for your honesty."

She walked gracefully, carried the orange hat like a bag. The flush left her cheeks and throat.

"Perhaps we should part here? I mean for this day."

"Forgive the grump, Gyla. I'm dying to see your place."

We drove saying little. Entered the apartment silently, the room bare but for a desk and a couple of chairs.

"We will inaugurate this inkpot," she said shyly.

I pulled a wall bed down. The foot teetered a few inches above the floor. The sheetless mattress was bright blue.

We were too reasonable. I teased her back zipper down unstampeded. She let her dress fall. With no urgency I took off the rest of her clothes.

Her lips were dry, though warm. Soft, restful friendliness, well mannered. Her breasts smelled of Spanish sandalwood perfume.

Not lust, compassion overwhelmed me. I hugged her, kissed the blush on her cheek.

"Gyla," I whispered, "you are beautiful, loving, and wonderful."

She hugged my back.

"I love the feel of you. In, out."

Her upper teeth were biting her lower lip. In full passion I would not have seen. What did Nina look like then? A billow, a tremor, a burst of light.

Bastard, to have such thoughts.

"Were we here alone?"

"What does that mean?"

"Our mutual friend was, perhaps, just a little in attendance?"

"You are here, Gyla. And I."

"None other?"

"Pandora's box is always everywhere."

With foot poised over the last step of Gyla's landing I remembered a chill in the pit of my stomach, the feverish throbbing desire which sent me running toward Nina: we always came together like two crisscrossing cresting waves.

Gyla called for me to enter.

She spoke on the phone in some strange tongue, raspy, vulgar, her soft mouth twisted crudely.

She sat in profile, cheekbones shiny pink, her head dipped down like a young filly.

I reached to pull off her shoe. She offered her other foot. I raised her, still talking, out of her chair, slid her to the floor. Her sweater was next, one arm free, then the free hand took the receiver, and she gave her other arm.

"Mother should only know," she whispered.

"Ask if it's O.K. for me to kiss you everywhere?"

She growled that strangely peasant tongue into the phone, stroking, kissing. Shook me off, pointed, frowning, to the door. I locked and chained it.

I kissed her mouth. Long eyelashes brushed my cheek. She trembled. Shaking violently, a girl all poise, high of manner in sunlight.

We made love with no urgency. No hunger. No terrible violent drive toward a wild and lovely end. We didn't make for each other the great thing wanting.

I sat over her as light drained out of the window. Twilight: time for two leavetakings.

"I'm wrong for this kind of thing." she said, "I should get a kick out of our being in league. Bagatelle doesn't excite me. Adultery even less."

"Should we go back to dreaming?"

"If it *matters*, we should change our lives. If it's less, we're wicked. Humanly, do you understand?"

"I do."

"I can never understand *lovers*. That's mere time-deferral. Marriage underlines."

"Gyla, why so profound?"

"You have thought these things too. Please reach out to my weeping soul? I am not what I seem."

"Let's begin with a corrected playback. I'll sit on the patio and you'll come to me without the orange hat. No oblique talk about a mutual friend. No fencing, no seduction chatter. Let's begin right here and now."

"Are you going to reward me with wild passion because I have been a good serious girl?"

"Yes."

She laughed.

"You know what I think? You would have been prepared to live in Eden without Eve. You gave up a rib because you needed not just her warm body but her wonder, which only you could minister to. You want me to know what you knew, or saw, first. And if I — Eve — prove exceptional, you in gratitude tear my clothes off and ram me into the mattress. And tell me again I'm beautiful."

I put my arms around her.

She threw them off.

"You cannot injure and comfort me with the same gesture! I may be on the threshold of a new world you are dying to experience. But — please look at me — you are not willing to enter this world with me."

In dusk her eyes shaded hurt. Boy-girl rules called for instant denial: those eyes begged something else.

"We found each other out," she said, "having an American affair. Remain strangers. Is that not the injunction? I have almost broken the code. To go on in my manner we would have to be more than bed pals. So I take it back. Tomorrow let us meet, same time, same bed. Not quite tabula rasa, of course. Neither lover forgets a rule was broken. But I am a well-mannered young lady. Though I am not sorry I behaved unAmerican."

"Nor I."

"Thus *à demain*, Adam."

"Thus *à demain*, sweet surprising Eve."

"Don't fall in love with surprise or sweetness."

We sat shyly knee to knee. She wore a shirt open at the collar, sleeves pushed up. Her hair just washed, glowing soft and brown.

"Yesterday," I said, "I met you for the first time."

"I did not meet *you* for the first time."

"Hey, peace."

"Tell me," she said suddenly, "what will I be? Ten years from now. Will I end up a pancake?"

"Turned and warm and nibbled and sweet?"

"No — flat and pale and dry, and turned *only* if somebody turns me."

"What's wrong with turning when somebody turns you?"

She pressed her face against mine.

"What do you *know* about me?"

"You speak a thousand languages, you're gorgeous — and tough."

"Tough?"

"Minded."

"Where was I during the war?"

"I don't know."

"I have you now in a Socratic box. How old am I?"

"Twenty-five, -six?"

"Perhaps. Perhaps less. How old was I when war broke out — in Europe, I mean?"

"Ten, perhaps eleven?"

I pulled the wall bed down with a slam.

"You want to make love to me?"

"God yes."

"Only to get out of the Socratic quandary!"

"Only to get out of nothing."

"I'll confess then. Everything was calculated to fill you with burning ardor."

I slid her shirt off her shoulders, flipped down her bra.

"My arms are caught."

"You are now a helpless female."

"Don't you want to know where I was during the war?"

"In the midst of pulling these clothes off you?"

"Untouched American! Innocent!"

"You look magnificent!"

"Oh, take me, take me," she mocked, and fell back, laughing.

"What should I know that I could not suspect?"

"That I too fled Hitler."

"Too?"

"Like our mutual friend."

"Did you know her there?"

"Shame on you! About which of us do you want to know?"

She heard the big city fall in sound which was not lightning-thunder. Mother came and sat. Father left the house. The sky speckled, wrinkled. Ugly furrows changing, fast, so angry. Bombs. Things with runners, tanks, went slow, shot loud hard. Every one was German.

Same house, same blankets, same mother. Outside, horses neighed. A sound — fright — big people's fright. A house was like a boat. Warm inside the cold sea. Storms washed foam over decks, ships humped, dipped, nosed up. Sometimes a ship went under.

Mother was crying.

"What is war, mother? Parades!"

"Against Jews there are two wars," her mother said.

"We will have peace after. Don't worry."

They ran in a flow, as if every horse had in his teeth the tail of the horse in front of him, white black brown stream, soldiers laying over, dirty bandage and slings, black brown gray red right through the town, clop clop clop day and night and airplanes and hard cannon and hard bombs hard in her chest. Germans wanted hurt. Bombs exploded deep holes. Old men old women children sheep cows dogs followed the horses. Deep holes broke where they passed. Moaning clop clop faster and screams. At night the sky glowed. No firemen came ever. Smoke and char and cloth burning. And roasting sheep baby lambs. And old old horses. Burning burning. The town was burning.

Mother made her leave bed. Put *that* on. Black, hard, on a chain. Mother never wore anything around the neck. And told her, oh in an angry voice.

"You are *not* pretending, Gyla. Kiss this cross. It is your only doll. Love the nuns. Do what the nuns tell. I will wear a cross too. Father when he can come back will wear a cross. Gyla, you must not fail us."

"I will not fail, mother."

"Kiss the cross now."

Cold.

All black back and mostly black front. White faces. Theirs were silver. Black beads mother almost forgot to give. You counted and told, not as often as the nuns. They rustled scary. One was nice. But some not. Jew kids, that one said, eat Christian children's food. Gyla learned to make herself small — eat only a little, shrink back into shadows, pray softly, never hit back, never cry when they pinched. You couldn't stand sideways for everybody. When there were faces all around, somebody had to see all of you. You could pretend to be a playing card, thin as the edge. Tuck the braid down the back of the dress.

Germans. The blacker ones were worse. Hate mouths black open. Hate eyes pop to bursting.

Mother sneaked out of that nice barn with eggs. Nun Twitchtipnose took them without thank you. And stared at mother.

Mother was very thin. Her face was dirty. Her eyes pulled in. A smaller voice.

Older nun told the Germans every day that no Jews were there. Nun Twitchtipnose bowed her head. Like boys when they were scolded.

"Mother," Gyla whispered, "make yourself more tiny. Stand sideways always."

Mother went away. Bad nun didn't say goodbye. And stared after mother too long. A German came in the night.

"You have Yid kids here?"

"There are no Jews here," bad nun said again. "Only Christians."

Gyla wondered if bad nun made a secret signe. And felt her cheeks burn for an hour. And went through it again, and again, during a hundred hundred other nights, and days.

She thought of herself as Snegourka, the snowmaiden.

Snegylaka.

Her most beautiful story. Without a happy end.

The war was the sun Snegourka hid from. High hot flames melting everybody. The children didn't know why Snegylaka stayed in the shade and had dark tiny hiding places and couldn't be found. At night the children forgot motorcycles and hooting horns and the feet and shouts, and laughed together. Snegylaka slid under the covers. That terrible smashing, wood, and glass. A tank rising slowly, iron breaking walls. Chestbursting, earpounding. The world was German. But Snegourka was beautiful and a blessing on her old mother and old father, and spoke gently and in every way was wonderful and sweet and loving, except the hot summer was too strong. Snegourka couldn't hide forever; suddenly she was gone. She did not come back. In real life a mother and a father would hide Snegourka under a baking apron.

Day was night, summer was fall and winter and spring, everything running together in hide. Hide day, hide all night all seasons. How many hides in a year? And how many years? And how many old? Ten eleven twelve thirteen — did mother come only twice a month or twice a year? Without eggs or bread or honey. And which was the dream, *before* the big city fell, when summer was flowers and no black shadows hid the sun? That dream: once she spoke in a loud voice, and ran down the middle of a street. The dream world was the one with colors. They came out a wave of black crosses and frightened her hiding behind her father who was laughing. Now *she* was in the middle of their black, and around *her* throat this was swinging. Far away was worse. All bones, or nothing left. Black tunnel. Was there such a story, of children in sunlight finding a cave and going inside? Dark at *both* ends. That cave. That tunnel. Germans were invisible in the dark. They must have been there always. Like the people who watched for them.

Bad nun looked. She could give you away. Being a nun you shouldn't, but some nuns did.

During that night they brought two new girls. And why during the night if they weren't Jewish. In the morning she saw cousin Elsie. Who wet. And cried. And always smelled of wet. But Aunt had told Elsie about Gyla, and Elsie looked frightened, but dropped her eyes. She smelled terrible. Bad nun scolded. It was good nobody knew someone who still wet was Gyla's cousin.

Bad nun grabbed her hand.

"Come child, to the chapel."

And dragged her across the yard though everyone was eating.

Threw her on her knees roughly, but not as if punishing.

"Pray for Elsie," bad nun said.

Gyla prayed. Such sudden praying. For Elsie not to wet again? It could not go wasted, such a prayer. But bad nun was crying. So Gyla cried too. Bad nun helped her up, still quite rough. Mother came, weeks or was it years later, and said Aunt's purse was taken, and a nun's note about Elsie wetting found. And Gyla prayed for Elsie again. And asked God's forgiveness for hating that smell. But not for hating *them*, who really did kill children. And prayed hard that someone would flash a silver crucifix, or drive a wooden stake through their hearts.

They told bad nun if she didn't give them up they would kill *all* the girls. And bad nun told farmer who was hiding mother. Bad nun said Russians were even worse. Gyla asked if Russians killed children, and black nun said millions.

When there was a worst, there was a still worst. A darker tunnel.

Mother came in the dark and they got in farmer's hay mother had cheese and tiny crumbs they scrunched up tiny eating like mousies while bombs and cannon a day or two days and stopping only to go but then farmer said no further and out from under the hay in moonlight with mother's hand a crumb of cheese more and a crumb of bread and crusted snow and Russians fired west and Germans fired east far red closer orange and mother was same old mother one skinny hand on her shoulder telling all the stories even when cheese was in her mouth and oh mother forgot years had gone and Gyla was older and mother was mother before the hiding and those baby fairy stories inside her months and years like

the white horse who was dawn and the red horse who was sun and
the skulls with lights in them and Gyla was not Snegourka or
Snegylaka but Vasilisa and for the dolly in her pocket saved a
crumb of her crumb and if you kept moving feet wouldn't be cold
and sleepiness couldn't come and mother sang in the night under
the moon and crusted snow the sun melted to glass and mother's
foot cracked like a pistol shot and she almost fell and wouldn't
admit her foot was soaking or even look down but kept telling like
Scheherazade who wanted to keep someone else alive Gyla in the
night cold and so frightening but something of a holiday in it being
able to look up at the moon and the dark hiding place farther and
farther away and mother a little silly saying we can't stop only a
little bit farther when there wasn't anything in the world which
would have made Gyla stop and so she listened politely and egged
mother on though she too could tell stories but in her heart she
knew mother's old too-young stories were better.

I hugged Gyla to me, pressed together like survivors of a disaster,
wordless, grateful. Survival made her something fiercely female.

"I adore you," I said.

"As something symbolic only?"

"As somebody gorgeous."

"But still keep yourself in hiding."

"I would not describe me as hiding a thing at this moment."

"Oh you poor vulnerable darlings. Infants! Destructive lovable
infants!"

"Destructive?"

"You all were brutal in Japan."

"You include me?"

"Naturally. I am all women, you are all America — poof! Listen
— look at me — I *know* you have survived something, right?"

"I have survived."

"No, you're fencing. I mean something terrible. A crisis, a trial.
You keep asking yourself if this day is worth the one which kept

you alive. I know you. I've seen the value you put on ordinary
things. They're mine. I know how I came by seeing the sky.
Haven't we been sending each other secret messages?"

"Not so secret —"

"Oh you terrible person! You still deny me! Flesh against my
flesh and no sparks can fly — you hold that hidden self from me.
Are our chemistries that wrong?"

"No, sweet girl. I love being here —"

"Being here — that is a consolation prize — you people are so
dishonest but your language is full of brutal frank words."

"I think you are magnificent."

"I am hurt by you, do you feel that? You are still loyal — I think
we must break it up. Maybe you will be loyal to me too. I don't
think your loyalty is such a virtue. Tomorrow, the day after, we'll
look back at this and think — a poor affair, but it was ours, all ours.
Right? I mean the American minute our tame love lasted."

The day after was too full of sun.

Pale pale sky, unclouded unshaded predictable sun.

It seemed a time to go.

Gyla was not the cause. Nina was not the cause. Perhaps such
motion has no exact cause. As Tolstoi had it, at particular times
bodies of men move from West to East, at others from East to
West.

I left those Lombard buildings, drove into that parking lot in
bright sunlight. No car resembled Nina's. No mockingbird sang.
No orange hat sat at the outdoor tables down the hill. I drove past
Percy Guralin's street, the garage where Levitt backed his car to-
ward Hettie. Walked past Uncle Baer's lemontree, glanced up at
Lila's patio sunlit and deserted.

Maggie was waiting.

"Hey," I said "how about chucking this town?"

"Great! I've been waiting for you to say something like this."

She stretched her arms easily, leaned back with a graceful bend. Her hair was soft, her nose newly freckled.

"You've been ignoring me, do you know that? If I didn't know you were working so hard I would think that black bitch Zora was in town."

"You were supposed to expunge Zora —"

"Don't you know my life here has been miserable? I can't stand another week of Aunt Teena. You've been studying. I didn't want to worry you. She's been bugging me. Now I know what happened to Tamara —"

"Don't be a bitch —"

"You wouldn't know. You left me to Gad and Gersh and Bitner and Christopher — ask them about Aunt Teena. Ask them anything about me. They're the ones who know me, you bastard."

"O.K.," I said, "we'll go East and make a life."

"Terrific!"

She stretched her arms higher, turned her head to one side, looked at me, smiled quizzically.

Uncle Baer wept. Aunt Teena's thick glasses clouded. My brother Gad tried to say something but Uncle Baer got to his feet and stood in the center of the room.

"I'm gonny tell you something," he said. "You are old enough to make decisions and me and aunty and Gad ain't gonny interfere. You travel all over the country — you're young, you should. But we got God's garden growing here. Stay away long as you gotty. And when you want to come back you're gonny get a welcome like they give generals and emperors. Young people got to see the world. Aunty especially wants you to see everything, my princess! And you, Maggie make him happy like she makes me — look at her, natural beauty, angel. God knows I don't deserve her!"

EAST

space spun

W<small>E</small> drove out through a burial ground for the unmentioned losers, failed Eastern dreamers who never quite made it to the Pacific. The other frontier. Tombstones wind-eroded bore no trace of names; abandoned mineshafts overgrown with dry hanging vines; treadless tractors precarious on pitched hillsides. Burnt-out barns set in a ring of charred field; foundations unbuilt on; fences falling, their circle never closed, senseless in the bleak setting of trees choked by twisting grapevines themselves dry and dead.

Higher further inland, even the domestic doom marks were missing. On Mono Lake a thin bird pecked at its dark reflection in the slaggy water. The world was moon or Mars, horizon jagged with inverted stone funnels, played-out volcanoes, mere shells now filled with dead space. Black stone hung on the gray water, sheer basalt waterfall crinkled at the margin with lava and flowers of funereal coke.

A day we climbed, the land momentarily green, but the Carson Sink pulled us back into sand, volcanic ash. Our long colorless road grew red with animal death. Shadowcasting birds unraveled bloodraw innards, old old scavengers in new ecological partnership with man's accommodating autos.

We drove where sand and sun and sky differentiated no century. Space bent, heat-clogged, inert, primordial slime crystallized.

I pulled Maggie closer.

The car's motor, groaning like Sisyphus, pushed on up its metal-coated boulder.

A green mirage of Tetons cut the sky, target for our labored chase upward in hairpin turns which sent shale skidding in sheer drop over the unprotected ledge.

Halfway up a truck roared in charge toward us, horn blowing, open doors the flapping ears of a runaway elephant. The driver yipped like a broncobuster. I wrenched the wheel violently to one side, wrestled the car to a steep climb. It shook like a kettle lid. Bucked and threatened backing. I pulled over to a small plateau as steam hissed from the bobbing hood. All space boiled loose.

Then settled. Like a curtain parting.

Sun flew at us. Flashed on milky ice clinging to rock in massive shields. Sun richocheted mischievously, dazzling, as if a thousand small boys played at light with blinding mirrors.

Sun rode with us eastward, blank white in the squinty morning, dodging out of rocky canyons. It steamed us at noon. Warmed our backs toward evening, red in the rearview mirror, darkening, suddenly gone.

We rode rims of rock, rock shelves pink and red and chalky. Rock buckling, tumbling, sheer with evergreen slides, buried deep in gray dirt, red, brown soil, disappearing finally under sea-level loam foaming black. Familiar earth slanty with windruffled wheat. Grain elevators were land lighthouses, twin blank tablets of the Law impressed on prairie topsoil. Over meshed silos small birds hovered in neutral, chained to a small square of space.

Land lost flatness, suddenly undulated, rolling in corn. Towns washed against our windshield, gasoline pumps in two's like salt and pepper shakers. On side spurs old railway cars tricked into being diners.

It was all space. For us it had no history.

I should have known time's dancers were leaping on that hood.

The river was its first signal, and powerline derricks, skeleton transmitters, rail lines crowding closer, overhung with city-thick strands of wire silvergreengold, Lippoldloveliness. Above the crisscross tracks ceramic insulators, brown and shiny, were disc cultivators harrowing the sky.

Drivers read the city rhythm and raced their motors. Mufflerless Fords and Mercurys turned the road suddenly into a drag strip, roaring by in the outside lane like horses in all-out sprint. I too tensed for the stretch, wheel to wheel with a similarly hung-up stranger.

Till I saw the Bridge.

Slim, graygreen, tube held up by graceful greengray pegs.

I raced for the walled city.

The Bridge held the sun in ropes of metal. Imprisoned all that glow in bars of steel shade. Light rushed to the water silvery beneath it, glanced off its towers in a scatter of gold. On its long shaded avenue of tall metal trees sun ran against girders like a small boy's stick on a picket fence.

The city. Never before did I know a city. Or such a church, pointed stone arrow ornate and feathered. A skyful of hubris. Concrete Indian ropetricks hung in the sky.

I read the city's sign: *Abandon all imagination, ye who enter here.*

It was all there in New York, whatever I had dreamed when I pressed my nose against my window glass and saw little or nothing. Here a world kaleidoscoped with every turn of my head. One tiny corner of one insignificant building could have kept me going for hours. In a city-second we were at a masque, a bazaar, circus, flea-market; open or canopied, junkheap, labyrinth, ratrun, geek gallery, gem setting, Eden, Sodom, Arden, thumbflick of unmatched cards flashed by a teasing gambler.

At 125th Street black girders crisscrossed over our heads, smoke-surrounded cathedral floating hollow-walled, shunning light. A train charge through the sky shivered abutments, roared retreat, vanished in an instant. A gaggle of Negro rollerskaters whipped in a turn off Broadway. A siren, kid crying, made trio with a garbage truck moaning. A hard ball bounced off a buckled aluminum door.

Over an acetylene torch hooded men straddled broken stand-pipes, dog pools full of cigar butts. A dumptruck's unhooked gate let fall a white mountain of gypsum.

Crosstown I looked for news of the sun. Dark valley where trucks leaned one wheel on the curb, crippled. Volleys exploded, thunderclaps, from handball courts sheer above our heads, windowladdered walls higher than my car-enclosed eye could see. Subways beneath us roared. All around us smashage, breakage, toppled-over bulks and masses. Anywhere else one such sound alone would have stopped all motion.

A face from El Greco gawked crazily as I drove by. A man stood at an angle I thought possible only in Soutine. A redfaced executive threw up politely into a freshly painted trashbasket, his bowler clasped cleverly to his sick head.

I stopped.

Twenty horns roared me *go!*

A cop pointed at me.

If any one wall bore a new message of Sinai I would not have been able to stop to take it in. Like the Dutch hero sailing into port to do battle with the crouching enemy, only to be swept out to sea by the unaccommodating wind.

At a cross street the light turned red. When it changed I entered the intersection.

Forgotten sun poured into the streets. Windswept, buffeted, dustflaked it gusted the avenues, struck fire in dull chrome, speckled glass, rocked on canopies, sprang yellowgreen from windowboxed plants, and potted trees.

Faces turned upward to be warmed.

Windows swung wide, scattering sun another window reflected, window to window, towering scaffold of climbing gold. Sun gyrated in mist northward. Black turned color, crosshatchings un-

earthed, hidden diagonals, brickscorch, wall cracks. For one second
the city froze in etching.

But horns honked me back into line, and the walled sky took
over.

I brought a paper, and found the world hidden to L.A.'s eye.
The Pacific's MacArthur, whose jaw jutted, who wore a white
ascot, whose hat was a South American generalissimo's, was an el-
derly Manhattan civilian in herringbone and homburg. Without
his dark glasses I would never have known him.

I burrowed the city, came out on its eastern side.

Night town, IBM card, windows punched slits. The Empire State
Building glowed like a grotesque commercial for spark plugs.

Signs said "WEST — NEW YORK."

The Sound held my shadow long and thin in the car beam, fading into darkness. My bare foot squished frothy bubbles filling a
six-foot rut an earthmover tire dug. Seaweed nodules were lit-up
pearls in the high beam's green light. Fish schooled around me as I
waded in, swirling phosphorescent streaks, lightning bugs darting
in tag, circling, gone. A hundred silverflecks of minnow at my ankles, beneath them two leathery horseshoe crabs ghostly, floating
on wavery shadows.

I dived into graygreen suffusion, Sound aquarium. Water rolling
off my face trickled into the night of peepers, cicadas, and shrill
truck tires.

Over Maggie's bent head a North Shore train slithered like an
illuminated two-dimensional snake on a black screen of oaks.

She waited on shore, holding a towel out to me, her knees bare
in the car's beam, strained white.

Running at, not fearing, consequences. Loinloose. We'd never
known nakedness. Prevent nothing. Passed through every looking

glass. Past soundspeed, lightspeed, moonwash, tidewash. Dizzy
dazzled two spun onespun brainthroatgroinknee spunfree hurtling
hangon brokeyokebrokewhiteallinashellallgainedallawashallamix.

Maggie slid her hands over her round white belly. Beautiful cat-
terpillar marveling at miraculous slow transformation to beautiful
butterfly.

"I look great!"

She rubbed her nipples with a thick terrytowel. Lost in work. A
champion swimmer preparing her body for a channel crossing.

"My mother didn't, but by God, I'm going to."

Her nipples stood up, reddened past their usual pink. Maggie
blew her bangs off her forehead with an upward jet. Bit down on
her lower lip, resumed rubbing.

She walked ahead of Christopher and me, her feet turned out
like Chaplin. Her hand checking her great belly heaved like a
moored boat.

"By God, Mag," Christopher said, "you're that creamy mother
type, greatest-looking pregnant woman the world's ever seen."

Grabbed her hand. With the other took mine.

"Listen," he burst out, "that bitch Sammie's gone!"

He patted her pillow. Her head wasn't there.

She brushed her hair before the sunlit window. Dressed for a
party. Seven A.M. The baby dressed for outside.

She lobbed something through the air. A braid, her hair. Cut
through, like the severed ends of a ship's mooring.

"You crazy bitch, you cut that off."

"Lend it to me when I need it, Chris."

He flew out of bed.

"That's not yours to cut! That's *my* hair."

"I'm leaving it with you."

"Put that back on, goddam it! Scalping yourself! Is the whole world nuts with masochistic symbolism."

"Blind bastard — I've been wearing it as a switch for weeks."

Her hair came to her shoulders, caught up in a dark headband. Chris squinted. Now she looked like only another California girl.

"I'm leaving, Chris," she said.

"Leaving me? The greatest fucker ever?"

"Dumby, this is serious. You'll never see me again."

"You require me."

"Chris, I've been working as a model for months. You haven't noticed. Tell the truth now."

"You've been showing those gorgeous tits?"

"No, idiot. Chintzy chintzy modeling. Hairstyles."

"So why cut my hair?"

"He made me do it."

"Didn't you tell him to fuck himself?"

"He pays me piles of money."

"Since when do you need piles of money?"

"Since you white sonsofbitches stole my country from me!"

Two red leather cases on the walk, her cornhusk doll deadmansfloat over them. Dried, yellowed. Bark canoe. Sealmask the kid screamed at in fright. Indian kids don't cry, eh.

"It's another guy, isn't it?"

"You mean one of my own kind?"

"You know goddam well what I mean, paranoid bitch!"

She tugged at his ear.

"I can't stand your *world*. But you're different, honey."

Christopher couldn't laugh back.

"I'll tell my relatives some of my best friends are palefaces."

"Get your goddam clothes off!"

"Chris, I'm through passing."

"You've been with some self-pitying spades."

"I'm through being the highbrow Halfbreed Katie, grateful some drunk miner shacks up with her for a week."

"If I'm the miner in the analogy I'll throw up. If I'm not I'll beat the shit out of the guy who is."

She held her hand out. Lovely beauty spot on her wrist. Another on her left breast.

"Your mommy can't shake this without thinking T.B. or syphilis."

"What does mother have to do with this?"

"I was born beautiful. So I got a bye. Halfbreed Katie stands in for me."

"I've heard enough bullshit. What is the matter with you?"

"I'm rejecting you, white man. You could never make it in my village."

"What will you do, train the braves to lie down in front of bull-dozers?"

"I'll teach them double-entry bookkeeping — I learned it at night school."

"You?"

"You think responsibility in a good lay is cute."

"One beautiful girl can't hold back my paleface tide."

"I can stop their Baptist whining."

"At least substitute the Internationale, not some goddam war chant."

Without another word she sat the baby in her yellow papoose-bag woven in Sweden.

In the front seat she checked the belt around the baby, kicked off her heels, wiggled her painted toes on the floorboard pedals. White Minnie Mouse sunglasses hid her eyes. Yellow Finnish shift stuffed into the leather totebag.

She ducked her head to pin her braid in.

Indian chants, poems, missionaries' memories. Buried truths in

Baptist archives. *Give us your cornthings for these autographed photos of Christ.*

Princess Samalatis forelady, who once withdrew into anthropology and a white shack-up, is returning. Therapist princess. Rehabilitationer, chauffeur, manager, most modern schiz. *Now I lay my fatties down to sleep. I pray the lord their hair to keep.*

Hairotron. Filaments. Man putting his head against it might not notice. But let him lay a hand there! Bourgeois contraception: the number of babies fag hairdressers prevented! Poor Marvin, cock shot down by a can of spray.

The tarpaper shacks insulated with *Los Angeles Sunday Times.* Two toothless old men in the roofless Model A's front seat. What she and Chris would blow on a dinner could hold them six months. Beautiful old men. Dry lips. Shadows on cheeks.

Sammie will save.

Modern dance notation. Merce Cunningham ritual Indian dance.

God I'm absurd!

Three little girls danced in the dust. Lousy drums the old men made. Handicrafts. Phony phony phony. Sammie the forelady rarely rejects. New concept for the sosh market. My people lived too long with reinforcement.

The old men had the blackboard mounted cockeyed.

All the kids will write on a slant. My A, my B. The older ones my walk. *My* talk. *My* song. Otherwise, nothing.

Princess Samalatis and her true original restored Indian village. Pitiful handmade imitations of beautifully crafted phoniness. My real Indians will sign Hong Kong totems with surplus ballpoints.

Her straw bag between her teeth, bare feet jigging, wiggle waggle wiggle waggle, kids laughing so hard their mouths open and bags fall into the dust.

Her hair piece lashed slowly from shoulder to shoulder. And keep the bellydance twitch out of your authentic ass, princess.

Sammie in jeans doing the doggydance. Just don't *sit*. Boneyard of Model A's, two dying grandfathers propped in the front seat, two dying grandmothers in the back.

Genocide incomplete, the rest sat and waited.

Bastards bastards paleface bastards.

A small hand tugged at her shirt's flying tails.

"Samalatis, please, can we stop now? My foots is dirty, my legs is tired."

The avocado seed smoothdryround, parted cleanly, its shoot an arrow, cleft it in two. Christopher's hands cupped the mottled glass planter.

"Mag, the mysterious East is it for you. Green thumb shows all over."

I put my hand on her firm warm belly; her flesh danced. Familiar sky, watched on the night a new planet is expected.

When Maggie's belly twitched we spoke in whispers.

"Time me."

I counted seconds, minutes, contractions, tremors, a fault line's message, superfluous as a clocker on the sidelines when some runner, lungs bursting, crashes through a four-minute mile.

My ear on the couch arm heard that dark hissing, shrieking rush of windtunnel time. Crumbling mountain, beatdown desert, discarded idols, fragmented golden calf. I would board arks and chase covenanting rainbows. Deal with such imps as knew how to make it with witches.

Blacker than dark, one remembered nightmare, black snowflakes falling, white birch-tree bark curled with char. Mindless of world end a gray ape was planning a mischief, though on his head the sky was falling shattered.

I yelled in that nightmare.

"Dumb lunatic ape, it's too late for evil!"

He didn't stop his business. Snow fell, blacker, those burning birch trees, gap-trunked, limb-stunted, were consumed in darkness.

The hospital woke me.

I drove under a sky swirling upward over a black road between blanksocketed nightdarkened factory walls. Windgusts peppered my metal with handfuls of rocksalt, churned snow up against my wheels like pursuing tumbleweed.

Roads unrolled, long asphalt contract snowswept with flaked smallprint clauses. I subscribed to everything. Offered a witch the wanted hair, promised the devil anything needed on the futures market.

This hospital.

Time, air squeezed out between clapping hands, collapsed. My metal chart that mousenight, and Mac's night, my mother's night, clashed on charts in the long corridor. An old elevator crashed gates in metal-bound mesh.

The waiting room's enameled shell, hollow, mounted at a switchboard this old lady, her hair tinycurl blackdye, creased face thin and chinless. A black snorkel tube grew up out of her chest. Over her a high Gothic window ornate as a pipe organ, black as predawn.

The phone was ringing, so dry, so dead. Her plug-in cut it off. Dry words to the dry tube. Her mouth a web.

Clotho?

Lachesis?

Please, please, never that other!

Babies cried behind blank walls. Sudden gasping screams, then silence.

Her blackdye curls were hard with hair spray.

"May I go in?" my voice somehow found strength to ask.

She blinked.

"We don't allow."

"How's my wife?"

"I ain't left. How'd I know?"

The phone rattled at her throat. She fumbled with a plug, jacked it in.

"Same room as Father Dominian?"

She clucked. The phone rustled back a sound.

"You sure?"

The sound rose.

"I only mean it would be better if he had went a hour or two later."

She hunched over the snorkel.

"It don't make no difference to them. I never seen Protestant ministers working here nights."

She stared at me.

"I oncet called one from the yellow pages but every family has their favorite."

She beckoned her headphones toward me.

"Sonny, a Protestant man is just dead upstairs. I got to find a good funeral parlor. Take over a sec. Your wife won't give birth while I'm gone."

The earphones were warm. Damp. The mouthpiece smelled garlic, whiskey, cloves.

"Things happen between shifts. Maybe with your wife, too, sonny. While the nights goes off and mornings ain't quite on."

Her glasses reflected the board's yellow light.

"See, nobody called."

I pleaded with my eyes.

"Doctor's in some kind of trouble. He's using high instruments."

She took the headphones from my dying hands.

A rinsing sweat, chill, life draining, loinwasting. Morning would not hold back. Mocking lying sunrise.

"Bad news," I heard her croak, "always comes in three's. You know Father Dominian. Then this Protestant man."

I found my fingers pinching my windpipe. Something missed. Gift borne for someone, the boat departed. On a wharf, trying to will the ship's return.

A misty face, all red, his glasses steamed, his surgeon's gown smeared with blood, his old scrubbed hands trembling, held out to shake mine.

"We got her," he said. "Fished for her."

Maggie's palms were red with indentations. I kissed her sour-smelling forehead, her swollen lips. She took my hands, pulled me down toward her, hesitated, gently placed my head to one side of her breasts.

"You were great," I said.

Face still full of business. Bones sharp under her soft transparent skin. Strain frozen in furrows, dug into creases.

I kissed her closed eyes. She lay flexed, still in the delivery room stance. Tumbling, in her dream I imagined, halfway home from this hurtling of the moon.

I followed the ancient bobbing head, guided by the white arm and trembling forefinger. White baskets, with slots, white cards with quickly scrawled names. On tiptoe, pressed against nursery glass I tried to see her. Could not tell. Could not have told, without that finger's point, and the bluepenned name.

Her.

She.

Who was fished for. Mouth open, gulping air, truly tiny, dark hair matted, caked in a wet whirl. Marred, smeared, bruised, dented. Sound asleep. Slept the instant born.

The doctor put old hands on my shoulders.

"What, you look shocked — did you want a son?"

For a moment I could not comprehend. In that waiting-room I had forgotten a child had to be one or the other.

Christopher drove, Maggie beside him, and in that back seat I held her, Bailla, in a cocoon of easily unwrapped blankets.

Ontological Bailla, asleep in my arms. Cleaned and polished, bonneted. Skinfuzz from another country. Faded bruises. Tiny brows. True lips.

In space.

Tell me again old preacher, there's nothing new under the sun.

The girl walked shyly, toes turned in. Her dress too big, drop-hemmed at the calf. Old woman's cotton. She stopped under the high hickory.

"Oh, that's a beautiful baby."

"Thank you," Maggie smiled.

"I live up the hill. If ever you need a sitter. I read all the time anyway."

She smiled at me too. Scrubfaced, hair in a ponytail, who could have been Nina's plainer stand-in, or sister. She poked carefully to tuck in Bailla's blankets.

"I make great omelettes. I lived in France."

"You sound like a want-ad," I said, and grinned.

She jumped back.

"Oh, I didn't mean for money. For this beautiful baby I wouldn't take money."

Color ran into her cheeks, wine film on the sides of a glass.

"That was supposed to be a friendly joke," I said.

"I thought you were being mean."

"He was kidding," Maggie said.

"But I *did* sound like a want-ad."

I held out my hand. The color in her cheeks deepened. Quickly, elbow up in Miss-Porter's-School style, she shook mine.

"I've watched the three of you," she said softly. "You look happy. I knew you'd be friendly types."

"Any time you want to make those omelettes," Maggie said, "come on over."

"Oh, tomorrow!"

"There's no rush."

"Tomorrow's perfect!"

Mavra.

Nobody knew anything about her.

That too-big dress said a fire, some kind of disaster, or escape. Mavra smiled at all speculations, affirmed none.

Her hill was an allegory. A brownthatch dark house full of designers and window trimmers. Two ranch houses further lived women whose heads seemed cast — shoulders pulled up, cigarette held burning-end in, between thumb and circled forefinger. Two huge old saltboxes taken over by college students. The largest house leased by the state asylum for people who puttered in sunshine. Two or three cottages held frizzyhaired ladies who walked their failing collie dogs, and vanished with evening.

She knew the calls of birds, the names of plants and trees, edible from poisonous mushrooms. When she caught sight of a familiar flower, she knelt to it. Ran with an awkwardness, a heaviness be-

yond her size, ponytail bobbing, her face open, expectant. Walked
with an odd laboring gait, as if climbing a hill.

At night she came to hold Bailla and sing her to sleep, voice high
and sweet, in lullaby, folk song, campsong. Knew Bach and Vi-
valdi, Handel and Mozart, solo or chorus.

"I pretend all the time," she said, making omelettes, "I pretend
I'm part of this family. Sometimes I even pretend Bailla is *my*
child. That everything she'll *be* she'll get from me."

Maggie stood at the screen door, tugging at her gloves.

"I don't have her number," Maggie said. "We always arrange
the sitting when she comes by."

"I'll go get her."

"Where?"

"Where she lives."

"Where is that?"

"Didn't she ever say which house was hers?"

Maggie tapped her gloved fingers against the screen.

I walked up the hill swiftly. Slowed at the crest. I hoped she
didn't live with the asylum boarders. She couldn't be in the house
of lesbians. I didn't want her with those weird old women and
their ailing dogs.

A man near the road tied down tomato plants.

"Excuse me, sir," I said, as if I were suddenly trapped in a quest-
ing tale, "I'm looking for our babysitter —"

"You mean Mavra?"

"Right."

"These three rows are her radishes."

"May I go in and get her?"

"In where?"

"Here."

"Oh, she come by at seeding. I let her have the rows. Don't
know where she lives. Someplace, I suppose."

The sun hadn't set. I walked in the middle of a road in full view of all the houses. But felt I was prying.

I waved at a girl with long hair. She waved back, came toward me.

She wasn't Mavra.

"Wrong number," she said with a smile.

"Do you know Mavra?"

"It figures."

"What?"

"That you'd be looking for Mavra."

"She's our babysitter."

"She'd never be late for you. There must be a reason. Try the bottom of the hill. I see her there all the time. Sometimes she's in Louie's carriagebarn."

I hurried to the carriagebarn labeled Louie's. A small doll-like garden ran along the walk. I imagined Mavra crouching over shoots and leaves, crying large tears. Her Raggedy Ann ripped on the side, one leg missing.

I knocked. Nobody answered. I called Mavra's name through a screen window.

The door was open. I pushed in.

Mavra lay on a low bed, face down, feet hanging over the end, arms thrown out, one hand touching the floor. Her open mouth left a wet mark on the rough blanket. Her face was welted red.

I shook her by the shoulder.

A man's cotton rainhat lay on a chair. A half-eaten Almond Joy. Two coffee cups, almost touching.

I had walked through her looking glass. Uninvited. It would have been terrible not to let her know.

I placed both hands on her shoulders. She groaned, ground her face into the blanket. I pulled her stiff body into a sitting position. Her eyes opened, closed again. Propped up against my hands she snored softly. Her breath was sleepy sweet.

"Mavra, get up. Your baby's waiting."

Her head rolled free of my hand, snapped to one side. She opened startled eyes, twisted out of my grasp to fall back full length on the bed. I grabbed her shoulder. She twisted her head, bit out with a snap of teeth. I yanked her up again, brushed at her face with the back of my hand. Her eyes opened, her hands paddled the air.

"Hey, wake up," I shouted into her ear, "babysitter, up!"

Her eyes opened wider.

"Oh my God — what are you doing here?"

"Getting you."

"Oh my God."

She backed away, ran with that headflopping motion into the bathroom. I heard her mumbling through the closed door. Water gushed.

She opened the door slowly.

"You. Oh my God. I could die. Look at me. Look at this place. Everything disfigured."

She put her hand over the reddened cheek.

"You still want me to sit with that beautiful baby?"

She began to brush at her hair, sharp harsh strokes, her clasp in her mouth.

"I sleep and sleep and sleep."

"Are you sick?"

"I'm a neurotic little bitch. I walk on water one second, then hot choking waves pull me under. Except with Bailla. Oh, I'm so grateful. Thank you for coming for me. You could have washed your hands of me. I'd never see any of you again."

"Come on. Cheer up. We're late."

"I'm not uncheered. I'm in a family now, did I tell you? Your family. I'm your cousin. Or Maggie's."

Squirming under an oversized flannel gown, crosslegged, a huge bowl her ashtray, croissant butterloaded, scrubbed cheeks widely grinning. Maggie and I grinned back from under the covers. When Marva shifted her weight, we moved our feet.

"Oh I love it here!"

She bit into the croissant, faked a puff at the cigarette.

"I *belong*, right? If you were to take an official family photograph you'd include me. I pretend — oh I've told you so many times. I'm the country mouse. You two had to go on a long journey, and called, and I looked after Bailla for weeks, months, oh it ran into years. Auntie Mavra were her first words. When you came back she was full of curtsies and nods, and you were so pleased. The next time you had to go, you called me again, over and over for the rest of my life."

"What did your husband say?"

"Oh, I'll never get married. I ran away from all that."

"When?" Maggie said.

Mavra's teeth locked on the croissant.

"I've lost a year some place. Isn't that pathetic? I was sixteen, or fourteen — I just don't know. I used to go into analysis from time to time. See if I could lay my hands on that year. I can't stand numbers or fractions. Sooner or later these things come down to my missing months."

She held the croissant out in both hands.

"Look at me shake. Just thinking about it! Nutsy, isn't it?"

She got out of the old Pontiac. A man in a cotton hat was behind the wheel.

"I've come to say goodbye," she said.

The glass on the windshield was a mirror hiding the man's face. He nodded, but didn't get out.

She was wearing an old yellow shirt of mine. Jeans. Sandals. Her hair was caught up in two featherdusters.

I followed her into the house. Maggie was diapering Bailla.

"Here, let me," Mavra said. "One last wet, Bailee old friend. For the road."

"Why don't you ask your friend to come in," Maggie said.

"I don't want him in here. This is mine."

She kissed Bailla on the tummy, pulled her undershirt low, caught it with diaper and pin. Two large tears rolled down her cheeks, hung there. Another tear clung to the tip of her nose.

"I don't know what I'm doing," she said weakly, "but I'm doing it all the same. I'll probably marry him. Anything can happen in Juarez."

"If you feel like this," Maggie said, "why go?"

"I'm almost twenty-two. I can't babysit forever."

Maggie mopped at her cheeks and nose with a diaper. Mavra sniffed a thank-you.

"I've been in Mexico before," she whimpered. "It won't even be that, a big thing. We'll hole up in a fleabag. He'll convince me it's the only place with drinkable water. I'm such a drag."

"Don't go," Maggie said. "Stay here till you decide what to do."

"Oh, I can't. Bailla would find me out, wouldn't you, sweetheart?"

She kissed Bailla again, and Maggie.

"Josh," she said, "when Maggie writes me will you add a hello? I'll need all the help I can get out there."

She held her face up.

I kissed her on the lips.

She opened her eyes wide. I laughed.

"I come from a kissing family," I said. "I'm generally friendly. I'll make you a handbook for fending off Latin creeps."

"I think maybe I could use it on this trip," Mavra said, and glanced outside.

She carried Bailla out to the car, but framed her back to the man at the wheel.

"I'll find you something fitting in Mexico, baby," she said, and nuzzled Bailla with her forehead. "A mountain maybe. Or a working shrine."

She handed Bailla to Maggie.

The man behind the wheel nodded, started up the motor. Mavra climbed in beside him, her head leaning out the window. A tear rolled down one cheek, fell, like a raindrop spattering, to dimple the driveway dust.

A married woman, mother-woman, doesn't need a fairy godmother. Life-welcomed. The *in* sorority. Maternal instinct fulfilled. Dark barren sea, life's sea, skiff-covered, all barks womanned by mothers. If you could be in light what you felt in the dark. Millions of great dreaming generals; only a couple who make it under fire. Walk over hot coals, hold breath under water. Do it if you train for it. Great analogy unapplied: childbirth. Didn't think I had that in me. Did. So if that, why not all the rest? General Zora, have at you! And this one? Paranoid. Just a nice kid all screwed up in the egg. Mavra out of Marian. Lady O' War. Good six furlong, best at a distance. *I* gave birth, not Zora. Not her. Nobody else could have done that. Fact. My child, my labor, my doing. Mastery. I split. Two out of one. With help, with help. But still. Now you see me, now me and another. Great! Soaring! Inevitable to come down. How not? One second as the greatest there ever was. When the pain and ecstasy and high falls, everything could go with it. Woe to women. Mystery. Some hit skids and never ever make it back again. Mother Lazarus. Is *that* what can be? Is this what it's like after?

Lackluster.

Unused.

Israeli women, the moral equivalent of childbirth. Stay at high pitch. If you can't make it destroy it. No depression.

Bailla's mother. Me. Jump rope without missing ever. Undefeated at hopscotch. Best of class. Best of breed. Blueribbon Maggie, prettiest sweetest hottest brainiest charmingest ballbelle queen of everywhere.

Salmon do it best.

Romantic bullshit. Those whose eyes tear when they hear of a suicide. Back to L.A., short course with Lila. Could put those arms around tipping Atlas and straighten him right up. Doesn't know beats and golden girls mock her. Lila, be my fairy godmother? Fairy godmother, me? Mafia enforcer tears ten guys apart between 9 A.M. and 11, bows to Lila. Maybe key is come on strong. World too mysterious. Lila, Nate.

Rise together. Scales fall from our eyes. Mrs. Lazarus arrived from Sinai with husband and child. Woman warmth. Lila believes it. Some day Bailla asks. Like, can you see God? Can you see life? Can anyone see it? Can you make it? If any good I'll remember to say yes. Somebody somewhere can.

"Joshua, level with me. You still believe a great love could heal a hip."

"I thought you were too tough for such mystic notions."

"Can you admit you might have married a flop?"

"A great love might coincide with a healed hip — do you believe in *kiss my booboo?*"

"God yes!"

He too does. Not from me. Expectations went by me on the outside. Zora — why Zora? Private inverse Pantheon. Blame-shelf. I would have been but but.

Fantasy put-down. Saks's bra counter. Casual, back turned to Zora. Let her order first. Thirty-six B-cup. Then loud, still not turning — thirty-eight, C-cup. No good. Anybody could see not. Buy it anyway. Inconvenience small price for such triumph.

Dear Maggie and Josh,

Report from the Mexican front. One year has passed — or more? I count time by the crud visitations. The truest way to lose pounds. Who says the locals are immune? They accept the bad cards they were dealt. Those paintings with peons bent double: I used to think that was pastoral.

Hey, Josh, where's my creep handbook? Louie is keeping a diary. He says Mexico is a castrating country. So is Iceland. Which means it isn't a matter of temperature. On some rainy day I'll remember to ask him. It may have something to do with the raunchy Cugat type who swives his señora dutifully, then runs, still buttoning, to a local dance hall for a teenage puta (is that the word?). By the way — though why should you two be interested? — Louie and I had our first real fight. He said I sounded like my old man, and I said he looked like my old man. Shouldn't that be considered a tie?

Oh, what the hell! I love Louie, I guess. I don't think I like him yet.

We got married — did I write that before? I may even be pregnant. Not passion. Laziness.

Bailla looks taller with every picture. Time flies, don't it? Even in this ass drag of a country. Teach Bailla my name. The music-camp phony one will do.

Louie's smiling at me. I bet he wrote something nasty in his diary. Ten minutes ago he killed a fat mosquito with his hat: it's still squished there, like a badge.

Ugh.

Cheer me up. Reinforce me. And don't think it's too late for the creep handbook, Josh. A girl needs all the help she can get.

Kiss Bailla for me. Hug her hug her hug her.

In afternoon sunlight my rural mailbox shadow was a crumpled Russian hammer. Squirrels under lush dogwood leaves snapped off green buttons. Terrible sound. Rifleshots in the distance; signal summer is over.

I pulled out three envelopes addressed in pencil, stamped purple. Mannerly handwriting. Mavra knew a finishing-school girl. Self-presenting. Nina's scrawl. Nina? Who is Nina? Someone signing her name today somewhere.

"Josh," Maggie whispered, "I think Bailla's asleep."

"Good."

"Let's sit outside. It's gorgeous, exciting."

We walked into the front yard, sank down on the grass.

"We should make another baby," Maggie said.

"You're right."

"I mean romantically — wildly — what would you like me to do?"

"Do?"

"I mean what wonderful thing should I do?"

"Like what?"

"Oh, come on — I bet there are a thousand things you'd like me to be. I've left Aunt Teena behind, and my mother. I'm the new Maggie — what would you like me to do?"

"I don't understand this *do* bit."

"It's dark, we're alone — would you like me to throw my clothes up into a tree and run through the grass?"

"Sure, if you feel like —"

"Not what I *feel* — Josh — don't you understand? What *you* feel! Make a demand on me. As if I were some gorgeous girl you'd never seen before in your life and fell for crazily. You couldn't pretend I'm great. Not for a second!"

Dear Mag and Josh,

Still here. Relief may be in sight. I've got the crud for the maybe fortieth time. Louie picked up his first seizure. He's in a clinic. We may be coming home. Louie has been collecting articles connecting dysentery with colitis. When I had the runs Louie wasn't ready to generalize yet.

Actually he's a nice man. He gets choked up thinking about doing something for somebody, and that gives him such pleasure he never has to do the thing. It doesn't seem to be a system.

Hey, the girl across the way puts my Marian-Mavra juggling to shame. She's Catholic and Spanish and has fourteen names! A keyboard full. On any particular day she can hit, say, six and nine, and be the person those two call for. Her own personal zodiac.

Louie is reading to me from his diary these days. And even from his letters. He's a great guy for shooting letters out to his buddies and old girl friends all over the place. His own press attaché. Every letter these days says the same thing — he's crazy lonely and miserable being in a goddam country like Mexico so alone. I clear my throat and try to remind him we're not only married but traveling companions.

Listen, this time I *am* pregnant. It's great. A terrible phony like me admitted to the race at last.

Maternal will be a new thing to be phony about. Every time I think of myself as a hopeless phony I remind me what country I come from, and I feel better. I'm as full of shit, no more, no less, than the State Department, the Pentagon, and those phonies in Congress — do you find my generalizations mature? Bailla does. She at least I know is on my side. I need all the allies I can get these days. One thing keeps haunting me: what if I gave all my child love to Bailla and when my own comes don't feel a thing?

Bailla held her face up to be kissed. Mavra's long dark hair hid her own expression, but she hugged and hugged and hugged, patting Bailla's back.

"I'll see you in the morning, sweetheart," she whispered.

"O.K.," said Bailla, and Maggie swept her off to bed.

Mavra's face was flushed. Her cheeks had filled out. She sat comically, legs apart, feet turned out, breathing heavily through her mouth.

"Josh," Mavra said, "I have to walk some before bed. You want to lead me?"

Her head bobbed as she labored half way up her old hill. The moon caught silver threads on her maternity jumper, flashed on her wide eyes. She headed for a stone bench in tree-shadow, sat down, dodging her face in and out of moonlight.

"God, I'm the outdoor athletic type. I used to wheel up this hill like nothing. Now I'm so heavy even Louie noticed the change."

"When do we meet Louie?"

"Here? Never!"

I laughed.

"You must think I'm nuts. I share my bed with the guy but not this house. He can't have any part of Bailla — or Maggie, or you.

You're mine! I'd kill him for his tricks here. In Mexico and at home I let his crap pass by."

She shifted her weight on the stone bench.

"God this thing is cold. You don't think I can do damage to the baby sitting here, do you, Josh? I'm shivering."

Clear white moonlight fell between our shadows on the night-grass. Our shadows pressed into one another. Mavra looked up.

"Maggie must have the coffee ready by now," I said.

"She must," said Mavra.

Bare feet slapped the hall floor. A door closed. Bed springs creaked. Bailla's sighs and small child breathing. Silence from the distant room. Mavra with her arms back on the pillow, her hands under her head, sleepless and excited. The night was black and full of happy dancers leaping dark through space. I found myself grinning. Imagined Mavra grinning back.

"Josh," Maggie said softly, "you awake?"

I dropped my arm across her waist. She was tense, stiff.

"Josh, are we out of our minds? What is this stranger doing in our house?"

"What stranger?"

"This strange pregnant girl who moved in on us. I've been laying here getting sorer by the minute. The relationship is all dreamed up. She plans to have her baby right here — Josh, are you listening? What the hell is this!"

The bedroom door creaked. Mavra's bare feet patted the wood floor. The bathroom door shut softly.

"And that Louie," Maggie whispered. "Did you ever get the feeling there is no Louie? She dreamed him up —"

"The pregnancy too?"

"She keeps saying she lies all the time. Maybe Louie is one of her lies."

"We saw Louie."

"We saw a guy driving a car. Every other detail comes from her. Josh, I've got a weird feeling about this girl. Don't you?"

"Nope."

"Come on. I'm serious. She dumped herself on us —"

Water running and flushing broke the still house's silence. Those feet beat a quick path back to the bedroom.

"Josh," Maggie said, "try voicing some of those stories she tells. Do it aloud when you're alone sometime. The only thing missing so far is an amusing anecdote about cannibalism."

"For chrissakes, Maggie, now who's being nuts?"

"Joshua, you fool — a pregnant girl has possession of our spare room. Everything else is hearsay."

Maggie's voice was tight, reedy.

"I take it all back, Josh. There's a Louie. God there's a Louie. Get over here. Do something about the sonofabitch!"

She hung up. I raced into the city.

Maggie was holding a small bugeyed man in her arms. His face was dark, his large eyes wet, his lower lip fallen.

"Pull yourself together, Louie," Maggie was saying.

She pointed him my way. He looked up.

"The kid — did you see the kid? His feet! Dusty. He walked all the way. Mavrie, sweet girl. She looks just like Ma. Ma gave birth — hair like that — I can't stand it. Those feet. My kid! Mavrie that plucky darling!"

Louie leaned his full weight on Maggie; her hands were in fists.

"Josh," she cried as Louie swung her past my ear, "knock him to the ground!"

"Louie, I'm Joshua," I said. "Congratulations!"

He swiveled out of Maggie's grip and fell on my neck.

"Kill him quickly," Maggie's voice whispered at me.

"My son. Ma's face. I looked just like that. I can show you pictures. Here, open my wallet —"

"Later, Louie," I said. "Now just stand up."

"I didn't think about Ma before. I'm in trauma. I can't go through this — that Mavrie — spunk! Her hair. Who ever thought I'd have this reaction? She understands such things. I need a day or two to recover. It's nothing permanent. Tell her not to worry. I'll be fine."

"Oh well," Mavra said.

Her dark hair was pulled tight off her brow. Her face was shining, welted red on her cheeks and throat. Maggie patted her brow with a washcloth.

"Birth, or anything connected with life gives Louie withdrawal symptoms," Mavra said. "I know he's a loving man underneath it all. I prefer you two with me anyway. Too bad we can't include Bailla."

Louie sat on the stoop of their old house, swatting at insects with his cotton hat.

"Hear that?" he said. "The kid's crying again. Mavra must be poisoning him with her milk. She's tit-proud. They get into a panic thinking they won't be feminine if they don't nurse. Poor thing, she throws a fit if I suggest growing tits at the expense of a kid isn't exactly nice. Ma didn't nurse. She had a magnificent bust. Six kids turned out O.K. I tell this to Mavra as kindly as I can. Maybe you can do something for her, pal."

"Bailla, help me burp our baby."

Bailla wriggled on Mavra's lap, spread her fingers wide and stiff, patted the baby's blanketed back softly, her arm straight out, rigid. Mavra folded her fingers, kissed them softly.

"Now we'll nurse, O.K., sweetheart?"

She draped a purple shawl over her shoulder, covered herself and the baby's head. Bailla backed into my arms, watching.

"I got a letter from Louie. He says he goes to bed at nine every night. He needed the shut-eye, he says. Life is one long recuperation, he tells me. Those three weeks in the mountains did wonders for him. He doesn't feel pale anymore. I thought I might send him flowers."

She drew the baby up to her diaper-covered shoulder, motioned Bailla to get closer.

"Are there such tribes, you think, who insist impregnation take place in the dark, between total strangers?"

"You want such a tribe? We'll invent one."

"When Mr. Right came along, could you resign?"

"Sure."

"Could the tribe believe, for starters, that men are men, women women, and nobody under pressure to prove anything?"

"Josh," Maggie said, "she's a great girl and I love her dearly but what are we doing with our lives?"

From the back room Mavra's soft singing, Bailla's loud whispered questioning. The baby sobbed, grew quiet, sobbed fitfully falling off to sleep.

"I can see it," Maggie said, "when Dov is sixteen Louie will have adjusted to fatherhood and Mavra will move back there."

I laughed.

"You may laugh," Maggie said. "But who invented Louie? When Mavra goes back to get clothes he comes here and cries on my shoulder. He said he's getting better. He's learning love on her. Josh, do you hear me? The prick actually said that! I mean as if when you're learning to play a recorder you just need a recorder to play on! God! And he calls her his pipeline into life. He calls *me* his sister. He's not to be believed."

"Things are improving," I whispered. "Starting Saturday she's going to spend weekends with Louie."

"Josh, try telling this to a sane stranger."

Division of labor. I will, baby cries. Programmed. Seventy seconds of Louie whine, baby wakes, howls, Louie takes off. Peace. Better to puff smell of something burning. Louie takes off, leaves us to professional firemen, explaining in all modesty a fireman he never was. Asleep now. Dropped off in middle of generalizing. What was it? At his best when in the hands of his therapist. Wants me to go to a shrink. Again? Not too involved if fall asleep in middle of own sermon. Like guy under pentathol. Talking, jabbed, conks out, comes to hours later still on same sentence. Now I lay me snore snore down to sleep. Do you stir, reverend? "Mavrie, we are too proud." Say more, sire. "We mustn't hide our inadequacies." Editorial *we* doesn't mean *I. You.* We don't piss on the floor, do we, dear? Why could you buy substitutes for army but not for this? My duties, madam? Assume my shell, give me a quick summary of all that transpired when I return from the blast at the Rainbow Room. What if your husband assumes the shell is you, madam, and tries to take his husbandly pleasure? Offer him a hot glass of tea and a backrub instead. Louie stirring again. Mouth open, half buried in pillow. "Lassitude — Mavrie, I don't mean to pull you down, but you are in considerable danger of becoming frigid." "Louie, are you trying to tell me I'm a lousy lay?" "Sweetheart, I'm not blaming you." "You mean I'm a bad lay but it's my old man's fault?" "There are many things in our psychology which we are not at fault —" On on on. Louie does have a system. Central blaming. Every inadequacy has its cause, a villain. The reason I am so full of shit this time is _____ . Form explanation: fill in names of guilty. Homefree Louie.

but we should be able to make something anyway no matter how fake just take hold overcome bypass destroy the formulas kick entropy in the ass dismiss every corny predictable niggling if can't get it up I castrate if gets it up and fizzles I lesbian those murderers his

therapists scaring him to death orgasm talk don't come big and a
growth a growth that's how cancer starts armor a growth hiding in
the muscles the nerves the tissues terrified little boy we could
knock it off all of it great new start nobody beats up on anybody
just look in eye tell truth Louie hear me my body no RelaxAcizor
no airdrome flesh warm flesh yours Louie take Louie not that way
not a sexual queue and wrong ticket and when own turn comes
wicket slams shut oh Louie life too important to kick to bits please
Louie skincrawls shoveloncement raspingfile teethsourgrape oh
pray become total schitz like army stores Louie at counter here
Louie take and this take and that Louie but leave the rest oh Louie
you can't want this teeth gritting don't Louie not a galosh a human
woman Louie I'm dying Louie dying help me help you God God
stop Louie that fucking therapist coached you Louie tell him to
screw himself I'm here Louie jesus jesus you can't you can't

We ate slowly, stopped, waited. Maggie shifted their place settings. A white rose drooped from a thin green vase before Mavra's
empty wine glass.

"I can imagine what's happening," Maggie said finally. "He's in
the midst of that tale again. How she never helps him. How everybody sells him out. How can a talented guy be so tasteless?"

She raised her spoon over her plate, let the vichyssoise drip back
slowly, untouched.

"I made this on purpose," she said. "Let him accuse me of trying
to poison him — the creep keeps confusing cholesterol with
cyanide."

I lit the candles in the center of the table: the two white plates
gleamed empty on the orange cloth.

"She tells me," Maggie said, "that she keeps herself going by
imagining his words are notes in *The Art of the Fugue*. The more
he yaps the more complicated the counterpoint. God, how could
you not feel sorry for her!"

We put our spoons down, and sat too still.

The phone made us both jump.

"That's Mavra — I know it in my bones!" Maggie said.

The line went dead.

We eyed the phone on its cradle. Again it rang. I grabbed for it.

"Josh," Mavra's voice said, "would it be possible for you to come over?"

I heard a click.

"What's happening, Josh?" Maggie said, following me to the door.

"She wants me over there."

"Josh, don't run into their web."

I opened the door. Maggie blocked my way.

"Sweetheart, I know this isn't the time — I have a terrible feeling —"

"Mag, he may be killing her —"

"They playact, Josh — don't be a sucker. Everybody's guts gets ripped out but those two stay whole. Josh, they kick the shit out of each other the way other people play a hand of gin rummy."

"You're out of your mind."

"O.K., go, but be careful. Watch it. When you feel your feet slipping grab onto me."

I pushed by her and slammed out the door.

Louie was swinging his hat at the tall grass in front of the house; at the sound of the car his face fell into a frown. Much hope there was for Louie, who believed his fine inner self could still give him away.

He waved the hat at me.

"You didn't have to rush, pal — you know how unstable the kid is. We had a physical struggle. Nothing. She clawed me. To calm her I threw her to the floor a little in self-defense."

I brushed by him and started up the front steps. His hand fell on my shoulder, lightly.

"No hurry — you know how broads are, pal? She's probably getting the shine off her nose. A little hysteria once in a while clears our lungs — my therapist makes me scream into a pillow —"

His hand tightened as I climbed the steps and entered the hall.

"She'll say I beat her up. Maybe I gave her a little nudge with my shoe when she fell on the floor — helped her collect herself. With her etiology she needs all the help she can get."

I opened the door to the basement kitchen. Mavra looked up from the bottom of the dark well. Her eyes were wet, she cradled the baby in one arm and shook milk from a bottle onto her wrist.

"That much taste you've got," Louie shouted at her. "I told her nursing after we had this little flap was a big madonna pitch."

Mavra lowered herself painfully into a rocker.

"You hurt me."

"I barely tapped you."

"You hit me with your hat."

"Look at the froth on her mouth," Louie said, "and tell me who is sane? I struggle and struggle for the ungrateful bitch, all she does is highhat me, the duchess!"

Mavra stood up, raised her sweater; three red fingerwelts stood out on her ribs.

"Josh," she said, "please take me to Maggie — I'm afraid to stay here."

Louie raised his hat in a threatening gesture.

"Leave, you bitch — go on, leave. See if you get back ever!"

I stepped between them.

"What do you want of me?" I said, and pushed them apart.

Louie pretended the hat was raised to strike at an insect. Mavra sank back in her rocker.

"Mavrie," he said, "you know I'm nuts about you, kid. What do we need this fighting for? Let's apologize, what do you say, baby?"

Mavra looked up at me. One full unfalling tear overspread each eye. Behind that watery shield hurt glittered.

Loaded paper bags in one arm, the wriggling baby in the other, laughing she used her head to butt the door open, pushed her knee in, swung her hip through. The grocery bag was splitting.

"Louie, hey, come quickly, give me a hand."

She hipped the baby into his highchair, let the slipping groceries slide off her thigh, her knee, her instep.

"Louie, where are you?"

Through the opening she saw him crouched over his soup bowl, slurping. In her black sweater, his cotton hat far down over his eyes. He grabbed frenchbread twohanded, bit violently, jammed damp white bread into his open mouth. Anger ran off him, dark, hysterical, slithering over the floor, squirming like a wet insect on her back.

"Louie, hi!"

Coveted anger, not surrendered, that kind of coveted, like a rare hard-on. His spoon baled the bowl. Violent angry baling. Spoon dug through plate through table through floor. Anger, universal solvent. Cutting through foundation, hemisphere, earthcore, digging into Mao's soup — ho ho, chop chop Louie!

Louie whirled and caught her smiling.

"What's amusing, whore? What's funny about making a husband wait for his meal?"

Spoon upraised, grabbed by his angry mouth. Down again for the next load, in.

She moved the highchair toward him, smiled his way, opened a tin of apricot, fed a small bit to the baby's waiting mouth. Hungry Dov, enthusiastic kid, clamped on the spoon, wouldn't let go, looked up, laughing.

"Where the hell were you at six?" Louie, fullmouthed, said.

"When?"

Crouched he scraped the soupbowl and with his free hand served himself more.

"Don't be so goddam smart —"

"It's now six twenty-one, and thirty seconds —"

"Don't give me lip, you bitch. I don't like your deportment."

"Honey, I'm not angry you began eating without me."

"*You're* not angry! Whore, I know you looked at your watch planning —"

"Louie, sweetheart, must we keep on with this boring shit?"

"I know your tricks —"

"Come on now, honey."

"You're like that old man of yours, big feetsmelling genius with shit all over his drawers."

"Louie, stop, O.K.? Before you say one other ugly thing."

"I'm talking to you!"

"Louie, for godssake eat your soup and shut up!"

"Who you telling to shut up?"

His chair scraped back, too late she looked up — Louie bugeyed, triumphant, crouched waiting for the opening she stupidly provided. His hand clutched at her shoulder. Something tore.

"Louie, sweetheart, we don't need this —"

Jingling carkeys christmasbell tinkling.

She jumped away from the baby, the spoon still in his mouth. Louie's hairyknuckle hand tore at her blouse. Acting out. Therapist in his corner, egging on. Phony lipdroop, make-up anger. Used. She backed away. His prop, his needed stimulus. Mouth pulled back, hate eyes. Two islands of yellow fat on his whitewhiskered chin. Darkmouthed, darklipped, swooning-eyed intruder, hand on her, ripping cloth, kicking out those whitebuck feet. Who was this stranger handling her?

A funnel, black gauze running from a dark roll, whipping between them, that darkfingered hand. She whirled to shake him off, bumped his table, his bread and board, backdrop, stage set. One lift, so easy, everything sliding, flipped, scattered over the floor — silver flowers glass soup tureen splattering red watermelon. Gapemouth Louie hung his Bosch head over her shoulder, spun her, grabbed her hair, christmasbell jingle, ringofkeys flashing, smashing in tinkle against her ear.

"Moll, gunmoll, everything you smashed, without provocation!"

Eyesbugged, mouthablackhole funereal gauze whipping out of it. Life, death. Louie could kill. She tried to get away. His hand tightened. She heard her hair tearing at the scalp, heard it then felt it. Screamed, tried to pull the screaming baby out of the high chair.

"You don't wreck a house with impunity, whore!"

"The baby!"

"Don't tell me the baby, whore!"

Karate chop at her neck, her head struck the flagstone. His shoe over her, pulled back, coming again — to scare. Even at this a faker! His foot pressed her head down, he tugged her hair into a stirrup.

Twisting she got up, tried to pull the baby out of the chair, too late saw Louie's foot flash out, cutting her feet from under her, crashing her to the stone floor. The jingling keys cut into her cheek.

"Louie, please, let me take the baby!"

"Slimytit sonofabitch, you don't take a kid out of his father's house!"

Leg braced she pulled the baby, his knees caught in the chair's traytop. Louie yanked her hair, tipped back her head. She tried to hold the baby out of his range, running, up the steps, fists clubbing her back. Broke outside, bobbing ponytail, gallop to car, threw Dov screaming into the back seat.

"Verminshit, you haven't paid yet!"

Louie stumbling after her. Blindly she backed down the steep driveway, scraping bushes, overhanging branches.

"You're trying to run me down, killer bitch!" Louie hollered, pursuing.

"I'll kill you, whore! Tear your heart out with these bare hands!"

Chasing her, smaller now in the windshield, feet scattering gravel, reaching to pick up a rock, throwing, hung in silhouette on the hill, voice lost to her gunning motor and the tire scrunch on gravel, Louie shouting faintly she was trying to run him down.

I knew from the horn, and ran out, Maggie behind me. Mavra crying, hair all over her face, head thrown back, spread-armed in the front seat. Her cheek was bleeding, one eye was bruised red. The baby twisted in his car harness, slid down.

Maggie grabbed him. I tried to help Mavra out of the car. She clung to the steering wheel.

"Please, put the baby back — I've got to get away — my hair — Josh, both his hands were full — lend me ten dollars, Josh — I've got to get away —"

Her hand at her ear was red with blood.

"I'll never make it — I can't — please put the baby back — I can't see. I can't drive. I've got to. Please help me, Josh."

The phone was ringing.

"It's him. Don't — no. Answer. Say I'm not here. Let me rest an hour. I can stay with my roommate. Oh my head, my ear. Madman actor. Acting, he'll kill. God, the baby saw it and heard it! What'll happen to him?"

Louie sounded cheerful on the phone.

"Another little fracas — we're both strained. You know how it is with husbands and wives, pal? I had to tap her a couple of times. Pulled the kitchen knife on me. Tried to run me down with the car — violent. Poor kid. There's a history of seizures in their blood."

"Louie," I said, "what can I do?"

Mavra, behind me, stared at his voice in the receiver.

"She took off. Doesn't even have a driver's license with her. Nice if she gets into a smash-up, huh? She can mangle the kid. God knows what else. And I won't have a leg to stand on."

"Louie, what do you want me to do?"

"She'll probably come by to borrow a few bucks. She wants money let her come back and get it. I'm no leper."

"O.K., Louie."

"I knew you'd understand, pal. Men know about such things. Mavra has endearing qualities —"

"Josh, I'm all shot — I'd smash us up. Drive me, please. Catch a train back."

Maggie held the baby and hid her face.

"Stay the night here, Mavra," she finally said.

"I want a million miles between us and that killer."

"Get Bailla, Mag," I said, "and come too."

She shook her head.

"I don't have my license or I'd try it alone," Mavra said. "I'm a pig to ask you."

"Drive her, Josh."

"He'll turn right around," said Mavra.

Two by two, headlights skittered across my windshield. Night exodus. Evacuation of a city. On the Upper Roadway, bridge girders cut Manhattan into riveted filmframes. The car's motion spliced them back whole. In darkness buildings massed together, one huge fortress, miles long at the East River line, rising tiered, windowslits and lookout posts, less monolith, peaks of red lights blinking a rhythmic semaphor in the moon-usurped sky.

Second Avenue's streetlamps twisted Mavra's eyes tight. She stirred, reached back, still asleep, to check on Dov. The cuts on her cheek were dark, dried.

"How are you now?" I asked.

She pressed her face forward, nose against the windshield.

"Oh I love this town."

"Are you O.K.?"

"I'm great."

She grabbed my hand, pressed it to her cheek.

"You know what I'd love to do now? Find a babysitter and head for the Plaza."

"I'm going right back or I'd volunteer to babysit —"

"I mean with you."

"Ten minutes ago you were dying."

"I'm quit of that creep for a while — I'm dying, but to celebrate. Anyway, let's not talk about him. Say something nice to me. How do I look?"

"Better."

"Are you glad you drove me in?"

"It had to be done."

"Come on, stop playing with me — are you glad you're here, in the night with me? Do I look beautiful?"

"You're beautiful —"

"I mean to you?"

The apartment stunk, dogshit, sour milk. I opened windows and night poured train soot, burnt coffee, freshbaked bread into the mix. One grayish light from an extravagantly abstract lamp made a pool on the high ceiling: mammoth action paintings contorted the wall.

Mavra in the back room was singing softly. I sat and waited to say goodnight. Sunday's silence muffled the city. No voices floated up from the street. The odd door slamming. Taxis rolling to a stop. A distant sanitation truck rotating brushes, hissing spray.

The singing stopped. The baby was asleep.

"Hey," I called softly to the back room, "I have to go."

"Shshshshsh."

Far away a siren started up. In a different key, another. Like converging tracer lights in darkness. Sounds like flaring fading meteorite tails, mere dreams with silence reimposed.

"Mavra, what the hell's with you? Did you fall asleep?"

Something white flitted past the pool of light. Mavra paused in the doorway, her breasts held forward. Her hair was down, her eyes glistening.

"Josh, I've been such an ugly animal all day."

"What's this about? You've been kind of —"

"Sister? Do I look to you now like anybody's sister?"

Her hands reached up to pull my face to hers; her belly pushed against the rough cloth of my suitcoat, her white thighs pressed into my pantlegs. Her head was to one side, her lips slightly open.

"Hey," I whispered, "it's been a lousy day for you."

"Come on, Josh, you don't have to be noble. I happen to know you're a wild man."

Our lips touched. Hers so soft, her tongue so soft, warm, her teeth tiny, lips and tongue zephyrsoft, her hands on my shirt unsure at unbuttoning. Her breasts ground into the tweed of my sportcoat, her thighs separated, my coat thrown off, pushing her gently down on couchcloth, her legs up, her hips bouncing, her lips squeezing my tongue, dark wet mouth, zephyrbreath quietsmell breastsmell thighsmell all a warm welling clothes strewn bodies met liquid and darkness and all one arms around and arms around legs around gorgeous twining all atouch quickening love felt love thrust breasts to chestwet ground together like kissing a nightsurge couchsail slamming love's insistence against the dark wall faster louder wilder surging onethrust onemouth groingrinding loinwet thighwet clungtogether hurledtogether dewy hovered sweetslam open opening felt for reached for softer swoondark swoonwet deep where love lies welling lurched and found in a couchcrash loingyre lovefunnel whirlwind headballsthroattongue whirled turning breastcunttongue spaceflapping darkswirl lightswath love a love this way found.

"I love you, Mavra."

"I knew it all the time. I love you and love you and love you."

Our wet bodies stuck together. We made no move to separate.

"Josh, actually I was terrified — what if you didn't like me? You're a terrible person to force a girl to make the first move."

"I'm dumb."

"I found you out, though, didn't I?"

"You mean my love was there all the time, hidden?"

"Yes — only I could have that love. Am I right, Josh? You wouldn't take any woman to bed — just because you and she were in an apartment together? I'll answer for you, sweetheart. It's safer that way."

On our sides, facing, armsaround, kissing, her breasts tight against me.

"It's great," I said, "falling in love with someone so familiar, someone you like. No strain, so easy. Drink me, eat me, everything open, soul mind heart and this gorgeous stuff —"

"I think we had a long engagement. I worked so hard — you were not nice to take so long. I wrote you all those loveletters from Mexico. I bet you didn't read one of those newsy chatty things between the lines?"

"Hey, no fair reminiscing about things less beautiful than this. Time started when we kissed. Let's do that."

"I did have you figured out — you'd like to make love till time ends. Never do one other thing. Erotic man, oh you are wicked!"

"I am also a father, remember?"

"Oh, God!"

Mavra jumped back.

"I went to bed with Bailla's father!"

"Knock off the horseshit, sweetheart. Let's not start faking each other out now. You and I have to stay clear, and on the same side."

"Just make love to me — around the clock only. And tell me how great I am, O.K.? Every time you think of something terrific about me, tell me. We neurotics need all the help we can get."

I put her head against my chest, pressed her cheek cool on my skin. Nina flashed into my mind. Her head here. I hugged Mavra closer.

"Josh, I want you to wash my hair. Immediately. This very second."

"O.K."

"It's a dream —"

"Behold the bridegroom cometh, with lather in hand."

"And unto her shall be given all manner of lover. But one shall come to bind her hair —"

"And set a foam in streams of water mounting. He shall lay hand on those dark tresses, and tremble at each touch. Knee to knee, breast to breast, closed eye to closed eye they shall be as one in porcelain and tile till fine rain wash them and she his bride will be again anointed. And again, and again."

"Oh I love you! So now please wash my hair."

Wringing wet we heard the telephone. I rubbed Mavra's hair dry with a thick black towel.

"Why not answer, sweetheart?"

"Josh, this is so beautiful. It's ours. I just don't want him horning in on it."

The ringing stopped.

"If we could find a screwdriver," Mavra said, "I learned long ago how to silence the bell."

Shampoo misted the apartment. Everything smelled wet and squeaky. Mavra sat on the couch, her back to me as I dried strands of wet hair in folds of towel.

space spun 271

"Would you believe I wanted this almost as much as making love with you, Josh?"

The phone rang again.

"He's sublunary, that Louie. I can't stand to think of his whine intruding. But it could be something else, I suppose."

"Answer it, sweetheart."

She picked the phone up slowly. Her mouth formed Louie's name. She made a dreadfully sour face, crossed her eyes.

"We were caught in Sunday traffic, Louie — not that I have to explain anything to a murderous shit like you."

She turned around to face me, sat yoga, then reached her bigtoe toward my belly.

"I am battered, Louie," she whimpered, winking, "I have taken one hell of a beating."

Her hand covered the mouthpiece.

"Oo my thighs! I don't think I'll walk again. Unless, sir, you can suggest immediate therapeutic remedies."

She looked up at the ceiling, shook her head, stuck her tongue out at the receiver.

"Louie's explaining," she said with a grin. "I figure it will take me months to recover — with the proper regimen, of course."

She put the phone to her mouth.

"Louie, what do you mean I'm not listening. Shmucky, I took a tranquilizer — you woke me from a sound sleep — I bet you had to ring a hundred times. See? Listen, you're a blackhearted killer, why not face up to that? How can I find it in my heart to forgive you? It's too soon, Louie."

"Bitch," I whispered.

"He loves penance, the phony. Here, listen to him whine. Come on. Hey, you really are noble."

"Not quite so noble as you and I thought."

She handed me the towel, swiveled, lay her damp hair over the towel in my lap.

"Louie," she said, settling down, "what do you want? From me, from life, from yourself? Maybe that's the question you're too full of shit to face, Louie, did that ever occur to you?"

Sunday's last train, well into Monday morning. Two Negro women dozing, on way back to their domestic stations. Blondecurl North Shore matron, homburged husband, home after a Sutton Place drunk. At the rear of the car a Merchant Marine Academy kid was fast asleep.

The train windows ran like lit filmstrips of silhouettes on the sheersloping banks.

Me. Feeling Mavra on my mouth, in my arms, all over.

Maggie's still face pinched in the blue reflection cast by bathroom light. One arm stiff behind her head. I kicked my shoes off.

"What took so long? That Sunday traffic — tell me about it? How is she?"

"O.K."

"Louie was here most of the night. He expected you sooner."

I climbed into bed, two chaste swordwidths between us.

"A whole night of Louie's keening. Was Mavra putting out too?"

"In a way."

"Josh, why do I have such a terrible feeling of doom? As if *our* life were being wrecked."

"Hey."

"What?"

"Knock off the Cassandra stuff."

"Put your arms around me."

Her hands were cold, her arms stiff.

"Josh, in cartoons — the cat gets a bump in one frame, in the next he's back as he was; he falls, he slams flat into a wall. He's always whole after."

"Maggie, let's get to sleep."

"It's not *general* psychopathy. I know what my doom feeling is about."

"Tell me, then sleep."

"Nothing — nothing matters. They can't carry something from one frame to the next. Louie's mind was a million light years from the whole thing. He didn't give Mavra or the baby a single thought. Josh, are you awake? I mean he couldn't have cared less."

"So?"

"What about Mavra — the moment she left she spit the whole thing out — right?"

"Probably."

"She acted as if nothing happened."

"I guess so."

"And we're dragged into this — you and I, shnooked."

Roland Kirk's horns hung from twisted straps. Unseeing he blew, fingerung, switched, turned, boreascheeked blew short high-pitched on a calling instrument, canopied the Five Spot wine canopy cupping sound over the bar. Mavra's wide black hat dipped his way, her rose rebosa tossed stylishly over one shoulder, her back bare. Eyes brilliantbluebrushed, blacklined, Villagelooped at the ears, putting down the Bard girls and secretaries passing; shoes of peacockblue, cigarette holder tipped up, signing herself into the sound the smoke the swirl of waitresses allblack scooping tips. Mavra Rooski Mavra spicspade Mavra ToledoMadridCannes rebosa raised, topping her hair, Roland Kirk blind Roland to her dark tower came like Orpheus, and she acknowledged the funeral musician, tragicbrowed, nodding. Threw back the rebosa to cheer Pamplona's bulls Roland Kirk unknowingly summoned. She made barstools her court, who carried trays her train. Half turned to me, pressing backwards softwarmsmoothbareshoulders, one halfoff pasteltoe lightly touching my calf, rubbing music horns might burst to catch. My hands on her leanedback shoulders, soft warmth spreading softwarm on the barstool closer, catching her under the arms, raising her up, out into nightair, crush lipglued oblivious of eightmillionnine, selfengirdling, spacespun over avenues greenlighted, an opening door, rebosa thrown high in a flashofflesh rocketing colors closed eyes lipwet tonguewet allwet all all and how could Roland Kirk know?

"Claim me, open me, own me, Josh. Anything, everything, make me measure up. We've bust out, Josh, gravity doesn't hold us, everything we need in the world is right here —"
"What about the baby?"
"Oh God, that's right."

Love's arrogance every lointhrust wilder a skymount a whirlwind, sundancer touched down on earth. FiftyNinthStreet's bridge, dissolving looking-glass, once through, everchanged, no turnback.
— Knock knock.
— Who's there?
— God.
— God who?

"Oh, did you happen to see Mavra in town?"
"Yes."
She took Bailla's hands, rubbed them in a folded towel, pushed her toward me. Arms out, squealing, Bailla ran into my arms. She yanked at my tie, pressed her forehead against mine.
"Where," said Maggie, "did you see her?"
"Under the clock at the Biltmore."
I put Bailla down. She clung to my leg.
"How," said Maggie, "is she?"

"O.K. I guess."

"Did you give her my best?"

"Josh, you're right, I am still full of fantasies. He's King Mark, and Maggie's the one with potions, and *we* drank."

"Great."

"In another you're the gardener."

"Christ!"

"I've had one where Maggie's Medea —"

"Are you sure she's not hated alter-ego Marian?"

"You can think *that* — after all this?"

"Yes."

"I to-o-o-o-o-old you that in strictest confidence."

"Uh uh, baby. You told it to Maggie and me, sitting at the foot of our bed."

"You are a sonofabitch, and a cad too."

"I'm keeper of poor battered reality —"

"I hate reality."

"It's where our bellies touch."

"I love reality."

In the dark sky, lit towers and cupolas hung like go-go-girl cages from a swinger ceiling. We climbed the bridge, behind us Manhattan rose like a carnival band from below stage level. Mavra leaned her head back to look up at the vaudeville moon. Rushing wind blew her hair streaming in a dark train.

"We should have rituals for lovers — you should carve my face —"

"Ugh."

"Oh I mean beautifully. Delicate. Not African stuff. Something gorgeous, even invisible — to everybody but those who *should* eat their hearts out."

"Love tempered with a little moral, a little vengeance."

"I'm telling you how much I'm in love. I want to wear us public as the Empire State Building — our mystic signature engraved, glowing like that 'Domino Sugar' sign."

"In primitive naval societies such feelings lead to tattoo."

"Stop mocking me! I'll never say what comes into my head. I'll only wonder if it's naïve, or corny."

"I'm sorry."

"Wouldn't you like a special sign on you?"

"I know what I would choose to wear."

"You're terrible."

She curled her head on my chest, my arm under her, her lovely face turned up.

"My muscles," she whispered, "God — here and here. My arch, of all things — go explain that. My chin is all chafed. My nose. Brute. You're supposed to shave before — Josh, I am dying to *tell* somebody — not just anybody — does that make me an exhibitionist? God, I mean as if this were the greatest of all Christmases and I got the most gorgeous gift—unexpected! I'm dying to tell Maggie. Do you think I'm crazy? She's not Louie. I know she's on the side of lovers."

I hugged her to my chest.

"Louie would think this was done *against* him — to spite him, poor man."

We swung a bowbend along the Sound. Ghost bridges hung northward in mist. The air was damp with seasmell, lobstersmell. It hung particled, in graywhite motes the carhood parted like the nose of a plane passing through a cloud.

South of the water, on higher land, the fog was gone. We drove over bumpy narrow roads past black fields treehumped, moonslit. Horsechestnuts heaped in the dark sky, and elbowboughed larch. Trunks shone silver in carlight as we rolled silently past the darkened mansion of Christopher's family estate.

"Josh — is this what you've never done with any other girl?"

"Shshshshsh."

White-lit corral fences crisscrossed the night. Birch bark black on white reversed, as in a negative.

"I think we're romantics," Mavra whispered. "Tough cynics like us."

"The price of romanticism could be an ass an-itch with ivy."

Twigsnapping our feet and knees. Nightshrill nightcroak peeper cicada leafrustle silk windcombing overhead oaks to shine moonlight glint eye blackshadow breasts moonflicker twigcrush darkneedle summer soft pinebed year upon year dry but nightdamp now when above all the peepers and this kiss octaves below or above mouthonmouth moaningkissingsong unsung unheard but under black lilypads answered, and echoed on moonflashed dark wings.

"I hate every woman you ever spoke to."

I pointed her hand at the shifting moon.

"Hate is the wrong subject, moonstuff."

"I don't want an affair — O.K., promise?"

"I love you, Mavra."

"How many times in your life have you said that?"

"Listen to it now. I love you."

"When I first saw you I knew — immediately. This is a guy who falls in love ten times a day. I didn't mean it nastily — it was so clear. You could never feel this is my love, only this —"

"This pause is not to be used for Maoist self-criticism, sweet."

"I won't have five seconds of your life unfilled by me."

In the dark we felt around for our things, naming what we found.

"Josh, could I leave a stocking here — like a victory flag? My scutcheon. I'd like to tie a stocking round the throat of every bitch you've been with. I'd start with Maggie. You are dreadfully loyal to her — I want you to bury her and join me in a dance on her grave."

"Thy love, sweet, is too much mixed with murder."

"It's all one, isn't it, Josh? If it means so much we go all out — not a thing held back. You give me anything."

"A child?"

"Children are different. This is a war thing. Maggie *has* to be cut up —"

"No she doesn't —"

"Why don't you feel the same thing about Louie? How can you stand to know he touches me? I can't abide the thought of any woman in bed with you — I feel a stab, a swordthrust right in my middle. Josh, listen — I'm not fooling. There's a spot — feel it — not my breasts not my heart not — oh, what's it called? Something awful. Sternum? Is that it? We're joined here, Josh. Bone to bone. If we separate ever I'll be like a Siamese twin and die immediately."

"Hate and death — what is this violence shit? Your clothes are poisoned, princess. You didn't sound this way before."

"Josh I want to be something special — magnificent. Could my love heal your hip?"

"Sweetheart, this is the twentieth century. We don't go for such things."

"*You* do."

"I did, but I don't now."

"Oh I know you do. I'm not wrong, am I? You've dreamed of that miracle. A love miracle. You'll meet some great warm girl and she'll work that miracle. That's what you're holding back from me, Josh, and I can't stand it. That patronizes me. I'm a lesser being. Don't you understand anything, Josh? I want that girl to be me."

Blackscreen darkened Maggie's face. Whiteframe and her chin held down. In the lower doorhalf Bailla bibbed in white was waving. The outside lights were still on. Sun made them weak and ugly.

"Josh, hurry!" Maggie shouted.

I ran in to pick Bailla up in my arms.

"Josh, your mother had a stroke."

I let Bailla down. My face was burning.

"Josh, did you hear? They want us there, right away — both of us — do you want me to go, Josh?"

"You said they want us both."

"Do *you* want me?"

"Maggie it's not a party —"

"You know what I mean — what's happening? Now isn't the time. Nothing ever is —"

"Get packed. I'll get us reservations —"

"You can phone for them, Josh."

"I've other things to do —"

"Here?"

"I'll be right back."

"Josh, for godsake, you've just come back. I haven't seen you for hours. Days."

"I'll be right back in minutes, Mag. Pack."

Mavra buried her face in her pillows, pulled the sheets over her head, screaming, terrorcry, caught in her throat, eyes screwed tight, fisted hands clinging to bedding. I pulled at her shoulders, twisted her head up. Tears and saliva ran over her cheeks.

"You can't. Josh, you can't you can't you can't. I made it, sweetheart. You know I made it. I deserve something. You absolutely must, you have to take me with you. You made me part of your family. That's what it's all about, Josh. I'm never left out of anything again. I'm your cherished. You couldn't leave me behind if you wanted to. Take Maggie too, sweetheart. But don't leave me. Ask me to do anything. Your mother will adore me. She'll see it in an instant. It was an accident of time only, sweetheart, that I didn't meet you before Maggie. Your mother is magnificent, Josh. She'll be sweet to Maggie. But we'll know she knows. This is mine,

Josh! Your family is mine! Your mother is mine! Her stroke is my business more than it's Maggie's."

"Sweetheart, we can't move in on this."

"Oh why did you say that? I hate you for saying that. I made it. You can't leave me here — don't you see? You can't reject me! You mustn't abandon me. Josh, look at me — see who I am. I made a world. We made a world. Listen to me! You're my leader. You won't do this. Tell me you won't."

"I'll be back in no time at all —"

She twisted out of my arms, heaped in the middle of the bed, tried again to pull the sheets over her head. I put my arms around her. She sat up.

"I'm wrong to be hysterical, sweetheart — I know I know I know. But I'm trembling inside. I came to life. You can't take my life away like this. Find us a potion, Josh. I'll drink it and grow terribly small. Carry me in your pocket all the way. When they're all asleep take me out, I'll become this me. We'll make love — no I mean just kiss and hug. And together we'll steal into your mother's room. Your father could be in on it too. Josh, we're a billion times more important than illness. Even your mother's. We're the greatest. We floated to the top of everything. We're married. More than married. Our great ceremonies — on that bridge, under those trees. I'm your ring. Just say the word, command me — I'll scream our love over Park Avenue, cry it in simultaneous translation at the U.N. You and I were born again. We can't ever turn us away from that, sweetheart. My body — your body. Touch any part of me, darling — oh, please. We created it all. I had no soul no body no heart — Josh, I was a murdering coldhearted castrating nymph — in Mexico, before that. I did it all in a black sleep. You woke me, darling. One kiss and you woke me. I'm spectacular, Josh, and you can take the credit. I could be mounted on the prow of a fighting ship."

"You are spectacular, lovely girl, and I didn't do a thing to make you so."

"You're cutting out of the credit so you can cut out of the responsibility. I'm nothing without you. I'm incomplete. You'll tear my heart right out if you go."

"Mavra, listen to me. What you feel is true, and right, but it's not —"

"Josh, you'll deny me and wipe me out. I'll be back to the old full-of-shit Mavra. I can't stand that. I deserve your mother's arms around me, don't I, Josh? Didn't I become a person? A real live real true mensch."

"You always were."

"No I wasn't. I wasn't and you know I wasn't. By saying something neutral you're shutting me out. I'm connected to you. Josh, you're hard. You're so terrible, so tough on me. Your arms are stiff. My face is here against your chest but my cheek feels bars and pikes — is it that I didn't make it at all?"

"Of course it isn't, lovely!"

"Was I fooling myself?"

"I'm not a judge, sweetheart. I'm not the one to pronounce on you. I'm your witness. I love you and everything spectacular about you —"

"What about the crumby things?"

"Those too."

"But you're protecting me — I feel it. I haven't got it, right? To be that girl who'd make you heal. That girl you wouldn't leave behind. You couldn't, Josh."

The public story given out was that she, like Aeneas, had her destiny to do. The tale we know best is Aeneas's, who had the gods on his side always, telling him of course he was right, and proving it with that famous success. She, in that very same legend, ends burning herself on a Carthaginian pyre.

I tell you a truer tale: the real story is Dido's, who had no trouble understanding why Aeneas did what he did, and when. She knew he was big with the gods, and they with him. And, being a queen, she knew gods and cities were quite high in the scales which lead to choosing. She put all those weightier things on the falling pan, and on the light one, rising, sat herself, alone. And being alone she registered an unheroic fact, that Aeneas had left her.

And cried, Dido, not like a queen, not like a heroic great lady who knows the score gods keep. She cried and her nose ran, her eyes grown red, swollen. She cried an abandoned child's unmuted despairing terrified angry shriek.

Queen Dido, left alone.

Idlewild's control tower floated, bubble of green glass, skylit operating room filled with bustling surgeons. A blacktailed BOAC jet thundered our cab's metal roof, swept over our heads, climbed skyward jerkily on four broken black smoke ropes. I raised Bailla to the window to watch a plane with teetering wings rumble across the overhead runway bridge. Like tightrope walkers a dozen piercingfinned jets rocked into an impatient queue, awaiting take-off. Yellow cars and cabs, square airport buses, limousines raced with us on the counterclockwise run. The Pan-American Terminal was a California drive-in where monster planes and not sports cars sat in stalls for service. Idlewild's powerplant hugged the ground like massed Léger sculptures of chalky pipes scrolling green and blue and orange around two white cement Buddhas, furnaces molded on squat daises.

I sat on the aisle, Maggie beside me, Bailla kneeling up at the window. Muzak tinkled teatime tune to cover the motor roar of readiness. Bailla sat back, grinning, her eyes open and excited and fearful. The music stopped. Planenose planetail did an about face, twin compasses with wheels for fixed feet. Whistling in a rush of sound and air the jet motors screamed the plane onto the runway. All senses drowned in sound. The shrieking rush of rockets and artillery firing. But in it, through it, I heard Mavra coughing out that desperate cry; my arms ached, my chest felt her head on it, and in it, as if a massive switchboard of multiple wires intertangled were being torn out and scrambled. The plane powered the runways. It ran at concrete, blew high weeds and bushes into a bend and bowing, turned upward, pillowed by underair, banked, gyrated, whipped higher and higher above cloud and earthview, pure blue, sunworld, where Mavra's cry muted, misted, fell in a shower, part of the plane's wake. Soundless, crying unbelief that this appointment would not keep. I ached with love. Till space absorbed the gliding plane and lost us in its blue-white golden infinities.

Maggie had taken the window seat. Her face reflected pale in the glass. Bailla nestled her head beside me. I in that flying arc crossed a midline. I wanted Mavra in my arms but the jet would not have it.

That stone corridor like a rut in space caught my pounding feet, onbeat, offbeat, and to my ear echoed an earlier step. Sealed stone canister holding my past for timed release. Rigid space. Bad and dark and old. Massed, turgid with what might dart into unsuspecting rooms to X men in beds, flash of black, smokywing, teakbeak.

I framed myself in the doorway. Bunched my muscles, tensed my legs and arms and shoulders to keep those corridor shadows out.

My father's face was sculpted terror. Hollow marble cheeks, eyes dark and deep as rounded glass. Sorrowing Ravenna king and emperor. My mother's face I saw in profile, tiny, white, silverdark hair roped and braided. I called to them. She cried her response. Hoarse, strained, untuned, almost soundless mock of that rising jet sound. Without strength, weakening more, the highest pitch of a violin string when the lower three are missing.

I rushed to put my arms around them. That cry was killing me. I fought to keep my hands away from my ears.

My father whispered.

"Don't look at her, Josh. She doesn't want you to see. She's all pulled to one side. She's afraid she'll scare you."

"Ma!" Something like a prayer broke from my throat.

She put her hands to her face and peeked out at me from her barring fingers.

"My tongue is a raw potato, Joshua. You can't understand one word I say. I can't even."

"Are you O.K.?" my father whispered. "Bailla? Maggie?"

"Great, we're all great."

"I'm a mess, Joshua — so be prepared. I cry or I laugh. I hear myself, like I'm in the next room. 'Poor crazy old woman,' I think, and pity her."

I put my arms around her. She pushed me away with her elbows, and wouldn't uncover her face.

"Maybe my craziness is catchy. You want to catch it? You want Bailla to have this lunatic's disease?"

"She wants to see you."

"Hold her up at the window. I'll look at her and hide."

Her hands pressed hard against her cheeks. I kissed them, dry, trembling, tiny. My father motioned me out to the corridor.

"Joshua," he said, and his dark eyes opened wet with pain and wonder, "she won't reverse."

"Pa, don't worry, I'm here."

"I know you're here, Joshie."

"I mean I'll take over."

"What will you take over, Joshua?"

I followed him to the dark sunporch. Fear pressed wires on his forehead and cheeks. He tried to light a cigarette. Malarial shudders shook his body.

"I just finished slopping coffee all over me," he said with a laugh. "Two hands together and I couldn't control a simple cup."

I lit his cigarette.

"Joshua," he burst out, "your Uncle Bim loved you. He talked about you — we did — listen, you remember that tweed coat with the velvet collar I bought you — I think about it — how old were you, four I think."

"Pa I don't want to remember me."

I turned to go back.

"Don't leave for a second, Josh. Calm me down. Let ma collect herself. Her sickness won't let a happy thing in yet. Listen, I want to tell you what Bim said —"

"Pa, please, I don't want to hear it. What did the doctor say?"

"Can't you see that, Joshua? She won't reverse. You won't ride in here like a hero — I wish you could. You can't put arms around her and kiss it and make better like she was a kid and fell and banged her knee. You and I are out of this, Joshie. I know you can't stand to hear it —"

In darkness when a flare explodes, illuminating everything, freezing reality for a twinkling of an eye, what's here is transmogrified. Space arrested. Beyond mere dimensions. Diestamped space. Shadow fresco, black urnfretting. Dark theater of action. My mother's face still in profile, good cheek to the door I stand by: powderwhite unpowdered skin, one seen eye shimmering with tranquilizer and tears. Over her my father is on watch, something dark and doglike in his eyes. White hair rises from his forehead like a mourning high priest's prayerhat.

Fear chills my black world. Fear flashes in the corridor like an unimpeded night jet slashing space high above a powerless country. Unbridgeable space separates my mother's bed and me fixed in the doorway. She floats on a dark floe. Breaking away, receding, pulling back into black water, whirling space darker and wider a nightpit nightchasm uncrossable between us.

Dear Maggie,

Things there must be hard for you. If it were possible, or right, I would fly out and take over. But I can't. That's why I am writing. It is as hard for me as it will be for you.

Josh and I are in love, Maggie.

We are lovers. I must tell you it was satisfying in every possible way. We didn't plan it. It happened, though details I'm sure are no great consolation to you.

Love isn't everything — as you yourself must know. Our love is overwhelmingly beautiful and exciting and life-giving, but when Josh was called he did not choose me. He chose you.

Louie, poor dear, knows nothing, of course, and can never be told. His analyst ordered my silence. Louie is as you know a mass of morbid fixes — his beginnings and all that (it's Louie's psyche and actually very private and must be respected). Potentially he is a loving man and it's only an accident he's not. I pity him. You must too. Not being the right stature is something nobody could hide from himself, not even somebody as self-involved as poor Louie. What I mean is that I'm back living with him. Sometimes he makes me jump out of my skin. One touch sets my teeth on edge. But his analyst is right. I'm at fault too. I *force* Louie to act like my father. That's being a terrible bitch. I have a natural talent for castrating, or so Louie's analyst tells me, poor guy. He's actually far more interested in me than a therapist is allowed by his ethics.

But to hell with Louie.

I'm writing about us, Maggie, and you may well be wondering where all this leaves us. I think we'll go on as we were. As if nothing crucial had happened. It will be our secret, and will make us even closer. I know no woman can read what I've written, dear, and not feel blown right out of the water. What's hardest for you, I know, is the knowledge that Josh and I have something which not even marriage can affect. Marriage is an external — it would be brutal to say another word on this subject. Josh and I are of one flesh. That couldn't change even if one of us died. So what I am saying, Maggie, is that I don't for a second question your role in his life. I am not Josh's wife, nor will I pretend to be that. He fathered Bailla in you. I think you were his first real love. My life with Louie is pretty well fixed. His call on me for the higher things is finished. He won't know that. His ego isn't tough enough to take truths like this. I'm his companion, his nurse, his cook who brings him tidbits while he's working. I even go to bed with him on the terrible occasions that's called for. I playact with him, the way you do with chronically ill children. You know what *he* would do if he got a letter like this?

Would I embarrass you if I said I couldn't possibly have written this before I met you? You taught me how to be truthful. I grew up believing the world swallowed anybody whole — who told the truth, I mean. What's in my ears is my liar voice. I used to be that way myself. Now I hear my voice and I sound like *you!* So don't think all siblings have to end up hating each other!

I hope Josh's mother gets better. Please give her and everybody else my best.

Love,
Mavra
P.S. I suggest that for all our sakes you burn this letter.

Darling Josh!

I hit on this great idea of a windowed envelope to make our lovetalk look like a bill. I do love you, denyer. I am dying.

Maggie may mention a letter. I wrote about us. She must have suspected all along — as Louie might say, things buried in the unconscious are dangerous to our health. I felt so great telling the truth! I never want to stop doing that.

She'll tell you I've gone back to live with Louie. It's an arrangement like any other arrangement. And you won't believe how the guy moons over me. It's rather disgusting. I think it's this thing you released in me. A love something. It started when I gave birth. A tiny trace. What I have now is like a release. I exude something primitively feminine. I stood in a corner at the Metropolitan yesterday, minding my own business, and the joint started jumping. Old guys, cloakroom attendants, guards, elevator men, everybody was *interested*. I could have gone off with any one of seven or eight of the most attractive arrogant sonsofbitches. I turned them off, the bastards. I used to play a different kind of game in Mexico. Sometimes I would, sometimes I wouldn't. That wasn't exuding. It was that I was a gringo chick and young and hung with a Louie albatross. You uncorked that new thing, bad man. On Fifth Avenue you would think I was girl pied piper to lovely boy children and all those Madison Ave rats.

Oh well.

I'm trying.

Being a good sport isn't easy. I keep thinking that bitch converted illness into a second honeymoon — I could tear her limb from limb. Please don't so much as spend ten seconds alone in the same room with her. You're *my man*. She has to have written permission to speak to you. Louie and I sleep on separate floors and I still feel dirty and disloyal to you. Apart from everything else I told Louie's analyst I am no sexual training camp for Louie. Let him find a whore who majors in rehabilitation.

God, I'm such a narcissistic bitch — and I talk about Louie! I shouldn't have said one thing about us. Only your mother, Josh sweetheart. I wish I could sneak out of Louie's bed in the middle of the night and you'd meet me at the airport. It's still late summer but it would be snowing big white flakes on my lashes (didn't you once take a hot walk with a bitch called Zora? Maggie told me about that). We'd bundle in the backseat of a cab and zip up to your mother's bedside. She'd cry and tell me how great I look. Your father would keep saying "Mavra you are beautiful — you are Josh's fate." They'd still be nice to Maggie. Your mother would say Bailla resembles me, and I'd tell her Dov has started to look like you. It would be a loving conspiracy. Your mother I bet would be better in days. She would never let me leave that city. Oh God my heart is pounding! I'm breaking out all over! Sheer delight to think such thoughts! Love love love — oh that warms me.

Kiss your mother a tiny tiny kiss and she'll know I sent that. I'm on a wavelength with her and your father and Bailla and you. Tune me in on the nightbands. All of me will expand in space. And all — or most — of you. Our bellies will touch sometime after four A.M. EST high above Lake Superior by my calculation (none too reliable). A feathery touch, sweetheart, since at times such as these the presiding angels allow no more. The world will record us in a meteorite shower like those Leonides but we won't reveal the true cause ever. Thousands will report a new sighting. Men may behave as magi, drop their worldly ways and vow pilgrimages. Astronomers haven't caught on yet. How come? I've looked in *The Times* and a thousand magazines for one report of the earth's gigantic upheaval that night you took me in your arms. We are still a guarded secret.

Maybe it's because I'm a witch. If you try getting into the sack with some longhaired girl you'll see! You won't be able to get it up. If you do you won't be able to make it. If you do that you'll positively hate it. Poor girl she'll die with shame. She'll say what's the matter and you'll tell her it's my gorgeous magnificent Mavra, a real woman, a billion times told lovelier than any ordinary female, and hotter, more gorgeous. She may slit her throat, so watch her, poor thing.

I can't stop writing, as if I hold on to you as long as my pen touches paper. I'll hide under the stamp in the shape of a kiss. That will close the stretching spaces between us. Too bad some engineer wasn't a problem solver for lovers. Why shouldn't Macy's sell a $19.95 magic carpet for lovers who qualify?

Think of it. Us separated.

I'll be thrown back to what do you call them — pre-*Oresteia* days. When love and justice were just a lot of shit and men lived a claw for a claw. I'll have my vengenace on you, you know, but don't think the guy who gets me will escape whipping. I'll leave nailmarks all over his bare back to record he sneaked into our circle by accident and rotten chance.

Oh this is no way to close, on such a crumby note. Forget this last bit. It's unworthy of me. Anything unworthy couldn't possibly be real, right? This is all so terrible. What I know and what you can never tell me isn't so is that if I were the great girl you've always dreamed about there would be no letter because there could never have been a separation.

Oh well. I may be unworthy but I do love you hugely.

Here, this is the way to make everything better, and conquer separating space. I kiss a border round these pages and touch each corner to me here. And in the center lies my love.

Llllloooovvvveeeelovlovlovlovlov!

M (now what does that stand for?)

Beatty too came, my mother's baby sister, from the green coast she came, her green eyes grayed with fear but shining as they shone in space the day they carried off my grandfather's turquoise eyes.

All eyes hooded.

Nightwatch. All nights joined. Continuous, risen like tidal water to cover our separated islands. Grandfather's night. Mac's night. Wilkoh's night. Swarming darkness in which we, lightilluminated, stood apart in vigil.

Not even my imagination could raise my mother from her bed,

prop her in a doorway or at a window. Reality would not be swept under. Only its airless breathless yawnfilled nightside merged with the darkness past.

Once, and then again, and again, a cry broke from my mother like a bird crashing loose of its cage, which, itself returning, breaks loose again, over and over.

My hands framed that then. But not this other, which in retrospect I had forced on me, with the glints and shadings I had almost missed. Just a simple leavetaking. He got out of the car, my father, with Beatty beside him. Sun lay abstract shadows at their feet. His eyes burned like brown pins in a blank map. A hundred other days of a hundred other — a hundred hundred other ordinary motions. He started up the steps. Beatty ran to catch up with his stride. Cars passed in a stream around me. The road stretched in asphalt band in front of the hospital; my graygleaming river ran parallel in back. The seminaries tipped their darkscreen porches toward the street. A priest allowed a running child to pass. My car hood shivered to my motor's idling. A template now, with twice-seen particles gathered in patterned charge. I imagine three birds winging in swallow-flight seconds before Hiroshima. Unconscious men and women cross the street as I wait for a light to change. I honk my going to my father. At the top of the white concrete steps he turns to wave.

Four minutes, five — measure them.

Three miles, five at the most, say.

See our reality. All other beings apart we skim the earth's circumferences. Flesh-enclosed. Our tale has only this telling, our telling. Space is empty but for this single track. One gray tarpatched road. And at the end of it Maggie, whom I didn't recognize for an instant, her hair streaming behind her, the silk of her dress clinging as she ran toward me. Hands wave. She shouts. I run from the car.

Beatty was on the phone, crying crying crying.

"Josh," I thought she shouted, "he's dead — your father, Josh —"

"Beatty," I shouted back, "you mean ma."

"Your father your father your father — Josh, quick, I'll die too."

I broke past Maggie drove over no road in no world, retraced my run in torn space, to start again, reverse it, cast it out. Heard the whores shriek maniacal as I stumbled over steps and broke inside, running through those stone corridors, one nun beside me, one nurse, and more, running, all running as if a tidal wave broke behind us.

My mother's room was locked.

Outside a closed door Beatty was bent and crying.

Doctors rose from him as I rushed in. He lay behind a peachcolor scrim screened in deathshadow. Feet bare, hornynailed. Gapemouthed, his lips fixed like bone.

I grabbed up his hand.

It was cold. Unfamiliar.

Pressed my lips to his forehead and told myself it was warmer. I could not believe him dead beyond our powers. Life was ebbed. Something remained. A pail knocked over, not everything spilled.

I patted his wrists. Life should run out of my hands. Youth. Love. Everything he needed.

The nun shook her head at me. The nurses turned away.

My dry voice cried wake to a dry ear. I could not even hold his lips back from curving inward on his teeth. Walls rose sheer and dry with those shadows, that silence.

I shook my father. Harder. He could not but rise and rub his eyes and ask what happened.

Kissed his forehead once more. It was cold with death.

A rip, a root torn from soil tendril by tendril, searing, milelong, pulled from my throat from my chest. Irreversible death. Knowledge that flayed. I could not be to my father as if he were Lazarus.

I stepped back.

His trousers rolled as if his bare feet were set to go wading. Death would not wave him away, or let him sink through the floor or be covered by a sheet. Death left me no easy exit. My father lay cold in a strange bed. Bony mouth without breath. I heard a sound escape my throat, ugly, weak, abject, pitiful. I swayed from it as from a hangman's cord.

So Orpheus wept to learn the limits of his lyre.

Beatty bent outside that other door couldn't stop crying. I put my arms around her.

"Josh, we can't."

"What?"

"Tell her."

She pressed both hands over her mouth to choke off sobbing. My hand with anonymous will reached for a doorknob. My leaden cheeks tried to describe a smile.

"Ma, hi!"

She struggled to sit up. Did not cover her twisted cheek.

"What happened to him?"

"He's probably coming down with something."

"Serious?"

"It might be, ma."

"Sit closer, Josh. I can't hear you."

I reached for her hand with my useless two. She lay back. Two tears hung at the corners of her eyes.

"You remember how he broke once, Josh?"

"That was long ago."

"This is the wrong place for him, Joshua. You don't know — he never could stand sickness. He hated coming to see you in hospitals. Think of a place we can send him till I get out."

Swolleneyed under dark glasses Gad stamped his foot, cursing shale in a buckshot scatter out of his path. Black arm against mine, moving aside a space, where she would have been, ahead of us, bowed in black. Slowstep black legs black shoes beside the black car with twisted posts like the legs of our old dining-room table. Six graygloved hands on the gray box, six graygloved hands swung at sides. Two graves. Did the diggers know the mound they made out of his was heaped on hers? Or Gad stamping his foot again, that those planks covered what was pieced for our mother?

Silent pulleys let it down, out of space, below time, beneath that rising song sadder than crying. Black whirlwind, shrieking bird climbing the sun, rising, black gyre bursting, raining down a mourner's darkness, violent sorrow pelting bowed heads.

Two fistfuls of driest dirt we threw into that pit, Gad's first, then mine, each grain a thundered nailblow on the gray coffin lid.

I could not mourn my father there. Terror dragged me from his graveside. I might hide his death from her, but not the death of the man who was her husband. Shortsleeved hospital gown gaped at the back, hair in white pigtails, her eyes on the shut door. Where could I find the strength to pass through it?

Sun warmed the blank stone.

His side there.

Hers.

That song sobbed itself out.

We turned round.

Reversed our way. Shadows fell behind us. Gad pounded his fist into his palm, silent in the back seat beside me. Slumped on a low stool, swearing to himself, stamping his stockinged feet.

I wanted to close my eyes and find cool darkness. Collapse in a corner and give my father the mourning I owed him. Burial should have covered both coffin and wound.

In times when nails tore at cheeks and men covered themselves with ashes, time moved on, mourning grew quiet, and dumb. Weepers retired from the whirlwind and, I think, slept.

It would have been beautiful just to sleep.

To wake without the appointed task, without agony, without this leaden fear. Chained to the inescapable. Gad could not stop his pounded cursing. My feet to the grave, from the grave, in the house of mourning, out, moved step by step closer to that horrifying moment. What messenger can carry this news ever?

My mother's illness cheated my father out of a death of his own. I could not remember what he looked like alive. Fear washed my memory free of his image.

Was there, I wondered, someone like Orpheus who comes from the dark side of Styx to lead the living out of the light?

I forced Uncle Bim's doctor son, Jeremiah, to check her room's oxygen, double her dosage of tranquilizer, and walk right behind me. A nurse in the stone corridor wheeled a white table. Starched linen covered sedation, stimulants, all measure of emergency.

Nothing lessened my fear. I walked openeyed but blind, a sleepwalker inhaling this cold jet from my lungs to my numb brain. Jeremiah's shoes squeaked in the hollow corridor. A voice chanted the same Rosary I'd heard a hundred times before on that same intercom. Prayer in an echo chamber, muffled, crackling static. In open rooms mumbled praying answered. Hands wrung. Hands in steeples. Evening webbed outwards from that darkest angel's underwings.

I had no breath. All my night terrors thundered within me. Scares locked away in closets, kicked under beds. In her doorway I was speechless, paralyzed coward.

She saw my face.

"He's gone?"

Something girlish broke out of her. Something sporty. An angry toss of her head as if I brought news of no more than a broken date. A magnificent young woman glared through paincreased skin.

Then she fell back. I shouted at Jeremiah. The nurse quickly wheeled in the table.

Reedthin her cry. Worn out, weak, weaker, trapped in that small room. Her head lay back.

"Jerry, do something!"

He looked out the window.

I began to shout, louder than her deafness needed, louder than the *Hail Marys* petering out in the stone hallways.

I shouted arguments, coaxings, family jingo, sentimentality, invoked God and the prophets, grandfather, greatgrandfather, words never mouthed by kings or counsellors, begged Jeremiah to swear to the truth spoken by Uncle Bim commanding inscription in the Book of Life.

She put her small hands over her ears.

"Josh," she cried out to the pillow, "please, for my sake, stop hollering."

"Only if you're on my side. Only if you promise."

She struggled to turn toward me. I gave her my hand. Hers was wet.

"What shall I promise, Josh, that I won't have another stroke?" Jeremiah put his hand on my shoulder.

"Promise you'll keep fighting —"

"I'm a rag, Joshua."

"You're a mother. You're a grandmother. You're a woman."

"Josh, look closer. I'm nothing."

"You're alive. You're here. That's everything."

"Sickness wrecked me — can't you see? I can't change back."

"Goddam it you don't have to change back!"

"Joshua stop your yelling! You'll scare the old ladies."

"You haven't promised."

"Idiot, stop that terrible hollering. They'll throw us all out of here in another minute. Listen — just shut up. In two seconds I may be crying again. Or laughing like a lunatic. I can't do a thing about it."

"I'm not asking you to do anything about anything."

"Josh you can't be straight with me. I'm telling you how things really are."

"What really is is that you're my mother and I'm your son. You kept me alive then."

"That was at the beginning of a long life. How can you compare this torn piece of cloth that's left?"

"Ma, goddam it, you owe it to me to stay alive!"

Jeremiah huddled with the nurse before the darkening window. I could hear my deafening bellow charge the stone halls.

My mother lay back again.

"Josh, never mind this campaign. You haven't told me — when did he die?"

"Immediately."

"You came in — he was already dead?"

"Yes —"

"Why didn't you tell me?"

"I was too frightened."

"It wasn't yours to keep, his death."

"Ma I simply was yellow."

She reached for my hand, patted it once.

"Ma, will you promise now?"

"Another stroke would make me a basket case."

"I don't care."

"It's not up to you, Josh, to decide how I should live."

She covered her face with her hands, and wept. Drawnout distant keening cry, hoarse, then soundless. A nun looked into the room, her glasses opaque as mirrors. Jeremiah stole into the corridor's yellow light. The nurse wheeled the table out behind him. Metal charts slammed on metal. Nurse heels beat urgency against the stone floor.

Worn and weary. Tinyshouldered. Weeping into her pillow.

I put my arms around her.

Then, only then, I remembered what he looked like, and cried for my dead father.

Josh love,

I'm thinking of taking a patent out on these envelopes. Love Inc. Statements sent monthly.

Why haven't I heard from you, terrible man? I know it's not

your mother. You must be having a ball, you bastard.

Oh well.

It's your irresponsibility which is responsible for me. I fell again.
I'm back to being the Mexican bitch I was before I met you and
became what you rejected and abandoned, bastard. Can you see a
loophole in my logic? I mean I've done things that are past praying
for. Nothing could possibly be worse. And if it's not worse, why
not do it? My new motto is for godsake lead me into temptation. I
could do just about anything, I think.

I've figured life out pretty well. We should always be proper on
the outside — none of this beat bullshit. Eat in gourmet restau-
rants, shop at Bendel's and Bergdorf's and those great old lady specialty shops, speak generously — clean tongue, clean heart, all that.
Behave correctly, with great manners, so that, well, you know,
people remember, like, "Dear Mavra, You may not recall the
old lady in the park ten years ago but you spoke so sweetly. I can
never forget. I am talking to you from the grave, dear Mavra. My
lawyers are instructed to settle ten thou a year on your head for
life." I am convinced rich things are the real pleasures in this society. Who ever suffers from somebody pissing away a buck?
God, wouldn't it be great if we were loaded! Unlimited money
would take the crimps out of our style. Those crumby sours who
hang on to their dough or spend it sensibly! Lock them up. Turn
their accounts over to me. One month for every soul in the Hamp-
tons — would that be an education!

I guess by now you understand I'm the all-or-nothing type.
When I was asleep everything was asleep. What did Joyce call it —
the Dante Alighieri (sp?) refrigerating apparatus — you know —
choked up, chill, and phony. You unleashed the woman under my
dead skin. You created me, you irresponsible creature. I used to
hate my body — oh I know I've told you this before — why
couldn't I have those Gina breasts, rippling ponds!

I was looking at a Rubens woman yesterday. Floating fatass. I've
got much greater stuff — in greater colors — than those Hals tit-
sies. I compete with all those Museum odalisques. I win every
time. So why aren't you right here using this stuff? Nobody can be
my absentee lord.

So look what happens — and all because of you.

I was comparing myself with someone's Aphrodite — not Botticelli's — you know the one — she's only got two hands, and three

things to cover. I gave up understuff for the duration so there I was
exuding and feeling all open and exciting and naked — I got out by
faking a quarrel and riding off in what Louie calls my aristocratic
huff, the shmuck. This guy stood beside me — kind of pock-
marked, a nobleman's pocks, and dressed like a Roman lord with a
lot of cuff and collar, silk, and leather. I always know when a guy
picks up my message — you don't mind my telling, sweetheart? I
am trying to be open. Well, so he's there. My heart was pounding.
I knew I meant business but couldn't tell if he knew. I'm looking
at Aphrodite but he says something about El Greco's colors on the
cardinal — not exactly to me but more to the guard. And steps
closer. He had a sports car illegally parked in front of the Museum.
Maybe I'm a cinch and took only the planned length of time. He
crushed a bill into a doorman's hand and I could tell from the
fawning thanks it had to be ten at least. His place was in the Fifties
in what looks like a commercial building only the elevator stops in
his livingroom. His mother was there but withdrew. I sat on a brocade couch and he took his sweet time pouring some cruddy stuff
into thin tall glasses. His walls had more on them than the Metropolitan. Picasso and Miró and Pollock. He talked and talked and I
didn't know quite how to tell him this couldn't be a European villa
go. Louie was out. The babysitter had to be home early. I threw
one leg up on the couch and he just had to stroke upwards. God
you should have seen him jump! European women must go around
trussed in elastic. There must be something schitzy in me. I was
like a spectator. Excited, but in a way out of it. One little twist and
the poor guy couldn't hold back. It's terrible to discover a guy with
elegant manners could be such a sexual hick.
  I was very polite, though. You would have been proud of me. I
tried to sound grateful but meanwhile switched my wedding band
back to my ring finger and told him with real tears in my eyes my
husband was coming back this very afternoon from the Saar but
that I would treasure this as a beautiful moment and he bowed
though it couldn't have been that great for him either or the least
he could do was take one little painting down off the wall and hand
it to me as memento. I would gladly have settled for his sports car
which with me in it would have stopped all the traffic in megapolis.
God it's terrible to remember every single thing. Every kiss, every
bed, every bathtub, every floor — that sink, you sonofabitch, I had
two faucetprints above my ass for weeks. There's a word for me —

one of those long kraut things which explains why girls degrade their bodies to get back at poppa. Things have changed. Twenty years ago my old man's generation thought if you found the right Freudian category that was the start of a happy ending. I'm of this generation, the new wave: we know the psychological shit can't transform one single thing.

Sweetheart, everything outside of us is a stupid game.

But if you dumped that bitch, and Louie went to a sauna to stay, and there were no Dov and no Bailla we could make love all day and all night till next noon when we would take a cab to the Palm Court (you'd be the only male and I the only hatless woman). The chef would come out and you'd whisper something and he'd look at us and smile and three drinks later carry out on a silver salver something freshkilled from New Guinea and we'd eat only one tiny delicious mouthful and it would come over us and we'd shoot up to our suite on the top floor (the first time somebody not a Vanderbilt or a Roosevelt had it) and we'd do everything, every single possible thing at least once and the best things ten times or more and it would be pretty late so we'd shower together and put on elegant formal clothes and float over to the Carlyle where all the women you ever slept with sat at surrounding tables (the most beautiful ones would of course be unescorted with their tongues hanging out). You would flaunt me but I'd be gracious and pretend I didn't notice they were eating their hearts out, the whores.

The Kennedys would stop at our table to ask us up to their suite for a drink but I'd remind you we had to meet the midnight flight in from Istanbul and the President would laugh boyishly and tell us to take a raincheck but Jackie would say oh no Jack let's make it definite. Then we'd sneak upstairs to our suite on the same floor as theirs and this time we'd invent lover things nobody in the world ever knew of. At dawn you'd fall asleep on my great breasts and wake in a couple minutes excited as if we'd never been with each other before. Day in day out we'd go this way, just be spectacular and never a moment older.

Oh well. What's terrible is knowing these crumby fantasies are only weak imitations of the magnificent things we've done together already. I could never make it with these poor jerks if I didn't always imagine the guy was you. I pray they don't speak or break the mood. They feel so clammy. I can't stand their smell. I don't mean BO or anything like that. Its just that they are not you. Oh

Josh I love you — warm shnoogly friendly familiar. I taste you and smell you and I want that! Oh I do I do I do. Food and ambrosia. How come we don't have atomizers of us for times such as these?

I'm lonely, sweetheart. Lonely I'm a mark. And just curious. I mean I can get something started and like a spectator watch it unfold — like a movie I've never seen. Think of it in another way and it could drive you crazy: I mean two people stand fully dressed in front of a picture and in minutes invade each other, totally naked! Strangers! It's wonderful in a way, and terribly romantic but sweetheart it's really insane, an assault on our private persons. I wanted to smash that guy in the face (though I led him to me) and yell what right do you have with me! I hated him. Being where you should be! And I hate Maggie and those other bitches who dared to take my place! Ordinary, less than sublunary! God, many the time when I'm in a guy's bed I go through a finishing-school act full of thanks and nuzzles. When actually I'm just tired and it's a bore and a strain.

Come get me. You take over. I've lost my leader, sweetheart. I need you. Sharing twenty-four hours with a playactor like Louie, and a bunch of assorted strangers is no life.

I need desperately to be straightened out!

Oh well. If nothing else this should take your mind off your woes there, and maybe amuse you a little too. I feel we can talk straight about anything. Lonely forerunners. People who bust out sexually and demonstrate life in love. Maybe we were meant to be a new evolutionary strain which can take anything — right between the eyes — use truth and reality like building blocks. Louie is the old tired out-of-date be-nice-and-I-reward don't-and-I-hold-back type, last of the oldform Freudian neurotics. Truth is a ratchet that clicks the deathclamp a notch tighter. We're new, precursors, Josh. We can do terrible things to each other, let strangers into our beds, but on the highest level be priest and priestess, shuck off dead snakeskin and be born again, younger, more beautiful. Please don't tell me — or think — this is rationale.

Again I can't stop writing. I'm all warm loved hugged and melting. I've spun a lovesleeve. I remember as a child making a house of bedclothes loving the smell and the warmth and the light and mine-ness of it. Now it's ours locked away from the world but full of gorgeous love and tons of food and nothing unworthy. We live at the top of our bent because God decreed us as a model for his angels who see us and cry to be corporeal (and, of course, uncelibate).

Don't shut me out, sweetheart. Even if things are awful and unbearable write me or call me and be terribly close.

Not a gnat's eyelash can get in between.

Miles apart but more one than any ever. If my awful ways depress you think how witty I am and beautiful and all yours.

Kiss your mother and Bailla and say something in my voice to your father. Include me.

Love, lover, and my wettest widest kiss,

M!!

Josh, Sweetheart, Love,

I got the message from the babysitter — I'm heartbroken, not to have been here when you called! What I wouldn't give to be with you now, arms around, and not shut-out, as I am, with that bitch pretending she's part of your family. My babysitter is Venezuelan and on top of it all dumb. She insists you said your father died. I have to get rid of her as soon as I can.

Darling I won't say one corny thing about death putting an end to your mother's suffering. Death is uniformly dreadful, no matter who dies under what conditions where. Oh I wish I had a mother a millionth as close.

I'm sure you're surrounded by enough gloom there, and don't need that from me. I'm *your* life-giver. And tell you truth.

Sweetheart, the reason I wasn't home when you called is this next-door neighbor guy whose livingroom window faces our kitchen. He's married to a Marian-type Junior Leaguer who does night duty at hospitals and that sort of thing. Which clears his place when mine isn't available. It's like a spy story. I learned to do this trompé bit in Mexico. We leave signs of ourselves in the corridor, scraps of paper and burnt matches — you know, one if by land, two if by sea. I read about using common things like that in some spy tale. In the middle of the night he gets horny and comes up my elevator and rattles the hall garbage chute and if Louie took a sleeping pill or I've sent him to a steambath for the night I rap on the wall to let Donnie know the coast is clear. I used to phone him, one short ring then hang up, but his wife isn't quite as dumb as Louie and figured something was up. When she's on one of her social remorse kicks I tell Louie I've got to get some air and sneak over to Donnie's (we look through the kitchen window and see Louie gorging himself, the liar, claiming he's on a starvation diet). I take so many showers rinsing off traces I think I may melt to nothing. If Donnie slams the chute and the coast isn't clear the darling goes almost crazy out in the hall. It's a wonder he doesn't get picked up as a prowler because he slams the chute ten twelve times in rage. I can't believe Louie is that unconscious. The hair rises on my head, pulses beat in my throat, but my kind of criminal type figures a new gimmick almost every day.

Maybe Louie knows. His kind always wants to dump responsibilities. He's probably grateful to Donnie for taking me off his hands. Donnie, between us, is a bore, and we make it together only because assignations are exciting, and there's the thrill and danger of being caught. He's actually no better than a highschool kid (I've even tried that in Mexico). Once a week Donnie gets delusions of grandeur and talks about us marrying. I must be the greatest playactor in the world. "Donnie, lover," I tell him "you'd be so bored with me as your wife. I'm a quicksilver type terrible on the long haul." Or I fall on the rug (I mean dressed) and cry real tears and tell him I could never leave Louie who is such a loving man in a very dangerous psychological state. I don't do too convincing a job otherwise Donnie might stop rattling the chute. (Sometimes I look at him with utter contempt and wonder how I let such an ordinary superficial creep into our universe.) I could spit this guy out in a second and duplicate him in two — though maybe not so conveniently situate — as the ads say — with window facing window so I can turn signal lights on and off, leave cookie jars and cornflakes packages like lamps in the window to say *come in* or *nix*.

Come snatch me up and I'll stop the chintzy bit, be a real woman, twenty-four hours a day. When you come back I'll have to let Donnie down lightly, though not completely. Once you've turned a guy on and told him this and that, what kind of persuasion can you use to stop it? I suppose if he rattled the chute and knew I was alone and I didn't signal back or open the door and he went into a rage in the hall and banged things around and came down with tertiary blueballs in the bargain, *that* would turn him off in time. I'm being castrating. Poor guy! Poor Louie and Maggie! That's what they deserve for coming between mighty similars. To drive Donnie nuts sometimes I tell him everything about you and me, only I attach Louie's name — like, "he's a bastard I know and

makes out with every dark longhaired bitch on the eastern sea-
board, but I have my weaknesses too, darling, and our love is so
strong it can absorb lovers and fuckmates." By now I know all the
things that can fizzle him. If he gets insistent I cool him and he
almost dies not being able to get it up. I'm terribly solicitous, of
course.

Such crap! All of it! Unworthy of us. Unserious. Maybe I'm telling you this to make it really pedestrian, and cut the romantic
ground out from under. Josh, help me! I feel so shut out! Your
mother's death makes me think only of Maggie and you in the
family pew, *her* arms around your father, your brother — you! How
can you let her get close to your father? I hate that most! take him
aside — even in his grief — tell him about us now, the minute you
get through reading this. Nobody can fail to be touched by our
love. And call me. Tuesday mornings from ten to twelve (N.Y.
time) Louie is with his therapists and goes for water therapy right
after (I suspect some therapeutic whore does something unspeak-
able like walk barefoot on his back or grind her ass into his groin).

I would love it if your father came to the phone and told me he
had a beautiful talk with you and was delighted (he'd do it with a
dignity and not take a thing away from Maggie).

That would draw the proper circle, and include *me*. I wouldn't
have another moment of blackest despair or think ever again that
I'm the most despicable castrating chippy the world has ever seen.

Poor neurotic, father-doomed to get her kicks imagining she's
rolling on the stage before an opening night Met audience — Josh,
you don't know! There's a cold still moment when I detach myself
from a guy and from my body and I'm in that Met audience just
looking, not even excited as a dirty old voyeur would be, given the
chance. I lose our space, I can't find our time, just a canister, orbit-
ing junk tumbling weightless and senseless. Playacting the sexpot
amusing full of great anecdotes always on the up never depressed I
look back and remember that was yesterday and this is today. Now
I drop another burnt-out match, and this requires a pill, and that
the diaphragm or the foam or the suppository and did I cover my
face with touch-up to hide the flush? I think of myself so gorgeous
and fleshly but suddenly I'm nothing but a sexual abstraction, a
vagina — how I hate that word!

God, am I using *you*, while *you're* in mourning, to dump this
sickness?

Forgive me, sweetheart. If there's anything genuine in me it comes to life only when I'm with you, or think of you. This unworthy body unworthy soul unworthy mind does have one tiny tiny corner that's genuine. Whoever touches everything else never gets within ten billion light years of this only thing in my world that's inviolate.

Do what I ask, sweetheart. Kiss Bailla (who has that other tiny incorruptible part of me). Let everyone in your family know that certain party who can't mourn with them is a lovely person, and sends them her love and softness and quiet.

Oh how I love you!

Please send me a number I can call (one *she* doesn't know about). I would have phoned, darling (or even had Louie do it) except I knew the sound of her voice would kill me.

> Love o love,
> Mavra-Josh

A nurse had dressed her, and put her in the wheelchair. Slumped to one side, her better hand holding her bad. Body shrunken in the coat and she in her body. Tiny braids wrapped her head like a gray crown. Someone passing in the corridor would see only a tiny weary worn old lady, one cheek disfigured. Motionless, tranquilized, or daydreaming. Shadows gather like dark fog, muffling her feet.

I wheeled her out through the corridor past that closed door she had forgotten she wanted to open. No shadow came in our wake.

"Boy," she said as I put her into the car, "I'm some matriarch!"

"You're the sly type. We never know you're asserting power."

"I'm so sly I may never sneak out of this coat if someone doesn't help me."

Over the small river, looking back, the graywhite banked building, those same dark seminaries and bleak residences, variants of messages terrifyingly repetitious. The gray of the hospital shadows washed in ripples against the river's graygreen banks. Clustered, gathered like dots in a newspaper engraving, one added to one, to change the hospital at evening into a mere image.

"How are you doing, ma?"

"I'm waiting for Dempsey."

My mother is that quantity of life, shrunken, dressed in time's accidental hangings. A remnant. What burgeoned in two is reduced to one, and her waning is clear. When they both lived I didn't think of the life they carried. Now she is something precious and powerful, weakening each morning. We see it clearly when two swift shells skim water, bow to bow, and any one falters. We mark the value of the one remaining.

"Ma," I shouted, "you're coming back to New York with me!"

"Drop me, Joshua, and keep on going. I don't want Bailla even to see me today — to live with me is forget it. No grandchild of mine is going to wake in the night and hear that crazy crying. I myself freeze at such a sound. Face it, Joshua: you can't stay in this town, and I can't leave it. I have nothing to start a new life with."

"Terrific, bravo, ma," I said. "Keep it up and we'll stop the speech therapy."

"Stop it anyway. Stop everything. It's all so phony and lying and such a terrible waste. My old dome is in pretty good shape. The trouble is it can't steer the rest of me."

Gad in his dark glasses held Bailla up at the front window. Came out on the steps with Bailla on his shoulder. Saw my mother sag to one side, lost in her outercoat, and stamped his foot once more, bouncing Bailla, Gad pounded the hollow wooden step for letting him see what he saw.

Tiptoeing in patent Maryjanes she bent forward, stiff-legged spindly in white tights, hands in fists, arms rigid, cheeks frozen in doll smile, getting closer, partydress starched stiff for a welcome, promised happy homecoming. Her dark eyes opened wide, shiny with fear. She paused, closer than an armlength, gave a sudden deep gasp inward, twohanded push against the invisible intervening wall. Struggling, trying not to look, not to see, but think holiday thoughts. Staring, for one eyeblink, at the drawn mouth, grandmother, broken like a puppet, propped, in black for grandfather, one arm held out, the other resting limp on the heldout wrist, a circle for Bailla to slip under, into.

"Hi, gramma, welcome home."

Shaky and quivering and her face up, breath held, trembling, frozen, arms like a scarecrow's, forcing themselves to bend, curve around grandmother's neck, and her braked feet, pulledback head, moved close, collapsing in fear but forced a hug and a kiss and offered one cheek to be kissed back. Stroked grandmother's hard stiff white braid, pressed rigid palms against grandmother's better cheek.

"Baillie you're a very sweet girl."

Grandmother a big sad broken old doll she wouldn't let be discarded ever. Hugged, more frightened, cheeks stiff with smiling. Grandmother's bad hand falling, splashing the chair. On her shoulder in her ear a howl, like something hurling and far away, two notes, a fifth, loo li, D A, under grandmother's hand pushed against the sound in her mouth, loo, li, liiiiiiiiiiiiiiiiiiiiiiiiiiiiiiiiiiiiiiiiiiiiiiiiiiiiii then just breath, as when you knew a baby still was crying, but hoped it had stopped, and it started again, louder, more hopeless: crying for grandfather, or maybe for being broken. It wouldn't be polite to step back, or move grandmother's chin pressed on her shoulder, making her party dress cold and wet.

It would be nice if somebody else took a turn.

Dear darling lover Josh,

God what you must think of me! How can I possibly make it up to you, my sweetheart? I almost killed that fuckface Donnie — I had to be in his place and the girl was here alone again — taking your message down in Spanish — sweetheart, I haven't left the telephone but for that once. Every time it rang I flew past Louie and padlocked the door. To get you to understand what I feel I should mutilate my face — if you didn't love me so I'd cut something off to prove to you I know when I've failed. And for whom — that shithead Donnie! That wiltcock! I sent your family the telegram and knew goddam well his wife was home (I saw her from my kitchen window) I told him if he didn't come over instantly it was all over. Then I rushed to the Museum and picked on the first guy I saw — believe me I don't even know what he looks like. How *I* trompéed that bastard Donnie, aroundtheworld, everything — the guy in the Museum still doesn't know what hit him. I was so furious I put my girdle on back to front and the garters just about killed me all the way home in the cab.

I cooked Louie a great thick soup with dry mushrooms and boiled beef and his favorite baked Alaska and gave him a treatment his therapists will marvel at for months. When the bastard Donnie came and rattled the garbage chute I sent Louie out in the hall (he didn't hear it on his own, the unconscious turd). He addressed Donnie as sir and said something formalassed. Donnie with his head down kept massaging his cock inside his pockets all the time Louie lectured. Good riddance to that clammy creep! We don't need that.

God, do you know how I love you! I'd even accept secondbest — nominally — enter into a maison à trois, polyerotic monamorous monogamy masking as polygamy — I don't give a shit about being number one always-come-first if-not-Mavra-who. Though I don't really trust you when those bigtit longhair whores sashay by. I could maybe stand you taking a bitch to bed. But if you loved her I'd slit my throat. I've told you a thousand times what I want most is to stop and make love in every room on every inch of ground you've loved someone else, or even kissed. I want a detailed checklist, to bury the past and establish my primacy (sp?).

You'd say sure Titsy was great and Snatchy was terrific and Dimple-ass was lovely but Mavra Mavra you are the greatest. The greatest everything — not just your sex-type goodies (I've been listening to disc jockeys), but your priceless wit and evanescent (I looked it up in the dict'ry) soul. I'd say how great was Titsy, really, and you'd say Titsy had a frozen pelvis and screwed as if she was in a dentist's chair, was middlebrow, smelled all wrong, had hair like a Barbie Doll's, was always dry, peed like a horse, put on a big show but never came once in her life, not even at her own hand. We'd bury them all like that, one after the other, and never send flowers.

Oh, I had to go to a party with Louie, full of asswrigglers I was glad *you* weren't there. French bitches are the worst — an American swinger at least wears a slip. One had on a sheer satin shift you could see her appendicitis scar. A filthy blonde bitch stood with one leg on a chair for five minutes with everybody having full view of City Hall. Lucky Louie is walleyed and could be a voyeur without anybody noticing.

Some lunatic with peaked eyebrows, full of stealth and bad news, told me he liked Louie (I give a shit), then brought around his wife, goggle-eyed, wearing contacts and afraid to blink. We chat and it's as though they're asking me to be a fourth at bridge only it's a *third* they want I suddenly realize. If they need a woman the least they could suggest is a flattering trio where she's the only female. I may lack scruples but not taste. I said what's the problem, who can't do what. And they said it was square to be only a this or a that. Since they liked Louie so much and weren't finicky about which was two, and which one, I suggested they try him.

I should have gone, just to see what that woman could possibly find for herself to *do.* They slunk off but later I saw them talking to a French bitch. Getting into an *à trois* with that one might have been a different matter!

Oh well.

Newsy little Mavra, trying to cheer you up. Though I shouldn't sound ever this superficial.

You have *real* pain. You lost somebody real. I've nobody in this world but you and Dov. A million people could die overnight and I wouldn't drop a tear. It's only death in your family I cry over. We must be related — way way back, through the woman I think you love best, Rebecca at the well. If I tried like Rebecca to carry an urn of water I'd slosh it all over the intermediaries. They'd say let Isaac marry that beautiful warm girl only if something can be done about her being such a slob.

Good thing this world doesn't have to rely on me. Sensuality doesn't allow for much else. It's only when cocks don't rise that cities and states do. Eighteen unbroken hours of sen-su-al-ity, the rest split between sleep and civilization — how does that suit you? God, the last thing I want to do is advocate. A night or two ago, after I had been with that shit Donnie (for the last time!) I hap-

pened to be in the kitchen and saw him giving his wife a short
course in the things *intime* he learned from me! Treacherous sonofabitch! Discipleship has its limits, though: him I gave D and her
I couldn't grade at all. Just when he was trying to get her to do
something special — so intimate I can't even write it — I called
their number. Can you imagine? The shnooks actually answered! If
he could teach that stiff ass the holds he would never have needed
me!

Babble babble Mavra babble!

I wish I could write a beautiful Donne kind of poem about your
father *he's gone he's gone and when you remember this* — no
that's not right — *he, he is dead, he's dead, and when thou knowest this thou knowest how dry a cinder this world is.* Beautiful sad
man! Would you write a great poem about me if I died? I'm so
sickeningly sentimental. I think all the time of dying beautifully
and gently while people disembowel themselves for treating me
like shit. It may sound corny but it sure moves *me!*

I get veto power then on who gets into heaven. Every bitch you
ever touched I blackball! My heaven is corporeal and sensual as hell
so you better be good to me or you won't get in.

Antony and Cleopatra wanted that, eternal dalliance — no
world to rule, no wives in Rome. Cleopatra must have been pretty
disgusting by that time. I don't think she ever bathed. Just kept
slopping perfumes over her old skin.

Oh Josh! Forget everything else! I love you, Josh! I'm a horror
but I know what's important. Whatever you have to do, do. And
come back. Day or night, with Louie asleep or awake, regardless of
consequences to me or you let's melt our souls and bodies mouth
to mouth. I'm never disloyal to our love. I have two bodies, and
lend the lesser one out, like a book which circulates while the mint
copy's shelved. Josh's I am, and wild for to hold though I seem
tame.

So please, darling, forgive my last letter, and hug your alive
mother *ten* times for me. Who but fuckyknuckles Mavra sends
condolence for the wrong parent?

Oh I'd love to wake one morning and find everything so far was
just a rehearsal. You could do it, Josh my darling, kiss and tell me I
was Sleeping Beauty. Rip the incriminating cards out of the world
files, shred them in teeny bits like Sybil's leaves.

I have such an ugly ugly side to me! Not even you could look at it without being revolted. The way I treated Louie on the phone that first time. That was really *me*, dirty *me*. Turning love into a murderous *anti* thing, to cut a sad man like Louie to bits. Let the analysts tell me it's all because of my backdrop. I *know* I'm a walking advertisement for psychopathy. Someone who thinks of herself as a beautiful litter runt so tries to carve up the real lovelies of the world.

Enough! I know this is heading ten thousand fathoms down into black despair. Darling, you *must* be bored by me me me! St Peter will axe me for my black sins, Lucifer whiteball me because of this prattle; I'm so stupid I'll never follow the directions which might take me to limbo. I'll bet you're thinking it's bad enough having to deal with her in the vale of tears, now I've got to put up with that in eternity?

Oh well.

Come back to me sweet sonofabitch and I'll remind you of compensations.

Let me know ahead of time so I can send Louie off to convalesce from something.

If you will take this kiss I will accept that. Closing up of space. Two loops = one circle. Heat and enough electric power to warm our newly charged world.

I love you, darling Josh.

Come see!

MmmmmmmmM

In nightwash, darkness rushing through halls and rooms, circular night wound to the black sky, swept back through a chimney. Darkness emptying his space, blackveiling a Corn Flakes carton, burial for his shoes. Slippers for shuffling and black for parties and brogues he once wore in streets, and older ones, muddied from gardening. All other clothes distributed, but never a man's shoes. Or toetip heeltip rubbers, broken buckle blackcanvas galoshes, hip boots for fish or flood. All heaped in one dark rubbersmelling carton. In empty dresser drawers death's darkness. Clothes closets swinging black skeleton wirehangers, empty brownpaper cleaning bag crushed and wrinkled.

Night buried the dead in ultimate burial. Rode off and left only presences behind.

Darkness like gas filled the rooms wholly. Far far away, as if I dreamed it, a woman was crying into her pillow. A baby's deep sigh, the struggle turning over. Gad snoring fitfully, his dangling fist rattling the floorboards.

Black wind blew nightbirds swooping over dark roofs. Black sea-shell darkened, hollow, dark distant waves night-hushed in my ear on night's black pillow. Submerged in sleepdark, nightsurfacing, dipped down in the black trough of a nightwave cresting.

He switched on a light as if I weren't sleeping, riffled the cleaning bags, his back to me.

"Josh," he whispered, "what happened to my suits?"

"Which, pa?"

"My new gray one."

I wouldn't tell him Gad had it made over.

He stood perplexed but not angry, waiting for an answer. The tweed coat neatly piled on a chair behind that sheet — he wore it; the same rust shirt (without the dark stain), the green cord pants.

"Josh, is anything wrong?"

"No, papa."

"Nothing happened to ma?"

"Nothing."

I wanted to signal Gad in the other room, tell him we'd made a terrible error — what lack of faith, to believe our father was dead!

"It's no big deal, Joshua. I can wear what I'm wearing."

I got out of bed.

"Pa, listen, you should have a brand new suit anyway."

"Isn't it Sunday?"

"We have your measurements."

"How come?"

"I don't know — we took all your measurements."

"Isn't that odd!"

In Gad's closet that gray suit was hanging, pa's raincoat, his hat.

I tried to sneak away, get them and hide them. If Gad wore any one thing pa would know right away that we thought he was dead.

"Josh," he said, "I see that you're worried. I shouldn't have brought the subject up. I'm prepared to wear these clothes the rest of my life if I have to."

He rattled the garmentbag paper, himself flattened like paper, wrinkled, fragmented, a paper wall shattering to flakes, and like flakes falling.

High and strained, like a distant trolley gliding, her cry drawn out, taut, hoarse, breathless, silent. I sat on the porch, lay on the couch to simulate the old seeing. The world outside was a door, a gate, a blank slide flashed on a screen while the show was preparing. No terror in it. No bad memory. The finite world fixed by the darkened houses across the street did not describe a universe which meant a thing to me. Two-dimensional memory, three-dimensional escape. Relativity's analogue in reverse, illustrating a flatworm's great liberation.

My mother's cry picked up, too feeble, struggled to become laugh, then brokenbacked, subsided.

Gad stood up, stretched his arms, walked outside into the night. A passing car struck the lenses of his dark glasses. He looked like a confused blindman on a strange street.

"Josh," Maggie said, "it would have been awful to mention anything before, but when do we start putting the pieces together in our own lives?"

"As soon as we want to."

"Your mother's home. She didn't die from the shock. We can't hold off — I've never mentioned receiving a letter —"

"From whom?"

"That's unworthy! You know from whom. The one that said shake well and refrain from using."

She tiptoed to the couch, sank down beside me.

"That girl has a book on me, Josh. She studied my strengths and my weaknesses, then built a matchless persona you could not resist."

"Maggie, I know you're wrong."

"And I know I'm not. She's too foxy, Josh, even for herself she's too foxy."

"I don't know what that means."

"It means she works everything out, layer below layer. She engineered the fights with Louie, the flight to the city; the whole scenario worked out as she wrote it, without one single hitch. She can manipulate settings, environments. Like a middling fighter, Josh, she picks her spots. You forget she used to talk to me of her gimmicks, freely. Always be the youngest most stylish girl in a crowd, or in a young crowd be the most sophisticated, the most elegant, the best informed. In her teen and adult life she didn't go to the bathroom without the trip being calculated to create some other kind of effect."

"You're nuts, Maggie. You've created a creature you can hate —"

"I don't hate her — that's what's so funny. I think she's almost as great as she thinks she is. It's only that my nostrils pick up a burning odor of sickening corruption."

"Come off it —"

"Josh, the point isn't really her, anyway, is it? It's you and me. What can we do to make a life? I suspect, nothing. I should have my head examined — Zora, and this one, and God knows what others in L.A. — forgive me if I do a double take on things there and grow sour with suspicion."

Gad's steps sounded on the cement walk. He rammed the fist of his right hand hard against the palm of his left. Again. And again.

"Josh," he called, "how about you and Maggie joining me in a walk — we can't go too far. Ma might want something."

"You go," Maggie said. "Was it wrong to bring us up so soon?"

"Of course not."

"I keep rereading that letter, Josh. One of these times I'll really figure out what she's up to."

She hung on to the same fences Wilkoh Joe made me cling to, on the same cement he walked me and wheeled that bike. I held out my hand, coaxed her forward like a parent trying to urge the first step out of a child. Mr. Boyczuk from his front window made cheering motions with his hollow toothless mouth. I looked up quickly at the solid pane I once stared through: in daylight, as in night, it was only a station abandoned, and pointedly unmanned. Jutted tarstreaks newmarked the old arena my eye automatically combed and catalogued. Car doors slammed that old unforgotten music, reminiscent wheels rolled over the badly fit manhole.

Two hands on a post, like a child hugging the goal in relievo, she squared her feet flatset on the sidewalk.

"Josh," she burst out, "I'm terribly tired."

Clung to the scrolled gate like that girl in leg braces. Old lady in stiffscreen black, tiny old lady, sagged darkly to one side. Where in time's space was the young girl of the album? Gray old lady untinted, dressed in colorless black.

"Soon it will be winter, ma," I said, "how would you like to take up skating again?"

"Are you crazy, Josh?"

"It's the kind of exercise the doctor prescribed."

"How many lives ago?"

I held her under her arms and helped her up the front steps. Bailla pretended not to see us, and ducked quickly inside.

"Josh," my mother cried, "you've tired me out!"

"I didn't want to do that."

"Can't you see I won't snap back!"

"You mustn't give up —"

"*You* give up. Recognize what's out of my reach, and yours."

"Nothing's out of reach."

"I want you to stop using yourself as my guide and model — just leave me alone, Josh! You admit you can't bring pa back. You can't bring me back either!"

"You want to give up?"

"I want you to stop bullying me. I'm being persecuted by your optimism."

"I want you strong enough to come back to New York with me."

Her voice fell to an indistinct whisper.

"Josh, are you blind? Or do you only want to blind me? Maybe I should believe too that you're happy with Maggie."

"Why are you saying this, ma?"

"I can't stand being treated like an idiot child. You pretend my body is whole and my mind is maimed. It's the other way around."

In the front doorway, taller than Gad, high above Beatty and Maggie, a gay flapperhat over one ear, in a long pink coat slipped back off her shoulders, someone familiar leaned awkward over my mother. Her coat was far too long and too old for her carriage.

She turned suddenly, stared at me, smiled, waiting. I smiled back politely.

She pulled off the black hat and frowning shook her thick gray-black hair.

"Oh, you bastard," she whispered, "I might die on the spot. You really didn't know me!"

Her voice tinkled that strange bell sound.

"Oh for chrissakes, Zora," I lied, "I knew you all the time. Not one thing is changed."

"So they say of Mount Rushmore."

I held out my hand and shook hers warmly.

"You bastard, again? I dreamed you would kiss me!"

"Do you live in town?"

"That's *three!* I live in *your* town, me and eight million others you couldn't recognize."

"When," I whispered, "did you cut your hair?"

"Oh you're not nice! My dream was different!"

Maggie walked over and took Zora's coat, playing unconsciously with her long hair on one shoulder. Pitiless appraisal. Then she and Beatty went out for a walk.

"You still like girls as much as you used to?" Zora said softly.

"Tell me about yourself," I said, "what have you been doing?"

"You used to fall in love on the hour, as I well remember. Has that changed?"

"You've a wedding ring."

"My husband is a sweet man. He likes *this* one girl only."

"You should think yourself lucky?"

"You *really* are not nice! Why treat me so cold during a friendly condolence call?"

"What's the connection between condolence and whether I still like girls?"

"Tell me just one thing — are you glad to see me?"

"Sure."

"Do I look great?"

"If I say 'yes' will you ask 'how great'?"

"What's with you, man? You're just sore I grew old."

She jammed her hat back on, flush as if it were a candlesnuffer. Bent over my mother curtly. I opened the door, she filled her lungs with air.

"Things," she said, "don't happen the way you dream them —"

She stood on the bottom step, pounding her hat flatter with the heel of her hand.

"One thing I know."

"What's that?"

"You won't like it."

She hopped off the step, wobbling on one foot, swung around slowly, her stiff leg extended.

"That, sir," she said, "is an unloved woman."

"Who?"

"Your bride."

"If that were true would you feel better?"

"God yes! I'd love to bury you both!"

The back of the long low building was damp with melted early snow. A black streak, like a mascara tearstain, ran from a dip in the roof down whitewash brick. Two trucks piled high with rolled bedding, wooden trunks, bruised valises held together with short knotted bits of string, belts, torn ties.

A bowed man led me through a long hall. Every door opened. Someone asked, in German, if I had come for him. The question, three doors down, was repeated in Polish by a boy of five.

I heard a grown man crying. Upstairs an old woman screamed.

The doors I passed quickly closed. Only the ones ahead remained hopeful and ajar.

The bowed man stopped at an open door. I walked in and narrowly missed hitting my head against two thickshod feet dangling from the upper of a bunk-filled room.

"Oh excuse," a man's voice said from the dark ridge above.

A pretty young woman looked shyly away, pretended to comb a small girl's recently brushed and ribboned hair. The young woman wore a formal evening dress of worn wine satin. Her legs were bare, her feet in new fluffy slippers. The little girl hid behind her mother.

My guide spoke gently — in Polish.

The boots over my head swung slowly down. A man dropped beside me, heavily, though he was quite small.

"You could leave us in charge of a bank," he said, "we lived like dogs but we are not dogs. You can trust us."

His wife hid her face. The man, Czernowski, had blackstained hands.

"Before they burned out us," he said, "the ma made I should run'— you see my papers?"

"Yes," I said.

"So small a young boy I hide by Russians. Print. Yes? See! Ink. I print. Everything. For Russian."

He patted my back.

"We look after your ma. When I run away, in Warsaw anybody look after mine ma —"

"Where is she?"

He shrugged his shoulders, threw up his hands.

"Joseph, please," his wife said in a German accent, "your mother is dead."

"No, no," he shook his head violently.

"They burned her," his wife whispered to me.

"Who?"

"Men."

We stopped in front of the house. My mother was a pale abstract in dark livingroom glass. Bailla peered out, her face from the band of putti.

"She will cry, Mr. Czernowski —"

"Please call Joseph —"

"Joseph, she cries, and she laughs. She can't help it."

"What," his wife said, staring at the dark window, "we do then?"

"Leave her alone —"

"If she cry more and more —"

"I don't let cry your ma," Joseph said, "I make good jokes."

"My arms it's alright to put her around?" his wife said.

"We put arms and she no more crying — only laugh," said Joseph.

The little girl hid her face in her mother's coat. Mrs. Czernowski spoke to her rapidly in Polish and German.

"What's her name?" I asked.

"Nina."

"That's a very pretty name, Nina." I said, "And you are a pretty little girl."

My mother stumbled trying to beat Maggie and Gad to the door, and fell against a chair, crying.

"Let's walk around the yard, Joseph," I said, "she wanted to greet you like a hostess. She wants you to be guests in her house."

"We," Joseph said, squeezing my arm, "will be what you — family — we will do — I have accordian — she music like, the ma? Nina dance — now she so shy, and scare — every day different room and difference voices."

We walked slowly, my mother's cry pursuing, past dahlias dry and dead, greendrained peony bushes, a leafless lilac sprouting ugly suckers from its exposed roots.

Joseph glanced back at their suitcases and cartons piled at our front steps. Waved and bowed to Maggie framed by the door, and Gad pounding the heel of his hand against the glass, in his dark glasses crying. Wearing out, as if far away, almost beyond the level of hearing, my mother's cry merged with the drone of planes and the crash of shunting in the distant railroad yards.

Bailla on the steps held out a new doll wrapped in white tissue. Nina hid behind her mother's skirt, drawnfaced dollchild who, with her past, should have been used to this sound, but fortunately wasn't.

She would be the one to hear it after Bailla was gone.

Between psychology's "You blame yourself too much," and the nobly confessed *mea culpa*, lies the act beyond explanation. My mother leaned on a black walking stick, precariously slanted, her eyes redrimmed, glassy, tranquilized and teared. Beside her, as in a composite photograph (from which Gad, or I, had been clipped, and this stranger substituted), stands a bald smiling man, short legs bent as if they had been broken. Joseph Czernowski, late of Poland, Russia, camps and billets, his neck shriveled and scrawny, his posture aged, leaden. His hand hovers an inch above her shivering shoulder. The other is at his side, rigid, at attention.

Hold them there, frozen. For one long imprinting.

Then let them move, for we too are moving, retreating, to the car which will take us away, Gad, and Maggie, and Bailla, and I. She tries to wave her bad hand, my mother, like an old queen leaned on her minister at the end of her day's last audience. She tries to switch the blackheaded cane to her bad hand, and wave vigorously with her good. The cane drops and ministering Joseph quickly retrieves it, puts it back in her good hand, which frustrates her wave.

Darkling, tiny, imprint on her white house.

Starting, our car motor rumbles space. We vibrate, she on Joseph's arm shudders.

The car moves. Space shifts. A white house blocks out my mother.

I should have remembered to tell you long before this: that spastic girl died in her sleep.

Bailla slept, Maggie slept, I dozed in sweaty darkness. The plane's effortless hum high in its cruising. My mother awake must be staring up at the ceiling of her long night's bedroom, enfolded by strangers.

Space outside was unmarked. Stretched silver rode a jet stream into night unmarked.

Too many stars for bearings.

Dearest darlingest lover Josh!

Say it's not an omen!

You can never reach me by phone, or I you! From now on let's dial our bellybuttons — is it *The Zohar*, some mystic thing says we all plug in. The universal phonenumber, is, I think, unlisted. Aleph aleph something something it must be.

This time I wasn't out with a guy. Worse! Louie's doing the head of this very fat grinner. He bites his nails down to the elbow but insists Louie make him a thinker, with long fingers, long elegant, manicured hands. He looks just like a Halloween Buddha, with some kind of nervous laugh thing. When we arrived he was just coming out of the men's room. His fly was wet (I couldn't decide if from piss or masturbation: which would be the more charitable interpretation?).

His buddies were in the middle of some kind of conference. Velvet eyes feeds ugly ideas into a computer, and clingy creeps add rationales. Greenfaces all around, sneaky-eyed, ringleted, and towing crewcut colonels cheery with yes-sir no-sir, our special contribution to civilization, the boyscout killer. One whiny little fag worked out a correlation between fear of DDT, fear of thalidomide, fear of fallout, fear of water and air pollution. He concluded not what you think, that this syndrome indicated a person in clear possession of his marbles.

When he was through everyone but me applauded, including, of course, Louie, who said things these days aren't bad for sculptors.

Wouldn't it be terrible, darling, if the world were in a middle stage, evolving the brain's kill-lobe *out* just at the moment the killers grabbed all the power! I feel so helpless, and involved — narcissist me!

There's no one to call.

Where power is held by lunatics, blow the whistle and all you get is more lunatics!

I listened and felt my skin crawl — no human being can hear talk about megadeaths and blinding lasers and antipersonnel burn and crop poisoning without feeling the vermin have taken over the sane earth. I felt horrible: the polite constructions, rationales, lies, embroideries, were familiar. That terrible little fag had my own cold whorish detachment.

God! Who needs my analogies? I'm explaining why I wasn't here again when you called.

I oscilate (sp?) or do I mean vascilate (sp??), always so friendly to myself. The same thing that depressed the hell out of me, a few hours later gets a gorgeous reinterpretation. So dedicated to the general welfare of humanity plucky Mavra oftentimes forgets whom she laid with yesterday. Straighter than Gide, rounder than Sartre, prettier than de Beauvoir! Bunoling with that many men she's actually playing house. She confesses to nicking a ball here — or there, but for every castrate she has made ten — thrice ten! — miraculously potent — for her pleasure and for the good of the race. Swollen with virility men have gone directly from game Mavra's bed to their wives (or somebody else's) and made them full with child. A woman who so fathers children is indeed to be honored! American homemaker of the year! Mistress America! Sew her image onto flags!

You've got a pretty nice rationale going too, now that I think of it. That you don't use it makes you even more suspect. Those gorgeous nurses who adored you. Sick bitches! Taking advantage of a young kid strung up in his bed! That's where you got the taste of us! Once that's there nobody can change it. Look at Medea: Jason was the only guy who could make her have orgasm, so would she let that go? I suppose a man is that way too, though men are bastards, and could come with anybody anywhere.

What is with me?

I've become so prurient (that I know how to spell). Next thing you know I'll collect erotica. That fat bastard Louie is sculpting is a fog. When he eyes you up and down you know what would make him happiest is a gift of your girdle.

Do you think man is evolving *this* way — too? We want to fuck fuck fuck because we're frightened to death of death. God, if I were a good person I wouldn't even mail this. Something must be wrong with me. I can't get my ass off the ground.

I do know what it is: *I can't stand the thought of Maggie there with your mother.*

Please think carefully how things have to be managed. You must bring your mother with you, and, please, darling, bring her to me. I've already looked at first-floor apartments. I'm tuned to her wavelength, the presence she needs. *Together* we'll heal her.

All my life I've been dying to do something magnificent for one other person. I want *your* mother. I could mount an invasion for her, be general of Helen's own destructive armies.

How much have you told your mother about me? The teeniest bit will do now — say only that I have a great heart, and with all of it adore *you!* She won't want to leave her house, of course, but she has to: a woman like that would die living with strangers.

When she comes I'm going to get rid of this music camp name once and for all. They — who? God, I think — changed Sarai to Sarah to celebrate her rebirth, right?

You I'll call Joshua. And I will be Hannah.

Joshua Joshua Joshua I love love love you!

Hannah (temp. reg. *Mavra*)

Nightflying nightsoaring nightwafted nightinvisible. Six miles high are you still in earth's world?

Trembling she threw her coat over the chair, pretended she was waiting. Old King Cole. Large room. Manhattan cutthroats winding down. Guaranteed fagfree. Almost. Lines aren't drawn that easily any more. Who shall abide the day of that one's coming? Dirtyminded bitch! Throw down the gauntlet and see who are men. Who am I to invoke this scale? Maybe there's some other way of looking at blackbirds.

She shook her dangling earrings, tinkled.

Hair to my ass, loops to my shoulders, in shades, leaned toward Josh, Sophia as the cameras clicked. Rome away from home.

The blonde chick has them that big. Bunny. Say that guy in Chicago auditions 'em all. A calling like any other calling.

Size, Blondie, isn't everything.

She folded her arms and upped them a notch. Cork. God! Imagine! Cosmetic surgery. Pack 'em with foam too. Right underneath so no scar. No cork for Sophia.

Oh well. Good specialty for a titman. But a lover would never allow us to be cut.

Bare arms. Raise. Stretch. Beautiful. And alone, no questions. Could be waiting for someone. Husband lover client. Mavra's motto — *see what happens.* Rusty Latin. Vide. Vidi. Videbemus

— some old Pope who stalled the Vatican into the Reformation.

If *ugly* and sit, King Cole soul not merry. Lonely women do. Are you waiting for another party, madam? Yes. Half an hour later — I'll have a drink while I'm waiting. Then oh he must have missed his train. I hope nothing happened. May I see a menu please. Otherwise TV or look out window at Manhattan cliffs. Some voyeur saw a guy climbing into somebody's twenty-sixth story. Called cops. What a civilization. Believes somebody up there is watching. Somebody down here too, buddy.

Couples drifted in.

The guys who tuck their heads down and put an arm around. Buddy buddy. Cloakroom types, fixers. King Cole's fiddlers. Minority leader, majority leader, whips, vice presidents. Now you know I wouldn't expect a favor without doing a little favor in return. Ping-pong. What if nothing left but Dirksen's voice and Vice President's arm? Georgie's bridge is falling down falling down falling down. Nobody remembers next says build it up with sticks and stones. Not here, anyway.

The waiter's trays circled six feet up. Bowls of peanuts. Cheese spread. Get what we want. All tough. Guarantee subsidize assure return. I lie. *Oter?* That's to hate.

I lie.

You lie.

He she or it lies.

He she or it swears to it.

Where were you Mavra? Shopping. Oh? Think fast — a bluff or does he know. Yes, shopping with Buffie. Who? Buffie, you remember her? Oh yes. Such a bullshitter. Can't remember a thing. Conned every time. Couldn't admit forgetting. What did you do after the stores closed? Buffie wanted to drive out to Queens to the discount houses. What did you buy? Oh darling it was just a lark, and everything was so expensive Buffie and I decided to save your money.

The end.

Three four days a week. Not of the best even as Pentagon scenarios go. So we do this and Mao does that and then we do this and then of course Mao must. And Josh abandoned me so I strike back and then Louie insists he has rights too so there's something more to strike back for. Escalation. Schemata for a civilization that believes in turning the other cheek. Leg up, Mavra old girl, and now turn — no no the *other* cheek.

Old Freud used to believe the fuckers would beat their rods into ploughshares. Soon learned. Himmel, what I heard from my neurotics! Pastoral therapy, to batten the hatches lock doors clamp tight the chastity belts. Probably preferred nightmares to daydreams at the end. Kinsey found one of everything. Put us on map. Well and here we have the midwest long winter nights nobody can get to town and froggy would awooing go — acourting? Family of man. And his animals. We can't lie down with lepers but we have a boy who's great with bobcats.

Lie. *Coucher*. That's the only kind. Chew 'n'Lie. Another yet.

A row of guys at the bar.

I look like a call girl? They'd run high here. Hundred. Two maybe. Italians and French executives want a Negro girl Donnie said — though how would he know? Tries to sound *in*. Disloyal sonofabitch! The intimate things Josh did with me he tries to do with that longline girdle! Who was the girl with weak wrists that wheelbarrowed broke her nose? Made that up probably. Thought it, so assumed it was true.

Mourning doves and cardinals, paired. Mates. Others would put those three thousand ejaculations into any old bird. Tread. Maybe Louie's part bird.

Starlings and grackles poach on the turf of lovers.

Guys at the bar mean business. The backs of the ones who just lush. Cocksman with leg flexed. Does every guy know he's in the same pose as every other guy?

All we do is raise our eyes once.

Eenie meanie minie mo — ugh! Ugly sonofabitch — no neck — foetus brow — red — God! Penis envy only to have something that shows we can be turned off. The secret. We can kill them and they can't us. Some girl in college supposed to have a clitoris like. Guy brushed by her she came. Myths. Same ones in every college.

Start at the other end. Eenie meanie.

Oh — saw me!

Halfsmile. Halfsmile back. Half of a half equals — brrr! Fractions.

Sending over a drink. Arrogant bastard.

Should have ring on finger. Told Louie we're in abeyance. Loves words like that. Let us declare a moratorium, Louie, on conjugal discussions. Ring would fox some of them. Not all. Something, those women. Hustle and hubby babysits. And those matrons who did it to charter a plane for the grand tour! God! Proves the fix isn't my invention.

Are there call girls who wear wedding rings?

Some guys do only call girls and whores. No entangle no breach of promise — they still do that? Come lay with — lie? Not *oter*, then what? *Falser. Falsir. Tromper* — that's different too. Maybe no way to say in French. We need all the ways we can get. Fudge fib bullshit — thousand others maybe.

Guy with strawberryblond hair. Kind who always says branch water. Fin for the kid who parks the car, sawbuck for the somme- lier, double sawbuck for the maitre d'. Escalation here too. Ten G's for the three-star general. Riviera villa in perpetuity — for any in- guy who finks or steers. Wife in Georgetown or Willow Run. Daughter Switzerland. Son West Point. God heaven. Can't make it unless mirrors. Can't piss unless water running.

The man turned his back to the bar. Drink set down she nodded thanks across the room. Rules in King Cole. Nobody turns down anybody's anything. Everybody a code. Where was it girl thrown out for not letting guy — East Eighties. Bartender said this is a family bar. What!! Family bar. Our executives come in same time same days. Expect girls who drink to carry through. Thrown out on her ass for breach of family ethics. And don't come back till you learn to behave decently!

What a country!

Hate the way they talk about it. *Have sex*. Never heard that from a real man or woman yet. Maybe they say *have sex* because they don't really know what they're supposed to do. Babies. Must be analogy with *have a bath*. That way no giver or taker. Whatever comes up. So terrible. Flat. Inhuman. If a guy wants a woman he should know that's what he wants. So many lovely ways to say it. Their way it's a dead sick miserable category. Only one term in Mavra Commandments: if he says *have sex* the game never begins.

The man leaned, elbows behind him. Chain on vest. Phi Bete? Wouldn't be Elks or anything prol. Type who has somebody else shave him. Sauna. Redskin, skis in summer. Golfs all winter.

He held his glass up in toast.

Mavra dropped her eyes. No call girl here, buddy boy.

Sipped. What if a potion slipped into it? Guy too arrogant.

Coolly the man raised his glass.

An alternative. A room full of alternatives. Alternative has to be alternative *to* something. Existential disaster — alternatives from alternatives. Eight million alternatives — no, only half are male. So four. Half too old. Two. Half too young. One. Half too dumb half more too ugly. Fractions! Some too boring, some too nutty. O.K. Say thirty thousand live ones. Could have a gallery. Issue ID's. That madam in New Jersey with list of businessmen desires and fetishes. Estelle? Something like that. *Daily News* dark glasses. Looked like buyer from Indianapolis ladies' wear. A pro. No different from a chef — Vanderbilts like it rare, Rockefellers medium. Carnegie, that was a welldoner. Corporate structure. Write-off. One of business counterholds to income tax. Hierarchy, Estelle.

Assistant managers specify only blonde or brunette. Chairman of board gives cup size, standing kneeling heelsonwall — sing *America* when coming.

The man was ready. Twice pushed off from bar, leaned back to sip a little longer.

Peripheral vision good. How many degree range? Twenty thirty tables. Breughel. Paw lean titstare fartmouthbragger halfslumplush twothirds handonelbow handonass handunderass. Beehive frenchknot flip guiche two wigged bitches one drunk or wigged out. Half with rooms upstairs, others go back quiet two's to Plaza Carlyle Waldorf. What at this moment are the poor people doing? Don't even allow panhandlers around Fifties and Sixties. Once Bowery guy outside Savoy. Cops before grabbing were like Audubon Society seeing robin in February.

Now.

Pushed off. Coming. Glass steady. Eyes front.

Call girls at two intervening tables looked up, smiled. Fur. Sparkly. Fetish too. My wife's clothes but move the ass briskly.

Cologne. One table over she smelled it. Just showered. Rubdown maybe. O.K. Josh you bastard. You made me what I am today, I hope you're satisfied. Sounds best in cockney. Oh Mavra once so sweet, stood pigeontoed. Now everything open. Wasn't I sweet once? Outside only, blackhearted whore. Blessed with a rotten memory.

Men's cologne. Louie has some. Maybe even I gave. This guy's wife wouldn't. Calfbound works of Churchill.

Standing over her. Strong cologne, to make us swoon.

"Would you consider it presumptuous — and forward — if I suggested the theater tonight — before you say no, may I sit down?"

Cold nod. She looked straight ahead.

"I beg your pardon. If you're expecting someone — I mean — no offense — you are a regular doll, you know that, I take it. My colleague can't get out of Washington. I'm stuck with two tickets to Olivier."

Say show me and he'll die. Types me near-highbrow. Otherwise would have tickets for sold-out musical.

"May I sit?"

"*N'importe.*"

"Ah, you're French!"

Silent, she sipped. *N'importe* gave nothing away. Still time to choose. Marian. Mavra. Maggie — wouldn't that be great? Mystic? Fey — a fungirl? Bergman smile, something tragic in my past. Lover killed in Korea. Bergman night. No nonsense. Mature voice. No verbal contractions. If you wish to take me to bed why do you not say so. I am a grown girl. Bergman is Hannah. But Hannah is Josh's mother's.

She smiled cool at his cool smile.

He sat down. Strange accent. Not Scottish quite. North Carolina? Not that either. Definitely not Fifth Avenue and Fifty-Ninth.

"We could dine first."

"First?"

"Ah, wicked girl! I meant before the theater."

Eyes down she sipped. Next line. I happen to have a few cold cuts in my suite on the penthouse floor.

"I am expecting a call from my colleagues. I should be in my room right now waiting."

Not a bad metaphor for cold cuts.

"Would you care to come up and wait with me? We could order dinner in the suite."

She looked down at her pendant watch. Timed in less than nine minutes from drink to prop.

No call girl. Neither a cinch.

"They will be glad to bring the phone to your table."

"Terribly confidential stuff. Shouldn't even be taking it through the switchboard."

When question used to be *why?* and couldn't come up with answer, did nothing. Since she changed to *why not?* the lack of an
answer was no handicap.

Poor Mavra.

Only suffering phony in the room.

From the airport booth tucked in the men's room I rang and
rang and rang and it was Louie's sleep voice I told I had a wrong
number.

And got her, two seconds, message: her roommate's (whispered)
and I love (whispered) and "wrong number" shouted, voice familiar, voice new, but all old feelings awakened, love and lust and
feverish groincramping desire, testicular fire and phallic flame,
scorched reality, burning bridges not yet come to, running outside
(two hours too early), knowing something hot and hysterical was
cutting all moorings, freeing boats and balloons before the sailers
were ready. Wild as a soldier home from long wars, someone released after half a lifetime in prison. Mad and futile for wise
friendly hermits to warn of consequences to potentially immortal
souls. Such heat could not but believe theology on its side, saints
with haloes in hand giving three and a tiger.

No sooner the elevator stopped than the apartment door
opened, and Mavra was crying, silly and gorgeous in another girl's
oversize dress, shivering beneath it, legs and feet bare, crying and
arms out, moaning as someone lost who has given up weeps when
rescued. Crying confessing explaining kissing, saltlips saltcheeks
saltthroat saltbreasts saltbelly, couchrough chairsmooth rugrough,
armsaround tonguesaround inaround, love's hurtling violence
catching up, for word, for promise not to be paperwritten, old
savor oldtouch new and neverbefore, great for mouth to stay this

mouth and breasts — tongue thigh belly slytouch slylip partsoft partsong caughtup wet and hugging violadamore wetringlet meet and wrap and part and open heelshigh kneesbent thighwide wetbellyslap headsnap breastquake rockroom poundfloor blurface flyhair flyhead losetongue losemouth joined only here only closer closer wetter fly over fly over locked or over closer and rocked flying thudding this too this too irreversible hurtling warmer and hot and flying anchored hotanchored wetanchored love's hands love's cry love's landing breastchest thighthigh mouthmouth rejoined.

Her hair spread out blacker on the black beneath her, darkness floorless, bottomless, space proved by the sheen of us, faintreflecting. Unseen unheard ungeigercountered. Womanbody manbody suspended manyfloors up; nothing to the senses, the place, time of it. Prove by this breastfold this chest these fingers that this is the twentieth century. Night-generalized. Manwomanspace — a measure. Soontofall. Puppetsrings and belting connections scattered like clothes over the timeless dark floor. And soon with clothes to be put back on: a thousand and one nights of no talk, no tale, but the thousand and second night comes, and, with it, the fall.

In the dark before dawn, Mavra's face in profile, featureless black silhouette, by the rising sun was differentiated hair by hair, pore by pore, identified, timemarked, spacemarked. A claim at every bend of cheek and curve of brow. Fashionclasped, historymarked, footshackled. In night, Eve. In light, Mavra.

We could not bear to turn on a lamp, and cry the world into this room. We knew the sun would end night's cover whether we willed it or not.

Sighing Mavra pulled on her halfslip.

"Josh," she said, "I wish I had two bodies."

"Then I would wish for another cock."

"Oh, I mean something."

She knelt where I sat, her knees stretched and round, her breasts flattening on her chest, parted.

"I mean all *that* would have happened to another body, not this. And I could despise that whorish carcass for living a sublunary-lover's life."

She stood up, dressed hurriedly, panting, groaning.

"Tell me, did you like the feel of me?"

"I love the feel of you."

"Knowing I've been such a nymphing bitch? I don't believe it. You'll never forget. Now when you want to display me you'll think — this is a common property — Mavra the community lay —"

"Mavra — I hate it —"

"Tell me you didn't take that bitch to bed with you all this time — go on, lie, Josh. And tell me you didn't find some loving unfucked-up girl to take your mind off me and Maggie."

She opened her handbag angrily. Crying to herself. Groping, her hand lost. Hair streaming down. Covering her face and her arms.

"I know what I did. Ruined it. Why didn't you carve your initials in me? Take an ad in *The Times*. On WNYC, interrupt the missing persons and tell everybody *your* Mavra's been found. You sonofabitch, I'd wear a bowlingshirt with your name embroidered on the back."

"It wouldn't count unless you wore it to Le Pavillon."

Combing, head to one side, tiptoe in a triangular mirror examining her face.

"God, look at this color. I'll be arrested. Bags under my eyes. Everything sagging and drooping. Can you believe I'm the girl who turned up one day to babysit? I'll bet you believed even then the blackhearted bitch in me was slouching toward The Museum to be born."

"When you're literary you're not at the top of your tragic bent."

"See? Goddam it! There you go again! You can't stand your responsibility, you fucker! You play with me. As soon as I get serious you turn me off. Do you think I'd go to the St. Regis and bask in the admiration of a hundred horny sales executives if you told me I was spectacular every hour on the hour?"

"That's a fulltime job."

"I'm not worth a fulltime job?"

"I can't stand you fucking around, but I can't stand you playing my victim."

"And I can't stand you and women! Other than your father and brother, did you have one friend who wasn't female? You can't be out of a woman's company for five minutes. I knew that years ago. What are you? You were in a goddam hospital and nurses loved you. That was long ago and in another country and at least a dozen of those wenches must be dead."

"I'm Josh, you frenzied bitch, and I love you."

"I'm — Josh! My God! I forgot to ask! Where's your mother? I didn't get an apartment or anything yet."

"She's not here —"

"Josh, you're lying."

"She's not."

"You sonofabitch, she's with Maggie."

"Mavra, listen — she wouldn't leave."

"I don't believe it. You'd never abandon her."

"She was too sad and too sick —"

"You're lying through your teeth. Your kind of family never throws anybody aside —"

"I didn't —"

"Josh. Were you really such a bastard that you left her there?"

"I've told you."

"Because I was whoring around — don't protect me. You couldn't bring your mother to a slut. Josh — answer."

"You weren't even in it."

"That's the biggest lie of all! You couldn't tell her you were in love with an ass-wagging bitch — God, did you at least tell your father about me before he died?"

"I couldn't —"

"You bastard! You denied me! Denied denied denied! Those St. Regis bastards affirm me more!"

"You bloody narcissistic lunatic! What the fuck did I care about your existential problem when real people were dying?"

She turned, snatched up a heavy alarm clock on the table, threw it mouthopen teethbared handaimed hairflying, smashed my forearm, shot fire through my arm, sickened my stomach. With my left arm I grabbed her and held her writhing down.

"Real people," she screamed though her hair and my muffling arm, "that's it, you bastard! I *am* a freak! You'll never rescue me."

"Shut up, for chrisakes. There was a time to think about you and a time that swept you and everything else out of my mind —"

"If you really loved me, you bastard, how could that be? I'm inadequate — let me go — I'm all right now — let me go I'm sorry — Oh, God, I broke your arm!"

"Screw yourself, you sentimental bitch!"

"Josh, I'm sorry — I'll cut my throat — tell me to do it —"

I pushed her away. My hand was numb.

"Not twenty minutes ago, you crazy whore, we sailed over the top of everything — look at us now. This fucking world born on Monday, fell on Tuesday. If it depends on you and me will never make it to the Sabbath."

"You're a lunatic, Josh. Kidding yourself to the top of your bent — Proteus. Lifegiver. Lovegiver. You're as bad as I am — worse. You won't press your precious die on me."

"We — you and I — drove this wedge between us. Fishman fishwife playing merman and mermaid."

"Bullshit — you hate yourself! You couldn't do it! Your Proteus love had limits. Where's the love which lies down with a leper, Saint Joshua? If I'm an unsalvageable nympho, isn't there something human and gorgeous in me that's worth saving?"

She grabbed my swelling arm. Kissed the rising lump. Licked at it, her wet hair over her face.

I put my good arm around her.

"If I were burned — unrecognizable — if some terrible fever robbed me of my brain — would you have thrown me aside when you came back? This is that kind of thing, Josh. Something exploded in me when you left."

I put my throbbing arm around her shoulders.

"Mavra, let's stop it all —"

"What, Josh?"

"The madness."

"You mean my screwing. If I give up my guys, what will you give up?"

"Let's sit at the table if we have to talk subsections and clauses."

"The vengeance is war — I told you I'm no better than that Halloween Buddha. I'm so blind to sweet alternatives I don't know how to get out."

"Just stop."

"Oh, God — will you turn back my time — get me a different old man, a different mother, a different persona, longer legs, bigger tits, a husband who doesn't feel pale in darkness —"

"You've fed the wrong data into the computer, you dumb bitch — so naturally it plays back this nympho necessity —"

"This world is so easy on itself. St. Julien lies with a leper and the running sores and the hideous ugliness turn out to be Christ. The real test would have been to lie down with a leper who was only a leper. I mean it. Any love that stops short is phony."

"Is that what the fucking is all about — blacken yourself into a beyond-salvation sinner and see if love can escalate to take care of that?"

"Josh, sometimes I think my century is me."

"Mavra, never mind confessionals — my arm is hurting."

"Sweetheart — here — I know what to do."

In that kitchen where pain and dogsmell dizzied my head she

broke open trays of soursmelling ice tinged yellow, specked with bits of meat. She lay the cubes in a dishtowel, and packed my burning arm.

I lay my head in her lap.

"How did we ever lose what we had when you opened the door? I did it, didn't I? Cold killer bitch. It's true. I *pretend* it's courtly love. Know what I really am? Middle class American college girl. Screws everybody on her Village weekends then marries the Yale boy — Josh, your arm is killing you. Let me kiss it. Take us back to the dark, after the *real* hot lay — how I must bore you, Josh — my sorrows, confessions, recriminations — always ready to hit the sawdust trail — my country 'tis of thee — drop another on Nagasaki — now we've *done* the worst there's no reason to hold back *anything!*"

"Sweetheart, shut up. You *are* boring. And my arm is smashed —"

"OK OK OK."

She leaned her face over mine. A hot smell of belly and thigh between her breasts.

"I've confessed it's boring — I can't see a way out — help me!"

Wet square tears overspread her eyes. Brimful. Shivering light, precarious glitter.

"Let me say just one more thing, Josh — please. Can I reclaim something? My bitchery is a lesson — a symptom of the times —"

"The symbolism of *you?* Mythic Mavra parallels?"

"If I came across a kid building something and he didn't let me build I kicked his blocks down — I'm terrified I don't have it. All lunatics are full of energy. They can't explode *for* something so they rip the world apart."

I pulled her face down over mine. Two large tears splattered my cheeks. I wiped at her eyes with my good hand.

"What do you want me to do, sweetheart?"

"Help me change. Bring your mother to me, let me start all over."

"Sweetheart, I've told you. It's final."

"Then I'm finished."

Melting ice ran chills over my chest. Mavra's blouse was dark and wet. My face washed over by her tears.

"Josh, let's not leave here ever."

"I should have this arm looked at."

"We'll go over to Brooklyn — anonymously — Mr and Mrs what — think of a good lovers' name for Brooklyn. I'll never go back to Louie. We'll live close. Utterly devoted."

"What about Dov?"

"Louie will have to solve that."

"You'd leave Dov —"

"For this I would. Wouldn't you leave Bailla?"

"No."

"*I'd* be here, all alone with you. You'd give up everything and everybody for me, wouldn't you? *I* would come first.

"You are the first —"

"I want to be so terrific you give the sun up for me — water — food —"

Glassy eyes. A flicker on the unwatery inner eye. Teletype message passing in darkness. Eyeblink. Retreat from here-and-now. Switch out. Signals, semaphores, codes, secrets clashing in her brain. Garbage chute maildrop, burnt-out papermatches too common to be recognized by anyone but 007, family and lover to Mata Mavra, head-of-class, head-of-list, come-first, number-one. Gears shifted. Her head jerked ever so slightly. A trance passing. I called her out of it again. She smiled behind the glaze. Deep sigh, shoulders dropped.

"Josh?"

"Welcome back."

"Don't tease."

"Those violent oscillations. Too too dark in the deep pit — the leap to sun and angelic whiteness — fail, fall — too too dark in the deep pit — declaring self an emotional basket case."

"You mean me?"

"You."

"That's not friendly."

"Neither is it self-pitying."

"I'm my country. My country is me."

"I am dying, Schoharie, dying."

"What does that mean?"

"Neither theological deflation nor cosmological ballooning can approximate this gorgeousness my face is pressed against."

"You care about my body?"

"We start somewhere, dopey girl."

"But it's all corrupted —"

"Oh spare me — the reel is starting up again — let's go, right now —"

"You can't stand to be alone with me another second —"

"Right."

He wound my arm in plaster, old doctor puffing on an unfilled pipe. Released that smell, domestic, pedestrian, deflating plaster. Vaudeville team, you Abraham, I Isaac. The ram's head was plaster.

"Tell me again," he said, "for the report."

"I slipped —"

"It's like a hockey injury — puck hit above the glovepad line."

"My husband slipped," Mavra said, "and fell into an ornamental doorknob."

But if the water come to him . . . argal. . . .

Noon sun overhead on Fifth Avenue, glittering the black spears fencing the Park. The cast on my arm shone white where cabs emptied the crutched, the slinged, pregnant women, hobbling men. Outpatients passed, good newsed and bad. Backs to the warm sun, dark shoulders huddled. Off the posh street a bus discharging lame and halt.

Mavra shuddered.

"Let's go to the Plaza, Josh."

"To celebrate this broken arm?"

"We can get back after lunch."

"They must be worried out of their minds —"

"I'll tell Louie I was with Buffie — I'll bawl him out for never remembering what I say."

"I've heard all this before. You are less cute than you think."

"While he was wrapping the plaster you were wincing. You couldn't take your eyes off me. Tell me what you saw."

I pointed my good hand up at the sun.

"Hey," I said, "do we deserve that?"

"Don't change the subject, Josh."

She ran beside me to keep in stride. Fifth Avenue whitewalled, sunwindowed. I put my arm around her.

"Weren't you staring at the lines around my eyes?"

"What will you fear when you reach thirty?"

"So many beautiful young women in this town!"

"Narcissist, self-involvenik — somewhere in this universe is something not you. Find it. Contemplate it."

"You mean I'm selfish?"

I gave up, and kissed her. A plumrobed doorman saluted.

The apartment warm, full of curry, steaming blackpepper, sesame bread baked in Atlantic Avenue belowground stone kilns. Cartons gone, junk thrown out, a gold damask cloth over the refectory table. The action paintings played their color to airy windows full of city light.

Mavra was smiling.

"Isn't this what your mother did on Fridays?"

"Cooked."

"Took over. Gathered you all in. This is her family, starting today. Dov, you, and I. Bailla when you can sneak her over. And when it's all set — your mother. My roommate won't be back for six months — didn't I tell you? I moved out on that Louie. He's too much. Didn't notice I hadn't come home last night."

"Liar."

"OK OK OK — so I hoked up a quarrel and walked off in a huff. Louie thinks I'm at my mother's. Dream up something to cover *your* tracks."

"Creatures of stealth."

"Lovers trying to make it out of a tangled world."

Hair matted, caught up quickly in an askew barette, Maggie stood in the dark doorway, arms over her head, waving surrender.

"Sybil, Cassandra, idiot — I foresaw. This crappy doom — it was right there, a shy innocent girl wandering down a road. I've told you. She has more strategy than a thousand generals, is better at tactics than jungle fighters, guerrillas, paratroopers, the CIA. Why couldn't she put all this to work for the Pentagon? Look at her victory! She has you. Louie has the story of his maim. And me? Here-we-go-again department! Zora was an angel. This madwoman. Ponytailed poison! Worse than Medea — or what Medea brewed."

"Oh Josh — you're early."

"I'm not."

"God — have you been waiting long?"

"It could be an hour —"

"I had shopping to do."

"With Buffie?"

"With Nancy."

"Whose money did you save?"

"You must be psychic — I didn't buy a thing!"

She scrubbed Dov's face with a washcloth.

"Traffic was terrible."

"Who was doing the driving?"

"Marilyn."

"Not Nancy?"

"Who said anything about Nancy?"

"Didn't you say you were shopping with Nancy?"

"I was shopping with Marilyn."

"At discount stores on the Island?"

"Wrong. We went to White Plains."

She turned toward me, rubbed hard at an imaginary hive on her cheek.

"Bastard — you expect me to give up everything — I won't!"

"What won't you give up?"

"Never mind. You're like my old man —"

"So soon?"

"He wanted my mother to give me up."

"I know who I am in the analogy, and you're your mother. But who is *you?*"

"You're trying to trap me. *Gaslight* — *Angel Street* — say I said Nancy when you *know* I said Marilyn. And the Island —"

"Not White Plains?"

"Yes — White Plains — you're mixing me up — would I lie?"

"Only if your memory were infallible."

"I was shopping for presents. Little surprises, for Dov and Bailla and you —"

Large tears formed in her eyes. Her lower lip quivered. She wiped at her nose with Dov's washcloth. Her voice was tiny, squeaky. Margaret O'Brien ready-to-cry mouth.

"You treated me shabbily when I was doing a beautiful surprise thing? I'm embroidering a doily for your mother — wine velvet with hundreds of gold tiny tiny little stitches — I may go blind from it — if I lose my sight making a secret gift for your mother, then how will you feel?"

I heard steps outside the door. Opened. A man was on his knees making an "M" out of used Q-Tips. He jumped up, threw his hands in front of his face. He looked a little like Louie, walleyed, goggling, fatter — beer belly, bowed legs, shortish denim trousers showing white cotton socks.

Behind me Mavra blinked a message. The man's mouth dropped open. He shrugged, made signs to show he was a mute. Mavra breathed out.

I toed the Q-Tips. He bolted through an exit, clattered down the emergency stairs. I closed the door behind me.

"You think that had anything to do with me? Poor old man, you frightened him to death. He was going to write a note asking for directions."

I sat down in the living room, picked up a book.

"I know what you're thinking, Josh — why don't you come right out and say it."

"You say it."

"You're hallucinating — do you know that? What's that girl you told me about — Evvie — you're like her — you dreamt up a whole conversation — I told you I went to White Plains with Buffie — I didn't say such a thing — people with guilt feelings always hallucinate — you can't face up to it. You took me away from Dov's father — that poor loving man. He sits there crying day and night now — a lot you care. You *know* a child can be permanently wrecked being separated from his male parent. A guy comes near the front door and you accuse me of screwing with him. Just because I wrote you letters to amuse you, and concocted diverting stories about me and Dickie —"

"Donnie —"

"Do-o-o-n — I did not say his name was Do-o-o-n — Oh, you didn't burn my letters — you and Maggie had a lot of laughs thinking of me with this ugly old clown. Don't you know *anything* about me? If I were going to screw with some guy he'd really have to be something. Handsome and witty, maybe titled — would I let an ugly old lush use my — your — sweetheart — I'm your chalice — did you forget?"

I held the book open.

Mavra took it out of my hands.

"You're tired of me, Josh."

"Right."

She laughed.

"Here, put your hands on me — right there — isn't that better than quarreling?"

She opened her eyes wide. Theatric muscle quivering. One eyelid puckered self-consciousness.

"We should never wear clothes and never talk — talk leads to trouble — just grab me, throw me on my back — when you don't I think you've found someone great who isn't neurotic and crazy like me."

"I once invented an American contest that guaranteed no winners — talk for three minutes straight, and never mention money."

"You mean I can't talk about anything but me — take your hands off me — I came offering peace."

"On your back, martyr!"

"OK OK — that's better — why don't you know by now? I'm stupid and insecure. Use me! Beat me up if you have to!"

"Masochist martyr — do you include shake well in your directions?"

She ducked her head in hiding, closed her eyes. Red welts formed on her shoulders. Her face a flame.

"Josh, promise you won't let me out of your sight. Ugly miserable bastards! Men! Nobody's going to catch me out!"

"Mavra —"

I shook her.

Her head wobbled, her mouth fell open.

"Help me, Josh! I'm *really* a castrating bitch! Do something, make me human!"

Down below, sanitation trucks whining, mad nightdrivers horn-honking, one truck two at distance, revving, garbage cans slamming, helpers' shouts, motor roar the truck moving, taxitires sticky on freshsprayed streets, cleaning trucks' brushes whirling drytwigs, lowkeyed, water hissed to roll tires stickier. Ambulance siren at dreampitch, police siren, fire siren, tremulo, callback, fadeout, planesound, sirenshriek.

Mavra breathed the labored subsnore of feigned sleep. Tensed. Battlestations alerted.

Did Daedalus imagine the maze of Minos would be his own entombing? A guard shackled to a prisoner is the prisoner's prisoner. One more pow at the tarbaby — one head left.

Mavra rolled over.

"You awake?" I said.

"Wha wha where am I?"

She fell back, openmouthed.

"Are you afraid I'll dream about some guy?"

Pastime. Start a little war. You all gonna fight and kill each other for li'l ol' me? Blank appointment calendar 3:00 to 4:00 A.M. — fill in with alarums. Let drums and heads roll.

I put my hand over her mouth. Gently.

"You're choking me!".

I laughed, sitting up.

"Why are you laughing at me? You had your hands around my throat. You were thinking about choking me — tell me —"

"Will that shut your mouth?"

"Own up who you're screwing."

"Our hour of truth?"

"One thing I want you to know. Outside of Louie I've never let anyone get within miles of me — I swear on Dov's head — on my

unborn children — if I'm lying let them be born armless and leg-
less —"

"Go to sleep, baby."

"You woke me and got me started — I don't turn off that easily."

"O.K. In the same spirit as your confession; outside of you I've
never been to bed with any other woman."

"Smartass! I swore on the heads of unborn children. On Dov's
head — go on, swear on Bailla's — the truth — go on, go on. You
think I'm a lesbian, a nympho, a child murderer — brainwash me.
I almost believed you. If other persons didn't show me I was
normal — girl friends —"

"Buffie and Marilyn —"

"You know damn well there is nobody named Marilyn, that I
made her up to fool Louie —"

At the stove she stirred Dov's oatmeal. Singing. Head thrown
back, forehead in frown, on pitch. Feet correctly placed, as taught.
Hair flowing down her back, cheeks red, up, smiling.

Old Mavra.

"Josh, come on, sing with me — that was a lot of shit, wasn't it?
We were awful. Psychodrama for two voices. I got that from
Louie. You got it from that bitch. It disfigures us to yell like mad-
men. Promise the next time you'll kick me in the ass and throw me
in a tub of cold water. There's nothing wrong with me, Josh. I'm
too idle. Think up a thousand things that need brilliant solutions.
I'll do them all — in one day. Tomorrow think up a thousand
others."

"I have to do the laundry."

I nodded.

"You want to come with me?"

"No."

"I want you to."

"Leave Dov here alone?"

"I don't want you to think I'll duck into some guy's apartment — I haven't so much as a nodding acquaintance with the neighbors."

At the window I watched a youngish woman cross the street. Two arms, two legs. Voice, Tell me, dear lady, what day is this? Tuesday. And it *is* Tuesday. There are such women. Name space, speak naturally of time. Not angels. How would that be? Hear a voice, believe it.

"O.K., *you* take the laundry — someone has to do it — you think I'll get on the phone the second you leave — or knock on some guy's door. I don't know a soul on this floor. I swear. What do we do?"

"The laundry!"

She stood behind me at the window, wound her arms around my neck.

"O.K. I'll be right back, huh, honey?"

"Right."

"What are you looking at down there — some gorgeous bitch with elegant legs?"

"New York City."

"You don't look at anything but great tits and twitchy asses, even way down there — why don't you run down and grab somebody? If you took the laundry down you'd find some girl hanging around — it's the assignation place here — as you damn well know. I've had the eye from a dozen guys around this place. One snap of my fingers is all it would take. You can forget about using *my* laundry to cover for you. Do what you want to — I'm not going to be a little fool while you're cutting up."

If, in limbo, those stinging insects pursuing, one could merely shut a door and close them out forever: if that poor driven beast could with one sudden burst elude the gadfly: if an entombed miner could give one push and find cool lightdrenched air, so I, getting away from Mavra. Stepping into an elevator, dropping below her turgid space. I stumbled into sunlight, amazed to find it still there, the beautiful, miraculous, ordinary world. Everything looked as it once had, through my window: a cracking sidewalk, an azalea in a stone pot. A policeman's voice I heard as thunder, his message gnomic and in the language of prophets. Fifth Avenue was a sunswept steel river where a kid with transistor flew at me music of spheres. I patted hydrants and lamp posts, nudged the solid miracle of a postbox. A janitor brushed red and gray dust out of a doorway, a message in each speck. What genius molded the curbstone, what Capaneus bolt chipped it at the intersection, what mystic animal pissed a stain against it?

Women poured out of buildings to greet me. Lovely eyes and sungleam arms flashing codes on the Nina scale. It was only the lunch hour. But I felt their hailing, worldglittered throngs streaming in welcome from bastions and sheer shells, sultry sirens who beat their heels like tambourines.

Lazarus, Lazarus, one by wearing a green picturehat shouted, *this I bought for you.*

That old common ordinary world-in-hiding. Waiting there all the time for anyone liberated. Nina. Gyla. Me. Falcons unhooded.

I stopped a beautiful girl.

"Hi," I said.

She looked puzzled.

"No, you don't know me. You're beautiful, and I wanted to hear a voice."

"Gobble gobble gobble!"

"Beautiful!"

"And you're not drunk — are you from Mars or somewhere?"

"Somewhere — say 'today is Thursday.' "

"But it's not!"

"Great, great, you're the greatest!"

I glanced back at the building I had run from. Mavra up there. Wasn't this abandoning her? As though she *were* a leper.

I could not move me with the thought. The recovered sun was warm on my cheeks.

Later, I thought — and breathed oh, deeply — later I'll think if I escaped, or abandoned Mavra.

Astraddle the sundrenched street I felt the globe turning under my feet. Heelmarked and hoofmarked and bellymarked. Palimpsestic avenue, manrecording, creaturerecording. Space inscribed by time. Who walked here and breathed here and died here. Palimpsest of history, prehistory. Primordial. The first mark of motion. Doomcrack birthcrack. On this civilized avenue which once, perhaps, was saltwashed.

I trod the earth as if it were a log in water, trudged it to a rhythmic roll.

Step, toe, retrace the tread of all those who loved a mad girl. See, eye, what was recorded as a lover's madness. It's all there, transparent spider threads weaving a palimpsestic tale.

Miracles I carry in my bones. Not when voice spoke out of whirlwind; or seas parted; or man was swallowed then spewed by a whale.

When Abraham went out was a miracle.

And Rebecca walked to the well.

And Jacob again saw Joseph.

Time by ticking passed an endless stream of camels through the needle's eye.

Maggie framed herself in the doorway.

"Your ladylove's line is busy —"

Bailla ran past her and jumped into my arms.

"Where have you *been*, Daddo?"

"In the city."

"Can I go back with you?"

"You stay here —"

"I don't mean forever —"

Maggie sent her off for a book.

"She has the phone off the hook," Maggie whispered, "what do you think that signifies?"

"That the receiver isn't on the cradle."

"She's planning World War III, I think. That bitch wouldn't settle for less."

"*Why* were you calling?"

"Your mother may have had another stroke —"

"May?"

"I'm not your mother's keeper. Get your bitch on the job — see what she can find out. I'm no taker of messages for Lothario."

"Did they want me to come?"

"Beatty didn't say."

"Why was she calling?"

"To tell you there is something real in this world that you and Lady Macbeth can't lie about or wriggle out of —"

Bailla ran back into the room. The book under her arm was slipping out.

"Read me," she said.

She looked from one to the other.

"Kiss!"

Maggie and I brushed faces — fingers like talons on each other's shoulders.

"Both of you read me — I'll sit between."

"Daddy can read to you — I've done nothing but."

"Read me!" Bailla ordered.

"O.K."

She wriggled up close to me, leaned her head on my chest, looked up, waiting.

"Where shall I start?" I said.

"Anywhere. I've read it a hundred times —"

The phone rang. Bailla slid off the couch, ran slipperslap to the phone. Maggie had it.

"Long distance —"

The line was dead but for the electronic charge music.

"Josh —"

"Beatty?"

"Mavra — don't you know me —"

"What is it?"

"Come back — please — I'm dying — I behaved like a cold whore — I must have looked ugly — Josh, can you stand to think of me — I've ruined it —"

Maggie swooped Bailla up in her arms, slammed out of the room.

"My mother may have had another stroke —"

"You're making that up — you'll never see me again — you'll find excuses — your mother — Bailla — anything. I can't stand this, Josh — so ugly ugly ugly. I didn't *do* anything — I swear on Dov's head. I couldn't. I'm yours — it's my curse. Come back for five seconds — you won't even put your arms around me — just look at me and don't run out as if I had you trapped in Auschwitz. Take my hand — five seconds — just long enough for me to touch reality — I'll never bother you again after — I swear, Josh. Liberate me. How can you hear the woman you love suffer, and not come running to her rescue?"

"I have to phone —"

"Who?"

"My mother."

"Did you make that up to get me off the line? If it's true you still can't go off without seeing me — claim me — put your stamp on me — you haven't told me I'm beautiful for hours. One last night together, Josh — then tell me to go to hell —"

"I'll call you —"

"Josh — swear you won't go without seeing me —"

"O.K."

"Swear!"

"I said O.K."

I reached Beatty on the phone.

"She's gone down, Josh. You'd never recognize her, Joseph picked her off the floor in the middle of the night. She was laughing to herself. Not the loud crazy thing — to herself. She weakened —"

"Is it a stroke?"

"Nobody knows."

"Should I come?"

"That's up to you."

"What does Jeremiah say —"

"He didn't see her."

"Call him."

"Oh, Josh — it's too late for that —"

"What haven't you told me, Beatty?"

"Nothing."

"She's gone down?"

"Yes — terribly —"

"Does *she* want to see me?"

"Why else did I call?"

"Is it urgent?"

"Nobody can say. You'd have to see her yourself, Josh."

I turned from the phone to Maggie, her eyes blazing. Bailla's record player sounded in the distance.

"Beatty keeps saying she's gone down. I don't understand what that means," I said. "I'd better go."

"Where?"

"To my mother —"

"You're lying. That brazen whore — who the hell is she to call you here? I could kill the both of you barehanded. Murdering romantics."

Slightly frosted glass. Greencoated he slid a panel open. Cold funereal smell. Green smell. Biting. Rich roses. Floor of wreaths. Rolls of ribbon. Blackedged cards. Flatgreen paper.

"Bright yellow," I said.

"Spiders."

"Right."

"Someone has given birth?"

"No."

"Ah — a successful operation —"

"Something like that. I want each one wired, each flower must face her way —"

"Her?"

"My mother."

"Ah. A very artistic arrangement."

Glasses mirroring flowers. Yellow, white. He held a spider chrysanthemum bent slightly forward.

"Ah — as if they watch out for her — one learns in business from everyone."

"Rush them."

"I will phone immediately, sir."

"I'm flying there myself in a few hours —"

"Ah — so these stand in but for a moment."

Precisely, loudly, he phoned flowers in for her bedside, bobbing his head, assuring me she would have them by the time I walked three blocks.

The man who looked like Louie waddled out the building, redfaced, furtive, casing the street walleyed. I made a sudden motion with my hands. He broke into a gallop. Zipper jacket flying behind him. Trousers hitched at his white sock calf.

A laugh coughed out of me.

Mavra took a long time coming to the door.

"Oh, Josh, I was taking a little bath —"

Her face hurriedly covered with filmy make-up. The upper half of her quite dry.

She looked at me.

"It was a sitzbath — I have terrible trouble with my spine — you did that to me, you rapist! I'll sue you for assault with a deadly weapon!"

"Mavra —"

"What?"

"Did you hear what I said on the phone?"

"That your mother *may* have had another stroke — I heard you — I'm being dumped."

I put my arms around her.

"Mavra, come on — stop."

"Tell me, did your cast frighten Bailla?"

"I kept it covered."

The phone rang. Mavra jumped.

"Damn — another wrong number — this number must be like some other —"

It kept ringing.

"Shall I answer?" I said.

Mavra dived for the phone. Picked the receiver up casually, pressed it hard against her ear.

"You have the wrong number, lady," she said loudly.

Smiled at me. Listening intently. White forehead in fixed frown.

"I *said* you have the wrong number, lady — there is nobody called Angie here."

She slammed the receiver.

"Aren't people weird — tell them they have the wrong number and they have to keep yapping."

"Mavra, I'm going."

She pressed her cheek between thumb and middle finger. Eyes lowered.

"God, I see it — a wipe-out. As though I never existed. You don't have so much as a picture to show your mother. Josh, *we've* gone down! Phony — you don't have a flight —"

"Right."

"You'll go out to that airport and sit by yourself all night till planes start flying?"

"How else will I get there?"

"You don't feel a thing — letting me stand here, dressed, like a stranger. I read your eyes. You thought that phone call for Abbie was some guy calling me. You thought you walked in on me douching."

She reached for my face, small hands, soft hands. I kissed her quickly. She jumped back — rubbed at her lips with outspread fingers.

"That was no kiss! You can't stand the smell of me — you've lost your feeling."

"Mavra, get your face out of the picture for once!"

"This is your face — you used to love this face!"

"I love it now. But listen for one bloody second — I've got to get to my mother —"

"Oh why couldn't you whip in here and tell me to fly back with you!"

"Can't you shut up?"

"OK OK OK — you know how to get me off myself — kisses and hugs and spectacular things. I'm so dumb and primitive — OK OK OK — so I can't stop talking about myself — take me with you, Josh. She'll clap her hands to see me! I'll hug you, you'll kiss me — she'll see what we feel for each other. Nobody could look at that and not be filled with life!"

"I have to go immediately, gorgeous Narcissa."

"Not before you reinforce me. I can call reclining —"

She dialed, then held the receiver toward me, a busy signal, fast, for tied-up circuits.

"Call another airline —"

"OK OK OK — I'm your Japanese type."

Tinny distant an automatic voice spoke its recorded message.

"You'll never fly out tonight, Josh. God's on my side."

She pressed her breasts upward, wriggled her belly against me.

"Sir, you're oversartorialized. I am swelling with passion, you sonofabitch! Don't you acknowledge stuff when it's offered to you?"

"Try the airline again."

She caught the phone between her shoulder and her ear, hair streaming dark to one side. One hand for dialing, the other undoing buttons on my shirt. Again the canned voice spoke.

"Josh, it's hopeless — please, just lie beside me — every hour on the hour I'll call. If there's still no flight wrap me up, bulge out the walls, quake the continent. Unusual high tides will be reported, and switchboards jammed. Let's assert love's precedence — you *love me* —"

"Bitch, that's never been in doubt —"

"OK OK OK — so to hell with the rest —"

"What about my promise?"

"Which? Oh, God, you mean your mother!"

When Beatty rang, shrill in the night, my chest and Mavra's breasts hotwet, sticky, darkness rushing cool over us, I didn't have to be told. I had it explode a searing light — as when Maggie ran to tell what I really knew — below surprise, below shock — that *he* was dead, *who could not live with terror, my father*. My mother could not live with words.

For if they fall, the one will lift up his fellow:
but woe to him that is alone when he falleth.

Mavra threw herself face down on the dark floor. But she still heard Beatty's voice, and Beatty crying.

"For the longest time — are you there, Josh? — she pulled every ounce together and looked out the door convinced you were going to surprise her — you *brought* those yellow flowers — Josh — are you there? Your card said you'd *follow in an instant*. She said: 'Josh, that sport, I know he's right here.' She wouldn't lay back till Jeremiah came and said there was nobody outside the door."

Mavra twisted her cheek into the rough rug, crying high and raw and loud.

I tried to get her to her feet. She scrunched up, shivering.

"Leper — now I am your leper. You'll hate me — hot hate — soul hate — I made you sell her out —"

"Sweetheart, get up —"

"I can't stand to see your face. Selfish this poisonous pig self —"

"Mavra, sweetheart, here, I'll tuck you in —"

"You don't hate my narcissistic guts?"

Indistinct in darkness the sheen of tear trails, the glint of watery eyes.

"Oh I can't stand not being dressed now."

I helped her into her nightgown. She shivered.

"Josh, I won't cry any more — I know what's coming. When you're at her grave you'll hate me with all your heart —"

I made her lay her head on the pillow. Kissed her wet cheek.

"Sweetheart," I said, "I won't even blame me. She died. *I wasn't there.* Just that. In her room. In that space. I wasn't."

"Josh, that sport," she said, "I *know* he's here."

Beatty told her I was not yet. And again read her the card.

"When he says 'an instant' he really means soon — *almost* immediately — like maybe tomorrow."

Jeremiah in his surgeon's gown poked his head in the doorway.

"Nobody's out here, old girl."

Slumped on her pillow, she dozed. Woke with both hands too heavy.

"Josh, is he here yet?"

"Still not," said Beatty.

"Footsteps — I hear his in the hall."

"Somebody else's —"

"Wake me when he comes."

"I will."

"Even if it's the middle of the night."

"I will."

"Such beautiful flowers — it's a shame —"

"What?"

"Spiders — especially the yellow, live forever."

"You'll take them home with you."

"Wake me, Beatty darling. I'll hear him, but if I shouldn't — can you understand my cotton batting tongue. I can always tell Joshua's walk, one light, one lighter — so wake me."

"I will, darling."

"Gad can't come — did you know that, Beatsie? What does Joshua's card say again, Beatsie?"

"That these flowers will pour sun on you, and Joshua is following right behind —"

"Did a plane crash anywhere?"

"Of course not, darling —"

"He'll come straight here from the airport — won't have eaten a thing — you look after him —"

"Oh I will."

"Beatsie, *I* told them to go. Why do dying people want their children —"

"Shshshshshsh — you're not dying —"

"Like water —"

"What's like water, swetheart?"

"He'll yell at me to get up, Joshua — tell him to take it easy. This time I'm doctor."

And lay her face on her child's hands making a steeple.

Nuns rustled outside her door. Joseph Czernowski, hat in hand, looked and left. Nurses glided in, took her pulse, stared at unmoving Beatty.

Bluewhite nightlight.

Grained on her clay cheek.

Claiming shadows. Below her. Thronged black in corners. Nightwings. Graywings. Whitewings. Angel with angel wrestling.

And Beatty dozing thought she herself heard footsteps. Sat up, straining. Metal charts clashed, water flushed with explosive suddenness, nurseheels beat dull marches on night's routine rounds.

Touched that dry forehead. Cool. Soft. Waking her. Barely turned her head to Beatty's side. Indistinct rush. Breath and word undifferentiated.

"Joshua, is Joshua here?"

"Any minute now."

"What time is it?"

"Four."

"Morning or afternoon?"

"It's dark —"

"Make it till morning —"

"Make what?"

"Will we?"

"Make it to morning?"

"Planes land now?"

"Not for a while."

"Can Jeremiah keep me going long enough?"

"Shshshsh — sleep, sweetheart —"

"With kings and counsellors?"

"What?"

"Joseph — he found me on the floor? Dressed?"

"Yes — of course dressed —"

"In case I don't — I should leave a message — I can't think. Telegrams. Cards. I never knew what to say."

"Sleep now — when you wake he'll be here —"

"How come, Beatsie? We believe they *can* keep us alive. Joshua's hand. Beatsie — don't be hurt."

"Hurt?"

"Too dumb. Nothing to say — or give."

"Josh will help you talk."

"Yes, Joshua."

"Is Joshua coming?"

"Joshua is coming."

"If I'm gone —"

"Shshshshshsh."

"Tell him how hard I waited."

I went to a funeral where a gray box was buried, in a familiar city with the gray box already closed. My brother Gad came in a duplicate jet of silver. During the service a man who spoke kind words about my mother gestured toward that gray box. Gad and I, on his word, followed it to an iron-gated enclosure. All of us walked on a shale path, and heard her sisters crying. I saw a man in black, Joseph Czernowski, pat the gray box with his inkstained hand. Tiny Beatty shrieked, much bent were my mother's older sisters. Her brothers cried too. Gad and I over the gray box were dry-eyed.

It sounded far off, that song sadder than crying.

We covered the lid with handfuls of dirt, below ground, gray box descended. A stone plaque with my father's name on it suggested the box was in a grave reserved for my mother.

And after, we sat in her house, that house, his house, on low stools, in black, her sisters and brothers, Gad and I, and, as if they were hiding, Joseph Czernowski, his wife, and shy child. I tried to comfort Beatty, who couldn't stop crying. Her green eyes shone like wet stones set in black.

"I should have *urged* —" she whispered. "It's my fault. I was afraid I'd sound hysterical."

"I heard you, sweetheart —"

"All I could say was she'd gone down. Joshua, did you know she was already dead — there's no other way to describe it. On the inside she was dead."

Joseph Czernowski, framed in the doorway, motioned to Gad and me to come into a back room.

"Josh," Beatty said, "I'm such a fool. I expected you to read between the lines —"

"I heard what you were saying."

"And still didn't come in time?"

Gad stood up, pointing to himself, then to me, motioned to Joseph that we were coming.

"She had a crazy thought in her head — she believed you could keep her alive. Not actually, maybe. In some funny way — I can't describe it —"

"Beatty, I couldn't."

"I don't think so either."

Nina hid behind her mother's black dress, and Joseph motioned us in, and closed the door. One small shaded lamp lit the room, and Gad's eyes lost in black behind those glasses.

"You give hand?" Joseph whispered.

We held our right hands out.

"You no think we no good look after?"

"Of course not," I said.

Gad shook his head.

"Oho, we all — wife same, same Nina, same me — look good after. She no hear. Woice she no hear. She hear accordion. Sit in pink chair and I play."

His wife nudged him gently. He stepped to the side.

"Boys, you know I be good her? And wife same good?"

"You were wonderful to her."

"She fall, I jump out bed — bare foot — pick up —"

"We know."

"Nobody can make hear. I make hear accordion. She do like so with hand — loo la la, loo la la — her face laugh — no cry —"

His wife shook her head sharply.

"Joseph, no no — she no move hand. Never say —"

"Oho, Gad, Joshua, you listen — she tap foot — both foot — so — loo la la, loo la la — waltz — same night she fall she tap foots, make so with hand — oho, she happy old woman, she like me make her joke and music —"

"God forgive Joseph! Please, no listen," his wife tried to pull him onto a settee.

"Boys, I tell true."

"Joseph, no — is dream — more dream. Please to forgive my Joseph, Joshua, Gad — he say like same his ma is no burn."

"Oho, Joshua, Gad, look it me. I show."

And listed, slanted, his one hand limp, his face drawn up hideously, stumbling, pumping his knees, to comfort us, dancing.

When all others were gone, in this her mourner's house, and Joseph slept, and his wife, and his child, and Gad breathed heavily in the corner, awake or asleep, it came back to me what house I lay in, what space was enclosed here, etched, three-dimension palimpsest, where every motion — like a filament once glowed, now out — burned its signature. I slid off this bed, struck that foot of floor. Space nicked. Agony-scored.

I listened to night. Same ear. Same night. New sounds. Joined, continuous, windtunnel time. Every pane every glass every dish shattered continued to shatter the length of my years. One long steam-hissing kettleboil should this be the night Uncle Bim, or a bridegroom, come.

In carved space he sprang from his own heelmark left years earlier, old eaglefaced man, waving his arms to discount the finite. Time later, his shaking hand let a teadrop fall, tannic splash etched into one single oak board. Over it a hundred heels passed, never fading his imprint. Nor other space markings diamondcut on glass.

Housecreaks crash in my ear a million times magnified, doomcrack, earthrumble. Space's prisoners clamber to escape this suffocating pit and stampeded toward an opening of air.

Long night yearsdrawn slippershuffle lightswitch onoff onoff:

lady, I did you no kind service. Gentle madam I could never dream I had used you so. Guilt, dear lady, puts it paltry — *shame for mis-using the mysteries* says it all.

Pocked earth. Tastefully covered over. Below space hidden. Below time. Even Bibul they brought back, after his ending. And Uncle Bim, bare marker over shale, near Dobrushyn, crowned with earth's finest marble.

Neither have they any more a portion for ever in any thing that is done under the sun.

Space. Deathcrowded museum.

My father's buried there. My mother. The I who was son.

So much buried. That beautiful girl in velvet who once lay in this bed, and the I in love with her, at my porch window winnowing the world.

Long unbroken nightbreath. Merged. Breath within breath. Those who breathe darkness were not always here — saint, Joseph Czernowski, my lady's juggler. Who knew the burners, but dreams they weren't real. Livid flame, long night of fires, Carthages burning. Alexandria. Warsaw. Successive cities clouddoomed. Burners abounding, and night growing darker. Busy, the burners; hawking their freak show. For fifty cents extra see Shakespeare the geek.

Last night in my house.

A dead leaf scraped the house's cement foundation. Dry bare elmtwigs tapped the tin gutter. Gently. As one taps a friend's shoulder, reminding.

Windwash.

Nightwash.

Time, like space, has its museum. In such darkness every Oliver holds his bowl out, offering more.

May I say it now, sunlit is loveliest.

Nina, my phantom.

Mavra, my player.

Maggie, my hider.

For to him that is joined to all the living there is hope.

We defy entropy. There *is* special providence in the fall of a soft warmbreasted sparrow.

Sad sour beautiful old preacher, could I possibly have read your message wrong?

If two lie together, then they have heat
How can one be warm alone?

I went to a lecture given by Lazarus; the only excluded topic was death. He was an old old man speaking a tongue known only to new angels. His remarks were off the record (but enough about that). His old chalky hand held ready for writing: he moved his wrist and chalk sprang imaginary petals on unseen flowers. Those who were lucky breathed that invisible gorgeousness in. It's rumored his theories, like those about light, may soon be taken over by burners. They are beautiful now, and need our attention. In the particle of particles there is no before or after. But shshshshsh shsh — our secret, that wild possibility.

You yourself are enough of a Lazarus. Nina a Lazarus, Gyla, Mavra, Fran, Orpheus, Daedalus, those who had breath or luck to sing in this dark. I myself heard the Lazarus message early, as I've already told you. From an eaglefaced man saying *son of man, you were born.*

Burners abound — I say it again to remind us.

My old Uncle Bim defied their victories. The burners are pursuing, but never let them take over the dark and sunlit taling.

I came back not to stay.

I came back to tell you here this unfinishing tale, cast images in frames, of swift metamorphoses.

Did I possibly dream it? Mouse, blood, sun, all. Did I dream, or did you, of a President shot down in sunlight? Did you dream, or I, that burners can fly? I might have dreamt almost everything, except what's broken, here, and still unhealed.

When men end such tales they must forbear trumpeting. Even defiance of entropy in time's a bad bet. Man lives bounded by death: that by itself sobers his parties.

Should we end celebrating the mouse we began with? All others in my tale might possibly have partisans. He, poor long-dead mouse, has, alas, only me. Salute him with me, and then I fly eastward, where sun rises tomorrow, as I hope to see.

THE NEW CANADIAN LIBRARY

n 1. OVER PRAIRIE TRAILS / Frederick Philip Grove
n 2. SUCH IS MY BELOVED / Morley Callaghan
n 3. LITERARY LAPSES / Stephen Leacock
n 4. AS FOR ME AND MY HOUSE / Sinclair Ross
n 5. THE TIN FLUTE / Gabrielle Roy
n 6. THE CLOCKMAKER / Thomas Chandler Haliburton
n 7. THE LAST BARRIER AND OTHER STORIES / Charles G. D. Roberts
n 8. BAROMETER RISING / Hugh MacLennan
n 9. AT THE TIDE'S TURN AND OTHER STORIES / Thomas H. Raddall
n10. ARCADIAN ADVENTURES WITH THE IDLE RICH / Stephen Leacock
n11. HABITANT POEMS / William Henry Drummond
n12. THIRTY ACRES / Ringuet
n13. EARTH AND HIGH HEAVEN / Gwethalyn Graham
n14. THE MAN FROM GLENGARRY / Ralph Connor
n15. SUNSHINE SKETCHES OF A LITTLE TOWN / Stephen Leacock
n16. THE STEPSURE LETTERS / Thomas McCulloch
n17. MORE JOY IN HEAVEN / Morley Callaghan
n18. WILD GEESE / Martha Ostenso
n19. THE MASTER OF THE MILL / Frederick Philip Grove
n20. THE IMPERIALIST / Sara Jeannette Duncan
n21. DELIGHT / Mazo de la Roche
n22. THE SECOND SCROLL / A. M. Klein
n23. THE MOUNTAIN AND THE VALLEY / Ernest Buckler
n24. THE RICH MAN / Henry Kreisel
n25. WHERE NESTS THE WATER HEN / Gabrielle Roy
n26. THE TOWN BELOW / Roger Lemelin
n27. THE HISTORY OF EMILY MONTAGUE / Frances Brooke
n28. MY DISCOVERY OF ENGLAND / Stephen Leacock
n29. SWAMP ANGEL / Ethel Wilson
n30. EACH MAN'S SON / Hugh MacLennan
n31. ROUGHING IT IN THE BUSH / Susanna Moodie
n32. WHITE NARCISSUS / Raymond Knister
n33. THEY SHALL INHERIT THE EARTH / Morley Callaghan
n34. TURVEY / Earle Birney
n35. NONSENSE NOVELS / Stephen Leacock
n36. GRAIN / R. J. C. Stead
n37. LAST OF THE CURLEWS / Fred Bodsworth
n38. THE NYMPH AND THE LAMP / Thomas H. Raddall
n39. JUDITH HEARNE / Brian Moore
n40. THE CASHIER / Gabrielle Roy
n41. UNDER THE RIBS OF DEATH / John Marlyn
n42. WOODSMEN OF THE WEST / M. Allerdale Grainger
n43. MOONBEAMS FROM THE LARGER LUNACY / Stephen Leacock
n44. SARAH BINKS / Paul Hiebert
n45. SON OF A SMALLER HERO / Mordecai Richler
n46. WINTER STUDIES AND SUMMER RAMBLES / Anna Jameson
n47. REMEMBER ME / Edward Meade
n48. FRENZIED FICTION / Stephen Leacock
n49. FRUITS OF THE EARTH / Frederick Philip Grove
n50. SETTLERS OF THE MARSH / Frederick Philip Grove
n51. THE BACKWOODS OF CANADA / Catharine Parr Traill
n52. MUSIC AT THE CLOSE / Edward McCourt
n53. MY REMARKABLE UNCLE / Stephen Leacock
n54. THE DOUBLE HOOK / Sheila Watson
n55. TIGER DUNLOP'S UPPER CANADA / William Dunlop

n56. STREET OF RICHES / Gabrielle Roy
n57. SHORT CIRCUITS / Stephen Leacock
n58. WACOUSTA / John Richardson
n59. THE STONE ANGEL / Margaret Laurence
n60. FURTHER FOOLISHNESS / Stephen Leacock
n61. MARCHBANKS' ALMANACK / Robertson Davies
n62. THE LAMP AT NOON AND OTHER STORIES / Sinclair Ross
n63. THE HARBOUR MASTER / Theodore Goodridge Roberts
n64. THE CANADIAN SETTLER'S GUIDE / Catharine Parr Traill
n65. THE GOLDEN DOG / William Kirby
n66. THE APPRENTICESHIP OF DUDDY KRAVITZ / Mordecai Richler
n67. BEHIND THE BEYOND / Stephen Leacock
n68. A STRANGE MANUSCRIPT FOUND IN A COPPER CYLINDER /
      James De Mille
n69. LAST LEAVES / Stephen Leacock
n70. THE TOMORROW-TAMER / Margaret Laurence
n71. ODYSSEUS EVER RETURNING / George Woodcock
n72. THE CURÉ OF ST. PHILIPPE / Francis William Grey
n73. THE FAVOURITE GAME / Leonard Cohen
n74. WINNOWED WISDOM / Stephen Leacock
n75. THE SEATS OF THE MIGHTY / Gilbert Parker
n76. A SEARCH FOR AMERICA / Frederick Philip Grove
n77. THE BETRAYAL / Henry Kreisel
n78. MAD SHADOWS / Marie-Claire Blais
n79. THE INCOMPARABLE ATUK / Mordecai Richler
n80. THE LUCK OF GINGER COFFEY / Brian Moore
n81. JOHN SUTHERLAND: ESSAYS, CONTROVERSIES AND POEMS /
      Miriam Waddington
n82. PEACE SHALL DESTROY MANY / Rudy Henry Wiebe
n83. A VOICE FROM THE ATTIC / Robertson Davies
n84. PROCHAIN EPISODE / Hubert Aquin
n85. ROGER SUDDEN / Thomas H. Raddall
n86. MIST ON THE RIVER / Hubert Evans
n87. THE FIRE-DWELLERS / Margaret Laurence
n88. THE DESERTER / Douglas LePan
n89. ANTOINETTE DE MIRECOURT / Rosanna Leprohon
n90. ALLEGRO / Felix Leclerc
n91. THE END OF THE WORLD AND OTHER STORIES / Mavis Gallant
n92. IN THE VILLAGE OF VIGER AND OTHER STORIES /
      Duncan Campbell Scott
n93. THE EDIBLE WOMAN / Margaret Atwood
n94. IN SEARCH OF MYSELF / Frederick Philip Grove
n95. FEAST OF STEPHEN / Robertson Davies
n96. A BIRD IN THE HOUSE / Margaret Laurence
n97.
n98. PRIDE'S FANCY / Thomas Raddall
n99. OX BELLS AND FIREFLIES / Ernest Buckler
n100. ABOVE GROUND / Jack Ludwig
n101. NEW PRIEST IN CONCEPTION BAY / Robert Traill Spence Lowell
n102. THE FLYING YEARS / Frederick Niven
n103. WIND WITHOUT RAIN / Selwyn Dewdney
n104. TETE BLANCHE / Marie-Claire Blais
n105. TAY JOHN / Howard O'Hagan
n106. CANADIANS OF OLD / Charles G. D. Roberts
n107. HEADWATERS OF CANADIAN LITERATURE / Andrew MacMechan
n108.
n109. THE HIDDEN MOUNTAIN / Gabrielle Roy
n110. THE HEART OF THE ANCIENT WOOD / Charles G. D. Roberts

n111. JEST OF GOD / Margaret Laurence
n112. SELF CONDEMNED / Wyndham Lewis
n113. DUST OVER THE CITY / André Langevin

o 2. MASKS OF FICTION: CANADIAN CRITICS ON CANADIAN PROSE /
       edited by A. J. M. Smith
o 3. MASKS OF POETRY: CANADIAN CRITICS ON CANADIAN VERSE /
       edited by A. J. M. Smith

POETS OF CANADA:

o 1. VOL. I: POETS OF THE CONFEDERATION / edited by Malcolm Ross
o 4. VOL. III: POETRY OF MIDCENTURY / edited by Milton Wilson
o 5. VOL. II: POETS BETWEEN THE WARS / edited by Milton Wilson
o 6. THE POEMS OF EARLE BIRNEY /
o 7. VOL. IV: POETS OF CONTEMPORARY CANADA /
       edited by Eli Mandel
o 8. VOL. V: NINETEENTH-CENTURY NARRATIVE POEMS / edited by
       David Sinclair

CANADIAN WRITERS

w 1. MARSHALL MCLUHAN / Dennis Duffy
w 2. E. J. PRATT / Milton Wilson
w 3. MARGARET LAURENCE / Clara Thomas
w 4. FREDERICK PHILIP GROVE / Ronald Sutherland
w 5. LEONARD COHEN / Michael Ondaatje
w 6. MORDECAI RICHLER / George Woodcock
w 7. STEPHEN LEACOCK / Robertson Davis
w 8. HUGH MACLENNAN / Alec Lucas
w 9. EARLE BIRNEY / Richard Robillard
w10. NORTHROP FRYE / Ronald Bates
w11. MALCOLM LOWRY / William H. New
w12. JAMES REANEY / Ross G. Woodman
w13. GEORGE WOODCOCK / Peter Hughes